Death Sees Most Of The Game

ANNABEL FRAZER

Death Sees Most of the Game

by Annabel Frazer

Book 1 in the Crooked House series

Also available as an ebook from www.Amazon.co.uk

ISBN:
ISBN 978-1-9160505-0-1

BLYTHWICH PRESS

CONTENTS

PROLOGUE

It was midsummer and just for once, London had the weather to prove it. The Tube trains sweltered, the buses sweated and the streets melted, their black asphalt transforming into a sticky substance like tar. Only the chilled ice palaces of cinemas and department stores offered any escape from the heat. Meanwhile, tennis at Wimbledon was under way and in the cricket, England had collapsed.

At Westminster, Parliament was dragging itself towards recess. The opposition had given up trying to create any real challenge – that could wait until the autumn conference season in some breezy seaside town – and the party in government were occupied with a high-level scandal which looked liable to precipitate a leadership contest.

The Palace of Westminster, itself sinking every day a little further into the marshland upon which it had been originally constructed, seemed a more inadequate a home than ever for democracy. Dead flies choked the window-ledges, lured in by the miasma of squalor that rose from the rotting foundations, and condensation slimed up the walls.

Not far away in St James's Park, an elderly man in a blue Panama hat fed the pelicans, offering them pieces of bread one by one. He liked the ridiculous way they waddled and the way their vast beaks gaped open. Whose idea had it been to put these absurd-looking birds in a London park? Now they were as much part of the scene as the sparrows.

Focusing on the pelicans made it easier not to think about what had happened, but his mind had a way of drawing him back to it. Lunch at the Ritz. Rather a treat for someone like him who had dropped out of things since retiring. But now, looking back at it, he felt no pleasure. It had been idiotic behaviour – fancying himself clever, dropping things into the conversation to see if they got home.

Well, something had got home, he had been left in no doubt about that. The question was, what would they do about it? As he broke off another piece of bread for the pelicans, he felt an acute spasm of what might or might not be indigestion – his stomach always reacted badly when he was upset.

The question was, should he go to Wimbledon? It would be a risk now. But he had been looking forward to it for months. The ticket was tucked carefully behind the clock on the mantelpiece waiting for the big day.

At the thought of Wimbledon – the ivy-clad courts, the green lawns, the quiet thunk of ball on racquet – he felt calmer. Perhaps he had been imagining things. There was really nothing to be worried about. At that moment, his stomach gave another untimely twinge and he told himself firmly that it was the artisanal bread at the Ritz that was to blame.

CHAPTER 1

The man calling himself Xan Ross was going home. A young man with fair hair darkened by the sun, eyes an odd shade between brown and green and a long scar down the left side of his jaw, he sat in the window seat of an empty row on the under-subscribed Oman-London plane.

It didn't feel like going home – but then, perhaps it never did unless you had people and places waiting for you. Xan had no one waiting for him – not in England, not anywhere. And he had been away so long that his memories were faded and forlorn.

The country he now saw featuring on the international news channels seemed entirely different to the one he remembered. It had sporadic successes in rugby and cricket but dependably lost at football. The Royal Family endlessly shook hands with smiling people on visits and were presented with unlikely gifts.

The air steward came down the aisle giving out newspapers now and Xan accepted one. He scanned the front page with a sense of complete disconnection. PALACE OF WESTMINSTER REPAIRS DELAYED AGAIN. CITY BIG THREE AGREE DEAL. PARTY LEADERSHIP CONTEST IMMINENT.

Xan's work never took him anywhere near England. In the private security industry, there were many places with better opportunities. Against his will, his mind was dragged back a space of ten days, to the city of Fez.

It had been meant to be a perfectly straightforward operation. (Homeland insisted on calling them operations, as though this was the Army. That was the point, after all, to give reassurance to people badly in need of it and willing to pay.) But it was in Fez that things had gone wrong. The dark, narrow streets with their endless variety of ornate doors and pillared facades, often with very little behind them. A good place for an ambush, Fez.

Should he have known – insisted on going some other way? But there was no other practical way except through the desert, where one tyre blow-out could lead to a long, lingering death from heat and thirst.

Nowadays, of course, mobile phones meant you could call up assistance fairly fast, but the people he had been working for had not been anxious to draw attention to themselves. He should have arranged for back-up from Homeland – Mr De Leiter wouldn't have wanted to pay for the extra warm bodies, but he should have insisted all the same – pointed out the likely saving in cold bodies, including that of De Leiter himself.

Spinnetti had been philosophical about the disastrous end to the operation. "You can trust homegrown gangsters to over-accessorise," was all he had said, regretfully eyeing the shot-up Mercedes. The fact that he and Xan were the only survivors did not seem to trouble him.

Homeland had sent people to Tangiers to debrief Xan and Spinnetti, although they had to drag the latter out of a bar to do it. There had been days of questioning – and then almost in seconds they had suddenly seemed to lose interest. Spinnetti had been given a new assignment. Xan had been offered an assignment too, but something had prompted him to decline it. After all, he argued, he had not had a break in months.

The people from Homeland seemed to see the sense in his reasoning, but when they asked where he intended to go, he had been evasive. One thing about working for a security firm was that you couldn't trust them not to keep checking up on you.

So he had trawled destination options at a café with bright Formica tables and a bank of computer terminals offering cheap and untraceable broadband. Untraceable to a point, anyway. It was perfectly possible, of course, to use both close access and remote techniques to get any internet connection point to yield its secrets. The safety lay in the difficulty of anyone knowing which connection point to look at.

On the travel websites, a sense of ennui seemed to ooze from every destination, with their identikit blue pools, sun-glare and cocktails. But then the café-owner had come padding past to grudgingly pour him more coffee and had cast an interested look at the computer screen. "You are going on holiday?"

And Xan had shrugged and pushed the screen away a little. "I don't know."

"You should not go on holiday. You should go home."

"I don't have a home."

"Everyone has a home."

So he had bought a one-way ticket to London – in cash, so that Homeland couldn't track the purchase. (Another thing about his unusual line of work was that you got into the habit of carrying a lot of cash on you.)

And now, sitting in the London-bound plane staring out at a cold grey fog of sky, he wondered what he had been thinking of. Home – to a country he barely remembered.

CHAPTER 2

Xan gave his passport to the immigration officer and almost stumbled over his unfamiliar name when it was given back to him with a cheerful: "Welcome to the UK, Mr Ross."

He would have to do better than that, he thought. He might be off duty, but that did not mean he could afford any mistakes.

He emerged into Arrivals to a forest of signs and eager faces, none of them watching for him. And then from the window of a slow train, he watched the airport buildings give way to the brutality of square warehouses and acres of industrial car park.

Beyond the airport, there was a relentless march of small, boxy houses over what had once been fields. But as they reached open country, the view improved. A stone arched bridge crossed a stream. A tractor toiled in a field. In the distance, the spire of a church pierced the sky. It prompted a reassuring sense of childish recognition.

Xan's own time in England had been far from reassuring. He remembered no father and his mother had died when he was eight. After that, his formative years had been spent in a series of boarding-schools overseas, mostly in the Far East. So why this sense of instant recognition?

Fragments of memory teased him – pictures in a book, his mother's voice asking him to name birds and animals. The illustrations had been remarkably detailed, capturing a rural landscape of blackbirds perched on walls, willows over water and cows at the water-trough. It was this landscape he was looking at now.

The colours – pale grass, wispy clouds – were muted compared to the brilliance of a Sahara spring. He studied the field boundaries and the way they took dramatic diversions to skirt a tangled dell of blackberry bushes or the outthrust elbow of a neighbouring farm. This spoke of civilisation built up over slow, measured millennia and of an assurance, rather questionable, that what had been so would always continue to be so.

London, when he reached it, was grey and dreary by comparison. A medieval town unceremoniously bullied into the twenty-first century through the introduction of glaringly ugly concrete, steel and glass. But of course, he wouldn't stay in London very long.

The question was, should he go to Blythwich? They would all be long gone, the people who would remember a young woman and a small boy living in cheap rooms on the edge of town. You moved on but places remained where they were and other people occupied the spaces where your memories had been. No, he wouldn't go to Blythwich.

After two days, Xan had seen London, or at any rate as much as he wanted to. His work for Homeland had left him with some invisible scars to go with the visible one and he had a particular aversion to crowds and shut-in places.

He had taken a room at a business hotel in the Square Mile. Financial districts tended to be relatively free of tourists and quiet at night and he liked the anonymity and predictability of business hotels, compared to their quirky boutique cousins. Business hotels were always the same – cream and muted neutral shades, unnecessary cushions and throws on the bed and a buffet breakfast in a room without any windows.

He had also adapted his wardrobe for the purposes of protective coloration. His usual work attire would not do here. But then, nor did he want to emulate the men he saw jostling each other off the pavements in their eagerness to reach the office, all unimaginatively attired in black and grey suiting, often with a discreet pin-stripe.

He went to a traditional gentlemen's outfitters in one of the quieter streets. The staff there seemed to understand him. What their customer required was the wardrobe of the English gentleman of leisure. They were too polite to do more than raise an eyebrow when the customer rejected expensive brogues in favour of soft-soled sneakers.

Xan did not trouble to explain. He disliked the idea of anyone being able to hear him walking at night. Many promising Homeland careers had been cut short through not paying attention to this simple consideration.

It must have been sheer boredom that took him along the dingy alley incongruously named Flower Street that evening. Cities were by their nature places where things happened – but apparently not to a young man of leisure staying at a dull business hotel.

Halfway along the alley stood a public house with its front covered in scaffolding. It looked like the sort of place his kind of people habitually drank in, which was reason enough for going straight past, but a man ducking through the rather low doorway paused and stared at him and he recognised Paul Latrelle's white, fox-like face.

He ought to have taken evasive action, Xan thought afterwards. Throwing off surveillance was something they both knew all about, after all. But, perhaps because he was bored, he stopped instead. And once they had got over the business of names, Latrelle shrugged and indicated the pub doorway with his elbow, as though it were inevitable.

Inside, it was the sort of place where old acquaintances seem to hover like shadows in every corner, only to fade away when you looked them in the eye – but there was no denying the corporeal reality of Billy Dangerfield when he turned round from the bar, his brutal brick-shape struggling to make progress through the crowd.

The two pint-glasses, one in each hand, didn't help. They were both for Billy. In the old days, drinking hadn't seemed to impair his operational efficiency, but age told and he had retired several years ago. If he had thought about it at all, Xan had imagined Billy drinking his way through a sunny retirement in Spain or South America, yet here he was.

It was Paul Latrelle who pressed the old boy on the matter, once they'd done the names again. He was drinking vodka and tonics himself, but very slowly and Xan remembered he had always been like that – urging drinks on others and taking little himself, but then remembering everything everyone said afterwards.

"Why London? You're a Scotsman. Everyone goes home in the end, don't they, like salmon upriver."

Billy took a mouthful of beer before replying. "A spot of consultancy work. It'll help to fund the golf club fees."

Billy would have to hurry to cram in much golf between his 'consultancy work' and the huge coronary episode that edged closer with every pint, Xan thought. He considered posing a question about the consultancy work but stopped himself in time. He had learned not to be too curious about other people in the business – leave that to Latrelle's type.

The Frenchman seemed to smell a rat all right, his quick eyes moving between them. Billy drank his pint in glowering silence. Xan was just reflecting that this kind of dull and awkward scene was exactly the reason he normally avoided people in the business when Latrelle turned his attention to him.

"What about you, then? Why are *you* here? Family troubles?"

"He doesn't have any family," Billy wheezed into his beer-glass.

"On a job? I didn't think your people did jobs in this country."

"They don't."

Latrelle studied his empty glass and appeared to draw a conclusion. "My round. What do you gentlemen want?"

Billy waited until he had gone. "He should have asked you about the name. What's wrong with your usual ones? You know what happens when you get too creative with cover names. Better practise it a bit. It doesn't sound right yet."

Xan laughed suddenly. "I'll be careful."

At that moment, Billy sat up as though someone had nudged him. "What are you doing here?"

"I thought we'd covered that."

"I mean, what are you *doing*? Job-hunting? Sight-seeing? Visiting family? You must have some idea."

"Sight-seeing, I suppose. I thought I'd travel around a bit."

"There's plenty to do in London."

"I don't like crowds, remember?"

"So you don't. Time you got over that. It will hold you back in your career."

"There are plenty of empty places."

Billy reached ineffectually towards his jacket pocket. "Got an idea. Aversion therapy. Not my kind of thing. No esprit de corps." He succeeded in dragging a stiff-looking envelope out of his pocket. "You take it. Green lawns, afternoon tea. You've missed all that."

Missed all what?

"And you've got the public-school manner. Playing fields of Eton. Fit right in."

It was impossible not to take the proffered envelope, so Xan took it. Then Billy's face drew back and his eyes went as blank as a factory wall as a clink of glasses and a splash of spilled beer signalled Latrelle's return, his thin face eager with curiosity and his tongue ready with his next set of questions.

It seemed a bare minute before Billy's pint glass was empty again. It was never any good trying to match him, Xan knew. But getting the next round in would get him away from Latrelle's constant probing.

He made his way to the bar and gave his order. While he was waiting for it, a man seated on a barrel drinking what looked like neat gin appeared to take him for an old friend. "Tried to sit in Paternoster Square today," he said affably. "They moved me on. Said you weren't allowed to loiter there. Explained that I was sitting, not loitering, but they wouldn't have it. What's all that about?"

Xan said apologetically that he was a stranger here. The three bottles of beer he had ordered, as being more practical than pint-glasses for transport through a busy throng of drinkers, had materialised beside him, but a glance at the crowd now packing the room made him reluctant to move.

"It's the same thing all along the river now. They say it's private land. Security guards move you on. I blame the Government," the man with the glass of gin went on, apparently untroubled by the originality of this thought.

A hasty man with the intemperate look of the thirsty punter whose next pint is further away than he would like barged through to the bar. "Service! I'll have some service!"

"You'll have to wait your turn," said the man with the

glass of gin. “They’re busy tonight.”

The hasty man gave him a look of dislike. “I didn’t ask you.”

The usual trouble brewing, Xan thought wearily. He volunteered his own space at the bar and, on another thought, Billy’s beer, which he saw no chance of getting to him in any case. “Here, have this and stop making a scene.”

A bar-boy, young and with a nervous look, was trying to make his way through the crowd. In his hurry, he knocked into the hasty man, who turned around slowly and blearily like a cargo tanker manoeuvring in a busy port, and considered the boy as though he saw more than one of him.

“You served me short last time,” he pronounced distinctly.

The boy shook his head, the whites of his eyes showing like a nervous horse.

The hasty man’s shoulder depressed and his arm swung back. What he intended was never clear, because unexpectedly he found his wrist caught in a hard grip and he was shoved against the bar.

“You’ve had enough in any case,” Xan said shortly. He let go with his right hand so that the hasty man could straighten up. A stream of expletives straggled from the hasty man’s lips.

“Reckon he has.” An older bar-man who had appeared by magic at the sound of trouble, assessed his customer with one expert glance. “Out you go, Bob, you don’t do any good here."

He assisted Xan in ejecting the hasty man out into the street, then turned to glance at the young bar-boy, who wilted under his look. "Still think you're ready front of house service, George? You'd best go behind the bar and finish that inventory for me."

The boy looked only too thankful to scurry from sight. The landlord shook his head. "Another drink, sir? Yours went in the scuffle. Very fast reactions, sir, if I may say so."

"No, thank you. I think I need some air. Those beers belong at table six." Xan had suddenly decided that Billy and Paul Latrelle would both get along fine without him. As he left, he heard the man with the glass of gin chuckle quietly to himself.

Outside, the entirety of London seemed stuffy and airless and it was raining. Red buses skirmished past him along the dark street, the raindrops illuminating their headlights, all offering inviting shelter. He disregarded them.

He should have stayed out of it. Why get himself into a cheap and unnecessary bar brawl? But he didn't like cheap and unnecessary violence. And as Billy would no doubt point out, that wasn't a selling point in their industry.

Billy himself had been one of the best in his day. That wasn't quite the recommendation it sounded and, in any case, his day had been a long time ago now. It was tough to achieve an honourable discharge from their line of business – the best and the worst tended to quit by death in service and it was only the mediocre who outlasted the steadily-worsening assignments and found their way out. But outlasting was a Billy speciality and here he was.

There must be something important to keep him in London. But what did it matter, Xan reminded himself? One of the pleasures of being currently 'available for hire', like the succession of black taxis crawling past him like giant blackbeetles, was that one didn't have to worry about what other people were doing.

Back in his hotel room, he opened all the windows to exchange canned, air-conditioned air for the real thing (or as real as it got, siphoned between skyscrapers above the boiling city streets). It was only then that he remembered the envelope Billy had pressed on him.

The envelope was thick and pale and expensive-looking. It had no name on it and had not been through the post, intimating that it was not the original container of whatever was inside.

Inside was a stiff card in purple and green which looked expensive. Elaborately italic printed lettering announced that the communication was from the *All England Lawn Tennis & Croquet Club*.

This meant nothing to Xan. He turned over the card and received a blizzard of precise orientation. *Centre Court, Level 2, Row S, Seat 40, Saturday 2nd July*. Tomorrow. And finally, the one word that told him what this was. Wimbledon.

Xan's knowledge of Wimbledon was limited to a hazy association with strawberries and cream and the upper-class brand of Englishness that was peculiarly popular overseas – the words that Homeland's wealthy clientele produced like hopeful passwords when they had to deal with 'the Englishman'.

"Yes, yes. Wimbledon. Goodwood. Ascot. Rolls Royce. Jermyn Street. Eton." Xan remembered Pierre Ho rattling off the words with a roll of the eyes in the Hong Kong bar where they had first met. Pierre had admitted candidly that he had been appalled when Homeland assigned him 'the Englishman'. "You people. You are finished, are you not?"

Somehow, they had rubbed along quite well in the end, the two of them. Pierre was still alive, anyway, which was the best Homeland could do in positive trading examples to offer the auditors, always supposing that Homeland had any auditors. He was settled in Portugal, enjoying the food and the sunshine and the extra lease of life. And Xan was here, in England – *Wimbledon, Goodwood, Ascot, Rolls Royce, Jermyn Street, Eton* – looking at a ticket to the high life.

CHAPTER 3

The Underground train to SW19 swarmed with people dressed in pastel hues and lugging wicker hampers. Xan retreated to the last carriage and effaced himself behind his newspaper. This must be what Billy had meant by aversion therapy.

He had almost consigned the ticket to the wastebasket overnight. He had no interest in tennis and after all, he had been foisted with the ticket through sleight of hand, as the dupe in a card game finds himself holding the poorest-scoring cards at the end of the round. However, a combination of factors – a sudden treacherous inclination to find out what the English were like at leisure, the memory of his own complaint of boredom – had changed his mind. Now here he was, on his way to Wimbledon.

When the train finally drew in to Wimbledon Station, a frantic disembarking began, involving misplaced flowery hats and hampers wedged too securely between seats to be easily dislodged. The colourful tide of people flowed up the station stairs and spilled out across the streets, where a sea of red buses and black cabs were cheerfully profiting from the chaos.

An overheated-looking policeman outside the station greeted Xan's dismayed expression with some pity. "First time, sir?"

"How on earth do you get to the place?"

"Depends. You can share a taxi or the bus will drop you half a mile from the main entrance for four quid." The policeman looked Xan up and down with the professional appraisal of a fellow Services man. "But for you, sir, I'd suggest walking. Fifteen minutes – the first half's a steep haul uphill and most people can't handle it with a picnic basket."

The walk almost made things bearable again. As the constable had remarked, the road was too steep for the majority of the visitors and they streamed slowly past him in taxis and buses and private cars, looking hot and fed up. Although the road was certainly steep, it had wide pavements and shady trees and there was a cool breeze.

These were the trees you thought about when you were out of England for a long time. Tall, spreading chestnuts and oaks with their seamed trunks and strong uplifting branches and wide leaves turning towards you. There were no trees like this in Saudi or Qatar or Kuwait or any of the places where there was work for private security specialists.

Come to think of it, there had been no trees like this in the narrow streets where he had grown up. No room for them, he supposed. And the town planners had no doubt decided the occupants of those cramped terraces would be too busy working to look at such things.

Further up the hill, he caught glimpses of splendid Victorian houses behind the trees. Wealth was not always so discreet and retiring – he thought of blue swimming-pools and green lawns in the heart of the desert and a dozen identical black Jeeps lined up nose to tail on the front drive.

At last, a prospect of high walls, stewards in high-visibility jackets and a sudden rash of signs everywhere indicated that he had reached the Club. Along with other ticket-holders, he was directed to an entrance gate and 'security'.

As usual, the process triggered a brief flash of irritation. He wondered in a detached way what caused that instinctive feeling of resistance. After all, he knew the purpose of the security measures, knew the limitations of the stewards' powers, was part of the whole industry of fear himself.

Another part of him clinically assessed the measures. The gates were sturdy enough, but they wouldn't close quickly enough against a rush from a determined crowd or what was more likely, a ramraiding vehicle. Moreover, the guards looked under-trained. They took his word for what was in his pockets, didn't seem to know what they were looking for in the bags they were searching and chatted too much with the people they belonged to.

When you were really on the watch, you couldn't afford to be distracted for a second. And the whole thing was futile without a metal detector in any case.

Play was evidently already starting on the outside courts. He could hear the cork-popping sound of racquet thumping ball and the patter of applause. He made his way to the Centre Court. It was famously ivy-clad, but that could not disguise the awkwardness of its dark green bulk. It had been described as the most beautiful tennis court in the world, but they must surely mean on the inside, like a kiwi fruit?

Once he had found his way into the stands, he decided the analogy was sound. The velvety softness of the grass court, the white netting stretched across it, the subdued sage of the umpire's chair and the glossy yellow-green of the ivy climbing the structural supports were all pleasing to the eye. If something as utilitarian as a tennis court could be beautiful, this was probably it.

There were already scattered spectators unpacking elaborate picnics and arranging rugs. Xan found his way to Row S. He felt a prickling at the back of his neck as other spectators began to filter along the row behind him, squeezing along the narrow gap, stepping awkwardly over bags and hampers.

He was not on a job, he reminded himself, and he didn't have to worry about risk routes. The trouble was that while you could control the conscious mind, you couldn't switch off the subconscious. In the background, he was faintly aware of it quietly ticking away, taking in details. The aisle next to him on his right. The empty seat on his left. Beyond that, a pair of foreign girls (German, he thought, or perhaps Austrian) sporting artificially blonde hair and thick black eye make-up and flicking through a celebrity-heavy magazine. At the end of the row, a family, four of them amicably swapping picnic food. No one appeared to be remotely interested in tennis.

In the more problematic row behind him, there were only six or seven people, including an earnest little man directly behind Xan with a cherubic countenance and a closely-clutched match programme. Next came an elderly man in a pale blue Panama hat who rustled his newspaper and subjected Xan to a piercing frown of disapproval for the temerity of being comparatively tall. Then a trio of middle-aged ladies in floral dresses and a young couple.

It would be difficult to imagine a more tranquil and innocuous environment – yet the instinctive habit of wariness persisted. For how long – that was the question. It might not be possible to switch it off overnight but supposing he was to walk away from the industry, how long would it take him to stop looking over his shoulder? A year? Two years? Ten years? An eternity?

Down on the court, two tall young women strode onto the court flanked by ball-girls and referees. The sparse crowd snapped to attention. Picnic items disappeared into bags. Programmes and newspapers were disposed of under seats. The Austrian girls focused keenly on the court.

"There comes Saturnova," one murmured. "She looks nervous."

"Larsen has been playing well this season," the other responded. "She has a pretty good chance if she remembers to focus on the key points."

The man in the Panama hat in the row behind began to steeple his fingers restlessly at the extreme edge of Xan's peripheral vision – infuriating to the last degree when you had been trained to be aware of sudden movements.

The Englishwoman beyond the Germans murmured something inaudible to her husband, who shrugged. "Maybe Larsen will stand closer into the baseline today."

It seemed that his judgement had been unjust. These people really were here to watch tennis.

*

Half an hour later, Xan was watching Saturnova defeat a dispirited Larsen, who had stood closer into the baseline to no avail. The players trudged off to generous applause.

A good majority of the sparse crowd also got up and streamed out. By now, Xan had become accustomed to the minor exodus that occurred at each two-minute change of ends in the match and the minor commotion it provoked as spectators struggled past each other in and out of each row.

A few moments later, the officials were back on the court, evidently readying it for another match. While they did so, more spectators streamed into the court. The seat next to Xan was taken by a brisk and energetic-looking woman in her fifties with a huge flowered carpet-bag which she crammed ruthlessly into the available space. The spaces in the row behind him were taken by three business-men in suits and a prosperous-looking couple with a hamper and a good deal of fuss about which of their two seats was more likely to be hit by a slice of sun-light later in the afternoon.

The stands were now almost at capacity. Xan suppressed another twitch of anxiety. Places like this were a death-trap in the event of a panic such as a fire. The hysterical stampede for exits usually caused more injuries than the original cause of the disturbance. He had learned to avoid such killing grounds, but here he was. Automatically, he found himself checking the exits again.

When the players emerged, the roar of approval from the crowd indicated that one, a blonde Swede with a bashful grin, was a popular favourite. His opponent, a thin, sallow Spaniard, slouched onto court in an ungracious manner, paying no attention to the noisy fans. But some 45 minutes later, he took a closely-fought first set.

Xan took the opportunity to leave the court. So did many other spectators, most of whom disappeared into the washrooms or headed down the stairs to the soft-drink stalls outside. Two minutes later, the doors to the court were firmly closed by the stewards. Now the outer circle of the Centre Court was empty and echoing– the perfect place for a restless man to get over a sudden attack of claustrophobia.

Xan strolled clockwise round the silent upper walkway, automatically noting the stewards who guarded each entrance to the court and the handful of spectators loitering outside the doors.

There was a woman by the stairs at Exit 7 – short and ginger-haired, rummaging in a bulging rucksack. As he passed, she gave him a short, unfriendly glance, then looked away. At Exit 8, there was a young couple in matching denim jackets apparently absorbed by each other. At Exit 9, a tall man with a sad face, intently studying the screen of his mobile phone. At Exit 10, a dark man with a badly broken nose and a bald patch. Ordinary spectators enjoying their day at Wimbledon, no doubt. Only it was a little curious how they looked like a line of sentries, one for each stairwell.

It was on his second circuit that Xan noticed the spare figure in the pale blue hat walking in the opposite direction to himself. It was the elderly man from the row behind him, evidently another sufferer of claustrophobia or restlessness. He glanced at Xan sharply as he passed as though disconcerted by his presence.

On the next circuit, the man in the Panama hat had his eyes fixed anxiously on the ground. Xan was wondering idly what would come of a third encounter when, to his surprise, the older man slowed to a halt in front of him.

"Would you mind if I spoke to you for a moment?" The voice was stiff and apologetic at addressing a stranger unbidden.

"Of course." Xan added extra impressions. Age 68-70, very little hair under the hat, skin a little sunburned, very thick blue veins on the hands. A thin, ascetic face with dreaming eyes that at this moment were fixed on him with a look of appeal.

The most obvious explanation, other than the absurd notion of ambush, was an offer of employment. Perhaps someone in Homeland, despite all Xan's precautions, knew where he was. Perhaps the man in the Panama hat ran an oil concession in the UAE or had a labour relations problem – although admittedly he did not look like a man with a labour problem.

The old man cleared his throat. "My name is Maybury. Giles Maybury."

It was at this moment that Xan realised Mr Maybury was really very nervy indeed. He was constantly looking around, noting movements and noises, but not efficiently. He gave himself no time to analyse observations, it was all hurried scanning.

"Is there something wrong, Mr Maybury?"

"It's just – you're a stranger to the country, I suppose?" the old man said rather surprisingly.

"I'm over from the Gulf for a few weeks."

"But you *are* English."

"Yes, I'm English."

"It's just that I –." Maybury looked wistful. "I thought you looked like the kind of man things happen to."

"Things happen to everyone, Mr Maybury."

Maybury nodded earnestly. "That's true – truer than I knew a week ago. I didn't believe it at first, of course," the old man added in his papery voice. "But in my experience, men of that profession, despite their concerns about the next world, are not prone to over-imagination in this one. And a photograph can't lie, you know. So, I looked into it – and I found out something. Something no one was supposed to know."

Xan looked attentively at the old man. Out in the bleak moonscapes where Homeland Security operated, he had come across paranoia and insanity many times – but he had also come across people who had good reason to be scared. He said: "If you're in some kind of trouble –."

"That's the thing," Maybury said eagerly. "It sounds absurd, doesn't it? So melodramatic. But I saw them myself – two of them, in the train coming up from Egham and again in the taxi queue. I'm all right here, of course, but they won't let me leave."

Suddenly, the doors to the court were flung open and spectators began flooding out. Mr Maybury drew back hurriedly. "I must apologise – I've been boring you with my troubles and you'll want to get back to the match. Perhaps you'd care to have my newspaper. I've finished with it."

"That's very kind, but –."

But the old man held it out insistently, and as the crowd surged towards them, the easiest thing seemed to take the unwanted newspaper. As he did so, Xan looked up sharply to meet the old man's eyes, which were suddenly focused and intent. Maybury nodded briskly and moved away towards the entrance that led to their section of the stands.

Xan gave him a moment and then followed. Ahead of him, as the old man neared the entrance, a swirl of people closed around him. Xan's eyes narrowed, but there was nothing he could catch hold of. Then the crowd thinned again and he could see Maybury making his way onto court.

The umpire was already calling Time. Xan climbed the stairs and dropped into his seat, careful not to glance at the spare figure once more hunched in the row behind. But as play restarted on court, he sat only half-attending. He was thinking about the little book, about the size of a pocket diary, which had been concealed within the folds of the newspaper and which now reposed in his own pocket.

The second set was well under way. 2-1 to the Spaniard, Fernandez. In the course of a quick service game followed by a long game on his opponent's serve which went to deuce four times, Fernandez entrenched his position to lead 3-2.

At the change of ends, only a scattering of people left the court to fetch refreshments. Giles Maybury sat hunched and silent, fiddling with what peripheral vision confirmed was a fountain-pen.

Xan was occupied by the question of the diary. Why had Maybury deliberately passed it to him under cover of the newspaper? Paranoia? Madness? But while Maybury had certainly been agitated, he had also seemed lucid. Of course, plenty of outwardly calm people nurtured crazy theories about dangerous international plots which they would share with you if you gave them half a chance.

More practically, what to do about it? Was it feasible to return the diary to Maybury at the end of the match? But if the old man was truly paranoid, he wouldn't accept it. Perhaps it would be better to return it without the old man's knowledge – basic pickpocket stuff, easy enough for someone with his training.

In the next game, the Spaniard opened the serving. An

early double-fault looked unpromising, but he collected himself sufficiently to win the game. 4-2. He then lost the first two points of the next game, promising an easy hold for the popular Swede, Johansson, but then unexpectedly fired a returning winner down the line, followed next point by a tricky drop-shot that trickled out of court before the Swede could get his racquet to it. 30-all.

Another winning passing shot and suddenly the Spaniard had a break point against his opponent's serve. The court was silent, every pair of eyes apparently fixed on him as he prepared to serve. All but one. Giles Maybury was still playing with his fountain-pen – it gleamed when the sunlight caught it.

Thump. The ball from the Swede's racquet hit the line and bounced, but a little flatter than he might have wanted. The Spaniard hit the low ball hard – it drove into the opposite corner of the court and barely bounced at all before it was gone, out of court, unplayable.

A break of serve and 5-2 to Fernandez. This time, few of the crowd left the court at the changeover, fearful of missing the next two games. In Xan's row, no one moved, but behind him, he was conscious of a spectator squeezing along between the seats. A few moments later, there was a maddening clunk as the little man next to the aisle rose and his vacated seat tipped up.

Down on the court, the two players prowled like cats, restless in their allotted spaces, unable to benefit from the recharging time.

In the next game, the Swede made a ferocious attack on

the Spaniard's service. After scraping the first point, the Spaniard lost the next two, one on a careless drop shot and the second on a wild lob. Sensing the chance to break back, the Swede pressed forward.

Fernandez hit a weak first serve, scrabbled to reach the return and couldn't put it away. Johansson struck a half-volley which hit the net-cord, bounced into court and trickled away into oblivion. Break point for the Swede. At which point, Fernandez produced what looked like an ace, but the Swede's racquet somehow scraped it from the grass and slammed a beautiful passing shot that bounced on the white service-line behind the astonished Fernandez like a coin clicking into the slot for the jackpot. 5-3.

Now, the crowd were silent. They scarcely seemed to breathe. There was nothing to distract the mind from the drama unfolding on the tennis-court – yet suddenly, Xan found himself distracted. Something – somewhere – was wrong.

The Swede finished deliberating over the balls he was being offered and came out to serve, sunlight glinting on his blond hair.

He assumed his trademark awkward-looking position at the baseline, one running shoe placed exactly to the line so that it looked as though he would overbalance on the ball toss and earn himself a foot-fault.

At that moment, at the edge of his vision, Xan became aware of the Panama hat in the seat behind him tilting sideways. He glanced over his shoulder. Surely now was an extraordinary moment for Maybury to fall asleep. In fact, it seemed scarcely believable.

It was unbelievable. Maybury's head had flopped sideways at an untenable angle. His eyes were glazed and unseeing.

Much later, when the police had finished with him for the day, Xan concluded that the correct response – the Wimbledon response – would have been that adopted by his neighbours, studiously ignoring the uncouth fellow whose indisposition so thoughtlessly threatened to disturb the spell of the Centre Court. At the time, however, it did not occur to him to do anything other than jump to his feet and kneel down beside the slumped figure.

The aisle seat was fortunately empty, giving him space. He had guessed at a sudden seizure of some kind, but to his astonishment, he saw a dark patch flowering in almost the exact centre of the old man's dark blue shirt. When he touched it, his fingers came away sticky.

Glancing sharply at Maybury's face, Xan saw that the eyes, which a moment ago had been glazed, were now sharply focused, perhaps with the urgency of knowing what was happening. The lips moved.

Xan knelt closer. Words were slipping between the slack lips, faint as breath. A half-intelligible phrase in a foreign tongue he was astonished to realise he recognised. He dragged off his jacket to put pressure on the dying man's chest but he could already see that it wasn't going to be any good.

*

From the view of the television commentators and the spectators at home, the whole thing must have seemed inexplicable. One moment, Fernandez was waiting to receive serve in his favourite position three feet back from the baseline. Johansson threw up the ball. At the other end, the Spaniard's shoulders tensed. Then, astonishingly, the Swede caught the ball and lowered his racquet, shaking his head.

"There's something wrong," the BBC commentator said. "I can't exactly see what –."

The Hydra-headed cameras apparently could not see either. They had a brief moment of indecision, switching from one view to another. The Swede was addressing the umpire, pointing up into the stands. A camera followed the direction of his irritable, outflung arm. A small knot of people were standing up in front of their seats, the sound of their arguing voices floating down to court-level.

"Some people are standing up – there's some kind of disturbance," said the BBC commentator, reduced to the basic journalist principle of reporting what he saw. "An extraordinary time for it. Very unfortunate for the two players."

Down on court, a polite pandemonium began to build. Both players were arguing with the umpire, who had his hand covering the microphone. The realisation that something was wrong began to sweep around the court like a grim parody of a Mexican wave.

The umpire leaned forward and removed his hand from

the microphone. He cleared his throat. "Ladies and gentlemen, play is temporarily suspended." The crowd gave a tremendous, rolling sigh. And the Spanish player began an energetic exchange with the umpire which could not be heard by anyone.

The crowd animal did not know what to do. The instinct to be elsewhere when trouble strikes struggled against the desire to get their money's worth. Some got up to leave, some remained in their seats.

A couple of security guards struggled against the tide. They had begun to talk agitatedly into their radios long before they reached Row S and once they did, they hardly glanced at the dead man. Instead, they looked at Xan.

"I'm afraid you'll have to come with us, sir."

Afraid was hardly the word – the guard looked terrified, Xan thought. Only then, looking down at the blood staining his shirt, did he realise it was he that they were afraid of.

He stood up and picked up his jacket and newspaper. Et in Arcadia ego. Death at Wimbledon – and just when he thought he had left death behind him in this green and pleasant land.

CHAPTER 4

"To talk to these people," Inspector Nash said bitterly, "you would think tennis was the only thing that mattered. All they can think about is when their precious match will be rescheduled and whether their tickets will be valid. Maybe too much tennis numbs the mind. Give me a late league away game with a relegation threat any day."

It had taken the police some time to get into the Club, due to the intractability of the entrance guards about their lack of valid tickets. They had then discovered a chaotic scene, with ticket-holders streaming out of the courts with little attempt to hold or search them and news reporters and camera-people milling eagerly around the grounds.

For Inspector Nash, it felt almost impossible to get a foot-hold, as it were, on the situation. A spectator stabbed in the middle of a tennis match, surrounded by hundreds of other fans – not to mention the TV cameras – and no one with apparently any idea of how or why or even when it had happened. Quite a conjuring trick.

The inspector's initial supposition, formulated in the car on the way to the Club as patchy information came in over radio, had been that an excitable fan had attacked a fellow-spectator over some imagined slight, then fled before anyone could hold him. The inspector's game was football and what went on in the stands at a Swansea match was past thinking about sometimes.

Upon arriving at Wimbledon, the inspector learned that the dead man's wallet was missing. He formulated a rival theory involving a sneak-thief committing murder for a well-stuffed wallet and bolting precipitately from the stands. But the tournament director ridiculed both ideas politely. "I'm afraid not, Inspector. It is not permitted to leave your seat during play."

At the inspector's mention of stewards, the director shook his head dismissively. "The crowd, Inspector. They would not stand for it for a moment. He would have had to wait for the change of ends."

So much for the Excitable Fan and the Sneak-Thief.

Inspector Nash next attempted to establish some kind of time window for the crime. The club doctor who was the first to examine the dead man had offered his opinion that he had been stabbed between five and twenty minutes before the alarm was raised. The weapon was lying on the floor at the victim's feet. An ordinary pen-knife – nasty business. No fingerprints.

The inspector had some hopes initially of the TV footage, until the BBC crew reminded him that all the cameras were pointed at the court. Some crowd footage might be obtainable eventually, but the chances of the relevant block of seats having been caught on film at the relevant time were almost infinitesimally small.

A handful of statements from the few spectators who had remained in their seats were unhelpful. As with the cameras, all human eyes had been focused on the tennis-court. No one seemed to have noticed the unfortunate man, dead or alive.

"They were there to watch the tennis, sir," Sergeant Monroe argued reasonably. "And what is there to notice about someone being stabbed, unless it's a glancing blow and they get up and start staggering about?"

"A compelling image, Sergeant," returned the inspector, a sandy-haired Welshman with a soft twang to his voice. In any case, he thought, homo sapiens had an instinctive preference for avoiding unpleasantness and that included not noticing people dying if it was more convenient not to do so. "At any rate, we can follow up with the rest of the people sitting nearest the dead man later."

But it was at this point that Inspector Nash learned that this was not as simple as he thought. While the Club retained records of ticket-holders who had entered the main draw, it was more difficult to identify individuals using tickets allocated through corporate arrangements and via tennis-clubs and they could not account at all for tickets sold illegally through touts.

The stewards had however managed to hold the ticket-holders sitting immediately to the left and right of the dead man and Inspector Nash proceeded to see them next.

The occupant of the seat to the right of the dead man, next to the aisle, had been absent from the court at the point when the death was discovered – a circumstance he was keen to emphasise and which perhaps helped to explain why no one had given the alarm earlier. Mr Colin

Brass had a shiny domed forehead and a cherubic countenance which looked at this moment anything but benign. His explanation was simple and emphatic. He had been out of his seat when it happened and none of it was anything to do with him.

"When exactly did it happen, then, sir?" Inspector Nash asked acutely.

"Well, I wasn't there, so I've no idea, have I? All I know is when I tried to go back in, they stopped me at the door. I kicked up quite a fuss, I can tell you. And then they had the cheek to detain me when I tried to leave." There was a rosy tinge to Mr Brass's face.

"It must have been very frustrating for you," Inspector Nash agreed soothingly, judging that placating Mr Brass's irascible temperament would be his best chance of getting any information from him. "So when did you go out, sir?"

"Let me see, now." Mr Brass frowned, his cherubic countenance crumpling. "It would have been at exactly 5-2."Encountering baffled looks from both the inspector and the sergeant, he added impatiently: "That was the score. 5-2 in the second. It was all getting rather exciting. But then, they stopped play. Fancy stopping at the end of the business end of a set like that. I wonder what they'll do about finishing the match," he mused hopefully.

Inspector Nash refused to be distracted. "What time would that have been, sir?"

"Heavens, I don't know. D'you think we spend our time looking at our watches after spending upwards of £100 for a ticket?"

Reflecting that they could get the actual time from the TV footage, Inspector Nash abandoned the point. "About the deceased. Do you remember anything about him?"

"Old codger in a hat," returned Mr Brass unfeelingly. "Looked dull as ditchwater."

"So, you didn't notice anything odd about him at any point?"

"What was there to notice? Ordinary sort of bloke."

"And he was alive when you left the stands at 5-2?"

"As far as I know. But I didn't check his pulse, you know."

It was hardly the sort of cast-iron testimony that would gratify the police surgeon seeking to narrow down the time window.

"Did you notice him leave the stands at all?"

Mr Brass advanced the theory that the old duffer had gone out some time earlier, perhaps in the first set, and had made quite a song and dance about squeezing past him. "I never get up for people. Let them manage for themselves, I say. But he seemed to think I should have done."

Such was the extent of Mr Brass's evidence.

The couple who had been seated on the left of Giles Maybury were interviewed next. Harlan Eastward was a bulky, bull-necked man with strongly curling hair and a pugnacious chin.

"Don't know why you have to keep us hanging about. It's a disgrace what's going on in the country today. No chance for the common man to get on."

Inspector Nash said that he was here to inquire into a murder.

"People shouldn't come to tennis-matches to get themselves murdered. Probably some sort of gang warfare. The authorities oughtn't to allow it," Mr Eastward said quarrelsomely.

Sarah Eastward supported her husband's statement and provided additional insight on Giles Maybury's earlier absence from court. "He went out at the end of the first set. I remember noticing because half our row did. People do, you know."

The inspector didn't know.

"The games at the beginning of the set are dead games," she explained kindly. "They usually go with serve and even if they don't, it doesn't mean much because there's plenty of time for the other player to break back."

"And when did he come back?"

"They don't let anyone in until the first three games of the set are done so he must have come back in then."

"Do you remember anything Mr Maybury did after that?"

But there, Mrs Eastward's memory failed her.

"I told you we didn't see anything," Mr Eastward said triumphantly. "Unlike some people, *we* were there to watch tennis."

"So, you didn't notice when Mr Maybury was – er – taken ill?"

"Thought he'd gone to sleep. Beats me why people

want to pay a fortune for a ticket and then doze off. But that's what I thought. Didn't give him another thought until someone started shouting out for a doctor." Mr Eastward's voice betrayed no qualms at his failure of care towards a fellow-human being.

Such was the extent of the Eastwards' evidence.

The spectators sitting immediately behind Giles Maybury had regrettably not been held for questioning. All these people would need to be, if possible, tracked down and interviewed. And they would almost certainly volunteer nothing except details of the match and criticisms of their fellow spectators, Inspector Nash thought wearily.

"There's one more to see," Sergeant Monroe said. "The man who raised the alarm."

"Is he making any trouble about the wait?"

"No, sir," Monroe said. "I had a look at him through the glass. He's very quiet. Too quiet if you ask me. Like he's not surprised to be here. Tough-looking customer too."

"Where was he sitting?" Inspector Nash demanded alertly.

"In front of the deceased. He could have done it all right."

"Hmmm." Inspector Nash visualised the scene in his mind's eye – a landscape which over the last hour or so had become extensively populated with homicidal tennis spectators. "It would have been quite a reach. Bit obvious, I'd have thought."

"Not necessarily, sir. I've been thinking it out and if he pretended the victim had dropped his newspaper or something, he could have done it. He *had* a newspaper."

"A damning indictment," Inspector Nash agreed.

When the inspector opened the door of the interview room, he could not at first see what his subordinate was getting at. The young man seated in front of the desk looked harmlessly law-abiding, apart from his blood-stained shirt, which gave him an incongruously piratical air. Fair hair. Regular features. The sort of man you'd find in a country pub being knowledgeable about fishing and dogs.

But as the inspector pulled up his own chair and sat down, he revised his thinking. The young man's hair was not naturally blond but mid-brown bleached lighter by the sun. Conversely, his skin had been darkened by the same exposure. He had the lean, hard physique of those whose job keeps them mainly outside and on the move. A white line ran down the side of his jaw – a scar of some kind? And although he was wearing a conventional suit, it looked newly bought. A man from a warmer climate, then, over here temporarily on business or pleasure and giving little clue as to his occupation.

The Inspector glanced down at the list of names that Sergeant Monroe had provided at the beginning of this irksome process. "Mr – er – Ross?"

The young man glanced up. His eyes, an unusual shade of hazel, were steady. "Yes."

"And you're staying at the Coronado City Hotel, EC1, I see. Any permanent address in this country?"

"No. I live overseas."

"Doing what?"

"Private consulting."

Xan had been wondering how this was going to go. Would his identity hold up? Keep it simple was the usual advice, make yourself as unremarkable as possible. He directed a mental reproach to himself for getting into this mess in the first place. Billy and his fairy-tales about esprit de corps and the playing-fields of Eton.

He was inclined to leave all of that out of it, along with Giles Maybury's rambling confidences – and most of all, Maybury's diary, which felt as though it were burning a hole in his pocket. He should have slipped it back into the old man's pocket before the security guards arrived. He had now gone too far along this road to admit to having it – a dangerous position.

The inspector glanced down at his notes. "You were seated in Row S. In front of the deceased – Mr Maybury."

"He was behind me and to my right," Xan corrected.

"You were the person who gave the alarm, I understand."

"Yes."

"I'm surprised you noticed anything was wrong, at such an important stage of the match."

"He had slid over in the seat. It didn't look natural. I thought he had had a heart attack. It was only when I got to him that I realised what had happened."

"Quite. And then?"

"I tried to stop the bleeding, but it wasn't any good."

"Quite," the inspector said again. "Did he say anything?"

Xan hesitated. "He said a few words in Greek. Ancient Greek, as a matter of fact."

"*Greek?* What words, exactly?"

Xan paused to be sure he had the words right. "Ἀνδρῶν γὰρ επιφανῶν πᾶσα γῆ τάφος, if I remember correctly."

Sergeant Monroe's pen paused irresolutely in its scribbling and Inspector Nash raised an eyebrow. "And what's that supposed to mean?"

"My school Greek is rather rusty, I'm afraid, but it means roughly that the tomb of an illustrious man is the whole of the Earth," Xan translated obligingly.

"Well, what's that got to do with Mr Maybury's death? Was he an illustrious man?"

"You tell me, inspector."

"Did he say anything else?"

"Nothing that made any sense."

The inspector did not pursue the point. Instead, he looked down, frowning, at the scribbled plan he had drawn on his spiral pad. Neat rows of seats, with in the middle of them a circle. "What else do you remember about Mr Maybury?"

It was no part of Xan's plan to appear particularly observant or to give the police more than he was required to give them. On the other hand, it would be unwise to withhold anything that they had other methods of finding out.

He said cautiously: "As a matter of fact, he spoke to me when I was out at the change of ends."

"Did he now? About what?"

"He asked if I was enjoying the match. My impression was that he felt it would be rude not to acknowledge me since we were the only people there. And he offered me his newspaper."

The inspector looked up. "His newspaper was found by his seat."

"Yes, I had my own." Things seemed simpler this way.

"When did this conversation take place?"

"At the end of the first set."

Inspector Nash nodded. That accorded with Sarah Eastward's evidence. "Did he leave the court again?"

"No."

"And when was the last time you noticed him looking alive and well?"

Xan knew the significance of this question. "Just before the last change of ends at 5-2."

The sergeant started. Inspector Nash said sharply: "You're certain about this?"

"Yes. He was playing with his fountain-pen and it was catching the light."

The inspector sat back, frowning. This information, if it was reliable, narrowed the window of opportunity to something under ten minutes. He had wanted testimony that would start getting him somewhere, but it only went to show that you had to be careful what you wished for.

He tried not to make the next question sound leading. "What can you tell me about the people in the row behind you?"

Xan reflected. "There were four initially. A little man in

a red T-shirt behind me, then Mr Maybury, then a young couple at the other end of the row. Several more came in after the women's game. There were some businessmen and a couple with a hamper. The woman was originally sitting next to Mr Maybury but they switched places after the first set."

The inspector's eyebrows elevated a little and Xan was immediately annoyed with himself. "You notice a lot, don't you?"

"I couldn't help it – every time anyone came in or out, all the seats shook, especially if people stood up."

"All the same, I've already spoken to some of the other people who were in your match and you might as well ask them what was happening in the tea-tent at the time."

Xan shrugged. "The game was boring me."

"Well, what can you tell me about the two people sitting either side of Mr Maybury?"

Xan had already realised that he had burned his bridges. The fact that he had spoken to the dead man and been the first to attend to him when he was dying already meant that he was a significant witness, liable to be called for either prosecution or defence in a police case, depending on how things went. This presented some fairly serious consequences. And it meant that there was little point in making himself look suspicious by avoiding answering additional questions.

Without any discernible pause, he therefore answered: "The fat, little man on his right was listening to his headphones between games. He left at the last change of ends, so his seat was empty when I realised Mr Maybury was ill. The couple were on the other side – I told you they changed places."

"Why do you suppose they did that?"

Xan shrugged. "You'd have to ask them."

The inspector made a note to do so. He resumed: "Does it seem odd to you that nobody noticed Mr Maybury was dead?"

"On the whole, no, it doesn't. He was wearing a dark shirt and it hid the blood. There was the newspaper. And at a tennis match, no one looks at the other spectators."

The inspector looked down at his diagram and then up again. "Only a small group of people could have got to Mr Maybury, you know. You're one of them. You have the reach." He had had the time now to get Mr Ross's physical measure. A tough customer, as Monroe had said.

And he still didn't look rattled. "I was in the row in front. It would be pretty difficult for me to do it without anyone seeing, don't you think?"

"Difficult for some," Inspector Nash conceded. "You'd need to be fairly strong – and fast in your reactions."

Abruptly his hand jerked out of his pocket and something went spinning through the air towards the other man. The next second, it was gone and Xan's hand lay closed on the table. He opened it and both men looked at what lay glinting in his palm. Sergeant Monroe craned to see. It was a coin, solid and dull and able to inflict a surprisingly painful wound if it caught you on the edge.

"Well, well," the inspector said. "What job is it you said

you do, sir?"

"Private consulting."

"Where?"

"Saudi Arabia, Qatar, Yemen."

The inspector kept his eyes on the other man's face. "Working for one of those oil companies? Security and asset protection?"

"That kind of thing."

"Well, now," the inspector resumed. "As I said, I think you had the opportunity. On the other hand – well, I'm sure I don't need to point out to you the two points in your favour."

"I raised the alarm when I could have kept quiet and I've narrowed down your window of opportunity."

"Quite." Inspector Nash looked down at his notes again.

"I'd also need a motive, of course. Do you have any theories about that?"

The inspector cleared his throat. "Mr Maybury's wallet was stolen."

"And that could have been me, I suppose." Xan spared a moment to be thankful that no search had been suggested, with Giles Maybury's diary in his pocket. "But I think you'll find that didn't happen on court."

"What are you saying? That someone pinched it off the body?"

"I think it was taken on his way back into court at the beginning of the second set. He was a little ahead of me and he had to push through quite a crowd of people."

The inspector frowned. Sensing that a favourite theory

was going west, Xan maintained a tactful silence. At length, the inspector glanced again at his witness. "If you don't mind my asking, what are your own ideas about this, Mr Ross?"

"I don't think it happened during play. You'd be looking for a very cool murderer. He or she would have had to sit through at least two games close to a dead body, waiting for his opportunity to escape."

"Then how do you think it happened?"

"I think it was at the change of ends. People were standing up, moving around. It would be easier to get to him without being noticed."

"And motive?"

"Well, once you look at that, no one on that court makes any sense at all." Seeing the inspector's brow furrowing, Xan added: "I was reading the rules of the club while I was sitting around waiting for you. The tickets are allocated through a draw. No one can possibly know in advance who is going to be on the same court on a given day."

"What's that?"

"You'd better read it up for yourself. But I'm afraid it will make your job more difficult, Inspector."

Inspector Nash closed his notebook in some exasperation. The last thing he needed was a motiveless crime. All this wanted thinking out with a quiet pint of beer.

"Well, your assistance has been very valuable, Mr Ross." As always, he noted that this sentence failed to please those to whom it was addressed. "We'll be in touch." So did this one. "You'll be at this hotel of yours, I take it?"

"I had thought about travelling around a bit."

"In this country?"

"In this country," Xan conceded, since it was clear that any plans to leave England would now have to be postponed.

When the door shut behind him, Inspector Nash glanced quizzically at Sergeant Monroe. "Still think he's our man?"

"You're bound to admit he looks suspicious," Monroe said stubbornly. "Why pay all that money to go to a tennis match and then spend all your time looking around at other people?"

"Maybe he doesn't like tennis."

"Then why was he there at all?"

"I'm not saying you haven't got a point," the inspector conceded. "I think he's hiding something. But what it is and how important it is, I don't know. And just at the moment, I'm more interested in his evidence. If he's telling the truth, our window of opportunity's less than ten minutes. I'm wondering if our murderer counted on no one noticing quite as quickly as that. It was nearly the end of the set and from what Mrs Eastward says, dozens of people would have left the court then, confusing everything nicely. It could be that that piece of evidence is going to be inconvenient for someone."

Xan left the Wimbledon tennis club without fanfare. There was no media presence at the back door he left by and the fans already queueing for tomorrow's tickets (possibly with the opportunistic hope that a disarrayed schedule would work in their favour) did not pay him any attention.

So why did he suddenly feel like the person of interest in the surveillance footage, a white circle applied to his blurry silhouette in post-production for the benefit of those watching the tape?

CHAPTER 5

"About that tennis match."

It was the morning after Xan's ill-fated trip to the tennis. He was occupying an ancient oxblood Chesterfield armchair cloistered by bookshelves filled with leather-bound tomes. Both he and the books were in shadow, but faint gold bars of early sunlight segregated by the blinds striped the polished table between him and Billy Dangerfield.

Billy had proposed breakfast at his club. An elegant building on the Strand, it was a distinct improvement on their previous rendezvous. Billy, on the other hand, looked early-morning-ish, which wasn't any sort of improvement.

"What about it?" he said rather peevishly, running his forefinger along his forehead in the manner of a man who has a hangover but doesn't choose to admit it.

"I was there. As you should know. I spent an hour with the police explaining myself."

"Well, I'm sure your cover is more than adequate. They do *give* you cover?"

"Naturally." Only when you were on a job, but there was no need to go into that.

"And I do trust you didn't involve *me* in any of your

explanations?"

"Not yet."

"Then there's nothing to worry about."

"It's damned inconvenient. It means I'm stuck here for the time being, apart from anything else." Xan gave him a hard look. "Who gave you that ticket, Billy?"

Billy shifted his bulk rather uncomfortably, looking as though the excellent cooked breakfast he had recently devoured no longer agreed with him. "My dear fellow, people send me these things. No idea why, half the time. Gifts from old clients, that sort of thing. What of it?"

"It put me in the seat in front of a dead man. And no, they didn't arrest me straightaway, as you're about to point out, but what happens when they find whoever did kill him?"

Billy looked bovine, but his mind was quick. "You're worried they'll want you as a witness for a police case in three years' time and look to pull you back from whatever crime-soaked paradise you're working in. So what? They won't find you under that disposable name of yours."

"Then have you thought how Homeland will feel about the situation? They're not exactly tolerant of mistakes."

"You're worrying about nothing. People get murdered every day."

"Not at Wimbledon. It's not the sort of place you'd choose at all. I mean, have you *been* there?"

"I don't care for the place." Billy rumpled his features in a fashion that conveyed the inferiority of racquet sports to his beloved golf. "But I'd imagine it has sneak-thieves like anywhere else. His wallet was taken, wasn't it?"

"I don't think it happened on court. It's a sneak-thief's nightmare. All those layers of security between you and a fast exit."

"Well, what happened, then?"

"Someone probably took it off him in the crowd around the doors going in or out, some time before the murder."

Billy shrugged again. "A random attack, then. Plenty of disturbed individuals wander around with knives, looking for people to stick 'em into."

"Do they also sit through a solid couple of hours of top-level tennis before deciding to make their move? And then stay there afterwards, waiting for someone to raise the alarm?"

Billy gave one of his expansive gestures that spared coffee-cups but were liable to winnow down beer-glasses at a more convivial time of day. "What, then?"

"I'm asking you."

"Well, I say it's a mare's nest. Giles Maybury was a dull fellow." Billy added with a faint grin: "You could say he was the looker-on who saw most of the game. Until someone stuck a knife in him."

Xan looked up sharply. "Did you know him?"

"No. But you pick up a lot in my line of country. Senior civil servant at the defence and security department but he retired years ago. Married, no children. His wife isn't young or glamorous or extravagant or any of the things that lead anywhere. And it won't lead anywhere. They'll investigate it quietly for a while and let the matter drop.

It's only the setting which interests anyone as it is."

It didn't seem much of an epitaph. Surely even a retired senior civil servant who had liked tennis and crosswords deserved more.

Xan walked back along the river to his hotel, deep in thought. Through no fault of his own, he had achieved what Homeland called a local compromise.

Ordinarily such a thing could be fixed easily enough, providing your cover stood up long enough for 'them' to bribe the witnesses and the police and spirit you over the border. But here, in England, where they never operated? Homeland, it was fair to say, were going to be very unhappy if they ever got to hear about this.

The first thing they would ask, as Billy had, was whether his cover would hold up. He had assured Billy that it would. But was that true? There were three things the police would inquire into immediately. Firstly, passport. That ought to be all right. Secondly, place of business. He had represented himself as a consultant who worked for hire, which meant there was no employer to contact. A solid professional reference would be required, however and one of Homeland's useful middle-men would provide that. Thirdly, banking reference. That ought to be all right, too. The Swiss were the experts in that sort of thing but they had been in the business for so long that to hold a Swiss banking account was practically a certificate of iniquity in itself. Xan had always found it perfectly satisfactory to deal with Luxembourg.

That disposed of the police. What of Homeland itself?

Ordinarily, the machinery would swing into action as soon as one of their operatives was compromised. But this wasn't the ordinary run of things. Perhaps they would never even hear of this. But the longer the case remained open, with the attendant risk that witnesses might be hauled into court for a high-profile police case dragging on for months, the more precarious his position became. And he did not share Billy's view that this would become just another unsolved statistic of robbery with violence.

Taking all these thoughts into account, it began to look as though it was in his interests for the murder to be solved as rapidly as possible. This thought combined with a twinge of professional self-reproach – a man had been murdered within a couple of feet of him and he had seen nothing, which was not something he had relished admitting to the police. And along with reproach, there was also the stirring of an entirely unprofessional curiosity.

He stopped at a newsagent and bought a newspaper. He preferred them to the internet – you could buy them with cash and read them without a curious government or an intrusive commercial supplier apprising itself of what you had read and therefore thought. Then he turned into a café to read the early reporting on the Wimbledon murder.

It was immediately clear that the setting was the star. It was not until the second page that the unfortunate victim was even named, with an incongruous picture in a suit and tie. Maybury still looked mild and apologetic and the sort of man to whom nothing interesting ever happened. The looker-on who saw most of the game, as Billy had remarked. Certainly a man who would dislike his sudden notoriety.

On the subject of notoriety, Xan was gratified to see that there were no pictures of him and only one mention of his name, which would mean nothing to the slowly trawling algorithms of Homeland.

He read the rest of the report, which bypassed all question of *why* in favour of an enthusiastic dissection of *how*. A packed tennis-court, every seat taken. How could one possibly pull off a murder in such circumstances? And how could a weapon have been smuggled to the scene?

Xan considered that one. The security procedures were, as he had thought at the time, casual. Anyone could bring in a picnic-knife, an apple-peeler or some other type of blade in a hamper. Hampers were searched, it was true, but not very thoroughly. A small pocket knife of the sort that had apparently been used could be concealed in a sunglasses case. Did that suggest premeditation? And did premeditation make any sense, in the circumstances?

The man who had sat on the left of the dead man, Mr Colin Brass, had chosen to draw attention to his rather compromising position by giving an interview. It ran in a side column, complete with a blurry picture which might not enable the casual reader to pick Mr Brass out of a crowd but gave Xan no difficulty in recreating the image of the little man who had fidgeted with his headphones.

Mr Brass made much of his absence from court for the last two games, clearly feeling that it gave him an unbreakable alibi. He was then choleric on the subject of the inflexibility of the Club's security guards. Xan found that he himself came in for some criticism under the heading of 'a dashed interfering chap who got up in the middle of the game, if you please, and started ordering everyone around', with the further characterisation of 'unpleasant-looking fellow – looked like a dangerous piece of work'.

Of course, all of this could be dismissed as a smoke-screen designed to distract from the suspicious circumstances around Mr Brass himself. He must realise that he had had an excellent opportunity of doing the murder on his way out of court. But did the fact that he had left the court at such a dramatic moment of the match count against him or in his favour?

And what about the people the other side of Giles Maybury? The blonde woman did not seem a very likely contender for stabbing a man in the middle of a tennis match, but people did surprising things. Her husband had looked as if he had the physical strength required and had swapped places with her ahead of the crucial moment. But was the fact that they had remained in their seats until the alarm was raised, apparently not noticing anything was wrong, suspicious or a sign of innocence?

Xan had known killers with the ice-cold disposition to sit quietly beside a corpse waiting for someone else to notice it. Was it more suspicious on the whole to loiter around outside the locked doors of the Centre Court arguing with the security guards and generally making a feature out of your absence from your seat?

It seemed altogether more likely that the murderer of

Giles Maybury had not been sitting anywhere near him. Since committing murder during play was almost impossible, it must logically have been carried out at a change of ends, the only time when spectators were permitted to move around.

Memory presented the moment in that last change of ends when someone had passed along the row behind him. The uncomfortable fact now stood – this was when the murder had most likely been done. And he had not known.

Xan had already glanced over Giles Maybury's diary but now he took it out and looked over it again. It was not a remarkable piece of evidence in any way. The humble record of a humdrum life, jotted down in that maddening cryptic style that people used with no consideration for the difficulties it would cause investigators coming after them.

A small yellow ticket, the sort issued by cinemas and museums to paying customers, marked the page devoted to the previous week and Xan had studied this page with particular attention, but its secrets were opaque to him. *Tues – lunch with C. Wed – Ritz 12.30pm.* There was nothing here that would explain Giles Maybury's actions in passing the diary to him – except for the notable fact that he had had his pocket picked and his wallet stolen only minutes later.

Coincidence? But Xan didn't believe in coincidences. And besides, there were other indications. The deliberate selection of a stranger to the country. The wistful remark about someone ‘things happen to’. It seemed more and more clear that Giles Maybury had singled him out and deliberately planted the diary on him. And then, with a fine sense of timing, got himself murdered.

Xan discarded his newspaper and made his way back to his hotel. It was as he came into the wind-blown plaza surrounded by tower-blocks that he noticed the watcher. Young, casual, cigarette in mouth, hands shoved in pockets, headphones on but remembering not to respond to the audio feed in his ear, clad in the inevitable sports gear.

Tactfully, Xan did not look around for the others who must be nearby – at least two but probably more. For a travel job, the police would use a car or motorcycle, but not for this – they already knew where he was staying. He therefore did not bother to disguise his destination. Best to let them watch him for a while, then he could watch them too and learn their faces.

As he came into the hotel, the receptionist halted him. “Mr Ross, you have a letter.” A young woman for whom such a thing was an echo from a deeply retrograde past, her voice was faintly incredulous.

She handed him the letter, glancing at him admiringly. Her name was Leah and she thought Mr Ross was rather good-looking, so tall and bronzed and lean, with those queer green-brown eyes.

Unaware of her romantic train of thought, Xan stood and read the letter, which appeared to have been hand-delivered.

Her Majesty’s Court Service requires you to attend...

Only a Government would write on such beautiful stiff paper and use such an old-fashioned typeface and such an elaborate choice of words. He was invited to attend the inquest into the death of Giles Maybury. A set of caveats like small birds flying across the page indicated that his attendance was not optional.

CHAPTER 6

At about the time that Xan Ross was watching Billy Dangerfield deal with a full English breakfast, Inspector Nash was perching himself uncomfortably in the rows of spectator seating on an empty Centre Court.

The forensic people had done their work and the yellow crime scene ribbon had gone. There had been a good deal of unpleasantness about all of this with the Club, which held the view that a murder on its premises should be considered its misfortune rather than its fault and could not be allowed to inconvenience the match schedule.

The tournament director had button-holed the weary Inspector on the subject on the way into the Club. "Centre Court closed! My dear inspector, you can have no idea what problems it will cause if the schedule is delayed. We may even have to go into a third Monday."

Inspector Nash had replied soothingly that the crime scene work having now been completed, the court could be returned to use in time for the afternoon's matches. For now, he sat in isolated splendour surrounded by a sea of empty seats.

He experimented with a bit of leaning back and forth and established that the only seats which gave the reach to stab a man were those on either side of it and the three in front and behind. And this basic test took no account of the requirement to do it unseen.

In the afternoon, he returned to Centre Court when a match was in progress. This entailed further unpleasantness with the stewards as it necessitated a paying ticket-holder being moved to a more expensive seat.

On his way in, Inspector Nash observed the precision with which the attendant scrutinised his ticket. Clearly, it would be impossible to sneak in with a ticket for another court or day or no ticket at all. With a sigh, he crossed The Murderer With No Ticket Or The Wrong Ticket off his list of possible solutions.

During play, he repeated his experiments. He leaned forward, sideways and back, extricated things from a rucksack brought for the purpose, dropped newspapers and picked them up again. In each case, his neighbours' eyes were immediately fastened on him in curiosity or outrage.

It looked as though the idea of a psychological moment when no one would notice anything was a highly risky proposition. The heightened tension and the stillness and silence of the audience during play acted as a sensory stimulant, so that any sound or any visual activity at the edge of peripheral vision clamoured like an alarm bell.

He watched the pattern of crowd movements. Every two games, the players took two minutes' rest break at the side of the court, where they ate bananas, buried their face in a towel or jiggled a leg restlessly, according to temperament. At this time, spectators were free to leave their seats, but unless they could perform their errands – fetching drinks and so forth – in two minutes or less, they were unable to return to the court before the doors were closed and play resumed. (This was what had happened to Mr Brass.) Two games later, there was another change of ends and those outside dashed back to their seats while others departed in their place.

Inspector Nash considered Mr Brass, who was of an irritable disposition and had been out of his seat when the alarm was raised. But if it was him, the inspector thought inelegantly, why had he not left the Club at once rather than hanging around waiting to get back in? Inspector Nash toyed with the entertaining notion of a murderer so fascinated by the match he had come to watch that he couldn't tear himself away.

Down on the court, a high-quality match was taking place but Inspector Nash was aware of none of it. He was mentally visualising a train of events in which Colin Brass committed murder with unusual coolness and self-possession then left the court and waited outside for the emergency summons he knew would come.

Had Mr Brass's absence from court been intended to furnish him with some ingenious alibi? But if so, it had failed. Had something gone wrong? What would have happened, for instance, if Mr Ross had not noticed that Maybury was dead? Brass would have returned to the Centre Court at the next change of ends, someone else would have eventually noticed the corpse in their midst and it was unlikely that anyone would have remembered

Mr Brass's absence.

The inspector shook his head sadly. Brass needed an observant witness for his alibi and yet the one he had couldn't clear him. Xan Ross had said that the little man had left the court during the change of ends – and there was every chance that Giles Maybury had been killed then. Brass could have done it on his way out.

The seats on the other side of Mr Maybury were scarcely more promising in that respect. Sarah Eastward did not look as though she had the physical strength for the job. Her husband, on the other hand, did. But it would have been risky and Harlan Eastward did not strike him as the sort of man who took risks.

No, the most promising candidate by far was Mr Ross himself, who by all appearances had the required nerve both to do the job and to sit quietly afterwards and wait for the crime to be discovered – only he hadn't, which was odd and required explaining. The Inspector dwelt persuasively on Mr Ross's confessed dislike of tennis. But could one suspect a man for not liking tennis?

At the edge of his vision, a red-headed figure loomed. "Sir?" It was Sergeant Monroe. "We've found the wallet. It was in one of the litter bins on the premises."

The inspector's eyebrows rose. "Was it now?" It was, of course, only to be expected that a common thief would fling away an empty wallet once he had stripped it of what it held, but all the same … "Contents?"

"Cards but no cash."

And again, that was interesting. "Fingerprints?"

"It's being tested now."

The testing had to be done, naturally. But Inspector Nash did not expect to find the fingerprints of either Giles Maybury or his assailant.

"And the CCTV footage is ready for review."

This was the cleaned-up footage from the camera on the Centre Court walkway. The inspector sat and watched it in the darkened video suite. The time was displayed in an old-fashioned digital watch font in the left-hand corner. A second screen offered the recorded television coverage on the tennis court, as a means of cross-checking the times.

From 13:03:34, there was a sporadic fidget of cleaners and stewards. Once the court opened at 13:30:56, a trickle of spectators began to arrive. Colin Brass showed his ticket, his cherubic face pursed with displeasure at the slowness of the steward. Ten minutes later, Xan Ross went in, his face turned away from the camera.

More spectators streamed in and then it was the quieter period of the women's match, punctuated with bursts of activity at each change of ends when the doors were opened.

It was interesting to the student of human nature to study the behaviour of spectators suddenly released from the immobility of the tennis-court. Almost all of them reached immediately for the life-giving cranial refreshment of their mobile phone. The rest hastened towards either washrooms or drinks stalls, evidently without perceiving a feedback loop between these two requirements.

Those who remained on the walkways between games fell into two categories – phone-gazers who remained rooted to the spot and exercise-seekers who made brisk circuits of the court.

At 14:35:40, when the television coverage indicated that the women's match had finished, a stream of people flooded out of Entrance 7. A few minutes later, a much bigger crowd began to collect, all eager to enter the court simultaneously.

It seemed almost impossible to pick out an individual in a crowd like this – but a moment later, Inspector Nash felt a thrill of shock when he spotted the halting figure of the victim, almost hidden under his pale blue hat. It was like seeing a ghost. Apparently unconscious of his short time left in the world, the old man made his way in through the doors of Entrance 7.

As the men's match unfolded, its progress charted by the regular tide of spectators flowing in and out of the court at every change of ends, Inspector Nash's attention wandered. The important moment would be the 5-2 change of ends in the second set – but in the event, it was a disappointment. In the busy crowd that thronged in and out of the doors at 5-2, it was simply not possible for his untrained eye to pick out individuals. A round and slightly rubicund blur suggestive of an irritable Colin Brass was the best Inspector Nash could come up with.

The tape spooled on to a sudden urgent confabulation between the stewards, listening anxiously to their radios and then conferring. Taken with the abrupt halting of the tennis match on the recorded BBC feed, it was a complete, if oblique, representation of murder off.

CHAPTER 7

The Wimbledon Murder, as the press collectively called it, immediately seized the public interest. With no clear motive or suspect to consider, a riot of speculation was indulged in.

At the Department of Security and Defence, where Giles Maybury had been a senior civil servant before his retirement, there was a degree of nervous curiosity. They were not used to former colleagues dying in such a blaze of publicity and excitement – civil servants generally had the good taste to expire discreetly of natural causes, at such an ancient age that their service to their country had been long forgotten.

The Secretary of State's Office put some querulous questions about the matter in the Monday morning meeting and the Permanent Secretary's office promised to look into said matter, having no clear idea what they meant by that.

The Department press office was tasked with coming up with 'lines' on the situation in case asked. ("Although I don't know quite what we'd say if we *were* asked," the Head of Press said dubiously. "Except that it's nothing to do with us. But perhaps we won't be asked." And they weren't.)

After several days of feverish internal debate, the office of the Permanent Secretary came up with a short set of proposed actions, only one of which survived contact with the Secretary of State's office – to send a bouquet of flowers to Giles Maybury's widow, Elinor. And this was done.

As far as the All England Lawn & Croquet Club was concerned, things began to return slowly to normal. The match which had been disrupted by Giles Maybury's death had been completed and neither combatant seemed to have been adversely affected by the delay. (It had been won by the affable, crowd-pleasing Swede.) The benign weather meant that all matches were being completed to schedule. The Club settled back with relief to the usual media headlines of the Fortnight – questions over billing of the top seeds on the show courts and that perennial favourite, the price of strawberries and cream.

And after three days of excitable media coverage, the national press discovered simultaneously that a) a popular heritage biscuit brand was being discontinued due to a global shortage of the right sort of currants and b) swans on the River Thames were at risk from a new species of algae. Press interest therefore began to wane from the Wimbledon Murder.

CHAPTER 8

The inquest into the death of Giles Maybury was held early in the morning at a coroner's court in Lambeth. It was not expected that it would discuss the developing police case with any detail but would confine itself to establishing the initial details. A number of witnesses were called.

Colin Brass missed his usual Sunday evening choir practice in order to get a reasonable night's sleep. He retired to bed early but failed to allow for the fact that it was a hot June night and the church was only just across the green. It was far too warm to close the windows and his attempts at slumber were therefore sound-tracked by bells. They pursued him into his dreams and he woke late and short-tempered and missed the early train.

Xan Ross also slept badly. He had had the dream again. The place was the same every time – wide, flat sands, sluggish tides and a damp bank of mist rolling in from the sea. Birds crying and an indefinable sense of menace in the air. He always woke from the dream with an uneasy mind.

To shake off his oppression, he left his hotel early and walked westwards along the river, thankful to be bound against the traffic. The prevailing wind of commerce appeared to blow most Londoners from south to north and west to east.

Attending an inquest was yet another activity Homeland would frown on if they got to hear about it. Once again, he had the uncomfortable sensation of being halted and identified, like a chameleon pinned against a flower and obliged to stick at a single shade.

The inquest drew only a thin crowd and very few press journalists, perhaps thanks to the inconvenient hour. The coroner was a round-faced elderly man with a face that seemed designed for a permanent rosy beam until suddenly the smile vanished and two cold eyes focused on the court-room.

In his opening remarks, the coroner confined himself to a simple presentation of the facts. Giles Maybury had been stabbed to death on the Centre Court at Wimbledon during the second set of a gentlemen's singles match.

First witness, Mrs Maybury, an elderly lady with her hair in carefully-set grey curls. She took the stand with composure and gave her evidence crisply.

Giles was fond of tennis. He had been in a cheerful mood at breakfast and looking forward to his day at Wimbledon, although he had been troubled by a little indigestion. She had no idea what could possibly have prompted an unprovoked attack on him.

Second witness, Mr Brass, bouncing on his toes with eagerness to explain how he had paid no attention to his unfortunate neighbour and had been out of his seat for the crucial two games.

Third and fourth witnesses, Mr and Mrs Eastward – he with a truculent air of being inconvenienced, she with one of being slightly embarrassed by her pugnacious husband. Neither had anything to add to their previous statements.

Fifth witness, Mr Ross. Mr Ross had noticed Mr Maybury slump over in his seat. He had raised the alarm and attempted first aid.

Mr Justice Longfellow tapped out his favourite opera tune on the desk before him with a pencil, a habit of his when working. "When was the last time you noticed the deceased alive?"

"Just before the last change of ends. 5-2," Xan added obligingly.

"So, there would have been in fact only a ten-minute window within which someone might have committed the murder?"

Slight sensation in court. A sandy-haired man in the second row of the audience studied the faces of the other witnesses with interest, to see how they reacted to this intelligence.

"I believe so, yes."

Sixth witness, the police surgeon. The weapon used had been an ordinary folding pen-knife. The … [an interlude of highly technical medical evidence which hardly anyone in court understood and was of limited interest to the press]. The police surgeon further testified that only a handful of people could have reached the victim from a seated position.

The inquest brought in a verdict of murder by person or

persons unknown. The coroner added a rider that this tragic occurrence underlined the importance of combating petty crime and robbery through stronger sentences for first offences, thereby cementing the impression that this was a mere matter of pick-pocketing. Court adjourned.

As Xan stood to leave, he was conscious of a feeling of anti-climax. It had been a thoroughly inconclusive affair – the police were no doubt keeping their cards, if they held any, concealed for the time being. But what about the cards he himself held? The fact that Giles Maybury had claimed to be in fear of his life, for example?

He could not now easily offer up this information – or for that matter his possession of Maybury's diary. The call he had made on this in the first moments after Giles Maybury's death, when he was kicking his heels in the interview room waiting for the police, was beginning to look dangerously short-sighted. It had been the correct response according to Homeland's manual of tactical short-term procedure, but it was looking all wrong for the long game. And he was now in a long game.

As he made his way out of the courtroom, he noticed a man with a gloomy expression leaning his elbow on the balustrade of the stairs and staring at his phone. He had seen that sad face before somewhere – where?

Xan turned the matter over in his mind until quite suddenly, he had it. Wimbledon. Not on the Centre Court itself, nor in the muddled aftermath of the murder, but earlier. The man had been one of the loiterers Xan had thought resembled sentries manning the stairs.

Well, it was not beyond the realms of reason for someone to take an interest in a murder because they had chanced to be on the spot. Would it necessarily prompt you to attend the inquest, though? He filed the face away in his mind.

As he left the building, he was interrupted. "Are you in a hurry, Mr Ross?"

The inspector's Welsh twang was more distinctive than ever.

"Should I be?"

The inspector smiled. "I have a few questions I'd like to ask you – off the record, so to speak."

The two men repaired to a nearby coffee-shop. It was by now after nine and the place was an empty shell of the crammed and frantic venue that had been hissing steam and dispensing coffee and pastries at high speed an hour earlier.

"What do you make of that verdict, Mr Ross?"

"Hardly eye-opening."

"Well, at this stage, we're under no obligation to share what we know for the entertainment of the press. Or, for that matter, what we don't know."

"Yes, I see that. For instance, that wallet being found."

"A thief usually drops whatever he can as quickly as possible after the crime. But I daresay you know that."

Xan disregarded the implication. "Odd, though, that it was found inside the grounds. And the fact that the bank cards were still in it was awfully convenient for you."

"Yes," the inspector said thoughtfully. "I wondered

about that myself." He took a sip of his coffee. "But that's not what I wanted to ask you about. In point of fact, I have a missing witness. I'm hoping the inquest reports might bring him or her out, but there's been no response to our various appeals. The seat behind Mr Maybury. I was hoping you might remember something."

Xan frowned. "I think it was a man. Oldish, stoutish, in a suit."

"That doesn't exactly narrow things down."

"Sorry."

Inspector Nash sighed. "It's a start, anyway. If anything else comes back to you, perhaps you'd let me know. Not that it will help, probably. I've been spending a bit of time on Centre Court and I'm bound to say you're right."

Xan didn't pretend to misunderstand him. "You couldn't do it during play. Not without being seen, unless you're one of the two people sitting next to him – and if it was one of them, you ought to be able to prove it."

"Which leaves the change of ends at 5-2." The inspector frowned at his coffee again. "Colin Brass could have done it going out – and he's got an explanation for *why* he went out then, but I'm bound to say it's not a very good one. And besides, he's one of the only two people who could have done it from his seat, so that doesn't seem to help much. Otherwise, I still don't see how any of them could have done it without being seen, either coming out *or* coming back."

"It's pretty simple, I would have thought. You stumble or drop your newspaper as you go past. You'd be very close to Maybury – no one would be able to see what you were doing."

The inspector looked dubious. "You'd have to be very quick not to be seen."

"The aisle seat next to Maybury was empty and some in the row behind may have been. That would reduce the odds of someone seeing. Besides, they don't look at each other when they're going past."

"Yes, I've noticed that."

"The man who ought to have noticed something is the one who was sitting on the other side of Maybury. You might want to try him again. Maybe he was paying more attention than I was."

Inspector Nash glanced at Mr Ross. For the first time, the flicker of an emotion on what he had come to consider a good poker face. But too difficult to discern what the emotion might be. Instead, he said briskly: "Well, I'm sure you won't be surprised to learn that, with the single exception of Mr Brass, none of the people in that row admits to being out of their seat in that change of ends. And I know what you're thinking – they're lying because they're scared. But I don't think they *are* scared. I don't think it's occurred to many of them that they're suspects. They're too busy feeling hard done by because they missed the rest of the match and arguing with the Club about refunds."

"In any case, of course, it doesn't have to be someone who was sitting in Maybury's row at all. Anyone could have walked through the row during the change of ends."

Inspector Nash's face assumed the frowning scowl that was its habitual expression when he was thinking something out. "You don't think the other spectators would notice a stranger?"

"Let's not call him X," Xan said with a sudden smile. "I don't think so. They're either watching the court, even when there's no play, or reading or talking to the person they came with or most likely of all, looking at their phones. And they always look forward, whatever they're doing. They never look left to right."

"So you're talking about our murderer sitting quietly in another part of the court, then seizing his chance at the change of ends, walking along Mr Maybury's row as though they've got a seat there, stumbling over halfway along and stabbing him, then going out the other side and no one spotting them?"

"A shot to nothing," Xan said. "You call it off if the circumstances aren't right, try again later. But I wouldn't get too excited about the idea. It can't have been any of the ticket-holders, not if it was a premeditated crime. And as a matter of fact, your murderer doesn't need a seat on Centre Court at all."

Inspector Nash stared. "He doesn't?"

"Providing he knew where Giles Maybury was sitting, he could have come in at the change of ends, done the murder and gone out again before play started. In fact, it makes far more sense because it gives you a potential killer with a grudge against Maybury and a premeditated plan outside the court, rather than a Centre Court ticket-holder who impulsively decided to murder him."

Inspector Nash felt that this idea warranted some thought before he committed himself in speech. He took the opportunity to consume the sticky Danish pastry he had recklessly selected. At length, he returned to speech. "Well, it's ingenious. Maybe too ingenious. I can't see a jury buying it."

"It would have needed someone very quick and very ruthless," Xan conceded. "No hesitation and taking on a lot of risk. I'd say you're looking at a professional hit. Possibly involving a team."

"And how would this mythical hitman get onto the court if you're saying he didn't have a ticket?"

"I don't know," Xan admitted.

"Well, I'm glad to hear there's something you don't know." The inspector frowned at his notebook. "I'll get the CCTV people onto anyone who was hanging around that gangway between games. *You* didn't happen to notice anyone while you were out there, did you?"

The vision of a line of sentries rose once again in Xan's mind. "There was a woman with red hair and a rucksack. A couple in their twenties. And a man with a broken nose. Any of them could be your subject of interest. If it was the woman, she would have had to leave the rucksack somewhere – but she would probably have been working with someone else. I think any of them would have been."

The inspector nodded. "And any of them could have been law-abiding citizens just getting a breath of fresh air between games. But it's a possibility, always supposing I can find an answer about how they got onto the court without a ticket."

He put away his notebook and rose. "I'll put it to my superiors. But I'm bound to say you're still their favourite suspect and this method you've offered me doesn't rule *you* out by any means. And you already had a ticket."

CHAPTER 9

Elinor Maybury was curled up in an armchair watching a bumblebee buzzing in the flowers in the conservatory. Mostly lilies – ugly, papery things with a stench that made her head ache.

Why send flowers anyway? The mess, the fuss of chopping the wretched things in half, finding a vase that fitted, pulling the leaves off and then tidying the whole thing away when the petals started to wither. People should have more sense – but bereavements, Elinor had noticed, often sent people into a flat spin of indecisiveness about how to respond. So they sent flowers. Dead things, to a house of mourning.

At least now the funeral was out of the way, there shouldn't be any more bouquets arriving. And today was the day she would banish them all to the compost-heap at the far end of the garden.

Giles wouldn't approve, of course. His whole life had been a hymn to correctitude. A job in the civil service. A nice, restrained wedding in a church, even though neither he nor she were religious. A house in a mature residential area, not too far from a train station but not too close to the city.

A life of moderate pleasure, something to be inched

through. And then the sudden break in the pattern. Death at a tennis-match – of all the extraordinary, melodramatic things.

It didn't make sense. And now that the first shock of grief was beginning to – not recede, not yet, but settle, like rain into grass – Elinor found herself starting to turn over questions in her mind.

She looked at her watch. She had refused the offers friends had made to come and stay with her – the last thing you wanted at a time like this, other than lilies, was an unexpected house-guest. Yet it was undeniable that in the empty house, the time did seem to run down slowly, as though the clock itself had given up on things.

Eventually, she supposed, things would start up again. The seconds would begin to tick on more quickly. After all, she was not quite seventy years old and she probably had at least twenty years to go. At which moment in her reflections, she was thankful to be interrupted by the annoying electronic chime of the doorbell.

Outside was a young man who looked faintly familiar. She was relieved to note neither flowers nor a reporter's notebook (or worse, a dictaphone – some journalists had impertinently come armed with those), but his well-cut suit suggested an equally unwelcome intrusion.

"If it's about the pension, your people have already explained it very clearly to me."

The young man smiled cheerfully. "I'm not from the government."

Elinor Maybury favoured him with a very sharp glance

indeed. "No. Your suit's too new. And they always wear pinstripe and often mismatch navy with charcoal, something I can't abide."

Xan was not entirely sure what had brought him here. Death at Wimbledon, however personally inconvenient, was no business of his. There was, however, the question of the diary, which he had felt justified in holding back from the police, but not from Maybury's widow.

He also had not settled in advance on a story to give her. It would depend on what kind of woman Elinor Maybury was – something that the brief glimpse at the inquest had not been able to tell him. She might have been hysterical, angry or despairing, any of which would have prevented her from thinking straight. She might have been of that naturally unquestioning type that is a godsend to the investigator. Now he made up his mind.

"My name's Ross. I'm sorry to disturb you. I was at Wimbledon the day your husband –."

"You needn't dress it up," Elinor said. "The day Giles died. Of course, I remember you from the inquest. That's memory in old age for you – it's slow, but it gets there in the end." She frowned. "You haven't come to tell me about his last moments or anything like that? I can't stand sentiment."

"That's not why I'm here. But I would like to talk to you about your husband, if you don't mind."

And this was the moment at which one should find words along the lines of 'not today, thank you' and close the door. If Giles's sister was here being a spiritual rock as she had proposed, she would already have done it. There were several reasons why Elinor did not. Unthinkable to admit that boredom was one of them. But at the same time – he knew something about Giles. She could send him away, but the questions in her own mind might steadily become more clamorous over twenty years and she might come to regret it.

She made up her mind. “I was about to have some tea. You’d better come in and I’ll make something stronger.”

Of course, it probably wasn’t very appropriate at two in the afternoon, but if you couldn’t drink whisky in the middle of the day when your husband had just died, when could you? She established her visitor in the living-room and went away to fetch the whisky glasses.

Xan looked at the old-fashioned titles on the bookshelf by his elbow. Rider Haggard, Jules Verne, John Buchan. They were shabby, elderly editions which did not seem likely to appeal to his hostess.

On an impulse, he pulled one out and opened it. On the flyleaf, the name of Giles Maybury was scribbled in a schoolboy hand. Evidence perhaps of a childish longing for adventure which life had denied the book’s owner – until the end. That sleight of hand with the diary had come straight out of an old-fashioned spy thriller.

Almost in passing, he noticed that the book’s spine was surprisingly dust-free. There were other signs too, when one looked for them – indications that the armchairs had been shifted out of position, scratches around the lock of the bureau next to the fireplace.

Elinor Maybury came back into the room, carrying two heavy-cut glasses. She poured a generous finger of whisky into each, handed one to her guest, and poised herself lightly in a wing-back chair, looking as though she might blow away out of the French windows at any moment. Then she gave her unexpected guest a schoolmistressy glance. "Well?"

"I wondered what you thought of the inquest verdict."

"Murder by person or persons unknown. It covers a multitude of sins, doesn't it? I said so to my sister-in-law and I believe she thought I was being flippant. Of course, Giles would be mortified. He hated a fuss. And he would have been furious about missing the end of that match." She took a rather incautious mouthful of whisky. It was stronger than she had expected – come to think of it, had Giles usually mixed it with water? "The coroner seems convinced it was robbery, but it does seem an absurd amount of trouble to go to for a wallet."

"I don't think it was a robbery."

"Why not?"

"For the same reason you don't – far too much trouble and risk for what would be likely to be little reward. No one carries much cash on them these days."

Elinor took another sip of the whisky – it was much stronger than she had imagined and if she was going to go on drinking Giles's prized single malts, she was going to have to learn to mix them properly. "Then what do you suggest? I assume you have a theory. At any rate, we've established you're not here merely to commiserate."

Xan said apologetically: “Can you think of any reason why anyone might have wanted your husband dead? I know it sounds melodramatic, but sometimes people have secrets.”

“Giles wasn’t having an affair, if that’s what you’re thinking. He wasn’t that kind of person at all.” She added wryly: “I expect wives always say that.”

“I’d say wives always know, even if their husbands don’t realise.”

“Well, that’s intelligence at any rate. The journalists who turned up here seemed to think that a man of Giles’s age married to someone like me couldn’t possibly *not* be having an affair. One very persistent fellow kept asking me if any photograph had been found with Giles’s effects, as if he was the sort of man who keeps a photograph of his mistress next to his heart. So insulting, to Giles’s judgement apart from anything else.”

Xan found himself suddenly interested. “What was he like?”

“Who?”

“The journalist who asked about the photograph.”

“Oh, a shifty-looking fellow with a broken nose. It seemed an odd question to ask.”

Xan thought so too. He decided to drop the point. He said apologetically: “I’m afraid the questions don’t get any easier. What about finances? Did your husband have money problems?”

“Giles was careful with money. Besides, I went through all his papers and there was nothing. The police did, too.

And the pensions people who came in were very thorough. Too thorough, if you ask me. I could hardly get rid of them." She shook her head regretfully. "No, Giles had no secret vices. He didn't even drink very much – except for this," she added, raising her glass in an unintentional toast. "And even whisky he was maddeningly moderate about. Never more than a finger at a time, never more than two per night. I'm not helping you very much, I'm afraid."

"There's something else." Xan had come to Egham not sure how to approach this. "I had a rather curious conversation with your husband when we were out of our seats between games."

Elinor said sharply: "You didn't say so at the inquest."

"No. He spoke to me in confidence."

She didn't skewer the evasion as she might have done. "What did he say?"

Xan held out the diary. "He gave me this."

"Oh, so that's where it went! *Giles* did? But why on earth?"

"He didn't say."

"But that's extraordinary. What on earth can he have meant by it?"

Xan had been over the rambling words already in his mind. "He asked if I was a stranger to the country and then started to tell me about something he had discovered – but he clammed up before he got very far. He seemed worried about being overheard."

Elinor frowned. "Giles – with a sinister secret. It sounds

ridiculous. But come to think of it, he did seem a little preoccupied. I thought it was indigestion but it's possible he had something on his mind. I remember him saying that once you had been a public servant, you always had a responsibility. Very pompous, but that was Giles for you."

"When did he say that?"

"Oh, a few days before – before he went to the tennis. And I said that I couldn't see what good he would be to the public at 67. The curse of a sharp tongue."

Xan nodded, tactfully disregarding the sudden ring of bitterness in her voice. It all added another dimension to Giles Maybury. "He didn't say anything to you – about anything that was worrying him?"

"No, of course not."

"All the same," Xan said cautiously, "it's possible that he talked to someone else."

"Nothing more likely – I've always found men will tell another man something when they wouldn't dream of telling their wives. Such a lot of nonsense."

"Unfortunately, the diary isn't a lot of help in suggesting who he might have talked to. I mean, it might be to you, but it isn't to me."

Elinor looked amused. "So that's why you're really here. The translating ability of a loving wife. Well, I'll do my best."

She opened the diary. "Let's see. Yes, this is his typical round, very Giles."

"Meaning?"

"Oh, Giles liked to keep up with his old school friends and civil service chums. They're all to a man (and they're all men) stiff upper lip, old school tie types. They asked his advice about government affairs. Giles loved to be of use to people. I sometimes think he regretted retiring."

Xan wondered if all marriages were like this – one's mental processes rendered entirely transparent. He also wondered whether Giles Maybury had missed being of importance so much that he had manufactured a drama out of thin air – something to fill his inactive days. But that was not the impression he had got of the old man with the earnest, quavering voice.

"So, the week before he died?" he prompted. He had studied the entries himself but the cryptic scribbles were meaningless to him.

Elinor glanced down at the page. "Well, lunch with C would be Charles. Giles's accountant – at least that's what he called him, but it's a grand name for a company to take care of your pension. And 12.30 at the Ritz was a lunch-party for a theatre matinee. Mark and Fenella were there – Fenella and I go back years and Mark and Giles were at the same department. They didn't come to the funeral – Mark had a debate in Parliament – but Fenella wrote me a lovely note."

Xan did his best to sift through all this information that was coming at him rapid-fire. "And then?"

"On Wednesday, he was in bed all day. I remember that because I had to look after him. It was most inconvenient because I was hosting the reading group in the evening –

and how long it takes those people to struggle through an average-sized paperback, you have no idea."

"He was ill?"

"Gastric trouble, I'm afraid. Nothing very glamorous. Any kind of rich food set it off, so I daresay it was whatever he had at the Ritz. He was down with it the whole of Wednesday and Thursday and he was meant to go to a cocktail-party on the Friday but he ducked out of that too."

"But he went to Wimbledon the next day."

"Oh, yes. He didn't look fit for it in my view – had a nasty spasm of his trouble over breakfast – but he would never have missed the tennis."

Xan wondered how many people had known that about Giles Maybury. He also wondered about that curiously timed bout of illness.

Elinor was still turning the pages of the diary. "That's interesting, now I come to think of it."

"What is?" Anything out of the ordinary was meat and drink to the investigator.

She indicated a page of the diary. "This is the Thursday, the week before he died. He was going to an Etruscan ceramics exhibition in Oxford, or so he said. I wouldn't have thought he had any interest in the Etruscan period myself, but there it is. But he wrote down a telephone number on the same page. And in my experience, one doesn't ring up museums one's visiting." She added drily: "It is an Oxford number, so at least we can conclude that he did go there, whatever else he lied about."

"I'm afraid," Xan said carefully, "that digging around in someone's life after they die can be rather unpleasant." It was as close as he dared go. Elinor Maybury had made it clear that she did not welcome sympathy. Inwardly, he reflected that the trip to Oxford would be worth following up. Anything that Giles Maybury had lied to his wife about was likely to be significant.

Elinor shook her head impatiently as though to clear her mind of any momentary qualms. "Well, we're not going to get anywhere if we're too squeamish to ask questions." She leaned forward and handed the diary back to him. "You'd better keep that. He wanted you to have it."

"Are you sure?"

"Of course I'm sure. You'll need it when you go and talk to all these people." When he glanced at her rather quizzically, she said: "Well, you can't pretend you're not interested. That's why you're here, isn't it? In any case, I should like to think that someone was doing something. I'll give you introductions to them all. Charles was one of Giles's oldest friends. Mark and Fenella Romilly, too. He's a junior minister and he's frightfully self-important. Fenella isn't nearly such a fool as she looks."

Xan noticed suddenly that there was a tiredness in her voice. He thought he had taken up enough of her time for one day.

She showed him out, as delicate and fragile a figure as one of her own china shepherdesses. As he came down the steps, he turned to take a last fleeting look at the house. Hanging baskets with flowers he didn't know the names of. More flower-pots each side of the three steps. An imposing and thoroughly respectable residence. It didn't look like the kind of place that held secrets, but he sensed secrets all the same. Not here – somewhere else.

*

Back at his hotel, he considered what he had learned. As Billy had already disparagingly remarked, Giles Maybury had apparently been a man with no secrets of his own. But it began to look as though he had stumbled across someone else's secret.

Maybury had liked to keep up with old friends and had enjoyed listening to their problems and advising them. It was therefore likely that whatever he had discovered, it was from one of these friends.

Which of them? The diary might answer that question, if he went back far enough. But equally, it might not. The friend in question might be someone Maybury had run into casually and he had never recorded the meeting in his diary. And Elinor could not help – it was already clear that Maybury had not confided in his wife.

There was something else he had learned from the visit to Elinor Maybury. Whoever was behind her husband's death, they had also searched her house. The signs had been obvious to someone who knew what to look for. A pro had done the job, probably a team of them. Xan knew the drill. The white sheet spread out across the floor for the tools, the photographs before you started to make sure everything went back in the same place. These people had been sloppy. They had left scratches around the lock of the bureau, for instance.

What had they been looking for? The diary? Possibly. Then there was the journalist who had come to the house and asked about photographs. That seemed to connect with Maybury's own words. A photograph that 'couldn't lie'. But what was it and, far more importantly, where was it? In the wallet that been stolen? But if that was the case, Maybury's house would not have been searched for it after his death.

The real question was, Xan thought, what was he going to do about it. Did he seriously intend to take on unpaid work the police were already doing? This was not why he had come to this country. But once again, the frail figure in the Panama hat shambled before his eyes. Giles Maybury had known something. That knowledge had been dangerous and he had evidently been killed because of it. From such gossamer threads of speculation were a case begun.

CHAPTER 10

It was not eight-thirty in the morning yet. The early sun streamed through the window and illuminated the witness reports from the Wimbledon murder which Inspector Nash was re-reading.

He had dispatched field teams to interview a number of spectators from Giles Maybury's row and the row behind and it was these thoroughly unhelpful reports that he had just finished reviewing. All these witnesses united in having only the haziest of memories about anything which had not taken place on court, although most of them could have given a shot-by-shot account of the match itself and several had tried.

There were still a handful of possible witnesses who had not come forward. And as the tournament director had warned, while tickets that had been allotted directly to members of the public in the main draw could be easily traced, those distributed to corporate customers and regional tennis-clubs were a different matter.

The most maddening of these missing witnesses was the occupant of the seat directly behind Maybury, who had apparently got up and left as soon as the disturbance started and had not come forward despite several appeals for witnesses. The AELTC had established that this ticket had been allocated to a tennis club but had had not been able to discover what had happened to it since. Of course, it was not likely that this person was the murderer. Giles Maybury had been stabbed from the front. But there was hardly anyone who would have been in a better position to observe him.

Inspector Nash returned to the witness statements that had been taken on the day of the murder. In his view, you needed to get to know an interview record like an old friend, going over and over it until you were familiar enough to notice any jarring notes.

For instance, it was only now, reading Colin Brass's statement again, that he found himself drawn to the fact that Brass had left the court at the score of 5-2, when the next two games might finish the set. Sarah Eastward had explained that most people went out in the early games. Going out towards the end of a close set seemed an odd thing for a self-proclaimed aficionado of tennis to do.

It was worth asking Brass about it. But by the irritating logic of the tickets, he was unlikely to be the murderer. That role belonged to the shadowy Man Who Walked Along The Row At The Change Of Ends, a Pimpernel-esque figure who had come to loom greatly in Inspector Nash's mind.

The man (or woman) in question must have been bold and reckless. Also efficient, since he or she had apparently committed a violent crime in broad daylight without anyone seeing. He or she apparently possessed a flying carpet with which to sail over the outer perimeter fence into the

Wimbledon grounds and some further means of magic to get onto Centre Court without a ticket. But surely there must be some way of getting a handle on this omnipotent individual.

Inspector Nash had instructed the police CCTV team to go over the footage of the public walkways that ran round the outer perimeter of the Centre Court.

"All the walkways," he had clarified to Sergeant Monroe. "There are twelve entrances to the court, see, and twelve staircases down with a camera at each one."

"What is it we're looking for?" the sergeant wanted to know.

"People hanging around between the games looking suspicious on any of the cameras and anyone trying to get onto the court without a ticket. And there's something else." Inspector Nash explained what was required.

"But how are two operators watching two different feeds supposed to spot the same person coming in through one door and out through another? And how are they supposed to cross-check that across twelve feeds?"

"It's likely our target came in at Entrance 8 and out at 7 or possibly the other way round, so it's only those two cameras they'll need to cross-check." Of course, all of this depended on the testimony of Mr Ross, who had been the last person to notice Giles Maybury alive, but it couldn't be helped.

The CCTV team were dedicated professionals. They knew how to watch footage of a parking lot for hours at a time and not tune out and miss the brief flash of action.

But it took time. They had been at the task now for two days and the inspector's initial optimism was beginning to flag.

He turned to the question of the ticket. If the murderer had come in from outside and had therefore not needed a ticket for Centre Court, it also followed that he had not *got* a ticket for Centre Court. In which case, how had he got onto the court?

At that moment, there was a knock on the door and Sergeant Monroe entered, brandishing a CD.

"The CCTV team thought you would be interested in this, sir. It's what they call the active clips from the cameras on the walkways – that is, the ones with things happening in them."

"Thank you Sergeant, I know what an active clip is."

And as active clips went, these weren't very exciting, at least initially. Blurred figures came and went along the long walkways, mostly watching their phones. Then the inspector leaned forward as the distinctive figure of Giles Maybury emerged, walking slowly around the perimeter of the court, passing under each camera in turn.

"This is from when he came out at the end of the first set, sir."

After a moment, the inspector became aware of another walker, a taller figure keeping his face turned away from the cameras. The two figures met, conferred briefly, then the taller one moved out of view of the cameras, obliging his companion to follow.

Inspector Nash grinned. "No flies on *him*. But was that

just habit or did he have something to hide?"

"I'm not sure, sir," Sergeant Monroe said stolidly.

"And if that's what you wanted to show me –."

"It's not."

Sergeant Monroe picked up a pencil and tapped the screen. "The team say the shadows indicate there are other people on that walkway who are staying out of the camera's way deliberately."

"You mean people walking up and down?"

"No, sir, I don't. I mean, or rather the team mean, one by each stairwell. They never get in front of the camera but you can see their shadows sometimes. And," the sergeant added triumphantly, "you see other people look at them. Or move round them. It's quite clear."

Inspector Nash considered for a moment the prospect of offering his superiors, let alone a jury, invisible suspects whose presence could be deduced by the glances of other people going past them. "How does that help us ID a possible subject of interest?" he grumbled.

"It doesn't, sir, but some of the stewards who man the doors to the court may have noticed them."

"The doors to the court aren't aligned with the stairs. The stewards wouldn't have a sightline." And Inspector Nash felt at this moment as though the All England Club had designed their showpiece court in this fashion for the specific purpose of annoying him.

"Well, when they went off for their breaks, they might have noticed someone," Sergeant Monroe said hopefully. "Some of them are ex-Army or police – noticing sort of people, you might say. Or perhaps one of the spectators."

"No one would call any of the spectators noticing sort of people," Inspector Nash said resentfully. His mind prodded him with some contradictory evidence. Mr Ross had come up with descriptions of a couple of people hanging about on the walkway. "You'd better get some-one to talk to the stewards again," he said grudgingly. "I'll handle the spectators. There's one or two of them I'd like to talk to again anyway."

Before the sergeant could reply, there was another knock on the door. The head of the CCTV team put his head around the door. "We've found one, sir."

"Found what?" Inspector Nash demanded irritably.

"What you asked for, sir. Someone who came in at Entrance 7 and out at 8, in a single change of ends."

The inspector was incredulous. "Are you sure? I've watched the tape myself and I couldn't have picked out an elephant and a troupe of dancing girls."

"Well, no," the CCTV head said, as tactfully as he could manage. Sergeant Monroe concealed a sudden smile behind his hand. "It's not very clear, but I thought you'd like to have a look at it all the same."

And indeed, it was not very clear. But it was clear enough. A man of medium height and build with a broken nose, wearing a cheap-looking dark blue suit. His face was turned away from the cameras as he passed into the court through Entrance 7 but the lens brutally picked out his bald patch in a way that made every man in the room wince and rub the back of his own head.

The view switched to Entrance 8 and this time the man was facing the camera, looking down, as though he knew it was there. His shoulders were tensed, a subconsciously defensive posture.

Inspector Nash leaned forward. “What’s he holding?”

The CCTV manager leaned forward and stopped the tape, revealing a blurred piece of dark cloth. “We had a couple of looks at that. We think it’s a handkerchief.”

“Well, well,” the inspector said thoughtfully. “The pros mostly don’t use gloves these days. Too risky if you’re caught with them. It was different in the old days when everyone from the aristocracy to the card-sharpers wore silk gloves. Now it marks you out. But I’m inclined to think there are cases where a handkerchief is just as bad. You’d better clean up that picture as best you can and run it through our records. We’ll try it on the stewards too.”

“What about the Club’s ticket-holder records?”

The inspector shook his head. “They already made it very clear their records aren’t complete. If this man queued on the day and paid cash for a grounds ticket, there would be no reason for him to be in their database. I’m not saying I think he did. I think they came as a team and I think they probably got in over a wall.”

“Yes, sir,” Sergeant Monroe said stolidly. “But that doesn’t explain how he had a ticket for the right court.”

It didn’t. And without an idea as to how that could have been done, they didn’t have anything resembling a watertight case.

*

By the end of the day, the team had pieced together a jigsaw of footage to paint a murder happening off-stage. They also had a portrait of a murderer.

There he was in the crowd that surrounded Giles Maybury when he returned to the court after speaking with Xan Ross. There again strolling along the walkway and then disappearing into the over-excited throng of people emerging from Entrance 7. Reappearing from Entrance 8 a moment later, his face turned away from the cameras.

In the most significant shot of all, the man was pausing on his way to Entrance 7, looking down at a paper in his hand. The CCTV team had been able to do quite a lot in tidying this one up and they were justly proud of themselves. The closest zoom had been able to pull a visual off the paper. It was a series of letters and numbers, but not a phone number or a name.

L2RT39. Giles Maybury's seat number.

CHAPTER 11

"But I really don't know if there's anything I can tell you," said Fenella Romilly, opening her large brown eyes wide and gazing wistfully at her interlocutor. Then her attention was suddenly drawn away to the importuning of a small child. "It's no good looking at it, Jasper. If you haven't got the money, you had better go and ask your mother."

A village fete was not the ideal circumstance in which to interview what the pros called subjects of interest, but it had proved the only feasible way to approach Mark Romilly, who had been a friend of Giles Maybury and was a junior government minister.

Xan had learned that Parliament closed in the middle of July and did not open again until September. However, fortunately, Romilly's constituency was reasonably close to London, in rural Oxfordshire and Elinor Maybury had been able to suggest a suitable approach.

"There's a fete on Saturday. I know it sounds frightful, but it's the best chance you'll have to catch Mark. It would be hopeless to approach him formally through his Department."

Wimbledon, Harrods, cricket, and now a village fete,

Xan thought. You English at play, you are so amusing. Now he was being offered another slice of it.

To reach the village of Hamblefield involved a slow stopping train from London Waterloo. He bought a ticket for cash at the station, reflecting that the railway system was the only means of travel that still offered anonymity. Providing you were not so foolish as to pay with a credit card, your destination was a matter for you and your conscience alone.

Three shining new smartcard machines outside the ticket office suggested that the option to buy tickets with cash would soon disappear – all in the name of convenience of course and offering a steady stream of data to the smartcard operator. Were people conscious of these small but persistent erosions of their privacy? Perhaps it was something you only noticed if you were in the trade.

There was an unexpected pleasure in seeing the ugly suburbs of London peter out and a quiet, green, view gradually unroll itself outside the window. Cottages with gingerbread eaves. Horses in white-fenced paddocks. Spreading trees casting shade for cows in a field.

Hamblefield, when he reached it, was an attractively old-fashioned village. The church had been built on a hillside above the river. From a gloomy churchyard full of yew trees, he took a steep path down through a doorway in an ancient brick wall and entered a garden stretching down to the banks of the river. The house to which this splendour had belonged was evidently long since gone, but the avenue of trees, the formal parterre herb gardens and the immaculate terraced lawn had survived.

Ordinarily, it must be a peaceful spot, but today, the lawn was crammed with stalls offering entertainments and refreshments, while a space in the centre threatened at any moment to burst into life with amateur theatrical performances and traditional dancing.

Squeezed disadvantageously between a plant stall and homemade produce, the book-stall was a comparative oasis of quiet. It was presided over by an elegant woman in her forties with wide brown eyes and a sweet, rather undecided expression. This, Xan knew from his research, was Fenella Romilly. He therefore introduced himself by mentioning Giles Maybury and indicating that he was a friend of the family.

"How lovely," Fenella Romilly said vaguely, her eyes straying past him to possible customers.

Xan had met this sort of witness before. There was only one reliable way to get their attention. "I'm a detective," he said firmly. "I'm looking into Giles's death. Elinor isn't satisfied."

Her attention was caught at once. "How marvellous. Of course, dear Elinor never *is* satisfied – between you and me, I find her just a tiny bit terrifying. But she would know best about her own husband and it did seem such an extraordinary thing to happen. Perhaps poor Giles had secrets. Have you found any?" The big brown eyes gazed at him brightly.

"Not yet," was all he managed to say, before she was

off again.

"We couldn't *believe* it when we heard about it. Of all the extraordinary things to happen. Mark said it must have been someone who had a *grudge* against Giles."

Xan refrained from getting drawn into the problematic mechanics of this theory. "Was he the sort of man people had grudges against?"

Fenella Romilly uttered a little shriek. "Heavens, I do hope you're not going to take everything I say and use it in evidence against me."

"I'm not a policeman," Xan said patiently. "Why do you think someone might have had a grudge against Giles Maybury?"

"Oh, I don't," Fenella Romilly said, wide-eyed. "That was Mark's idea. I think the murderer got the wrong man. After all, men all dress the same for sporting events, don't they, and one old man wearing a hat would look very much like another."

Xan considered this admittedly ingenious proposition. It would be ironic to say the least if he was chasing the wrong hare.

"Now, do say you're doing some detecting here. Of course, you probably can't say if you are. But if it's any of our neighbours, I'd be only too happy to tell you simply outrageous things about them."

"As a matter of fact, I wondered if you or your husband could tell me anything helpful about Giles' frame of mind when you saw him the week before he died."

"I daresay Mark won't remember. You know what men

are like, so unobservant about each other – well, I'm sure *you're* not, of course. But poor Mark spends so much time remembering his key messages, he doesn't have room in his head for anything else. He says he dreams about someone waking him up in the middle of the night to ask him if he's been thinking the wrong things in his sleep. So Orwellian. But I can tell you lots. For a start, he said he had digestive trouble."

A shadow fell over the bookstall. "Who had digestive trouble?

Xan turned to see a man of slightly less than his own height but stockily built, with dark-brown hair going to salt and pepper at the sides and the bright blue eyes of the sailor. Seen close to, he looked younger than his internet picture suggested, perhaps forty-odd. Just now, he looked worried, and his next words gave an immediate indication of his preoccupation. "Look here, Fen, I'm supposed to be starting on the treasure-hunt in a minute – I wish you'd come and give me a hand."

"Mr Ross is a very old friend of the Mayburys," Mrs Romilly said, with a slight emphasis on the word 'very'.

There was a rapid switch from distracted stall-organiser to professional politician. Romilly produced a smile and offered his hand. "Of course, delighted," he said rather mechanically. "Poor old Giles. Damned shame what happened to him."

"But Mr Ross is a detective really and he's come to ask us lots of leading questions about Giles."

The politician looked thoughtfully at Xan. "What's

your background?"

"I work out in the Middle East."

"I expect it's awfully dangerous," Fenella Romilly said wistfully. "Is that where you got that scar?"

"No." Xan felt that having supplied some credentials, it was time to divert the focus from himself. He directed his next question impartially to both husband and wife. "I gather you talked to Giles shortly before he died."

"I say, that sounds very incriminating." Mark Romilly grinned. "We ran into Giles at a lunch-party at the Ritz, that's all."

"It was a party for a theatre matinee but of course Mark didn't have time to go to that," Fenella Romilly supplied. "They laid on things nicely at the lunch, though. Giles was at the buffet table when I went up to try and get rid of my salad – a load of huge salad leaves, impossible to eat neatly standing up. Why don't people think about these things?"

Xan declined to pursue this fascinating side-track. "Do you remember anything about his manner?"

"Well, of course it would be easy to say now that he seemed ill-at-ease but it might all be hindsight."

"So, he wasn't ill at ease?"

"Oh, he *was*. He was short with the waiter about his wine not being cold enough and he kept looking around in a peculiar way as though there was someone he wanted to avoid."

Xan glanced at the MP. "Did you think he seemed ill-at-ease?"

Romilly looked a trifle uncomfortable. "Well, I didn't really speak to him. I'm afraid I was more interested in getting something to eat. I had a long afternoon ahead of me and a debate in the House in the evening. But look here, are you seriously saying that he was deliberately killed? I thought the police had concluded it was a sneak thief."

"That's what I said," Fenella Romilly put in. "After all, who would want to kill poor old Giles? He never did anything apart from watch tennis."

"In any case, how could anyone get in to murder him? They control the doors pretty tightly at Wimbledon, I've always understood."

"It must have been another ticket-holder," Fenella said eagerly. "You can't trust these passionate tennis-goers."

"All the people in the other seats would have been complete strangers," Mark Romilly said impatiently. He turned to Xan. "Isn't that right?"

Xan obligingly assumed the role of Wimbledon security professional. "Yes."

Romilly shook his head. "Well, it's beyond me. What do the police think?"

"Mr Ross doesn't work for the police, darling, do keep up." Fenella turned to Xan brightly. "I'm sure *you* have a theory, though." But before he could answer, her attention was diverted by a couple of customers arguing over a cookery book.

"Well?" Mark Romilly said quietly. He seemed to be occupied in adjusting his watch – an expensive-looking, old-fashioned affair. But at this point, he glanced over intently. "Sounds to me as though you have a theory."

Xan took a moment to note that Romilly was more intelligent than his bluff good fellow persona suggested. "Not exactly."

"I only ask because although I said old Giles didn't say a word to me, I have a nasty feeling I let the old boy down rather."

Romilly paused. Behind them, the clamour of the fete bore on – raised voices, the mooing of megaphones, tinny musical accompaniment to children's races and some sort of country dancing affair involving sticks and bells.

"He said he wanted a chat with me if I had a moment. Well, one knows what that usually means – a charity subscription. I've got used to avoiding that particular type of conversation, I'm afraid. Propriety issues, you know. So, I must admit I didn't exactly go out of my way to catch him. I thought if I spoke to him on the way out, I could cut it short and plead a previous engagement."

"And did you?"

"Well, no. He rushed off before the dessert course, as a matter of fact. Said he wasn't feeling too good. He looked a bit green, actually – I wondered if something he'd eaten had disagreed with him. But I keep wondering what he wanted to tell me. I mean, what if it wasn't a subscription at all?"

At this moment, Fenella Romilly glanced at her watch and gave a little shriek. "Mark, you're meant to be on the treasure-hunt. The Committee chair said two o'clock sharp and you know what a stickler for timing she is."

"Well, I wish you'd come and help me, Fen. The sand's the wrong kind and those plastic spades we bought barely make a dent. They were supposed to dig through it ahead of time to get some air into it. Never be a politician," he added in a gloomy aside to Xan. "The things they make you do. Unbelievable."

He shook hands again and trudged away through the crowd, his shoulders squared to face the coming ordeal.

A vigorous wind had blown up and was doing its best to destabilize the various tents, flags and balloons. Someone staggered past bent almost double beneath a tall fern in a pot. It seemed a good moment for a quiet exit.

*

The train which brought Xan back to Waterloo was a slow one and it was after five before he got back to the hotel. As he entered the hotel foyer, Leah, who was on the phone, waved a hand to him. With an apologetic roll of the eyes, she indicated the door of the hotel lounge. "A visitor, Mr Ross. Wouldn't give his name."

Xan felt a prickle of caution as he crossed the foyer and went into the room. But he found nothing more sinister than a man in an impeccable suit studying the book-shelves with his hands behind his back.

The man turned quickly. "Mr Ross? I'm sorry to trouble you, but I wanted to have a word, if it's convenient. My name is Temperley."

Mr Temperley had neatly clipped silver-grey hair and finely-drawn features, but the authoritative eyes and mouth were comically undermined by the bulbous nose of a clown. He looked to be in his late fifties or early sixties. A retirement candidate, then, but judging by the suit, not fully retired. Xan was reminded of Elinor's strictures on pin-stripes.

"What can I do for you?"

His visitor, evidently taking this as an invitation, plumped himself down in one of the armchairs. "I'm here on behalf of – er – various interests. I'd like to ask you a few questions if I may."

Xan took another chair without speaking.

"You're very wise not to say anything," Temperley said. A slow smile lit up the clown-face. "But I can assure you I'm not from the police."

And indeed, Xan had guessed as much. His visitor smelled of quietly wealthy rooms with panelled walls and old leather armchairs and quiet connections made from those comfortable chairs.

"Then who do you represent?"

"I'm responsible for a part of the Government that has oversight of security matters. I also happen to be an old acquaintance of Giles Maybury's. Here's my card." Temperley leaned forward and offered a neat pile, like a conjuror, so that Xan could pick one. "Not that it will be much comfort to you."

Sir Miles Temperley, CBE,

Assistant Director of National Affairs

Xan turned the card over a couple of times. It looked genuine enough but there was no departmental or agency name and he found himself interested in the vagueness of that job title.

Temperley was watching him with amusement. "You're a cautious man, Mr Ross."

"Habit, I'm afraid." And it was perhaps an odd moment to notice that the books on the shelves which Temperley had been studying when he came in were in fact a two-dimensional trompe l'oeil in the form of wallpaper.

"I expect you're wondering why I'm here. As I mentioned, I was slightly acquainted with Giles Maybury, in the way one is in the senior civil service. When he retired, I lost sight of him. Again, one does." Temperley paused, as though for effect. "He wrote in to my office the week before his death, asking for an appointment."

"Did he say what it was about?"

"Unfortunately not. And my office were not particularly prompt to respond. But the day before his death, he rang up. I had no time free, but he said the matter was urgent, so I agreed to a private appointment the next day at my house. Unsurprisingly, he never kept it." Temperley leant forward. "The question is – what did he want to ask me? Or indeed to tell me?"

Xan wondered whether he was expected to answer this question. He remained non-committally silent.

Temperley said: "I'm concerned by what happened at

Wimbledon. I gather you're an acute observer. I've read the police report and it's pretty thorough, but I'd also be interested in your observations, if you don't mind."

Xan wondered if he minded and what would happen if he did. His visitor had said he was not from the police, but he might have influence over them all the same.

Temperley looked as though he knew what was in his mind. "If you would just oblige me by going over it from the beginning..."

Xan recounted the basics, as matter-of-factly as he could manage. He omitted the details of his conversation with Maybury and the matter of the diary. When he had finished, Temperley leaned back to summarise. "So, the only people who could have stabbed Giles Maybury from their seats were the spectators seated directly behind, in front and next to him."

"It's a little more complicated than that. The people behind could hardly have stabbed him in the chest. The people sitting in front, including me, could have done, but not without being seen. The people seated on either side had the best chance but would inevitably be first to be suspected. But in any case, suspecting any of the people with a seat near Maybury is nonsense since no one could have arranged to have a ticket for a seat near his."

Temperley smiled. "How did you come by your ticket, by the way, as a newcomer to these shores?"

And once again, Xan cursed Billy and his damned sleight of hand. "I bought it from a tout. Not strictly above board, but I understand it's often done."

"And so you couldn't have known you would be sitting near Giles Maybury." Another crooked smile. "By your reasoning, the tickets business clears you and everyone else who was sitting near Mr Maybury of murder. Or of premeditation, at any rate. But I presume you have your own ideas about what happened."

"Well, it seems logical to assume that the murderer came in from outside the court and took an opportunity during one of the set breaks."

Xan outlined the theory of the Man Who Walked Along The Row In The Change Of Ends. "I imagine he got a ticket to the grounds by queueing – or queue-jumping. Or he went over a wall. Easy enough for a professional. Once you're in the grounds, there's nothing stopping you from walking right inside the Centre Court building. You don't get your ticket checked until you're going onto the court itself."

Temperley nodded. "That sounds reasonable. But could anyone have known where a specific target was sitting?"

And here, Xan remained silent. There were various possibilities, for example, mobile phone tracking, but it was hardly his job to speculate.

Temperley sighed. "What I'm trying to establish, as I'm sure you can appreciate, is whether anyone who had a premeditated intention of making away with Mr Maybury could have done so. If they could, it places a more significant perspective on his appointment with me."

"For what it's worth, then, yes, I think they could."

Another nod, but a brisk one. "But what did Maybury

know about that was so urgent to keep quiet? The widow didn't come up with anything – at least, not to our people. Did she suggest anything to you?"

When Xan remained silent, he added sharply: "Come now, it's known you went to see her. Anything you find out – from Mrs Maybury or any other source – could be of the highest importance. I'm sure you understand the penalties under British law for concealing evidence. And incidentally, I'm intrigued to know your motivation for mixing yourself up in a police investigation."

Xan shrugged. "Boredom. And curiosity. If someone gets murdered within a few feet of you, you naturally want to know what's behind it."

Temperley smiled. "Not everyone would have the same instinct." Then the clown-face looked serious once more. "If you find what you're looking for, I'd be interested in hearing about it. Giles Maybury was a good man."

He took a fountain pen out of his pocket and scrawled something on his business card.

"That's my private number. Don't bother with the other ones. They're all monitored and recorded and I believe you'd find that inconvenient."

CHAPTER 12

Charles Latimer, Giles Maybury's friend and personal accountant, was employed by a firm named Lombard & Black which occupied premises off Gutter Lane in the Square Mile.

If Xan had imagined some Dickensian alleyway of dirty cobbles with lonely garrets above them lit by a single candle, he was disappointed. The medieval origins of Gutter Lane had long since vanished. The street was now delineated on both sides not by gabled roofs but huge buildings like giant telephone boxes which stood stupidly staring at each other with their blank eyes.

The only evidence of the street's history was a tall church at one end – and at the other, where it widened to a paved courtyard, a square of grass surrounded by railings. Inside was a cluster of ancient graves, disjointed from the church to which they no doubt belonged.

Lombard & Black occupied offices in a block on the eastern side of the courtyard. The gleaming glass walls, the stunted trees in pots at strategic corners, all told their tale of wealth and success, summed up by a huge metal sculpture of a bird with a blazing tail in front of the main entrance.

Xan paused in front of its sharp beak and angry eye. A

hawk of some kind, perhaps an eagle? No – a phoenix.

Through the sliding glass doors into a gleaming, white foyer, where young women with professionally blank smiles presided over a long reception desk. The standard, unimaginatively-furnished HQ reception, in fact, repeated from London to New York to Dubai.

Xan did not have to lift his eyes to know that above his head the space would stretch upwards to what must seem to the company's female employees a triumphant irony – a glass ceiling. An atrium had been a required fixture for every corporate headquarters for over a decade now and still no one seemed to grasp that glass was a security weak point.

To the investigator, the trend for a transparent material as a building block had come as a boon. And to terrorists, anarchists and penniless protestors, it was likewise an open invitation – most glass could be shattered by bullets, bombs or vehicles and some even by well-aimed office furniture.

Xan presented himself at the front desk, where the receptionist took him through the meaningless rigmarole of identity. "And who are you here to see?"

"Charles Latimer. I'm afraid he's not expecting me."

"I'll just check his diary and see if he's available. Is this your first visit to Phoenix House? Then if you could please watch this short safety video..."

She pressed a button on a touchscreen. An animated presentation began to play and a voiceover informed Xan that his health and safety were of paramount importance to Lombard & Black. "To ensure the safety of everyone in this building, please pay attention to the following instructions..."

Colourful animated figures scurried to and fro, chasing arrows along unfolding corridors in their quest to escape imaginary bursts of flame. Gratified by this useful insight into the building's layout, Xan paid close attention until the coloured dots triumphantly reunited in a jungle setting beyond the boundary of the building.

The receptionist picked up her phone and dialled a number, then glanced at Xan. "What company did you say you were from?"

"I'm not from a company. It's personal."

She looked a little blank. Perhaps the inhabitants of this tower uncommonly exhibited any personal life.

"It concerns a mutual friend, Giles Maybury," he added helpfully. "He's dead."

He judged rightly that this intelligence, relayed on the phone, would prompt Mr Latimer to act quickly to fore-stall any further confidences. Some movement above him attracted his attention and he glanced up instinctively – a face, heavy and pursed, was glaring down at him from the second floor. Then the receptionist put down the phone. "Mr Latimer will be down shortly."

Latimer was as good as his word. Within a few seconds, a lift – travelling from the fourth floor, not the second – had whirred down to ground level. The man who emerged did not own the heavy, bulldog face that had stared down from the glass a moment ago. He was older, perhaps late fifties, with salt and pepper hair and an aquiline profile. It was the sort of face clients would feel comfortable trusting with their money.

"Mr Ross?" Latimer's voice held just the right blend of politeness with a tinge of inquiry.

"I'm sorry to call in unexpectedly," Xan said equably. "But Mrs Maybury thought you would be happy to see me, in the circumstances."

"Of course, of course," Latimer said swiftly, hastily conducting his guest into the lift. He did not betray the puzzlement he must feel. "Naturally – an appalling thing to happen. Poor old Giles. How is Elinor?"

A few seconds later, the doors slid open on the fourth floor and Xan was ushered into a meeting-room. The walls were made of the inevitable glass – his eyes were beginning to tire of the glare – but at a touch of a button, the transparent surfaces changed to a smoky grey.

"I'm not sure if what you've got to say is private, but I always think it's better manners regardless," Latimer said. "I hate the feeling of people staring in at you like a goldfish bowl."

He indicated a table with four 'easy' chairs. "Sit down, Mr Ross. Those chairs aren't as uncomfortable as they look." He belied his own words by dropping cautiously into a chair as though it might suddenly fold up under the weight of his spare frame and adjusted his trouser-creases carefully.

Xan took a chair in his turn. "It's a simple matter. The fact is, Elinor isn't satisfied with the efforts the police have made."

"But surely – I mean, his wallet was stolen, wasn't it?"

"There are complications," Xan said mysteriously.

"I see."

But Latimer did not sound as though he saw. Nor did he ask what this had to do with him, as he might have done. Xan decided to help him out a little. "It's possible he was deliberately targeted. I've been talking to a few people who knew him. Trying to get a handle on his affairs."

"I see," Latimer said again, unhappily. Evidently, he was beginning to regret agreeing to see his uninvited guest. "Well, of course, I'll tell you anything I can. But I don't believe I can help much. I mean, poor old Giles never talked to me about much other than money. And frankly, he didn't understand that very well."

"Well," Xan said agreeably, "the main thing I'm looking into is motive. Whether anyone had a reason to want Giles Maybury out of the way – perhaps someone he knew something rather damaging about. He was a client of yours?"

Latimer managed a smile. "Are you allowed to ask leading questions? And do I have to answer them? But if I didn't, it would look suspicious, eh? As a matter of fact, Giles was just a legacy client from my days in private practice. I kept him on out of politeness, really. He and Elinor were hardly High Net Worth Individuals."

"But you had lunch together a week before he died."

A sudden clang on the glass wall made Latimer start again – the man was really intriguingly nervous. Xan followed his glance to the far wall, where a shadowy shape suggested a figure peering through. He looked back at Latimer and was startled to see a sudden paling of his face.

"You'll excuse me – I'm wanted outside. Do – er – read the newspaper or something."

"Of course." Xan was watching the wall. The sharpness of the initial summons suggested impatience and that meant there would be a second. Sure enough, a blurred hand approached the glass and knocked again. The metallic clang was, Xan now saw, caused by a signet ring.

Latimer closed the door. Xan stretched himself out in his chair with an appearance of indifference, turned away from the glass wall. He would not be able to see or hear anything useful through it anyway.

Latimer came back into the room. "Now, where were we?"

"You were going to tell me why Giles came to see you."

Evidently, Latimer had got his composure back. "Well, strictly speaking, it's not appropriate to do so. But I don't suppose it will do any harm now. The fact is, old Giles was fussing about his pension investments. Asked me if I could put him onto anything good."

"And did you?"

Latimer looked amused. "My dear chap, in our game, you learn not to just throw out recommendations. I didn't know what his aspirations were or his appetite for risk or anything like that. I said to come back with a clearer idea and some facts and figures. But of course, he died before he could, poor chap."

"Do you have any idea why he wanted to move his pension stocks?"

Latimer shrugged. "If you ask me, he just didn't have enough else to think about. Retirement didn't suit Giles."

Pensions, Xan thought. Elinor Maybury must have the management of that pension now. And she had mentioned 'the pensions people' coming to see her. This might hang together nicely – too nicely, perhaps?

"And then what?"

"We had a spot of lunch down the road."

"What did you talk about?"

"Oh, I don't know. This and that. Politics. Speculating about the next Party leader. Poor old Giles felt a bit out of the swim of things since he retired, I think." Latimer seemed to have relaxed a little now that he was no longer answering questions about financial matters.

"Anything else?"

"Not a lot. He had something on his mind, if you ask me. Seemed a bit preoccupied. But I'm afraid I didn't pay too much attention. I was worrying if I was going to be late for my afternoon client. Talking of which, is it worth my attempting to interest you in the services of Lombard & Black? You're based overseas, I gather. The Gulf, isn't that right?"

"Dubai and Abu Dhabi, mostly."

Latimer nodded. "I daresay you've already got a lawyer, but if you're going to be spending much time in this country, you could do with someone in London. You *are* planning to spend time here, I take it?"

"I don't know yet."

"Well, if you are, it's better to have someone to advise you from the start. Doesn't have to be us, of course, but we're pretty well regarded."

"Thank you, but I'm not a High Net Worth Individual either."

And nor had he mentioned that he worked in the Gulf. As he was ushered down in the lift, Xan reflected that Latimer must have received a briefing on him while he was out of the room.

CHAPTER 13

Outside Phoenix House, a cool wind was whispering through the square. Xan strolled down to the other end of the street, past the medieval church. Its grey stone bulk was a refreshing sight after all the plate glass. How had the building escaped the Great Fire, he wondered? A stone wedged into an outer wall testified to the efforts of local people with buckets of water.

Ahead of him, a small alleyway ran along past the church on a downward slant southwards to the river. The way crossed a thoroughfare, passed through a narrow gap made available (with almost palpable reluctance) between two corporate buildings and emerged on the brink of the river.

Here, there were old loading quays and an angry wave slapped at the stonework below his feet. A ferry speeding east was creating the wave. To his left, the ugly concrete foundations of London Bridge and to the right, a railway viaduct.

A sign screwed to the river wall indicated that this part of the riverside was private commercial property. There were to be NO BALL GAMES, NO PHOTOGRAPHY, NO VAGRANTS and of course, NO LOITERING.

He leaned against the river wall (NO LEANING?) and

took stock of what he had learned from Giles Maybury's friends.

The Romillys had told him, with many confusing contradictions and side-steps, that Maybury had been nervous at the lunch at the Ritz. He had looked around continually as though he was fearful of seeing someone, as he had at Wimbledon. He had wanted to speak to Mark Romilly about something important but had not got the chance.

Charles Latimer, meanwhile, had presented Giles Maybury as a man who was restless in retirement and rather thoughtlessly took up the time of his busier friends. When they met, Maybury had seemed preoccupied. Did that indicate that whatever Maybury had found out, it had been before their meeting?

At this point, Xan remembered about the Oxford phone-number. As Elinor had remarked, you didn't write down the phone number of a museum.

The traditional red phone-kiosks one saw in every shot of London on the foreign news channels were scattered generously throughout the Square Mile, no doubt for the amusement of tourists rather than for actual use, but still apparently functional. Xan found one and stepped inside, trying not to think what a perfect target he would make for an assassin with a rocket-launcher. The tall, red box, the illuminated yellow interior and the silhouette of the caller. You might as well paste up a cardboard cut-out from a shooting gallery.

He inserted a handful of coins and dialled the Oxford number from Giles Maybury's diary.

The call was answered at once by a choleric-sounding elderly man. "Porter's lodge, Coventry College."

Xan had not really expected a museum, but nor had he expected this. At a loss what to ask, he made a polite excuse and hung up. Then on impulse, since he still had credit in the kiosk machine, he dialled a second number.

This one too was answered promptly, but less professionally. "What do you want?"

"We need to talk."

"Is this to do with the – er – the tennis business?" Billy sounded wary.

"Does it matter?"

"It might."

"I want you to get hold of some information for me. I can't get it any other way – not here."

"Information is one of the commodities I deal in, old boy. A precious metal that can be bent to all sorts of uses and never tarnishes. But on the other hand, why should I? *I'm* not the one being followed around by policemen."

"Because you got me into this."

Billy exhaled down the phone. "We'd better meet in person. Three o'clock tomorrow at the Tower."

"All right." And he heard the connection break at the other end.

On his way back to the hotel, he stopped for an early dinner. Eating-houses in the City were expensive and by now, he had learned to drift east, towards the shabbier end of the Mile.

It was illuminating to watch the world of the haves fade

to that of the have-nots. Here, the tall brick buildings were blown with soot from centuries of prevailing winds and the facades were shabby and tired-looking. The small shops traded a mysterious mix of textiles, hot food and unattributable internet. Among them were small, quiet establishments where the hungry traveller could eat alone without being glanced at askance. Xan chose a table by the wall and the lamb and lentil curry and let his mind drift over the case so far.

Unlike the media, he was inclined to put 'how' to one side. As he had observed to Inspector Nash, Maybury's murder looked like a professional hit, probably involving more than one individual. Therefore, 'how' would not lead easily to 'why', which in normal circumstances led dependably to 'who'.

In any case, he already had a 'why', of sorts. Giles Maybury had claimed that he had discovered a secret – apparently a dangerous one. Someone must have known that. But the only way to find out who was to find out what that secret was. And the old man had left few clues behind him.

By the time Xan left the café, the streets were dark and quiet. The City retired to sleep early – the offices closed at six and the wine-bars at eight and after that, the streets were empty of everything but the roulette wheel of red buses and black taxis, spinning through the dead streets on their way to somewhere more exciting.

He cut through an alleyway which would take him close to the back entrance of the Coronado Hotel. He knew the narrow maze of streets well enough by now not to be fazed by the lack of signage or by the bizarre objets d'art that occasionally loomed incongruously in his path, gifts from corporate companies to their local environment – a steel angel's wing here, a set of organ pipes there.

Afterwards, he was not sure when he first became aware of the footsteps behind him. Of course, in a city like London, there would always be footsteps – but these were persistent and distinctive. And, by the time he became consciously aware of them, he knew that their owner had already been dogging him for over five minutes, despite several turns in his route.

Instinctively, he quickened his pace, taking a turning at random. Left, right, down some steps, along a narrow passageway where a late-night barber still plied his trade beneath his candy-striped pole. Beyond it, a square with on one side, a cafe that was lighted but with the chairs upside down on the tables; on the other, the glaring, blank windows of yet another corporate headquarters, this one boasting a rearing bronze horse before its glass doors.

He paused to listen. Nothing. Then ahead, he heard the scrape of boots not far away and knew that his pursuer was not alone. There was at least one person ahead and one behind. They were hunting him.

Homeland protocol was simple. You kept engagement to a minimum, aiming to avoid injury or identification. Which was all very well in a text-book and in training, but in practice, less straightforward.

The thing was to get away, to lose his pursuer in this

maze of passageways and blind corners. Thank heavens for soft-soled shoes. If he could get to one of the main roads, he could reach Liverpool Street Station. Stations were good places for what the pros called dry-cleaning – the process of shaking off unwanted pursuers.

The footsteps behind him were coming closer. He ducked into a doorway which looked as though it led nowhere. Inside was a narrow flight of steps leading up. He followed it and at the top, emerged to a dimly-lit vista of walkways and squares and walls with creepers falling down. An upper level of the city, half-suspended in mid-air.

Xan had explored this area before. It was a second maze, built above the other by well-meaning city planners in the Sixties, deploying vast amounts of the then-new material of concrete to replace the holes left by wartime bombs. Hidden within it were concert halls, council flats, art galleries, gardens, even a tennis-court. It was easy to get lost in and would be easy to lose other people in, too. He crossed the main square, aiming for the steps that led down to Moorgate. But as he reached the stairway, he stopped as he heard someone moving below.

Cautiously, he moved sideways to get a view down the stairs. Youngish, stockyish, back turned, shifting around with the boredom of being stuck on this stairwell and pushing his earpiece into his ear to better hear his instructions. They, whoever they were, evidently didn't train their operatives very well. He could have done better himself when he was starting his training. But it didn't make any difference. You didn't have to be well-trained to be dangerous.

He retreated, working his way with infinite patience round to the east, towards the Barbican Theatre. And once again, had to stop, as his route was cut off, this time by a couple apparently admiring the non-existent moonlight. And then he remembered the lines of sentries in the stairwells at Wimbledon. They had played this game before.

He found himself back in the big central square, in front of the closed and locked concert hall. Two of his exits were blocked. But he knew of a third, a narrow, stepped lane that dropped down past a church onto the main street. It was dangerously easy to ambush, but he had no choice.

He had descended the steps and was halfway along the lane when he saw the single figure moving carelessly at the far end. So, they had stopped this earth too. Then against the pale night sky, he saw the silhouette of the church spire and he turned thankfully into the hallowed ground of the churchyard. He knew by now that the old churches were like hollow spaces at the heart of the city, ringed around by newer buildings. There was almost certainly a second way out.

There was. The passageway spilled out into a courtyard, where a centuries-old stone fountain with moss on its baby cherubs dribbled water half-heartedly into a basin.

He paused. There was dead silence. He could hear nothing except the dripping of the water. Small black somethings skittered softly into the shadows.

There came the deep chime of a church clock, and as it finished, a soft sound, perhaps another rat. Xan paused, slightly puzzled. Was he alone, or wasn't he? He took a cautious step into the darkness, turning his head to listen. Then out of nowhere, something heavy connected violently with the side of his head. He reeled back and crashed into the stone basin of the fountain.

Someone there, invisible in the darkness. He ducked and rolled instinctively to dodge the expected second blow, then groped for the rim of the basin to pull himself groggily to his feet. At that moment, a sudden unexpected sound echoed through the courtyard. Laughing voices and clipping shoes signalling the all-clear. Office workers taking a short-cut through the churchyard.

He was alone by the time they passed through, two women and a man. They gave him a curious glance, perhaps taking him for a drunk unable to keep himself upright. But it gave him the opportunity he needed. At the end of the alley lights glimmered, signifying streetlamps, crowds, safety.

When he reached it, the main street seemed to rush at him, all yellow lights and roaring traffic. He paused, steadying himself. On the other side of the road, a line of queueing people outside a fried chicken shop were the potential witnesses who were now his bodyguards.

At nearby Liverpool Street Station, a train had just disgorged itself and it was busy, despite the late hour. No one had time to pay any attention to the young man with blood trickling down a cut from his head who moved through the station, taking advantage of its many exits and entrances, until he could be sure he was no longer being followed.

His head ached and the lines of streetlamps dazzled him until at last he made out the giant children's letters, in neon blue and green, that said City Coronado Hotel three times over in blurred type.

*

Leah looked aghast at him as he came in through the back entrance.

"Someone tried to take my wallet."

"That's terrible, Mr Ross. Do you want me to call the police?"

Xan shook his head and instantly regretted it. "It's fine. They'll be miles away by now."

He dragged himself painfully up to his room and set about reviewing the damage in the bathroom mirror. There was a swelling bruise on his left temple, but it could have been a lot worse. He shrugged and then winced as a repetitive throb of pain set up in his jawline.

What to make of this? A chance robbery attempt? He did not think so. He had been deliberately followed. Since when? From outside the headquarters of Lombard & Black? Before then?

What did they want? Did they suspect that Maybury had told him something important? But in that case, Xan thought ruefully, holding the towel wrapped in ice to the side of his head, it would be nice if he also knew what it was.

Or did they suspect that Maybury had given him something? The diary? Or perhaps they thought that he had the mysterious photograph.

Either way, when had they found out about him? At the inquest? Possibly, but if so, it was curious that they had waited so long to make their move.

Of course, he should just cut his losses now. Check out of the Coronado, walk out into the street with his luggage – no taxis, no credit cards, nothing traceable – and vanish. Leave the country. But if he did, he could never come back. He would be on a police watch list for eternity. He could get a new passport and find new places to go, but nothing he could do would be good enough to pass the test here.

And Xan wasn't ready to leave. This country with its wavering hedges, fields and shaded woods, soft shades like watercolours that had run when a glass of water had been upset over the paper.

It was absurd sentimentalism – the nagging voice of a childhood he scarcely remembered. But there it was – he did not want to leave.

CHAPTER 14

In the morning, Xan's head ached rather more than it had the evening before. The bruising on his temple had come up considerably, his right eye was bloodshot and any kind of ill-considered movement, such as walking, set off a repetitive jar of pain.

He made his way reluctantly down in the lift to the Coronado's breakfast buffet and gloomily rejected the Full English and other unpleasantly lavish platters for plain yogurt with chopped nuts, with a strong coffee. To hide his slightly battered appearance from the curious gaze of the other guests, he deployed Giles Maybury's days-old newspaper as a screen.

When the waitress came to clear his plate, keen to get a second look at the occupant of Room 213, who never came down for breakfast but whom Leah had described as 'ever so good-looking in a kind of adventurous way and awfully polite', her eye fastened at once on the out of date image accompanying last week's football preview.

"Oh, they've given you an old paper, sir. Let me take that away and get you a new one."

"It's quite all right," the young man from Room 213 said swiftly. "I'm quite happy with this one."

The waitress eyed him critically as she removed his

plate. Polite he might be, but whatever pretensions to good looks he might have were spoiled in her view by the fact that he seemed to have been in a fight. Adventurous indeed, she thought disparagingly.

Unconscious of her disapproval, Xan was staring incredulously at the classified Marriages, Births and Deaths announcements in the newspaper, one of which had been shakily circled using a leaking fountain-pen, as though it had been done in a train.

Reverend Adam Paradine, aged 73. Suddenly. In the fullness of his years. Sadly deceased & taken from us. At his home in Rotherfield Chase, Hampshire. Service at the St Benedict's Chapel and the Civic Crematorium of Everlasting Peace. In the midst of life, we are in death. No flowers, by request.

*

He had been a fool not to look at the newspaper more closely. If he had, he would have spotted that circled notice.

Maybury's own words were the first clue. He had talked about men of a profession who, despite their concerns about the next world, were not prone to over-imagination in this one. A vicar definitely qualified under that criteria. Moreover, Adam Paradine's age was close to Maybury's. They had probably been at school together. And as if that was not enough, there was the date of Paradine's death – four days before Maybury himself.

Xan tore out the notice from the newspaper and folded it away in his wallet, then drained his coffee. He had work to do. He was going to need more data.

The All-Day Sunshine Internet Café was situated in a cheap road off Whitechapel and was, in contradiction to its name, dark and dingy. As Xan came in, the proprietor gave him a gloomy look from his counter, as if to say *I know what you're up to*. Terrorists favoured these places, Xan knew, along with others of the criminal persuasion.

A line of computer terminals sat innocently in a row, promising anonymity however sinister your business. Xan opened up an obscure search engine, knowing better than to do business with the leading providers. And the information came flying onto the screen.

Adam Paradine was a retired vicar living in the village of Rotherfield Chase. He had been an enthusiastic swimmer and had constructed an outdoor pool in his garden. He had been found in this pool one morning by a neighbour, Mrs Julia Banner. Death had been ascribed to an overdose of chlorine used to clean the water.

Xan made thorough notes, then cleared the history and every other aspect of his activity that would leave any kind of digital footprint – the sort of habit you got into when you worked in his industry for any length of time.

He glanced at his watch, wincing slightly as he did so. He had an appointment. Open source information was all very well but to get anywhere in this sort of investigation, you needed human sources.

*

The tower wall was over one thousand years old and deserved greater respect than it was being given by the big man in the shabby suit who was leaning on the bridge over the moat, flicking cigarette ash into the water. A large raven watched him from the top of the wall, its head on one side.

Xan was late. He threaded his way impatiently through a maze of giant hotel-blocks, marvelling at the bloated stupidity that had put them here to spoil this medieval landscape. He walked down to the place where a gated arch was cut through the stone wall and a stream of black water flowed beneath. "What a place to choose."

Billy's breath was blue with smoke. "It's all for your benefit. You're here to see the sights, so you said. Well, here's a sight. Jewel in the crown of English history. It *has* crowns with jewels in, loads of them, if you don't mind queueing for an hour in the sun to see them."

"No, thanks."

"That's right, I forgot. It gets crowded inside." His laugh was more like a wheezing cough. "So, you went to see the widow, I hear. Get much out of her?"

"Not really." How did Billy know that?

The other man drew on his cigarette so forcibly that the lit end blazed in sparks. "What are you doing talking to anyone anyway? I think I recommended that you stay out of it."

"Well, whose fault is it that I'm a murder witness?"

Billy disregarded the question. He had been studying Xan's face with interest. Now he grinned. "Well, well, you've been doing more than talk to widows in cosy suburban settings."

"Someone mistook me for a tourist and tried to take my wallet." Xan shrugged. "It wasn't a big deal."

"Right. Either you're slipping or it wasn't the casual pick-pocket you suggest – otherwise, how did they get anywhere near you?"

"Well, maybe I am slipping."

"All the more reason to keep out of things that don't concern you."

"Look, there's something very odd going on here, Billy. Giles Maybury wasn't killed for his wallet. And until his murder's solved, I'm under a microscope."

Billy considered the glowing immolation of his cigarette. "So, you think you'll solve it for them?"

"It passes the time."

"And where do I come in?"

"You've got the access. You were a policeman here."

Billy stared down at the water flowing beneath his feet. "A long time ago."

"I know that world. They don't trust anyone they've known less than twenty years. They'll talk to you."

"About what, exactly?"

"About the Maybury case. Whether there's more to it than meets the eye. You know the sort of thing."

Billy did. But he looked oddly uneasy.

"There's something else. A man named Paradine. He was a vicar."

"Was?"

"He died about two weeks ago."

"And I'm sure you've already got everything you can from open source."

"I want Paradine's post-mortem report. The full inquest transcript. Anything to do with his death you can get."

"I told you, I don't have the access any more."

"You seemed to know all about Maybury."

"That's different."

"Why is it different?"

Billy was still staring down at the black water. Instead of answering the question, he said slowly: "You know what this waterway is? It's the way they brought Anne Boleyn into the Tower, before they cut her head off. It's called Traitor's Gate."

"I'm not interested in history."

"Maybe you should be."

"What the hell does that mean?"

"Nothing in particular. Incidentally, I hear that Carlos Spinnetti's dead. An op that went wrong. They do sometimes. Thought you ought to know."

Xan shrugged off his unease as he walked back along the river. Billy was right, of course. Operations did go wrong sometimes. Maybe Spinnetti had made a mistake. He had been prone to mistakes. So there was no reason at all to feel a sudden chill blowing off the river.

CHAPTER 15

The slow train to Winchester was quiet and there were few other passengers to notice the young man who sat and leaned back in a dark corner of the carriage as though he had a headache. There was an ugly welt beginning to fade across his left temple.

Rotherfield Chase consisted of a single long street with small cottages crammed in together, a village green, a duckpond and a pub called the Blue Boar. Xan asked at the pub about The Lodge and was directed to Heath Lane, a meandering street of larger houses which, as half-promised by the name, backed onto the heath. The Lodge was halfway along, a gabled affair in rather bright brick that suggested a red-faced obstinacy.

Xan looked at the house beyond, Cherry-Tree Cottage. There was no cherry tree in evidence but instead, little pots of flowers along the path and a hanging basket above the front door, hung so low that even a moderately tall visitor was at risk. Xan ducked cautiously past it and, seeing no doorbell, applied mild pressure to a wrought iron knocker in the shape of a lion's head.

The door was opened by a small woman, but what she lacked in height, she made up in her stoutness, the robust curl of her iron-grey hair and the twinkle in her eyes.

"Well, I never," she said, pressing a plump hand to her flowered blouse and breathing alarmingly hard. "To what do I owe this pleasure?"

"Mrs Banner?"

"Depends who's asking," she said with gleeful promptness. "I know you people with your energy comparisons and your party-political leaflets and your what have you."

"I wanted to ask you a few questions about Reverend Paradine."

"Press?" Mrs Banner said warily. "If so, you're a little late."

"Insurance," Xan said. An odd-sounding accident rather lent itself to this possibility.

"Well, I'm not surprised. Of all the unnatural things to happen. That horrible machine. Someone ought to bring a lawsuit."

This was mysterious but intriguing. Xan said: "If you could give me a moment of your time, I'd be very grateful."

Mrs Banner's entire frame shook with what appeared at first to be a racking cough but then transformed into a hearty laugh. "Dearie me. If the press had been half so nicely spoken, they might have got more out of me. You'd better come in and I'll put the kettle on."

Xan did not like tea but it seemed politic not to say so. He followed Mrs Banner in and was installed in the kitchen while she concocted a powerful dark brown brew in a teapot. The room was extremely warm, with sunlight flooding in through the picture window at one end of the room and a tabby cat stretched out asleep on the window-sill.

"Sugar's on the table." A cup of the alarming brew was placed in front of him and he looked at it without enthusiasm. However, it was clearly crucial to obtaining Mrs Banner's goodwill.

"Like I say, it was that horrible machine that did for him," Mrs Banner had compressed herself into a wooden chair with supporting arms which creaked when she leaned forward to sip her tea. "I won't have a moment's peace until the clearance people take it away. Gives me nightmares, it does, thinking of it sitting there brooding in that shed. I'll never forget looking out of my window and seeing him there in the water. All in his outdoor clothes, he was, with that horrible machine all wreathed round him like an octopus."

Xan resisted the temptation to ask further questions about the machine. The preferable course of action would be to examine it and to do that, he would need to gain the trust of his hostess. It seemed therefore best to start with more general questions. "Reverend Paradine lived alone, I understand."

"That's right. His wife died a few years back. And he wasn't the type to marry again – not that I'm saying I thought of it." Her eyes twinkled merrily with this piece of intelligence.

"Any children?"

Her eyes lost a little of their twinkle. "He had a son that passed some years ago, out in Egypt. In the Army, he was. The poor lamb wasn't above twenty and you'd think that would make a man question the ways of God, but the Reverend didn't seem to. He wasn't our vicar, of course. He moved here when he retired. Said he knew too much about his own neighbours. He seemed happy enough here, but quiet – not much of a man for visitors."

This was discouraging. To understand the truth about anyone, you needed to gather as much data as possible about their life – that was standard investigative practice. It was always unhelpful to learn that a subject of interest had lived alone and had no close ties.

"Did you see much of him?"

"He kept himself to himself. I kept his key if he went away. And fed the cat for him. Tiger," Mrs Banner said, and the tabby by the window blinked his amber eyes. "He's moved in with me. Cats know what suits them."

Xan persevered. "Did he have many friends?" There was nothing in this line of questioning that an investigator into an accident in a swimming-pool would be justified in asking but Xan had found that once you started asking people questions, they were liable to carry on answering.

"Not above the usual. Like I said, he kept himself to himself. At my time of life, Mrs B, you like to be quiet, he used to say. Saying that, there was a fellow who came over for lunch a few weeks before he died. Elderly gent in a Panama hat."

Xan did not move a muscle to indicate his satisfaction that this cast had found a target. "A close friend?"

"I couldn't tell you. They seemed to know each other

right enough. He looked like one of those fussy fellows that's always picking over their food. I wouldn't have taken any interest but they came out and had a look at the garden after lunch and I was pruning the roses right the other side of the fence. So I couldn't help but hear some of what they were saying."

"Of course you couldn't," Xan agreed diplomatically. "And it would be very helpful to know about Reverend Paradine's mood – if he seemed worried about anything, for instance."

"That's what I thought," Mrs Banner said rather promptly. "But I'm bound to say he sounded cheerful enough. Talked about the spring-cleaning. He'd been right through his attic and cleared it all out."

"Reverend Paradine had?"

"That's right. He must have had a lot of junk up there. Boxes for the dustmen all over his drive by the time he was through."

"Did it all get thrown out?"

She nodded. "I did say some of it might come in handy for the church bazaar but he wouldn't wait. Seemed to me he was in a hurry to get shot of it. Anyway, he told the other fellow that it had done him good to get through it all."

"Did he say anything else?"

"He must have given the other fellow something. Not that I could see what it was, but he said it seemed a funny thing to find. I'd like to know if there's anything to know, that's all, was all he said. And the other fellow said he quite understood and he'd do what he could."

"He said find, rather than find out?"

"As far as I remember."

"But he didn't say anything about what it was."

"Not he. He said it was the sort of thing that couldn't lie, that was all."

The kettle hissed on the stove and she got up and turned it off. Xan took a moment to absorb what he had learned. He dared not risk any more questions about the man in the Panama hat. He turned to the investigator's staple. "When was the last time you saw Reverend Paradine?"

"It was the evening before the poor man passed," she said promptly. "I saw him over the hedge, so I did just mention the bins. He was always very helpful about putting them on the street for me."

"And did he?"

Mrs Banner nodded briskly, setting her iron-grey curls dancing. "A good neighbour was the Reverend."

Xan glanced through the window at the blank windows of The Lodge and wondered what secrets lay inside it. "Do you know if he made a will?"

Mrs Banner's small eyes gleamed. "Left all his money and things to a charity. Didn't have anyone else to leave it to, poor fellow. There wasn't even anyone to organise the funeral. Good thing the Church stepped in. They put a nice notice in the paper, too."

"I suppose the house hasn't been cleared for sale yet?"

To his surprise, she nodded again. "The charity came and did it straightaway. Sent a nice team in."

Xan considered this. It seemed rather hurried, in the circumstances. He remembered Elinor Maybury's house and the faint indications that it had been searched. At any rate, it suggested that there was nothing to be found in The Lodge now. All the same… He risked another off-topic question. "Do you remember the name of the firm that did the clearance?"

Quite unsuspiciously, Mrs Banner reflected. "Now, what would it have been? Dunwood and Something. Bane, that was it. Dunwood & Bane."

"And I suppose you have a key to the house too?"

She hesitated. "The clearance firm asked for the keys. But if you ask me, it's not right to have no one local with a key to the place. What if there's a gas leak?" Her pursed mouth twitched. "So I gave them the Reverend's keys but I've still got my spare if you want to borrow it. There's no harm you can do in there – everything's been cleared out, apart from that horrible machine." She shuddered theatrically, making the chair creak protestingly. "Such a turn as it gave me. I keep wondering if he might have cried out, poor man, but there's no getting from it, my hearing isn't as good as it once was and with my window shut, I wouldn't have heard it."

*

Five minutes later, Xan stood on Reverend Paradine's lawn – which had once been lush and green but was now starting to revert to an unkempt meadow – looking down at the vicar's swimming-pool.

Julia Banner had not accompanied him. The provision of a second cup of strong tea generously provisioned with sugar had braced her up against the horrible memory of the machine but not enough, she declared, to set foot in the garden of The Lodge. "And I'm sure I don't know what looking at that pool will tell you."

"We have to look at the scene of the cr – death," Xan said. "It's an investigative principle."

Now his own words echoed in his head mockingly. What exactly was he going to learn from standing here? The deep scuff-marks over the overgrown lawn told their story of hurrying paramedics with stretchers – there would be no Holmesian revelations.

He looked from the closed French windows of the house to the paved stone terrace and the pool, with its faded orange sun-lounger. He was picturing the scene in his mind. The old man switching on his machine, then pottering around the pool peacefully.

The news reports had stated that Reverend Paradine had been found in the pool fully-clothed. They suggested that the unfortunate man had tripped over the hose and fallen into the pool, banging his head and knocking himself unconscious. This would account for his failure to switch the machine off before it reached a dangerously high level of chlorinity and the lethal embrace of the machine itself would explain the fact that Adam Paradine had not drowned. The hoses had held him at the surface. It was all very easy to explain, if you wanted it to be. But Xan was not satisfied.

If you fell over a cable, he thought, you would most likely hit your head on the terrace paving-stones, in which case you would be found lying there in the morning.

Alternatively, if you tumbled straight into the pool, the water would break your fall and you could quickly scramble out again. The only possible scenario that would fit the inquest verdict was that Paradine had hit his head on the side of the pool as he went in. A possible sequence of events, but surely an unusual one.

He examined the pool. The water level lay at least a foot below the surrounding paving-stones. It would be easy enough to jump (or fall) into the pool but difficult to get out, except at the ladder at one end. But this was not what interested Xan.

The stone edging was sharp. It would be difficult, in his opinion, to hit your head on the edge as you went down without breaking the skin. Had such a mark been found on the body? If it had, surely this would have been noted at the inquest and mentioned in the news reports.

In the corner of the garden stood what the Americans called a maintenance building and the English, uncompromisingly, a garden shed.

It was unlocked and he pushed it open with his elbow to avoid leaving fingerprints, revealing a dark space with dust motes hanging in the air. The abandoned gardening equipment – trowels and forks, oddments of twine, flower pots and sacks of compost – had a pathetic look to them.

In a corner of the shed sat 'the machine'. Mrs Banner's

description of an old-fashioned vacuum cleaner was close enough. Squat and round, it sat wrapped in its tentacles with a sinister air. Its mode of operation seemed clear enough. As Mrs Banner had described, you lowered it into the water and set it going, enabling it to trundle along the bottom of the pool while its hoses trailed behind it on the surface.

There did not seem any point in risking leaving fingerprints by examining the machine in detail. Instead, he looked at the other things stacked on shelves and boxes around the shed. The usual gardening and maintenance suspects – garden spade and fork, a hammer and saw. The tools were all too heavy and unwieldy for the purpose that Xan was thinking of and they had sharp edges which would leave a mark that the police surgeon would have noticed.

His attention moved on to an array of flower-pots, some filled with earth. A round-based heavy pot would be more suitable for the job of knocking an elderly man on the head – but it would almost certainly shatter, making a noise that might draw the attention of an interested neighbour and creating a mess that would need clearing up.

Beside the pots were bags of compost. Compost would probably not be heavy enough, he thought, except in very large and unwieldy proportions. But behind the bags of compost were a couple of medium-sized sacks containing builder's sand and cement. They sat there looking at him innocently.

He glanced at the gardening gloves – but fingerprints

could be left on the inside of gloves as well as on any other fabric and they were almost impossible to remove. Instead, he picked up an oily rag which he could take away with him and used it to drag out the cement sack by its corner. It shifted forward sullenly and reluctantly, a solid mass of clayish lumpenness.

The plastic covering was dusty, dirty and unremarkable. But at the bottom, where it almost couldn't be seen, there was a cluster of grey hairs. Frowning, Xan pushed the cement sack back into its place and closed the shed door.

Next, he made a careful search of the garden. The death had been certified as natural causes and there would have been no thorough forensic search. It was therefore possible that there was still something here to find.

A conscientious search took some time and yielded nothing but a paperback book, soft and pulpy from being out in the rain, lying half-hidden in one of the flowerbeds near the house. He picked it up and turned it over. An old Penguin paperback – The Case Of The Man Who Wasn't There. The corner of one page was folded over as a bookmark.

Presumably Reverend Paradine's book. Anyone might read a book in their garden on a summer's day and leave it there. But in that case, why had the book not been left on the sun-lounger? If it had been, of course, Mrs Banner would have moved it out of the rain. It was not obvious how a book might find itself discarded in a flower-bed.

Nonetheless, the crime was starting to take place in his mind. Someone (or more likely two someones) had come here bent on murder. How had they got in? The garden boundary was a tall brick wall. However, there was a promising side passage barred by a simple wooden door which could be easily vaulted. When Xan examined it, a series of scratches to the paintwork at the top of the door suggested a cautious support of this theory.

And then what? The most careful murderers preferred to use their victims' own tools for the purpose, avoiding the headache of transporting a lethal weapon to and from the scene of the crime. The unlocked garden shed would have been an inviting prospect, offering both a choice of weapons and a place of concealment.

Had the murderer waited there for the old man to come down to set his machine and attacked him then? Xan shook his head, dissatisfied with that idea. He or she would not necessarily have known about the machine or Paradine's regular habits and besides, it was likely that the machine was set before dusk and that the murderers would want to wait for the hours of darkness.

He glanced again at the discarded book he had found. Looking at the read portion, it was possible to identify pages with the faint imprint of a corner-fold indicating where Paradine had previously marked a page.

He seemed to be, as already established, a man of habit. He read around six or seven pages at a time and these chunks usually corresponded with a chapter. Yet the final bookmark was on the second page of a chapter. And it was larger and more carelessly folded than the previous, neater examples.

Taken with everything else, it suggested that Paradine had been reading, perhaps in his sitting-room after eating his dinner, and had been startled out of his reading by something – a noise in the garden? One could imagine him coming outside, book in one hand, and confronting his murderer. The machine in the pool, already trundling along on its task, would have furnished a quirky disposal method for the murderers.

Letting himself into the house through the French windows, Xan found that as Mrs Banner had warned him, the furnishings and possessions of Reverend Paradine had gone. A shabby cream carpet and plain magnolia walls were almost all that was left of his occupancy.

There would have been no family or friends to do what was needed when someone died – all the thousand and one tasks, some expected, some horribly disconcerting, none of which could be left undone. Against his will, his mind went back to the little house on the bleak east coast and he jerked it sharply forward again.

Reverend Paradine had had only a kindly, well-meaning neighbour. That and 'the Church', which had stepped in and organised the funeral. No one to communicate with friends such as Giles Paradine.

He prowled the downstairs rooms and then the upstairs floor with a growing sense of disappointment, frustrated by the clearance firm, whoever they were. The more he thought about it, the more suspicious that sounded. But in any case, they too had by the sounds of it been forestalled by the dead man's own decision to clear out his attic.

Last of all, he went to the front door, but did not open it. One of the interesting things about dead people was that they sometimes still received post. Of course, there was no telling if any letters had been removed by Mrs Banner or the dubious-sounding house clearance firm, but there had evidently been more deliveries since then. Three letters lay squarely on the doormat, along with a handful of glossy leaflets.

Technically, taking other people's letters was a crime. But it was also a crime that was quite unlikely to be found out. Without taking any more thought, he picked up the letters and put them in his jacket pocket. Then he retreated through the French windows and returned the keys to Mrs Banner.

"Thank you for letting me look around."

She sniffed. "For all the good it's done you. Curiosity killed the cat, if you ask me."

He smiled. "Perhaps."

The tabby cat was stretched along the garden wall. It slit its eyes at Xan as he took his departure, negotiating the hanging basket by now with practised efficiency, and he wondered what it had seen and what it knew.

CHAPTER 16

In the train that jolted him slowly back to London, Xan reconstructed the events leading up to Maybury's death in his mind. In early June, Maybury had lunched with his old friend Adam Paradine. Paradine had told him – what? That he had found something. Not found it out, but found it. That was an important distinction, which was why it had been worth risking Mrs Banner's suspicion by double-checking it.

Presumably, he had found it, whatever it was, when he was clearing his attic. It was surely not too much of a leap to suppose that it was a photograph and that Paradine had shown it to Maybury over lunch. Paradine had asked his old friend to 'look into it' and Maybury had only too willingly agreed.

Why would you 'look into' a photograph? Because it was evidence that things weren't as you thought they were. Evidence of what? He pushed away the questions of WHY again and went back to WHAT.

Maybury had looked into the matter and had discovered something unexpected. He had said as much. He had, everyone agreed, been preoccupied – worried, perhaps, about the implications of what he had discovered. But not seriously concerned about his own safety. But then at breakfast on the morning of his trip to Wimbledon, he had glanced through the *Times* as was his customary habit and seen the notice about his old friend's death.

He had covered up his reaction as a spasm of his gastric trouble, which had been convincing enough to satisfy Elinor. But it would, Xan thought, have come as a shock. Paradine had known what Maybury knew and Paradine was dead.

The old man had been stubborn. He would not miss his tennis if he could help it. So, he had gone to Wimbledon, confident that he was safe in the hallowed grounds of the Club. But they, whoever they were, had followed him to Wimbledon and they had got to him, just as they had got to Paradine.

Presumably, Xan thought, they had targeted both men at the same time. But while Reverend Paradine lived alone, Giles Maybury was married. His wife represented a potential awkward witness. To add to that, Maybury had come down with his 'gastric upset' which kept him housebound for three days. They, whoever they were, had had to wait.

Perhaps they had been waiting for the cocktail-party he was due to attend on Friday, but then he had pulled out of that too. But then Saturday had come and the trip to the tennis. And that had been enough to seal Maybury's fate.

It all held together nicely, Xan thought. But it left one question. What had happened to the photograph?

*

Hotel beds, with their vast size and snowy sheets, were excellent places to do forensic work. Xan sat on the edge of his – why did business hotels invariably consider king-size beds the appropriate provision for a single young man? – and looked at the letters he had removed from the house at Rotherfield Chase, which lay spread out on the counterpane.

Two of them were in brown window-format envelopes with the address printed on the letter inside, suggesting business communications. The third was hand-written.

Using one of the Coronado Hotel's spare pillow-cases to avoid leaving fingerprints, he opened the first of the business letters, which was addressed unpromisingly to The Occupant. It proved to be a request for confirmation of residency details from the local council.

The second letter was a badly-phrased but evidently keenly-felt offer to compare competitively with Reverend Paradine's current electricity service provider. Such was the lot of the investigator.

The third letter looked much more promising. A dusty envelope that looked as though it had been acquired from the sort of shop that only infrequently sold envelopes, the flap was barely stuck down.

Gently, he extracted the contents – a doubled-over page torn from a spiral notepad. The letter, such as it was, was scribbled with a leaky biro.

I've thought about what you said. There's something – I remembered it the other day. Don't know how much use it'll be, mind. But you're welcome to it.

I've moved, by the way. The boat's got a sunflower on it – come along the water at Mile End and you'll recognise it right enough.

The letter was signed not with a name but with a crude, scribbled sketch of some kind of small animal with long ears.

CHAPTER 17

"But I told you, I didn't see anything and I don't know anything." Colin Brass's tone was querulous. His house on the edge of the village green looked too idyllic to be associated with murder, as did the William Morris sofa and chairs the inspector and Sergeant Monroe were now solemnly perched on.

"You were seated next to the dead man," Inspector Nash persisted.

Mr Brass looked flustered. "But he was killed in the change of ends. I'd gone out by then."

"I thought you said you didn't have any idea when he was killed?"

Mr Brass's cheeks became a little purple. "They said at the inquest that was when it happened. It wasn't *my* idea."

"Well, assuming that's the case," the inspector said soothingly, "you must have gone out just before it happened. Do you remember anyone else going out?"

"No."

"Or coming in?"

"Someone barged past me coming down the stairs. Simple good manners cost nothing."

"What did they look like?"

"How should I remember?"

The inspector deployed his reserves of patience. "A man? A woman?"

"A man, I suppose," Mr Brass said sulkily.

Sergeant Monroe produced a set of photos, all of men of roughly similar appearance.

Mr Brass shook his head crossly. "*I* don't know. Could have been any of them." Then an idea seemed slowly to present itself to him. "Are you saying that was the *murderer*? And that he went right past me? Why, I might have been in danger!"

"I don't think so, sir," Inspector Nash said reassuringly.

"Well, why not? He might have decided to murder me instead. I don't usually carry much cash but I had over twenty-five pounds on me that day." Brass stared at the pictures with fascination.

Inspector Nash glanced at Monroe. As corroboration, it was nowhere near good enough. But he had another question. "There is one other matter, sir. Why did you go out when you did?"

Mr Brass stared. "To get a drink."

"Well, yes, sir. But it seems an odd time to choose, near the end of a set like that."

Mr Brass steepled his fingers edgily. "I can't help that. I was thirsty."

"Are you sure that was all you were doing?"

Mr Brass looked out of countenance. "Well, if you will insist, I was worried about Lola Valiant the Third."

"What?"

"She's a pedigree Angora – they're extremely delicate.

She was at the veterinarian for a most delicate procedure and they promised faithfully to call me the moment it was over and they didn't. So, I went out to call them." He glared at the policemen defiantly. "You can call the veterinarian surgery yourself if you don't believe me."

"An Angora rabbit," Inspector Nash said disgustedly to Monroe as they drove back to town. "And he couldn't ID our man. Or wouldn't."

"Mr Ross could."

"Use your head, Sergeant. Ross can put him on the stairwell and we already know he was there. He can't put him on court for us and that's what we need. We'll just have to hope that the Eastwards are more help."

But when they arrived at the Eastward house in the elegant suburb of Dulinghurst in south-east London, there was an unexpected setback. The elderly and somewhat flustered woman who opened the door to them regretted that Mr and Mrs Eastward were not at home.

"Will either of them be back soon, Mrs –?"

"Mrs Villiers. I'm Sarah's mother."

Inspector Nash glanced at his watch. "It's nearly half past three. Perhaps your daughter is collecting the children from school?"

"Well, no, as a matter of fact, they have to go to the dentist today." The old lady continued to look flustered.

"Then that's where they'll be. What's the address?"

"I – I'm afraid I don't know it."

Inspector Nash glanced at Mrs Villiers attentively. He was not unfamiliar with the sound of a witness who is lying. He had not expected to hear it here, but experience had taught him that deception comes in unexpected guises. He said authoritatively: “You’d better let us come in and look around.”

Mrs Villiers fell back nervously from the doorway as the two policemen passed into the house, Sergeant Monroe staring in astonishment at his superior. “You can’t seriously think –,” he began incredulously.

“I don’t know what I think,” Inspector Nash returned. “That’s why we’re having a look around.”

But there was nothing remarkable to see. The rooms were immaculate, with chintz covers on the chairs and not a thing out of place. Mrs Villiers accompanied them around the rooms, keeping up a gentle stream of running commentary about house prices and catchment areas to which Inspector Nash only half-attended.

As they reached the hall again, he said abruptly: “I’m sorry to have troubled you, Mrs Villiers. I can reach your daughter or your son-in-law on the phone, I expect. But please tell them that they can expect to hear from us.”

As Sergeant Monroe followed him to the car, his face wore a baffled look. “Won’t we be waiting for them, then?”

“There’s something not right,” Inspector Nash said briskly. “That house doesn’t have any children in it. There’s not a toy in it and none of the bedrooms look used. You’d better ring up Mr and Mrs Eastward on whatever mobile numbers you’ve got for them and say we want to talk to them urgently.”

But by the time they reached Headquarters, Mrs Villiers must have reached her daughter by phone. The Eastwards were waiting at the front desk – a chastened-looking pair. Gone was the broad-shouldered assertiveness of Harlan Eastward.

"We thought we'd better come and explain to you straightaway, Inspector," he said rather sheepishly. "Once Sarah's mother told us what had happened –."

"It's no good blaming Mummy," Mrs Eastward said sharply. "She always said something like this would happen."

"Something like *what* would happen?" Inspector Nash demanded.

"Something that would catch us out with the school, of course," Sarah Eastward said impatiently.

"What school?"

"Dulinghurst Church School of St Mary, where Teddy and Mia go. It's quite the best one in the district."

"That's the whole point," her husband said gloomily.

Inspector Nash leaned forward. "Mrs Eastward, there was no trace of any children in that house."

"Well, of course not," Sarah Eastward said. "We don't live there. It's Mummy's house."

"It's in the school catchment, you see," Mr Eastward explained. "We didn't stand a chance of getting them in if we didn't put an address that was closer than ours. We live a mile the wrong side of the boundary."

Inspector Nash breathed an exasperated sigh. "Are you saying you lied to the police and on oath at the inquest about your place of residence purely to get your children into the school you wanted?"

"The point is that we'd already lied," Sarah Eastward explained, as though that made it all perfectly reasonable. "Mummy's address is on record with the school. We just had to keep going."

The inspector took a deep breath and counted to ten. Of all the infuriating, maddening stories he had ever heard. Witnesses always had their own secrets to protect – that was one of the things that made detective work so complicated. But what a day – first an Angora rabbit and now this. "You do realise that you've put yourselves in all kinds of trouble with Her Majesty's Court Service? But you'll have to put that out of your minds now. Do you remember seeing any of these people at Wimbledon?"

And once again, Sergeant Monroe presented his rogues' gallery of photographs. The Eastwards bent over the pictures studiously, eager to make amends for their blotted copybook. Harlan Eastward shook his head regretfully. "I wasn't really paying attention to people in the crowd."

His wife looked more attentively at the photograph third from the right. "That one looks familiar. Now when did I see him? Oh, I know. He came past our seats at the change of ends. It was just before that rather nice-looking man got up and said Mr Maybury had been taken ill."

It wasn't exactly a smoking gun, as Sergeant Monroe observed later, but it was good enough.

CHAPTER 18

According to the map, the Mile End Road cut sharply through the East End of London from east to west. Half-way along it, a wavering blue line suggested a small tributary river or a canal.

Xan made his way east, to where the Square Mile's steel and glass gave way to the faded brick of the poorer East End district. Whitechapel brought a welcome burst of colour – a long street market clamoured with fabrics in every hue of the rainbow. Here and there, he saw hints that gentrification was spreading east. A big Victorian hospital dominated the long high street, but an estate agent sign announced that the old nurses' quarters were being turned into luxury flats.

So where would the nurses go, he wondered? What would happen when they came out from a shift at 2am and had to wait for a night-bus to take them to wherever they could afford to live? These old streets looked safe enough in daylight, but at night they would be lonely and this had been the heartland of Jack the Ripper.

The long ribbon of road edged by degrees into Mile End and at last he came to a bridge over the canal. He descended to the tow-path to find himself in what seemed a forgotten landscape. Old brick warehouse buildings and yards bounded the water, which looked dark and deep and no doubt full of bicycles and shopping trolleys. Evidently, this area had not yet been redeveloped. There were no cafes with hanging-baskets of flowers. Instead, under the bridge by which the Tube line crossed the canal, he found the collie.

It was hunched into a corner, a black-and-white bundle of shivering, matted fur. A stray, he thought at first, but upon seeing him, it struggled to its feet, its eyes hopeful. It tried to come forward, but he could see that it was limping, the back left paw hovering above the ground.

What did one do with stray and injured dogs in this country? Alert the police? A vet? But the chances were that it belonged to someone around here. It whined and instinctively, he reached a hand down and patted it. The tail wagged feebly. Of a friendly disposition, then.

When he straightened up, the animal whined, as if at the prospect of being left behind. Seeing that there was no alternative, Xan bent down and picked it up – it was small and light for its breed and weighed very little.

As he walked along the tow-path, he began to pass moored vessels. Some were narrow-boats decked out with tubs of flowers, others of less conventional build and uncompromisingly utilitarian in aspect. He noted the names as he passed – the *Wanderer*, the *Queen of the Waters*. He did not get the impression that these boats, despite their names, ever moved from this spot.

The fifth boat along stood out thanks to the quality of her paintwork, which could most kindly be described as hand-crafted. Her top half was a dull deep red, which had dripped down onto the yellow bottom half creating an unfortunate impression of bloodstains. A round yellow thing with wavering rays emerging from it suggested the sun.

The flat roof of the barge was piled with sacks of coal. A battered bicycle balanced precariously on top of an iron box, looking as though it might tumble into the canal at any moment. A rusting barbecue set with heavy fire irons on the flat cruise-deck and a couple of gas bottles at the stern suggested a basic, outdoors approach to cooking.

As he took in the scene, the cabin-door was shoved suddenly open and a face looked out. It was, Xan thought, a face from a nightmare. The features were all right – the face's owner had been lucky with whatever had made that unholy mess, it had missed the eyes – but the cuts that crisscrossed the skin, rendering it into an awkward jigsaw puzzle, could only have made by glass shards or a knife.

It seemed at first that the face only had the intention of observing, but upon seeing the dog, the door was pushed further open. The man who emerged looked young, perhaps only Xan's age, with fair hair and disorganised stubble. He was clad in scruffy combats and an ill-matched T-shirt with POLICE written across it. His voice when it came was hesitant and high. "What are you doing with that dog?"

Xan put the animal down with some relief. "It's hurt. Back left foot. Do you know who the owner is?"

The man swung himself swiftly over the side of his boat

and onto the tow-path. "He's mine. His name's Mags. Short for Magpie. Glory be to God for dappled things. That's Mags."

Xan said: "You'd better take a look at the back foot. Looks like a bad cut to me."

The man passed his tongue over dry lips uneasily. "I'm no good at things like that."

"What do you mean?"

A rueful grimace. "Can't stand the sight of blood. That's one of the reasons they kicked me out of the Army." He stared down at the dog glumly. "Can't even get a splinter out."

"I'll take a look," Xan said resignedly. "But you had better hold him in case he tries to bite me."

"Yes, he might do that," the man said thoughtfully, and in the circumstances, unhelpfully.

Xan knelt down beside the dog. Rather to his surprise, it sat still and allowed him to pick up the back paw for examination.

There was an angled shard of glass sticking out of the soft felt pad of the paw and congealed blood around it. Glancing up to make sure his unwilling veterinary partner had a firm hold of the dog's collar, Xan gently exerted some pressure on the piece of glass. The dog whined. His owner swallowed convulsively. The glass slid smoothly out of the wound.

Mags' owner looked grateful, if a little pale. He fished in his pocket and dragged out a battered cigarette packet. "Smoke?"

"No thanks."

"Cup of tea, then."

Xan sighed. It seemed the only way to ingratiate himself with people in this country. "Thank you."

The man vanished into the boat. A clinking of metal cans and cups could be heard inside. Surprisingly quickly, he reappeared, carrying two tin mugs. Xan reluctantly accepted one and took a sip of the brew – it was dark and bitter and looked suspiciously like the water listlessly swilling between the barge and the tow-path.

His host scratched his head and stretched. "Nothing like fresh air on the river," he announced. "My name's Rabbit, by the way." He pulled aside the collar of his T-shirt to reveal a tattoo of a small hopping animal on his shoulder.

Xan had already guessed it from the boat's hand-painted motif. "Mine's Xan. You've got a nice boat."

Rabbit nodded, patting the side of the *Sunflower* as though she were a horse. "She suits me and Mags." He looked dreamily along the canal, the still waters to which he had somehow safely drifted.

"So, you were in the Army?"

"Not for very long. You might say the life wasn't for me."

"Is that how you hurt your face?"

"Yeah. In a crash."

"Bad luck."

Rabbit shrugged, as though luck had nothing to do with it. Which might well, Xan thought, be true. "I wasn't the unlucky one."

There are times in the investigator's work when several pieces of information come together at once. This was one of those times. Without any discernible pause, Xan said: "You served with a man named Paradine, didn't you? Was he the unlucky one?"

Rabbit did not move, but his body was suddenly tense, his mug of tea held to his lips. His eyes strayed nervously around him.

Xan didn't move either. That glance around had not been aimless. The fire-irons would make handy weapons for a trained soldier who didn't like questions.

"Why do you want to know? You police?"

"No."

A quick upward glance, as though Rabbit was making a second assessment of his visitor. "Forces?"

"No."

And now the patchwork face relaxed a little. "Yes, then. What of it?"

"You were there when he died?"

Rabbit nodded.

"What happened to him?"

A boneless shrug. "I never knew anything about it. We were going down to Luxor. I was off duty, heading for a spot of leave. We took the tourist coach – it's cheapest. I'd had a lot of beer the night before. I fell asleep. Woke up to find myself wedged in the bottom of a ditch with glass all over my face. The coach had crashed. Next time I woke, I was in the hospital, screaming for water."

Xan grimaced. That familiar environment – the heat,

the fans, the flies, concerned faces, white coats, voices speaking languages you didn't understand and pain you could neither put words to or escape.

"That's when they told me David was dead," Rabbit went on unemotionally. "He'd been shot."

Xan looked up sharply. "I thought you said the coach had crashed."

"Because there'd been shooting," Rabbit said patiently. "They said he'd got into an argument over a card game for money. That was nonsense. David never played for money, his father was dead against it. He only played two-handed rummy, too. It was his favourite game. But that's what they said."

Xan considered this account. There was certainly a mystery of sorts here. Was his son's death the thing that Adam Paradine had wanted Maybury to 'look into'? But why now, so many years later? "You don't remember anything at all about the journey?"

Rabbit shrugged. "Nope. They asked me all of that at the time. Name, pack drill, all the rest of it you get when you've blotted your copybook and you don't know how. *You* know," Rabbit said, and there was a sudden directness in the appeal to his listener.

"Yes, I know."

"They seemed interested at first, then all of a sudden, they couldn't care less about it. They took me out of the regiment and put me on cooking instead. And then I got the discharge I'd been asking for more than two years, only on medical grounds. Seemed like they couldn't get me out fast enough."

He relapsed into silence, looking downriver. A cargo boat chugged past, low and flat and ugly. A sullen-looking man at the wheel and his equally scowling dog were the only crew.

"Why do you think that was?"

Rabbit shrugged. "Search me."

"And David's father?"

Rabbit shrugged. "I told him everything I could about it at the time, but I don't reckon he never got over it."

"You wrote to him about it recently though, didn't you?"

Rabbit showed the whites of his eyes like a frightened horse. "What makes you say that?"

Xan put down his unwanted mug of tea and pulled a paper out of his jacket pocket. Showing it to Rabbit was of course a risk but Rabbit did not strike him as the sort who had much respect for the minor laws of the land. "This is the letter you wrote to him."

"Why have you got it?"

"I found it at his house."

That frightened look again. "You mean he's dead."

"I'm afraid so. He drowned in his swimming-pool."

Another flickering look from the nervous eyes.

Xan said quietly: "This wasn't the first time you wrote to him, was it? You told him you had moved. Why did you write to him originally?"

For the first time since they had got onto the subject of Reverend Paradine, Rabbit showed a hint of animation.

"You've got it all wrong. He got in touch with me."

"When?"

"A couple of months ago."

"Why?"

Rabbit studied the water intently. "He didn't say. He just wanted to know anything I could remember about it. But I was asleep the whole time. Like I told you."

Xan watched the averted face. For the first time, he thought Rabbit was lying. He persisted: "Why had Adam Paradine started thinking about his son again? Had he discovered something? Found something?"

"I don't know."

"You said you had thought of something. What was that?"

"I remembered someone he could talk to – the Major. He's in a nursing home now. He was David's CO."

"What nursing home?"

"I don't know," Rabbit said again, sullenly. "What's it got to do with you, anyway?"

"I'm just looking into it – for a friend."

Rabbit nodded. "Nice to have friends who care about when you die. Now you and me, we won't have anyone to worry about us when we go. Apart from Mags, of course."

"What about the letter Reverend Paradine sent you? Have you still got it?"

Rabbit shook his head morosely. "I don't keep stuff. I showed it to the other one, though."

"What other one?"

"Old chap in a Panama hat. A bit doddery. Mind you,

he was all right up here." Rabbit tapped his forehead.

Xan paused, exasperated. Wherever he got to, that spare, upright figure with the worried blue eyes had been ahead of him. "He came to see you?"

"That's right. But I couldn't tell him any more than I've told you."

"Did he ask you about a photograph? Show you one, maybe?"

Rabbit shook his head. "He didn't show me nothing nor tell me nothing."

And Xan didn't believe him. He followed Rabbit's glance down into the still surface of the canal – so deep and still, but unseen things stirring down there for all that. There was something more Rabbit could tell him, he was certain of it. But he would get no more from him today.

"Thank you for the tea." He handed back the tin mug rather thankfully, most of its contents undrunk, and fished in his pocket for pen and paper. "If you think of anything else, you can get hold of me at this number."

Rabbit's eyes were steady and guileless. "I've told you everything I know."

And again, Xan didn't believe him.

CHAPTER 19

At last, Xan began to perceive the possible shape of this case – the bones emerging from the desert sand. It was a shape that he had not expected. But that was what happened when you started to dig without knowing what you were looking for.

It started with Reverend Paradine. Judging by what Mrs Banner had said, he had philosophically accepted his son's death at the time, perhaps helped by his faith. But years later, chance had played an unexpected card. Clearing out his attic, Adam Paradine had found something – a photograph? – probably among his son's stored possessions. Whatever it was, it had made him question what he had been told about his son's death.

Paradine had discussed the find with Giles Maybury, who had promised to look into the matter. Maybury had talked to Rabbit, who had served with David Paradine in Egypt, and perhaps to other people. And he had found out something – something he hadn't bargained for.

He had appeared preoccupied to his friends and dropped some of his engagements. He had arranged an urgent appointment with Sir Miles Temperley. And then – the visit to Wimbledon, long-planned and anticipated, impossible to cancel.

Perhaps on the journey up by train, he had realised he was being followed – or perhaps only imagined that he was. He had reached the Club safely, but he had believed that his enemies would not him leave. And so had come the desperate decision to confide in an outsider who had just arrived in the country and thus could not be involved. And then fate had caught up with Giles Maybury and he had left behind only a newspaper and a diary.

It was mostly conjecture, with a couple of rather wild leaps of logic. But surely, it must have been something like that. And now the only way to find out for sure was to follow in Maybury's footsteps and begin where he had started – with the death of David Paradine.

There was something in Xan that didn't want any part of this. A cold case involving the death of a soldier took him too close to his own past. There would be hard truths at the end of it. But then after all, who was he to pick and choose?

*

This time, he picked a different internet café, one that was buzzing with teenagers hanging around talking on their phones, bored in the summer holidays. No one paid any attention to him as he selected a terminal at random. And yet, as he entered the name of David Paradine into the search field, he felt something akin to the sensation of the scientist who gently tests a single strand of the web of a rare and poisonous spider.

UK SERVICEMAN KILLED IN BRAWL. BRITISH SOLDIER DIES ON TOURIST COACH. But beneath the excitable headlines, the actual facts were sparse.

A coach carrying mostly American and British tourists from Cairo to Luxor had crashed in the desert after an argument between a British soldier and an Egyptian got out of hand and shots were fired. Who had shot who and in what order was not explained.

A brief biography of the dead British soldier appeared alongside the article in a sidebar. Corporal Paradine had lived a short life but apparently a brave one. He had joined the British Army at eighteen. He had served overseas in Afghanistan and Iraq, always in the same regiment. A career without remark but equally without hitches, until in 2007 he had been posted to Cairo, where his history had ended abruptly and violently.

Paradine's Commanding Officer in the UK, a Major James Phelps, offered a quote of thoughtful blandness saluting Paradine's bravery and competence – the sort of thing, Xan knew, that every Army press office kept ready on the shelf for these occasions.

The Egyptian news reports included more details on the coach accident. Most of the passengers had been seated towards the front of the vehicle and had been oblivious to any problem until it abruptly swerved off the road.

One report mentioned another British passenger who had been taken to hospital injured, a Robert Hare. It was easy enough from a position of knowledge to recognise a source of Army humour and the faint trail that led to the

Mile End Road. Another story quoted a female passenger, a Miss Jane Griffin. "The two soldiers were playing cards. Then suddenly, the Egyptian man jumped up and started shouting. And I heard shots fired and the whole coach tilted over."

A third account attempted to recreate the crash as it had occurred, the wording suggesting that the writer had been given some information by the local police. "The coach plunged into the ditch on the left-hand side of the road, slid down a shallow incline and came to rest on its side in the valley. The whole of the window on that side was ripped out. The wheel-tracks –."

But Xan was not interested in the wheel-tracks. He looked at the photograph of the coach in its final resting-place, in a dust-dry valley that had perhaps once carried a river. The left-hand side of the coach was mostly hidden from view, but he could see the curved and bent frame of the window. Vehicle windows were nowadays designed to fall out in one piece, not to shatter. (Out of nowhere, he suddenly remembered Mr De Leiter jabbing at the rear passenger window with his revolver and swearing, until it suddenly got dislodged and fell outwards, and a hail of bullets came inwards.)

At any rate, it was evident from the news reports that little information on the incident had been released by either the British or Egyptian authorities. Yet there was indubitably more to know. How had David Paradine got into a dispute with a civilian in the first place? The news reports said cards, but Rabbit said very definitely that it had *not* been about a game of cards. And perhaps Reverend Paradine had thought the same. It was also odd how little information there was about the civilian in question – a man named Hassan Khalim.

No doubt, Adam Paradine had been given the official briefing on this incident at the time of his son's death. But it seemed to Xan unlikely that the official records would be much help now – at least anything that he could get his hands on. In any case, experience had taught him that to understand a cold incident many years back, written accounts, even those produced at the time, were of little help. You needed people. Witnesses.

There was no obvious way to identify the Jane Griffin who had been quoted in the news report. A quick internet search offered over a dozen people with her name in London alone, none with any apparent connection with Egypt. Conversely, there was not the faintest trail left by Rabbit. Council tax records, bank accounts, employer references, utility bills – all the usual flotsam and jetsam of life were entirely absent. Evidently, Rabbit was living off the grid. And yet Adam Paradine had evidently known where to find him.

Xan looked back through the news reports to find the name of Paradine's Commanding Officer. Major James Phelps. The internet offered a picture – a grizzled veteran with tufted eyebrows, leaning heavily on a stick. This was the man Rabbit had mentioned – and surely the man who had had the difficult task of breaking the news to Adam Paradine.

CHAPTER 20

The photographer who had taken the picture of Major James Phelps had an office address at Brunel Street in Shadhurst, a loop of south London tucked below the river.

Xan crossed the river at Tower Bridge, only to find that he was too far east. He worked his way west through a hostile neighbourhood of warehouses and goods yards, their gates firmly closed and their high walls protectively edged with barbed wire.

Brunel Street was, as one would expect, close to a rail line. In fact, the trains thundered alongside the road in an elevated position and then crossed the street via a bridge at the far end.

No 38 was halfway down the street, an unassuming building in a short row of commercial premises. As Xan got closer, he saw the bottom floor was a launderette. A separate door led to an upstairs office and a dusty card stuck against the glass announced the premises of

PAUL FLANNERY – PHOTOGRAPHY
Press - Weddings - Divorce
Discreet, confidential service

Xan spared a moment to reflect on the cynicism of a

business that offered services for both weddings and divorces, then entered the shabby premises. Inside, a flight of stairs led upwards. The door at the top of the stairs was ajar and he knocked for politeness' sake and entered without waiting for instruction.

The office within was bright and new in a gimcrack way. A cheap desk with a chair on each side of it and an easy-chair in the corner that did not look very easy. But the man behind the desk was more remarkable than his room.

He was vast, for one thing, his spreading bulk encased in an expansive denim shirt that seemed to go on forever. When he rose to his feet, it was with caution, as though he did not quite trust the load-bearing of his office floor. The youthful face atop the huge torso was professionally jovial.

He offered a hand, "How can I help you, Mr –?"

Xan knew he did not look like a customer in need of photographic services of any description. "West."

It was a mistake to be a Smith or a Jones. Names needed to be distinctive enough to sound real. But it probably didn't matter in this case. Mr Flannery was nodding indifferently as though he didn't believe a word of it.

"I'm Paul Flannery. Divorce, weddings, press, etcetera, etcetera. Do sit down, Mr Whatever. What will it be for you?"

"I need some information."

"Well," Flannery said cheerily, "doesn't everyone?" As he spoke, the small eyes were summing Xan up carefully.

"It'll cost you."

"That's fine." With some subjects of interest, a subtle approach was advisable, but Xan was pretty certain it would be wasted here. Paul Flannery, if that was his real name, came from the same side of the fence as he did. Hard cash was much more to the point.

Flannery exhaled, as though this was all going to be more trouble than he cared for. "Police?"

"No."

"Thought not. You'd be offering paperwork rather than cash. But you're that sort, aren't you?"

"I'm just a private individual."

Flannery eyed him acutely. "Then I can't see why you're poking around paying people for information you could get through straightforward means if you had any right to have it."

"It doesn't matter what you can't see though, does it?"

"No, it doesn't." Flannery named a sum. "That's for anything I already know and feel like sharing. If you want anything else found out, it'll be extra."

"I can handle anything else I want found out."

"I'm sure you can."

Xan produced a copy of the photograph of the soldiers. "You took this picture?"

Flannery glanced at it briefly. "What if I did?"

"You were sent there, as a press photographer?"

"That's right. Not really my beat, but a divorce job I had lined up fell through – reconciliation, would you believe it – so I went along like a good little boy. Dull as ditchwater." Flannery gloomed down at the photographs.

"Where was it taken?"

The photographer wheezed a ghost of a laugh. "You're not a Londoner, are you, Mr Whatever? That's Chelsea Barracks. Corner of."

"So that's where the soldiers were from. What about the veterans?"

Flannery shrugged. "Got to have veterans for a war memorial line-up. The more incapacitated-looking the better. Half of them look like they'd drop dead on their feet. What's the point of going on like that?" He considered the men in the photograph without sentiment.

Xan suppressed a sudden urge to knock Flannery's head against his mahogany-effect desk. It was no good taking offence at witnesses, however offensive. "Do you know where they came from?"

"Local nursing home in Nightingale Street. Not too far to walk to the Barracks." Flannery studied his client thoughtfully. "I'd love to know what you're after with all this. But as you're about to remark, I'm being paid in cash, not information. So, you're welcome to come across with that any time you like."

Xan came across. Flannery counted the money, then put it away in a drawer. He put his fingertips together in a parody of the successful executive. "Well, it's been a pleasure doing business with you. Or come to think of it, that might be going a bit too far."

And Xan had to concede that Paul Flannery of Photography Ltd had had the last word.

On his way back east, he decided to check out the clearance firm that Mrs Banner had mentioned, Dunwood & Bane. They appeared to be an innocuous business, part of an umbrella group of companies offering a range of dull-sounding administrative services. They had premises in EC1B 5TJ – a postcode in the central eastern London district, in other words within the Square Mile itself. It seemed reasonable to satisfy curiosity by going to look at them.

As he found when he reached the area in question, this was easier said than done. Postal codes were all very well for postmen but the only way for ordinary citizens to identify the streets grouped under this invisible label was to use the navigation function on a mobile phone.

Xan had a deep aversion to satellite navigation and, when a postman came stumping along the street, took the simpler expedient of stopping him and asking.

Left, right, right again, through an alleyway with a giant aluminium unicorn at the far end and into a street with a tall church at one end and at the other, a square of grass with a cluster of ancient graves. On the eastern side was a square and unattractive block and a metal sculpture of a bird with a blazing tail.

Xan checked the address to make sure he had it right. The postal address of Dunwood & Bane was Phoenix House, the headquarters of Lombard & Black.

CHAPTER 21

Nightingale Street was to be found in a smart district of west London where the river looped lazily along between the Barracks and a Victorian pleasure-park. Nightingale Street itself embodied Georgian elegance, giving way to modern steel and glass wherever World War II bombs had carved out a hole.

Xan trod the wide pavement gloomily. He didn't like nursing-homes, hospitals or any of the institutions into which people disappeared to become, mysteriously, less of themselves.

The Magnolia Trees Nursing Home occupied one of the surviving Georgian buildings on the street. The white-coated man on the reception desk offered no challenge when Xan asked for Major Phelps, perhaps taking him for a military colleague. Xan reflected that homes of this sort were probably not high-security environments, although the lack of visitor checks must surely open places like this up to targeting by small-time thieves, if nothing else.

A second orderly conducted him through the building and into a garden. Of course, it was only to be expected that these former family homes would have gardens. This one was a rectangle of overgrown grass, bordered by a wall of bricks so old that their colours had begun to flow into one another. And there were real magnolia trees, a quartet of them extending their bowl-shaped branches over the grass and the old brick walls. Xan's instinctive resistance began to fade.

The orderly brought him to a seat under one of the magnolia trees, where a grey-haired man was seated. He looked older than his picture had suggested.

"Major Phelps, a visitor to see you, sir," said the orderly and went away across the grass.

Bees murmured in the overgrown flowerbeds. It was entirely possible to suppose that time did not pass here. Then Major Phelps glanced curiously at his visitor and a frown deepened the furrow in his forehead.

"Major Phelps? My name's Ross. I have a few questions for you, if that's all right."

"Ask away." The major's voice was unexpectedly dry and amused. "But I have to warn you, I've forgotten a lot. Which is probably just as well."

"I wanted to ask you about a man named Paradine – David Paradine."

The Major glanced at him properly for the first time. "Are you a member of his family?"

"No. I'm here on behalf of his father." Xan's conscience prodded him and he told himself it was true.

"He's dead. Someone told me – I forget who."

"Yes, he died about a month ago."

Major Phelps nodded. "He couldn't understand what had happened. None of us could. I wasn't out there, of course. I was David's CO here. Young soldier on leave gets into an argument with a civilian – well, it happens. The civilian was carrying a gun and loosed off a couple of shots in a temper. I don't suppose he meant to kill him."

"There's very little information about Hassan Khalim – the civilian in question – in the news reports," Xan said. "That struck me as odd."

Major Phelps shook his head apologetically. "I'm afraid I can't help you there. I was only involved as David's CO. And I had nothing I could tell his father except that he had been shot in peacetime in a friendly country."

"How did he react? I mean," Xan added quickly, "was he angry? Did he ask questions? Blame anyone?"

The Major shook his head. "He seemed to accept it in a very measured way. Perhaps living close to God gives you that comfort. I haven't that privilege myself." He peered at his visitor. "I don't suppose you have either."

"No." Xan chose his next question carefully. "Reverend Paradine came to see you before he died, though, didn't he?"

Major Phelps frowned. "Did he? No, I don't believe he did. It was the other one who came here. Mayfield, or something, his name was. Wanted to know the same things you do."

There it was again. It was hard to know whether to find it reassuring or infuriating that everywhere he went, Maybury had been there before him. "Did he show you a photograph?"

"A photograph?" The major looked puzzled. "No."

"Did the soldiers routinely carry cameras?"

The puzzled look intensified. "No. What is all this about a photograph?"

Xan let it go. In any case, the major was not going to be able to tell him anything useful about David Paradine's death. He might, however, have some insight into his life. One of the most valuable things about human witnesses was what they could tell you about those who had gone beyond the reach of the investigator's notebook and the witness-box. Accordingly, he asked: "What was David Paradine like as a soldier?"

"He was a good recruit. Worked hard, passed his training levels."

"Was he happy in the Army?"

"He seemed to be. And you can generally tell when someone has any doubts."

"What about Robert Hare?"

Major Phelps chuckled and shook his head. "A shockingly bad shot. And couldn't stand the sight of blood. Rabbit was about as well-suited to the Army as this tree I'm sitting under."

Xan went away and found the orderly who had brought him. "Does Major Phelps get many visitors?"

The orderly shook his head. "Not usually."

"A friend of mine came about a month ago. Elderly man in a Panama hat?"

"That's right," the orderly said without interest. "One visitor a month is about right for him. He doesn't have any family."

Xan looked out to where the major still sat, gazing up

into the trees. "He has – everything he needs, I suppose?"

The orderly gave him the look you give unperceptive people who imagine that the world's ills can be cured through cash. "Yes, sir."

As he came down the nursing-home steps, Xan glanced across the road, instinctively noting the car waiting there – an expensive-looking one with a uniformed man at the wheel. He didn't like occupied stationery cars. But the man's livery suggested he was merely a chauffeur waiting for his employer who had business at one of these tall houses.

Only that wasn't right. There was already a passenger in the back seat. A heavy, pursed face glared out at him. The bulldog face he had seen looking down from the first floor at Lombard & Black.

CHAPTER 22

The tall power-station that dominated the London sky-scape above the river had once breathed smoke into the atmosphere, but times had changed and the building had long since been gutted of its internal workings. Now it housed significant works of modern art.

It was the day after Xan's interview with Major Phelps. He had been waiting here for half an hour already, watching the tourists coming and going and trying to disregard the brisk wind that blew off the river. This was another of Billy's ridiculous rendezvous suggestions – but if it was intended as a joke, this time the joke was on Billy. As he waddled briskly across the courtyard, a set of fountains sprang up out of nowhere, briefly soaking him.

Children who had a moment ago been playing in the treacherous water feature screamed with laughter at the fat man in his drenched suit. Their parents hurriedly hushed them. Xan tried to assemble an expression of gravity onto his features, but it was too late.

"I don't know what you think is so funny," Billy growled, stretching out his arms to watch the water drip from his sodden shirt-sleeves. He extracted a plastic folder from his inside jacket pocket. "It's your briefing material that nearly got pulped. Next time, you can do your own research."

"On that subject, there is something else. I want to know about a company named Lombard & Black."

"And what have a respectable City firm got to do with a murdered civil servant?"

"I don't know yet. Maybe nothing."

"Just as well. They'd sue you for the mere suggestion."

"Who are they, anyway?"

"They own a lot of land all over the country. Restaurant chains, insurance, pensions, hotels, you name it, they're in it."

"Yes, but who are they? I want to know who's behind them. Not the people listed on the board of directors, the ones who aren't named. People who are getting their mail there but aren't in the company reports, for instance."

"As it happens, I think I can help you there. But like I said, you'd do better staying out of it. I hear you're taking an interest in military cold cases now."

"Where did you hear that?"

"Nowhere in particular. But I'd be careful if I were you. You could be making some bad enemies."

"I don't know what you're talking about."

Billy shrugged. "Don't say I didn't warn you."

Xan walked along the river to a quieter spot, beyond the crowds. Here, there was a discreet affluence in the lines of former warehouses transformed into apartments. Only the occasional jogger or dog-walker passed along the path. The perfect spot for a murder, then – or was it? Xan was not sure, looking up at the hundred blank eyes of the windows. They might all be empty, but they might not. You could not be sure and if you were a careful murderer, you might not be inclined to risk it.

He leaned against a wall and read Adam Paradine's post-mortem report. It was not conclusive. The victim had died from chlorine overdose, as the coroner had observed. The report described bruising to the back of the head, which might be ascribed to hitting it on the edge of the pool as he went in but might not.

There had also been bruising to the upper arms. The skin around the mouth had been burned by the chemical contact. Was it possible, Xan wondered, that if that had not been the case, other bruising would have been seen there? In a surprise attack, the first thing you had to do was silence your victim. In this case, the killers had wanted the death to seem natural. They would probably have had to put a hand over his mouth to keep him quiet until the stun blow was administered.

These were ugly thoughts. But it was getting clearer that this was an ugly affair.

*

At the canal, the long line of boats swung idly on the water, which was never still, but stirred and eddied as though some monstrous creature lurked beneath the flat black surface. On a sunny late afternoon, it gave nothing away and only offered up your own reflection.

Xan paced around a little, scraping his boots on the

stones and generally making the kinds of noises that would disturb a watchful and alert ex-soldier. But there was no answering commotion from the boat, not even, and this was rather odd, a sound from the dog.

"He's gone." The occupant of the next boat along – a short man with a barrel chest – was watching Xan with unfriendly eyes. "Cleared off a few days ago, said he'd be gone for a while. Did you want something?" His voice said that Xan had better not.

As he trudged back along the tow-path, Xan cursed himself for not having questioned Rabbit more closely when he had first found him. He would not be an easy man to find again. Anyone who lived off the grid – no bank account, no job, no council tax – could disappear at will. Xan found some comfort in directing some of his reproaches towards Giles Maybury and the maddening opacity of his hints.

As he came into the hotel, Leah waved. "Another letter, Mr Ross."

He thanked her, mildly puzzled. This time, it could not be a summons to an inquest. And who else would write to him at the Coronado? Who knew he was staying here, other than the police?

The envelope was of thick, cream stock, but smeared and dusty. Originally there had been some kind of logo on the bottom left corner – this had been scored out violently with a thick black biro. His name was written on the envelope in ragged capitals.

He waited until he got to his room to open it. Inside was

a doubled-over sheet of paper. Like the envelope, it was of good quality stock. The top corner of the page had been torn off, by the looks of it to obscure a place-name and address, but it had been done carelessly, leaving half the words.

-zy
-mon.
-vercombe.

The message began without fanfare, just below it. It was written in the same black biro, scoring heavily into the paper.

Mister,

Just so you know, I've moved on. Some people came to see me. They wanted to know the same things you did. Mags didn't like them so we left.

This place is good enough for now. I'm working for cash and they don't ask too many questions. And Mags likes the sea air. Maybe the change will do us both good.

The message trailed off with a scribble that looked like a small hopping animal with long ears.

CHAPTER 23

The salesman at the car rental garage sized his customer up as an overseas tourist, perhaps American, who would like the biggest, shiniest and newest vehicle available.

Xan had not intended to drive while he was here. Whether you bought or hired a vehicle, it was the ideal way to bring yourself to the attention of the authorities. Both you and your car had to have paperwork and one minor traffic infraction could blow a month of cover. But if he was going to go looking for Rabbit, he would need a car.

The salesman waved his hand at a row of gleaming new BMWs and Mercedes. "Sat-nav comes as standard and of course, everything's digital inside."

But a car with computerised systems that talked to its manufacturers (and quite possibly others) was exactly what Xan didn't want. "Don't you have anything older?"

"We have a few older models, sir, but they don't have sat-nav. And no air-conditioning," he added warningly. "It's going to get up to the seventies tomorrow, they say."

To Xan, who was used to Dubai and Saudi Arabia, the prospect of 70 degrees Fahrenheit was scarcely alarming. He stopped by an old and dusty smoky blue Volvo estate. "What about this one?"

The Volvo was neither rakish nor new enough to attract attention. It would be good for a surveillance job – dull enough to avoid being noticed, big enough to be bearable for long hours and even sleeping in if things turned out that way.

The salesman opened his mouth to utter more warnings about the lack of a device pairing mode and other critical functionality, then shut it again. “Very well, sir.”

It had been Rabbit’s letter that had prompted Xan into action. Overnight, feelings of unease had begun to collect around it like a flock of ragged crows, birds of ill-omen. Unable to sleep, he had found himself switching on the light and looking again at the torn heading at the top of the page. What sort of places had headed notepaper these days? Hotels, for one. And Rabbit had been a cook in the Army, at least briefly.

He had gone down to the deserted hotel lounge and found a set of travel books, including a guide to hotels and inns of Great Britain. After half an hour of headache-inducing study under a reading-lamp, he had closed the heavy book, his question answered.

The Lazy Salmon Inn, Ilvercombe, Devon. Gourmet cuisine. Real ales. Food served all day. No dogs allowed in dining-room. Free car park. Sea air (no doubt).

However much Rabbit might object to the establishment’s position on dogs in dining-rooms, this must be the place.

*

It felt surprisingly good to be behind the wheel of a car again, although he had almost forgotten the eccentricities of manual transmission. The traffic-choked East London streets were frustrating and it was a relief when at last he turned onto the quieter road to the west.

It was a grey day, with a slow, invisible rain soaking the fields. At midday, he pulled over in a gateway and spread the road atlas over the steering-wheel to double-check his route. To the west, England gradually tapered to a point through Cornwall. Before that point lay three counties. Somerset to the north and Dorset to the south, then Devon sprawling from one coastline to the other.

Ilvercombe lay on the north coast – it looked a tiny place, although the map indicated that the railway called there. Perhaps, he thought, that was one of the reasons that had taken Rabbit there – a man living on a London narrow-boat would not own a car and like Xan, he would have been wary of the paperwork involved in getting one. Nor, probably, did he have the money.

Over the next hour, the rain petered out, as though its boundary line lay here and it could not transgress it. And once into Somerset, the roads grew narrower.

He followed a twisting route that meandered through sunken lanes between high hedges and then climbed to an upland world of wide skies, rough grass, and purple and yellow gorse.

He stopped the car again on a rough chalk track evidently intended for farm vehicles and got out to look at the view.

Although the breeze was presently mild, the tortured shape of the thorn-bushes attested to the savage winds that must sweep across this plain for much of the year.

This, he knew from the map, was Exmoor. Now that he had become attuned to the silence, he could hear birdsong in the distant sky. Two moorland ponies watched him and tossed their heads in the contemptuous way of horses.

A gently descending lane with fields on either side brought him underneath an ugly railway bridge, past the sleepy-looking station and down towards the sea. As he checked the car to allow a pair of brightly-hued hikers to scramble past him without being pitched into the ditch, he felt a sudden and disconcerting pang of something – what? It could not be memory. He had never been taken on seaside holidays as a child. So why this treacherous wave of longing for a past he had never known?

Ilvercombe proved to be little more than a row of what had once been fishermen's cottages, most now converted to holiday dwellings, facing the sea. No boats waited here now for the chance to go out for a catch. A church with a squat tower stood on the hillside. In the middle of the row of houses stood the Lazy Salmon, an old-fashioned inn.

He headed inside. The place was done up in pale wood panelling and plaster walls washed in pastel colours. A hurrying waitress carrying plates glanced at him curiously and he wondered at the hurry, rather than the glance – the dining-room was almost empty. It was long past lunchtime and only a handful of diners, mostly families and hikers, were engaging with what might be afternoon tea or even an early dinner.

Behind the bar itself, a jovial teddy-bear of a man in an apron was drying glasses. A brass plate indicated in wavy Italic script the legend, *J. Bageshot. Proprietor*.

For the investigator, ordering drinks that took a long time to pour presented an excellent catalyst for conversation, so long as you did not consume too much of what you bought. Billy had never been very good at this. Now, Xan initiated a lengthy exchange on the merits of the various real ales before making a random selection.

"Passing through?" the landlord inquired mechanically as he poured the sludgy-looking liquid.

"More or less." Xan glanced out of the window at the grey, cloud-tossed sky. "Looks stormy out there."

Mr Bageshot seemed to take his remark as an affront to the desirability of Ilvercombe as a resort. "You say that, but it can clear up easy as winking when it likes," he said defensively. "Lovely climate hereabouts, much milder than you'll get down the coast."

"Seems like a nice place you've got," Xan offered as a conciliatory gesture. "Can't be easy getting staff though, out here."

"You could say that," Mr Bageshot said gloomily as he handed over his customer's pint. "Youngsters these days want everything on a plate. Only bother to do a job of work when they're short of cash."

Xan took a reluctant sip of his ale and advanced the opinion that national service would have sorted a lot of that type out.

"It's funny you should say that, sir. A few days ago, I needed an extra pair of hands in the kitchen and found a fellow who said he'd cooked in the Army. I wasn't sure that was any recommendation, mind. And his face was all carved up – we couldn't have had him front of house. But he said he was happier behind the scenes anyway."

"And is it working out?"

Mr Bageshot's face went a little purple. "Well, I thought it was. Needed some finesse with presentation, but he showed willing, no doubt about that. Didn't cause any trouble either, him or his dog."

Xan began to feel an uneasy sensation in his spine. "Well?"

"Didn't show up for work this morning," the proprietor said shortly. "Bed's not been slept in either. Now, I'm not an unreasonable man, but when you're running a place like this, reliability is what you need. We get dozens through here on a sunny day in the holiday season." He looked around his mostly-empty dining-room as though to make the point.

"Where would he have gone? Did he have a car?"

"Not he. Must have walked or hitched a lift to the nearest town and why he'd have done that when it's pay-day in two days and leaving all his kit here, I couldn't tell you. Looking for a good time, maybe. You would have thought the Army would knock that sort of behaviour out of a man, but I didn't think to ask him why he left, did I?" Mr Bageshot inquired rhetorically. "Probably, they kicked him out for the same reason. And now here I am, on a busy Saturday in August, having to help out with the food myself." Mr Bageshot shoved his chin forward and scowled at his interlocutor.

"Have you thought about the police?"

The proprietor snorted. "I have not. I don't have any time for that lot. Always sticking their noses into things that don't concern them."

Xan guessed at some previous run-in with the law that still rankled with the hotel-owner. He paid for his almost untouched beer and came out into a cold, brisk wind.

Had Rabbit taken fright and left without taking his things? For someone who had as little as Rabbit, that would be a choice made only out of desperation. And where would he have gone? There weren't many routes out of a small place like this. Might he have hiked up the steep road Xan had driven down, or, remembering his Army training, gone across country? But to where?

Xan glanced up at the inn's first-floor windows. What about Rabbit's room and belongings? It was a fairly risky proposition but he had carried out riskier searches – and an under-staffed public house serving gourmet cuisine would almost certainly not have time for staff to laze around in their own quarters during the day.

Public-houses always had several entrances. He chose an obscure door which faced out onto an almost empty car-park at the back and made his way past a set of visitor cloakrooms and other anterooms to the back stairs.

The upstairs rooms of the Lazy. Salmon would once have been used for paying guests, but few people stayed at gastropubs in dying, half-abandoned villages. No doubt, J Bageshot or another had concluded that offering rooms to staff would both attract employees who did not have homes locally and make it feasible to offer lower pay. At any rate, Rabbit had clearly been staying on the premises – Mr Bageshot had indicated as much.

Xan guessed that the room would not be locked, if Mr Bageshot had already checked it himself. The third door on the right as he came up the stairs was standing slightly open and he went in.

Inside, the covers had been stripped off the single bed and a shabby rucksack stood in a corner on the bare floor. A small chest of drawers represented the only storage and a grey zipped sweater he recognised hung on a chair.

There wasn't time for the proper discipline of covert searches as Homeland had taught it to him. Using a spare pillowcase to mask fingerprints, he went swiftly through the chest of drawers and checked under the slats of the bedstead.

Then he emptied out the contents of the rucksack. No photograph. Nothing but clothes and a couple of packets of dog treats. In the wardrobe, more clothes in a heap and at the bottom of the pile, unexpectedly, a book. He pulled it out and glanced at it in the dim light from the window.

A battered old hardback volume of poetry. He had to screw up his eyes to read the faint gold lettering on the blue cloth spine. Collected Poems of T S Eliot. More in Billy's line than his and certainly not something that he would have expected to find in Rabbit's belongings. He opened the cover. There was a name on the flyleaf – *Tom Riley*. The name meant nothing to him but he slipped the book into his jacket pocket anyway. Then he closed the door on the empty room, went quietly back through the hotel and emerged on the seafront.

The storm which J Bageshot, proprietor, had been at such pains to dismiss now seemed to be on its way. The sky was thick with massing clouds and a patter of rain drummed on the pavement. Shreds of litter were scudding up the street and the old-fashioned inn sign whipped back and forth on its hinges in the wind.

Beyond the road, the beach lay pale and empty, but in the distance, the incoming sea humped up in menacing swells.

Xan did not think that Rabbit had gone to the nearest town looking for entertainment, as Mr Bageshot seemed to believe. His empty room with its meagre belongings had had a bleak, abandoned feel. Somehow, he already sensed it – Rabbit was gone. He had slipped through the crack between the paving-stones and vanished.

He shaded his face against the wind and rain with his arm and measured along the bay with his eye. To the west, the shoreline lengthened in a slow curve, sliced into sections by long, low, wooden walls running into the sea which must have some local name and be intended to prevent the sweep of sand from the east side of the bay to the west. Making up his mind, he began to trudge along the shingle towards the west, the Lazy Salmon at his back.

Here, the houses gave way to a sandy heathland. A steep shingle bank dropped down to the sea. Heaps of splintered driftwood and tangles of seaweed, together with the occasional piece of netting or glass bottle, showed where the waves habitually abandoned their flotsam and jetsam.

Down on the foreshore, the tide was coming in, driven fast by the storm. The waves smacked angrily on the shingle. It looked to be about an hour off high tide.

As he paused to take in the scene, he saw a movement down at the waterline. It was a nightmare – a tableau that belonged in some surrealist art gallery. A cloaked black figure bending over a helpless dark shape in the surging water. Death caught in the act of plucking a soul for his kingdom.

It was a couple of seconds before he took in what he was seeing. Murder, or something close to it. He shouted, the words whipped away from him by the gale, and began to scramble down the shingle bank towards the water. At the same time, blown on the wind, there came the barking of a dog.

As he reached the water, another wave came surging up the beach. The figure staggered, thrown off-balance. Xan now saw that it was a girl, her face half-hidden by her long hair, her cloak now showing itself as nothing more sinister than a raincoat.

He had to shout to make himself heard over the wind and the waves. "What are you doing? There's a storm coming in."

She said, in a voice he could hardly catch: "There's someone in the water."

And when he looked down, the reversion repeated itself – here was the nightmare, as the shape in the waves rolled suddenly over to reveal a face that was blotched and swollen and gaping.

Still death, then, but not as he had thought. The body – whoever it was – was at least 12 hours dead. The girl drew in her breath sharply and turned away, stumbling a little with the difficulty of keeping her footing in the swirling tide.

The wave receded, making a hideous sucking noise. Another wave surged up the beach, dividing to pass the rock and swirling around on the other side. The sea was coming fast. He looked down again at the dark shape. It stirred in the water in a nauseating fashion. The dark clothes gave no clue to gender – in any case, any colour looked dark soaked with seawater.

The girl spoke uncertainly, her voice unnaturally loud. "Shouldn't we try and get it out of the water?"

Xan thought about that. Single-handedly, he would be hard pressed to drag the body above the high water line. It would be much heavier than it looked and you would have to manoeuvre it well beyond the top of the shingle bank to get it out of reach of the wind-whipped waves.

He also wondered what sort of help could realistically be summoned from the cosy, warm hotel or the fishing cottages along the seafront. The temptation was overpowering to simply let the hideous thing slide back into the sea and disappear forever.

"Well?" She was watching him.

"I'm not sure if it can be done, not with the storm coming up." He stood bracing himself against the dragging water and considered the possibilities.

It would be easier to take hold of the body at what might be termed the head end, by grasping under the shoulders – that would leave the second and stronger person to try to grip the heavy and awkward boots. But it also meant that the person at the head end would be in uncomfortable proximity with the unpleasant face and the no doubt equally unpleasant hands.

He knelt down beside the body. "If I lift it, could you try to take some of the weight at the other end?"

But even as he spoke, doubt assailed him. The real weight would fall in the middle of the body, not at the ends and even if she could lift the boots a few inches, that would not raise the rest of the body off the ground.

She said: "What if we were to drag it on something?"

"On what, exactly?"

"My coat." She was hurriedly unzipping it and pulling her arms free. She held it out to him. "There."

Silently, he knelt and tied the waterproof around the thing in the water, by the arms. It should now be possible to drag it up the sand to the high water mark.

All the same, the business was worse than he had thought. The body dragged in the water, a dead weight in every sense. The girl did her best. If it had not been for the sea doing some of their job for them, it would have been impossible. As it was, with every incoming wave, the dreadful burden was inched up the shoreline until it lay sprawled across the shingle, a few feet beyond the wavering high tide marker of driftwood and seaweed.

The girl stepped back, looking rather white. "I think I need to – that is, I think I'll go and wash my hands." She turned away hurriedly and went down to the waterline.

He turned back to the body on the sand. The grim task had made certain things clear to him. Although the dead man's face was unrecognisable, the height and general build, the clothing and the fair hair were all corroboration of a sort.

The next moment, confirmation came. A small, dark shadow came slinking forward, towards the body, then backed off sharply, and stood trembling, the body pressed into the ground. A dog – and not just any dog. A black and white collie, thin, with ruffled fur. Not admissible to a coroner as evidence but deeply persuasive.

Xan pulled aside the soaked pullover gently to expose the dead man's left shoulder-blade. Even in the poor light, it was clear enough – a hopping rabbit, one ear flopping back.

Reluctantly, he reached down and turned the head from one side to the other until he found what he was looking for. A discolouration on the back of the neck that did not look as though it was likely to have come from a battering on the rocks.

Xan shoved his hands hard in the pockets of his coat and turned away. Emotions he ordinarily kept at bay –

horror, self-reproach, anger – now had the mastery of his mind. This moment of the opportunity not taken, the life not saved, the dead end, was why he had walked away from Homeland after the De Leiter case, but here it was again. He should have known, at Wimbledon, where death had seemed so tidy and neat and unemotional like a puzzle, that death was never any of those things.

He shook himself impatiently. Act like a professional. Next step – examine the body. The thought didn't appeal. But he could at least take another look at that hideous, disfigured face and try to search the coat pockets. A brief, gingerly search revealed surprisingly little, apart from a handful of loose change. No wallet. No room key. No papers of any sort and no photograph.

As he turned away, he saw a glimmer of dull light on the shingle. A small handbag with a brass buckle, its sheen not yet damaged by the action of water, salt, wind or sun. He glanced down to where the girl was washing her hands, then bent and picked it up. It was open – inside were keys, purse, and an envelope stuffed with papers. He put it on a rock out of the reach of the water and went down to the surf to wash his own hands in the surging tide, then splashed over to the girl.

By now, the clouds had drifted apart a little to reveal a pale, watery sky. By its light, he could see that she had been anxiously studying the face of her watch, perhaps wondering if it was still working. Now she glanced at him apprehensively.

This was the point at which the Homeland Security

handbook dictated one ask a few hard-hitting questions. But he had little appetite for it. In any case, it would be foolish to stay here any longer than necessary. The thing they had pulled from the sea was a ticking time-bomb.

As though she were thinking the same thing, the girl said: "I suppose we ought to call the police or someone." Her voice made it a question and once again her eyes drifted uneasily to her watch and then up to the road.

He said, watching her carefully: "Well, we could. But they might ask some difficult questions – for instance, what were you doing here and how did you know the dead man."

She glanced at him nervously. "But I don't know him."

"I imagine you can guess who he was, though. And the police will want to know why you came down here."

"Perhaps I live here."

"Perhaps you do. But they can establish all of that quite quickly by asking for ID."

He looked past her towards the direction of the Lazy Salmon. A cluster of torches was bobbing down over the sands like disembodied phantom lights, until one made out the dark figures carrying them. Someone from one of the cottages must have seen something in the dim light and gone for help.

He turned back to the girl. "You've got some reason for not wanting to be mixed up in this, haven't you? Beyond not wanting to miss your train."

"I never said I came here by train."

No, but the restless movements of someone in a hurry

to leave are hard to disguise, and she had not made the driver's gesture of reaching for car-keys. Instead, she had looked at her watch and towards the road that led up the hill to the station.

"Besides, what about him?" She looked down at the huddled heap on the shingle.

"I'll deal with that."

"Why should you?"

When he didn't answer, she said uncertainly: "It's not what you think, you know. I'm not a complete coward. It's just – I've got to consider the Department."

She turned and began to clamber awkwardly up the shingle towards the road. He gave her a moment, then turned to remove the waterproof coat from underneath the thing that lay sprawled on the shingle. He rolled it up into an insignificant bundle to be disposed of later, then trudged over to meet the rescue-party.

They looked to be about a dozen strong, the landlord of the Lazy Salmon among them. Their faces were serious and professional. People who lived by the sea knew how this worked.

They did not waste any energy on questioning him but turned their attentions to the thing on the sand. They did not touch it, knowing as well as he did that there was nothing there to be saved, but concentrated on assuring themselves that it was far enough above high waterline to be safe even from a storm surge and on searching the rest of the beach. Xan guessed they were looking for drift-wood from a wrecked boat and further bodies. He did not think that they would find either.

And then there were sirens along the beach road and blue flashing lights and the search party repaired to the saloon bar of the Lazy Salmon, where Xan was offered a whisky he did not want by J Bageshot Proprietor, who had washed his hands (one hoped) and slipped back behind the bar, his metamorphosis from volunteer mortuary assistant to barman complete.

Once the party was busily engrossed in drinks and conversation, Xan quietly put down his glass. It was time to fade from the scene, before someone thought to take his name. They did not need his testimony as to Rabbit's identity – the police would find that out soon enough.

None of the men clustered round the bar paid any attention to his departure, but he was not to leave wholly unobserved. As he came out of the front door of the Lazy Salmon, a small shadow slipped across the road and trotted purposefully at his heels. A thin collie, his tail hopefully wagging.

CHAPTER 24

At about the time that Xan Ross was driving to Devon in the afternoon sunshine, a man with a broken nose sat and scowled at his pint of beer (which in his opinion had been poured badly and was at least half an inch short), at the small, unstable, mahogany-effect table it rested on and at the crowds thronging the Cheshire Cat pub. In his considered opinion, London was too crowded these days and with the wrong sort of people. It was time he got out of his line of work.

It wasn't as though the job had been easy. Murder on a tennis-court in front of a potential audience of thousands. If they hadn't been so slow to pass the instruction on, the team could have got to the old man on the train or the Tube. There had been any number of opportunities.

As it was, they had watched him shuffle into the queue for shared taxis knowing that their best, their easiest chances were gone. And if he himself hadn't had the good sense to crash the queue and get into the same taxi 'to make up the numbers', they would have been stuck.

He'd had the happy idea of asking the other people in the taxi what seats they had on court – a natural enough question. They had all proudly showed their tickets and he had got a look at the old man's. As soon as he reached the Club, he had written it down in case it came in useful – and it had.

He wouldn't personally have chosen to do it on court, but the instructions had been clear. Get it done at once. They were afraid of what the old man was going to do. He was well-connected. One phone call was all it take to blow things sky-high. And that was the only justification for something as crazy as murder on a tennis-court.

But now they were saying he had messed it up. The alarm had been given too soon and instead of a confused melee of people leaving the court at the end of the match and one man sprawled cold in his seat, the police had a handily short time-window and a set of CCTV stills. And now no one was happy with one of the neatest eliminations he had ever done.

A giggling couple bumped carelessly against his table and he looked up to direct his scowl at them. They had their backs turned, oblivious. He turned back to his pint. It was still foaming, further evidence of the bar girl's incompetence. He took a long swallow all the same.

Ten minutes later, he stumbled to the door of the Red Cow and peered out into the cobbled back-street. The evening sunlight blazed painfully into his eyes and he squinted, trying to get his bearings. Where was he anyway? He had stopped here impulsively, drawn by the noise of laughter and the football game and the sawdust-and-ale aroma.

He rather thought that the little back-street he was on was somewhere between Oxford Street and Marylebone

High Street. You never forgot these streets, hard-wired into your brain. But which way did he need to turn, that was the puzzle. The little cobbled alley-way looked exactly the same in both directions. In fact, when you looked at it hard, it ran off into a vanishing point, which was even worse. The cobbles began to run together. He had to take hold of the edge of the door to steady himself.

A man going out said: "If you don't mind," irritably and shoved past him. You couldn't stand in a pub doorway all day. Bad form.

He struck off down the street at random. The brick walls on either side of him played tricks, one moment closing in on him and the next veering off again. He stumbled to the end of the alley-way and lurched forwards, then stopped again.

Two huge yellow eyes and a screaming shriek of a horn told him, dimly, that he had almost been hit by a car. People hurried along, too busy to pay attention to the man stumbling along the pavement.

In the middle of all this mayhem, the bench presented itself. There were two people sitting on it already – they looked vaguely familiar, one plump and smiling, one hawk-nosed and serious. He sat down, carefully, between them.

They didn't comment on his arrival. He peered more closely at the fat one, who looked back at him, infinitely cheerful. Definitely something familiar about him. It was his last coherent thought.

The constable on duty in the Oxford Street area strolled

along South Audley Street in the early dusk. Halfway down the street was a bench – from a distance, it looked as though three people were sitting there in a row, motionless, staring straight ahead. It didn't look natural.

As he walked towards the bench, the tableau began to resolve itself but it wasn't until he was close up that he got the full picture. Two of the three men were statues – a cheery Winston Churchill and a sober-looking Roosevelt in earnest discussion. The third man was not a statue. He looked neither cheery nor sober and his throat had been cut.

CHAPTER 25

The weekend newspapers didn't carry Rabbit's death as a front-page headline. (Nor, incidentally, did they cover a knifing in Savile Row at all, due to police instruction.) Xan had to turn several pages to find the small headlines.

MAN'S BODY FOUND AT SEASIDE. EX-ARMY CHEF DROWNS AT HOLIDAY BAY.

The words read like a charge of dereliction of duty.

The café was brightly-lit and too busy for anyone to pay any particular attention to the tired, unshaven young man at the table by the back door with a plateful of breakfast he did not look inclined to eat.

After getting back to the Hotel Coronado late in the evening, he had not slept much and when he had, he had dreamed the dream again – the lonely estuary, the river running through the sands, the tide coming in.

This was why he had walked away from Homeland in the first place – the nagging sense of dread, the patterns that kept repeating. Now it had happened again. The sum had come out the same way it always did, which could only mean one thing. It was his pattern.

He forced himself to read the news story again. Could he have saved Rabbit? The ex-soldier must have sensed the threat coming. In his letter, he had mentioned callers to the *Sunflower*. He had taken his dog and cleared out of London.

Living off the grid as he did, it ought to have been easy for him to stay off his enemies' radar. He had travelled to somewhere that was not one of his own haunts and, wisely, he had taken a job that paid cash. So, what had gone wrong? How had they found him? And just what was the dangerous knowledge he held?

Wearily, Xan reran his conversation with Rabbit in his mind. He had known that the veteran was not telling him everything, but he hadn't pressed him. If he had, perhaps it might have saved his life – or at least provided some leads as to his killer. As it was, there was nothing to show for his single meeting with Rabbit except a dead body on the shoreline and a dog without an owner.

Also on his charge-sheet was the lesser indictment of carelessness at a crime scene. He had spoken to the manager at the Lazy Salmon and asked about his staffing problems. He had then become involved in the dredging up of the body from the sea, which he might sensibly have stayed clear of.

Should he have remained in Ilvercombe to speak to the police? Self-preservation and Homeland protocols had dictated that he clear the scene as quickly as possible – and there was certainly logic to that. Imagination saw him trying to explain to a disbelieving local police force the sequence of events that had taken him to Ilvercombe. A secret whispered at a tennis match, a dying man's last request, a cold case involving the death of a soldier ten years ago. It would have been pointless. He had no hard evidence to offer, nothing but theories. All the same, he did not feel easy about it.

And what about the girl? Who was she and what had brought her to Ilvercombe and sent her along the shore in time to find a dead body washing up at her feet?

He had not asked her those questions, being certain that she would not answer them. In any case, he was fairly confident that he could find her when he needed to – if he wanted to. And that was the real question, wasn't it? This wasn't a Homeland job. He didn't have to go on. Perhaps he should stop now, before anyone else got hurt.

He went back to thinking about Rabbit. He had served his country and then become a drifter, lonely and without connections, harming no one. And someone had brushed him out of life like a bothersome fly.

On the way back to the hotel, he considered the final item on his charge-sheet – the abstraction from the crime scene of a scruffy-looking dog and its conveyance, against all rules and regulations, into his room at the Coronado Hotel.

When he came into the foyer of the Coronado, Leah pounced on him at once. "Mr Ross?"

"Yes?" he said warily, thankful that he had, after all, not stopped to buy dog biscuits.

"You've got a visitor." In place of Leah's usual expression of gratified intrigue, there was a worried look. She dropped her voice. "I've put them in one of the meeting-rooms, out of the way round the back. The management don't like that sort of thing."

The police, he deduced. It was not unreasonable for a murder witness to receive visits from officers of the law, but it would hardly add to his standing in the eyes of the City Coronado. And there was the uneasy question of why they had chosen today to talk to him.

Leah looked at him glumly, as though sensing his disquiet. "Conference Room 4, Mr Ross."

The set of conference rooms at the back of the hotel were plain and unvarnished and looked unpleasantly to Xan like interview rooms at a police station. In the least roomy of them, he found Inspector Nash and his red-headed sergeant standing, rather than seated, which suggested a short visit – or something else.

"Apologies for the unexpected call, Mr Ross," Inspector Nash said in his soft voice. "I have a favour to ask of you, if you're not too busy. It's not, I'm afraid, a very pleasant task for a Sunday morning, but it can't be helped."

Xan could make nothing of this. He had nothing to say as he accompanied the two men out to the waiting police-car, discreetly parked at the back of the hotel.

Inspector Nash, occupying the front passenger-seat next to Sergeant Monroe, an excellent if sometimes over-cautious driver, was puzzled. You got all sorts in the back of a police-car but he wouldn't have expected Mr Ross to look – well, rattled was the only way to describe it. It was only a simple matter of ID, after all.

Xan looked up as the car drew up besides an ugly, square building in a dull part of Lambeth. "What's this?"

"It's part of the Met estate, Mr Ross. In point of fact, the morgue." Inspector Nash was glancing at his watch as he spoke and missed the sudden paleness that came over Xan's face. He began to speak and then stopped again. His jaw tightened as he followed the two policemen into the building.

Sergeant Monroe spoke briefly to the officer at the reception desk and they passed through a barrier and along a corridor that smelt of disinfectant and perhaps worse things. An ugly eternity of strip lighting stretched into a distant vanishing point.

"I hope you don't mind coming down here, Mr Ross," Inspector Nash said briskly. "It's simpler than trying to do it with photographs. They never reproduce properly in this situation."

Xan found nothing to say to this. The corridor seemed to go on forever. At last, they paused before a set of doors which seemed indistinguishable from the others they had passed. A man in white medical kit came out and nodded at the inspector. "He's in there."

His words seemed to echo hollowly. Xan could almost smell the horrible tang of salt and decaying seaweed.

The man in the white kit held the door open so the three men could pass through. Inside there was a single trolley with a single body under a single sheet, as Xan had known there must be. And Inspector Nash was saying cheerily: "This will only take a minute," as though they were all at the dentist. And then the sheet was drawn off and he found himself looking down, not at Rabbit, but at a man with a flat, brutal face and a broken nose and a gaping dark wound where his throat should be.

There was a wave of disorienting nausea. A sense of darkness where there should be light. Then suddenly he had control of himself again and the darkness cleared.

"What was it you wanted to ask me, Inspector?" he managed to say quietly.

The inspector nodded briefly at the man on the trolley. He was feeling even more puzzled now, but there was no need to advertise it. He said matter-of-factly: "This man was found just north of Oxford Street last night. Throat had been cut. Have you ever seen him before?"

Xan had himself in hand again. He made himself look carefully at the thing on the trolley. He said calmly enough: "I'm pretty sure he was one of the people I saw on the walkway outside Centre Court at Wimbledon."

Inspector Nash nodded in satisfaction. CCTV was one thing, but testimony from a witness was always better, providing they kept their heads on the stand and didn't go letting anyone put doubt in their minds.

Mr Ross wasn't that sort, although he was bound to say he had looked very strange a moment ago, almost as though he was about to faint – not what you expected of a man like him.

"We'd like that in writing if you don't mind, Mr Ross. It might not be a certain ID, but it'll come in handy on the witness stand, as will you."

Xan shoved his hands in his pockets and looked down again at the dead man. Someone had put him out of the way. Probably, he thought absently, the man had made a mistake. But what mistake exactly? "What? Yes, all right. When?"

"If you don't mind waiting a moment, I just need to go through a few things with Dr Hartwell here."

"If it's all the same to you, I'll wait outside. I need some fresh air. You can bring the paperwork out to me." If it's so damned important, he wanted to say, but he controlled himself with an effort.

Inspector Nash looked at him carefully. "Very well, Mr Ross. Monroe will show you out – you can't get out without a swipecard anyway," he added untruthfully. In his head, he was thinking that Mr Ross wasn't ordinarily the sort of man who would let a building layout disorient him, but right now he wasn't sure.

Xan knew the matter of the swipecard was a fiction. Silently, he followed the square shoulders of Sergeant Monroe. The red-headed sergeant looked stolid and as though he had no thought in his head, but all the same, he seemed to find a quicker way out of the building than the one they had come in by and moreover, one which opened on a silent square of grass and trees and beyond it, the river.

"You may as well wait here, sir, it's quieter than on the street."

Xan walked over to the river wall. Somewhere out of sight, church bells were ringing on the air, their message defiantly out of kilter with his surroundings. He was not sure how much time passed before he was aware that someone else had come outside.

"Mr Ross?" The inspector's voice was carefully non-committal.

Xan turned. He could pass it all off – say nothing, sign the blasted form and get out of here. But that would give himself the easy way out, and why should he do that? He said: "I suppose you're wondering what made me lose my balance just now."

"Well, now," Inspector Nash said tactfully.

"You needn't spare my pride. I damned near passed out. And you can't pretend you didn't notice, so you're bound to ask me about it. So, let's save time. You sprang it on me and I was expecting someone else's body."

Inspector Nash felt lost. He was not aware of any other body that could import itself into affairs so boldly. "Is that so?" he temporised feebly.

Xan smiled wanly. "Yes, it is so. And I'll save you some more questions. The body I was expecting to see was that of a man named Robert Hare who disappeared from London just under a week ago. Known as Rabbit to his friends. I pulled his body out of the sea yesterday evening in a little place called Ilvercombe."

"Ilvercombe," the inspector repeated thoughtfully.

"It's in Devon. I'm sure you'll find it on your database – there can't have been that many unexplained deaths in the last 24 hours. And both these two with a connection to me, as you're about to remark."

Inspector Nash felt that the truly surprising thing was not that Mr Ross was connected with so many dead bodies but that one of them appeared to have knocked him off his equilibrium. He said cautiously: "I'm sure you had your reasons for being on the spot."

"Because it was all my doing, Inspector, and not in the way you mean. I was playing detective and I put him in danger. That's why he left London but he didn't leave quick enough. Someone found him and I only got there in time to find his body."

There was no expecting Mr Ross's mood now. The words came quick and angry. Inspector Nash studied the distant view of tower-blocks tactfully.

"All right, so it's got me on the raw. I started interfering in this for all the wrong reasons. I was bored and I fancied myself at being good at solving puzzles. Instead, people got killed. Giles Maybury was bad enough but Rabbit would still be alive if I hadn't interfered."

"And how did he connect with the case?"

"Maybury was doing a favour for an old friend and looking into the death of his son. The son died in a shooting accident when he was in the Army. Rabbit was there." Xan spoke shortly and irritably.

"That's quite a hypothesis, Mr Ross."

"Well, it's only my theory that Maybury was murdered because of what he found out. But Rabbit's death adds weight to it. If I keep going, I can provide you with a whole list of dead witnesses you can't interrogate. You'd better give me that paper to sign."

Silently, Inspector Nash handed over the paper and a pen. Xan rested the paper on the mossy brickwork of the river-wall and scribbled his statement and signature onto it as best he could, then handed it back to Inspector Nash, who received the illegible return without comment.

A flicker of curiosity prompted Xan to ask: "How did you find him?"

"We didn't. Someone else saved us the trouble. We had his mugshot, thanks to your suggestion. He came in and out of the two entrances in a single change of ends. But we hadn't got so far as identifying him when someone decided to put him beyond questioning. He was found yesterday evening."

At about the time he had pulled Rabbit's body onto the shingle, Xan thought. "A professional?"

"It looks that way."

"I told you so. The rest of the team will be out there somewhere. But I don't know that I'd waste your energy looking for them."

"I don't suppose I'll get the chance." Inspector Nash paused, but when no prompt came, he continued anyway. "My superiors have it in mind to close the case."

"What?"

"Now that we've found our murderer."

"Your murderer. Your superiors don't have any interest in why it happened or what was behind it?"

"This man had a history of minor robbery and violence. That's enough for them." Inspector Nash folded the ID form away. "Thank you for coming here today, Mr Ross, you've been very helpful. Sergeant Monroe will drop you back at your hotel, if you like."

"But I sound as though I could do with the walk," Xan finished for him. He shook hands with the inspector, then turned away along the river-path.

*

The day had been dull and rainy and the last light was already dying out of the cloud-washed sky as Xan walked along the tow-path. The boats he passed were shut up and silent. Empty? Or was each one occupied by someone who chose not to advertise his or her presence?

In the dusk, the *Sunflower* looked lonely and uncared-for. The police tape around it confirmed its abandoned status. No wonder the occupants of the other boats were keeping out of the way.

The truculent man Xan had encountered on his previous visit stuck his head out from the cabin of his boat to stare, curiosity evidently trumping caution. "What do you want?"

"Just passing by," Xan said, truthfully enough. He had given up any intention of searching the *Sunflower* when he saw the police tape – they would already have found anything there was to find. Besides, Rabbit would have taken whatever he had with him to Ilvercombe.

The truculent man nodded at the *Sunflower*. "That's a crime scene. Owner got himself drowned down on the south coast the day before yesterday."

"Murdered?"

The truculent man scowled. "I didn't say so."

"You said it was a crime scene."

"Yeah, well. Figure of speech, that's all. He probably drowned himself."

"Why would he go all the way down there when there's water right here?"

The man shrugged. "People do odd things. If you ask me, it was those people came bothering him that drove him off."

"What people? Police?"

"Nope. Government types. Suits. Going on about council tax and forms and suchlike. He didn't have much truck with that stuff."

Xan nodded. That sounded like Rabbit.

"And then someone broke into the boat after he'd gone. He wasn't having any luck."

Again, this seemed a logical progression of events. But Xan was no longer interested in the *Sunflower*. Instead, he asked: "What happened to his dog?"

Another shrug. "Probably took it with him. Mangy-looking thing. Can't stand dogs, myself."

And the other thought which had brought Xan down here faded away. It looked as though he was stuck with Mags, at least for now.

CHAPTER 26

Elinor Maybury was dusting the slats of the kitchen window shutters. It was back-breaking work and she was thankful for the interruption of the door-bell and the sight of Xan propped against the porch.

"Well, goodness, I was beginning to wonder if you were ever coming back."

This time she took him through to the kitchen, where a wide oak farmhouse table seemed too big for the room. Xan stood at the kitchen window and looked out at the neat garden, with its square of lawn with bird-bath, a spreading and burdened apple-tree and a distant vegetable plot. It was all very neat, very respectable, very English.

He turned back from the window to see that Elinor was watching him, a small frown on her face. She began to fill the kettle, then paused. "You don't like tea, do you? And I don't suppose you came here for refreshments anyway. You came here because you had something to tell me."

As she spoke, doubts assailed her. With that look on his face, anything he had to tell her could only be bad news. And despite her assurance that Giles had had no secrets, one never really knew, did one, and her sister-in-law's assiduous hints had achieved the gradual wearing-down effect of dripping water. ("Don't you think it's rather odd that he never suggested you going with him when he went off to all those exhibitions and lunches and things?")

Xan took hold of himself. His decision to come here had been a sudden one and he had thought how it would look to his hostess.

"It's nothing about your husband," he said quickly. "At least, nothing definite. I haven't got very far, I'm afraid. But I can tell you what I have found out. It seems that one of his friends had asked him to look into something."

Elinor nodded briskly, to cover up her sudden attack of nerves. "Well, that sounds typical of Giles."

"The friend in question was a man named Paradine."

"Adam Paradine? Why, I didn't think Giles had seen him in years. He was an old school friend and rather a dull one."

"Do you know anything about his son?"

"David? Only that he joined the Army and was killed on active service. It was a tremendous shock to his father. But it was all a long time ago."

"Adam Paradine wasn't satisfied about what happened to his son. It looks as though he asked your husband to look into it."

"Why now? It must be ten years since David Paradine died."

"I don't know."

Elinor glanced at him thoughtfully. So far, the tale he had told was puzzling but not alarming. There was nothing in it to explain the look of strain she had seen on his face, quickly covered up. Of course, men were absurd in their pretensions, ashamed of showing a weakness. She said briskly: “You had much better just tell me whatever is worrying you. Is it something you’ve found out?”

The odd brown-green eyes met hers. “It’s something I failed to do. I found a witness and I didn’t protect him. He died.”

“What sort of witness?”

“A man named Rabbit. Ex-soldier. Ex a lot of things, probably. He lived alone on a boat because he couldn’t get along with people, and did without the basics like money and paperwork, but he got on quite nicely all the same until someone knocked him on the head and pushed him off a breakwater to drown.”

“Oh.” In her heart of hearts, Elinor felt that the possible witness did not sound like much of a loss to the world. But she had had decades of practice in not saying the wrong thing to Giles and old habits died hard.

Xan was not fooled by her silence. He met her eyes. “I expect you think I’m being pretty hypocritical, given my trade. But you see, I think I led them to Rabbit. And that’s why I’m not sure that I can do what you want.”

So that was what this was about. Men really were unfathomable. “Nonsense!” she said robustly. “If he knew something that was dangerous, that wasn’t your doing.”

About to add that one couldn’t make an omelette without breaking eggs, she caught herself in time. When men were indulging in feeling sorry for themselves, they didn’t take kindly to flippancy. Instead, she said firmly: “If these people are as ruthless as all that, they’ll carry on being a danger to society until they're stopped."

He looked up quizzically. "A danger to society?"

"That's what Giles would have called it. And while he could be a bumbling old fool at times, he had – *instincts* – about things. Old-fashioned values. And he would say that none of us had the right to stand aside when there's something wrong."

Xan was silenced. At last, he said what he had not in the least meant to say. "I don't suppose you'd like a dog, would you?"

"A dog?" Elinor stared at him as though he had become slightly unhinged. "I'm allergic to them."

"Never mind, it was just a thought."

*

In the evening, Xan smuggled the collie down the back stairs and walked him through the narrow City streets to the river, where the tourists had long since drifted away and the hazy twilit views across the river were lonely.

He walked for several miles along the river, the dog a thin, silent shadow at his heels. To drive away the ghosts that might otherwise have joined him – Rabbit, Giles Maybury, Mr De Leiter – he focused his mind on the practical question of what to do about Mags.

One couldn't keep a dog in a hotel room for any length of time. A rescue centre, then? But the idea seemed a double betrayal.

By the time they returned along the same route, the pale

grey of the sky was deepening into black and the traffic along the streets to his hotel was lessening. Back in his room, he stood at the window, staring across at the matrix view of dark tower-blocks and squares of yellow light as though it were a code he could learn to decipher.

Was he really going to give it all up? There was every reason to do so. Yet he seemed to sense Giles Maybury's stiff, upright figure watching him disapprovingly from the shadows. Is it all going to be for nothing, the old man seemed to ask?

"It isn't as though we've got any new clues to follow," he said aloud to Mags.

The dog cocked his head on one side. As one who knew plenty about following a trail, he evidently considered this an evasion.

"All right, all right," Xan said. "So there's the girl. But she might not have anything to do with it."

That wasn't true, admittedly. According to the crest on the envelope in her handbag, she was employed at the same government department that Giles Maybury had once been part of. And if she didn't know anything, why had she been on the beach when Rabbit's body came ashore?

CHAPTER 27

The government department for security and defence had its headquarters in Westminster House, a rather grand Georgian mansion tucked away in a quiet square close to the river, the Houses of Parliament and the Abbey.

This was the department where Giles Maybury had worked and where Mark Romilly was a junior minister. Was that significant? There was no obvious reason why it should be so, but Xan filed the fact away in his mind for consideration.

He had positioned himself on the opposite side of the street from Westminster House, where a dark and tree-crowded garden hemmed in by railings offered a useful backdrop for the loiterer. The garden itself could be of no use to anyone except the birds, thanks to the padlocked gate, but the railings made a handy repository for bicycles, signs telling people not to do things and individuals with a predilection for lounging.

No one really needed a visual alibi for lounging any more, of course. In the old-fashioned thrillers that Giles Maybury had read and even early in Xan's own career, investigative operatives had perused newspapers, smoked cigarettes or waited for imaginary buses. Now it was only necessary to study one's phone.

Accordingly, Xan leaned against the iron railings and took out his own. Practice enabled him to appear engrossed by the screen while keeping a watchful eye on everything else in the vicinity.

From his vantage point, he could count half a dozen security guards in the foyer of Westminster House. No one could simply stroll into a government building any more. 9/11 had put paid to that.

In fact, terrorists tended to prefer humanitarian targets that would cause greater public outrage, but that had not stopped companies that traded in defensive security equipment from marketing it to government buildings all over the world – along with corporate HQs, transport hubs, hospitals, schools, anyone who would pay.

Homeland had done pretty well out of the business. Equipment was more reliable than intelligence operatives. It didn't have to make decisions or maintain focus on the third dull day of a watching job or distinguish the guilty from the merely shifty-looking innocent. Or get a man from Marrakesh to Tangier without getting his head blown off in an ambush.

Xan shook off these uncomfortable reflections as the church and institutional clocks in the vicinity struck their various versions of quarter to five. Soon, the occupants of Westminster House would begin to emerge on their way home.

Just then, a telltale pattering began on leaves and grass. It was starting to rain. This was annoying. He didn't mind getting wet, but few excuses for loitering stood up well to rain. The Westminster House security guards would start to wonder about him.

He moved along a little to position himself under the inadequate shelter of a tall elm tree. And at that moment, the glass doors that ruined the Georgian façade of Westminster House slid open and a girl in a summer dress came hurrying out.

Xan had expected to be uncertain with the ID but in fact, there was no doubt at all. Slim, medium-height, with a pale face and sensitive, mobile features. The long dark brown hair was now restrained in some fashion and in place of a raincoat, she was wearing an inadequate-looking light jacket. But it was definitely her.

He drew back into the shadows of the trees overhanging the railings – it was no part of his plan to be recognised at this point. 'House them first' was the Homeland doctrine – once you knew where someone lived, you could take your time selecting a suitable approach.

*

Jemima Drury was employed as a junior officer with the Department's Records Branch. She always found that time passed particularly slowly during the Parliamentary recess, but today had dragged unbearably.

Certain facts, certain suspicions, weighed on her mind. The ritual enquiry from colleagues of 'did you have a good weekend?' had made her start nervously. Imagine if they could see the hideous series of technicolour pictures that presented themselves in answer. The dead body washing up on the shingle, torn clothes ballooning in the tide.

Now she was leaving the office a guilty few minutes before five – and as though it had been arranged to punish her, she saw that it was raining, which was the last straw, given that she had lost her coat at the beach and couldn't afford to buy another one until pay-day.

As she came down the steps, she buttoned up the useless blue velvet jacket, bought for spring days, and turned up the collar, as though that would do any good. It was only ten minutes to the Tube station, she told herself, and how wet could one get in ten minutes? She did not notice the young man on the other side of the road studying his phone who suddenly lost interest in it, slid it into his pocket and fell into step behind her, about thirty yards back.

On the busy road that led to Parliament Square, buses swished through the dusk. Jemima paid no regard to them – even in the rain, it was easier to walk to the station than board a bus and risk getting caught up in the traffic bottleneck around Parliament.

The wind was getting up, making the rain blow in treacherous gusts from different angles. People hurried past her, better-equipped with raincoats and umbrellas. She turned her face away from the rain and a dropped umbrella sailed towards her like a big, black bird of prey and bowled into the road in front of a speeding cyclist.

Jemima plunged after it in dismay, already knowing she

would be too late. Thankfully, she saw its progress arrested by another pedestrian. The cyclist swerved past, his brakes screeching, shouting something that was mercifully inaudible. Jemima turned to make an acerbic comment and found herself staring at the man from the beach at Ilvercombe.

Xan was annoyed with himself. What had he been thinking? He knew the drill. Now he had spoiled his cover – and a busy street on a rainy evening was no place for the difficult business of getting someone to trust you. He shook out the wet umbrella impatiently to give himself time to think and dropped it into a nearby litter-bin.

Jemima spoke quickly, to cover up the flash of dismay she was feeling. "That's a bit presumptuous – it might have been mine, for all you know."

And instead of saying something which would put this all back onto the safe footing of a chance encounter between two strangers on a London street, the young man said drily: "It wasn't yours, you weren't carrying one."

"So you were watching me!"

"Following you, to be exact. And if I was doing my job properly, I'd have kept out of sight."

He had already dismissed any idea of pretending this was a coincidental meeting. In some ways, this might be for the best. Women had their own excellent reasons for being wary around strangers. They acquired early and instinctively the habits of caution and observant fieldwork which professionals like him painstakingly learned on the job.

That being the case, perhaps after all a busy London street was a better place for this than a lonely beach – or for that matter, the encounter on the doorstep with the frightening corollary that you had been followed home. He said quickly: "My name's Xan Ross. I'm a private investigator."

Her eyes widened. They were rather striking, he noticed – clear grey with an unusual black ring around the iris. "You mean a *detective*?"

"Yes, but not here. I work overseas, mostly."

"And how did you know where I worked?"

"I searched your bag when you left it on the beach."

"You searched –." She paused. "Then you think the man on the beach was murdered."

"Well, what do you think?"

"I didn't know what to think. The news reports –. He might have just got swept away by waves. People do."

"But not everyone –. Never mind. The point is, I was there, you were there. That's quite a crowd in a lonely spot for someone who was off the grid. I think someone else got there before us. And you must know something – why else would you have gone down there?"

She drove her hands into the pockets of the thin jacket and said: "I oughtn't even to speak to you. It's breaking about five million civil service codes. But then, that man who died – I expect he was a nice person and someone somewhere was fond of him. And I keep thinking about his dog. Someone ought to have looked after him."

And in theory, his noncommittal silence at this point

should not have committed him to anything. But the grey eyes widened. "You took him with you."

"I did."

"Then what have you done with him?"

"He's at my hotel. But they don't allow dogs, so it's a little awkward."

"I can see that it would be. But you couldn't have just abandoned him. And he looked rather a nice dog – quite a lot of collie in there, I thought."

He looked at her with sudden renewed attention. "You like dogs?"

CHAPTER 28

The narrow street was lined with terraced houses, in an area of East London where the skyline was mostly patched with post-war council blocks. Columbine Road had evidently been missed by the bombers. Perhaps they had fallen instead on the grimy Victorian cemetery which ran the other side of the street, taking out stone angels and griffins instead of real flesh and blood.

It was a Saturday morning. One could hardly bring homeless dogs to people during the working week, so Xan had had perforce to wait four days, each day thinking that the staff at his hotel were about to ask him leading questions about dogs barking in the night.

No 47a was halfway down the street. He rang the door-bell of the upstairs flat. The girl answered the door. This time, her long hair was tied up and there was, puzzlingly, dust all over her jeans and T-shirt.

"I'm afraid I'm in the middle of something," she said rather mysteriously. She patted Mags. "You'd better come in."

They followed her into the house, past a door which must belong to another tenant and up a set of narrow and rickety-looking stairs. At the top was a long and wide landing, an echo of the original layout of the house. It was lined incongruously with empty bookshelves, perhaps to conceal lumpy, pea-green wallpaper. The skirting-boards and banisters were thickly painted in a clashing mint hue.

The girl led the way along the landing to a large front room.

"You'll have to excuse the décor. The landlord's choice and as you know, woodchip is an absolute nightmare to get off – well, perhaps you don't if you live abroad, it's something only we seem to have gone into. And in any case, tenants aren't allowed to do improvements, so here we are, resolutely unimproved."

She looked critically around the room, which boasted high ceilings, tall windows and a big fireplace at one end. A cheap futon did service as a sofa and a battered leather armchair hinted at broken springs. Three large bookcases were half-filled with books and there were more in a box on the floor.

"I'm moving them into the hall. The landlord wants to rent this room and you can't always be popping in to get a book you want if there's someone there. I'm dusting them at the same time. You have to do it a lot if you don't want it to settle into the pages and you need a special brush for it. In fact, if you don't mind, I might carry on, now I've started."

Xan glanced down at the box of books on the floor. "Do those need moving?"

"Yes, but I've been managing them in armfuls."

"I think I can improve on that."

The box was not difficult to carry, but it did transfer a

generous helping of dust over his shirt.

"I'm terribly sorry," she said in dismay. "I don't worry about my clothes, but men are always so very particular."

He smiled. "I'm not as particular as all that." And it was gratifying not to be offered tea, at any rate. He propped himself cautiously against the banisters, which looked like the original ones and rather fragile.

The girl knelt down beside the bookcase and began carefully to transfer the volumes in the box beside her onto the shelf, dusting each one in turn with a delicate wooden brush with soft bristles. The dog settled down beside her and watched with keen attention.

She glanced up. "So are you really a detective?"

"Yes, but not here. I'm on vacation."

"But you *are* English?"

"Yes."

"And is that your real name?"

"It's my real name," he said gravely.

"Mine's Jemima – Jemima Drury." She considered him carefully. "So, if you're on holiday, why are you involved in something like this?"

"I went to a tennis match and the man in the row behind me was murdered."

She stared at him. "I remember that. It was in the news. And Mr Maybury used to work for the Department, so the press office got in a flap. But I thought they said it was just robbery."

"That's what the police think," Xan said, with a slight twinge of conscience for maligning Inspector Nash. "But

I've been looking into his death. It looks as though he had found out something – something which got him killed."

"I see." She seemed to be turning something over in her mind. Abruptly, she said: "Who are you, exactly? I mean, where do you come from? You said you were English, but you're a stranger here."

"I was born in England. I moved away when I was eight, when my mother died."

He gave her the potted history, abridged version. Boarding school in Hong Kong. Consultancy of various types. He left out military service in a number of different countries, sometimes official, sometimes not, and he omitted Homeland altogether.

"So you don't have any connections here?"

"No."

"Family?"

"No. I don't have family anywhere."

She glanced at him, then went back to dusting the books. "Well, I think I'd better tell you where I fit in. If you already know about the Department, it seems stupid not to tell you the rest."

The dog had settled down on the floor, nose on his paws. Knowing that it was often easier to talk when no one was watching you, Xan fixed his eyes on the lumpy green wallpaper with an attention it did not deserve.

"I work in the records branch at the Department. We hold data on the military estate both here and overseas, financial accounts and so on. But the main thing is the personnel files. Some are electronic but a lot are paper files. Once you're dead, anyone can request your details, whether they're a relative or not. But of course, they might not get much information, depending on how long ago you served and where and they would have to pay the fee regardless, which puts a lot of people off." She glanced at him. "Shouldn't you be taking notes?"

"I've got a good memory. And it puts people off."

"Oh. Then perhaps you shouldn't admit the memory?"

He smiled. "Perhaps not, but the damage is done now."

"I suppose so. Well, about a month ago, a hard copy file came into the Branch that had been re-classified up to Secret. The name on it was David Paradine."

Xan waited.

Jemima picked up another book and began to dust the pages. Some of the dust blew into the dog's eyes and he sneezed reproachfully.

"It's unusual for such an old file to be re-classified. It means no one outside the department can ask for it, not even a relative. I had a look at it and there didn't seem to be any obvious reason. And when I checked the subject's next of kin, who was the only person likely to request his records, he had recently died himself, so I thought perhaps it didn't matter. Only then last week, it happened again – and this time it was a soldier who was still alive. His name was Robert Hare."

There was a pause, as though she thought Xan might speak. Mags lifted his head from his paws, then dropped it again and the girl resumed.

"I was worried. For a discharged soldier to have their

own records re-classified like that didn't make sense. It would mean he couldn't even request his own records – and there were no contact details for him on the file, so he couldn't have been told about it. But then I spoke to someone in Pensions Branch and they told me he had got in touch with them."

Xan frowned. "That doesn't sound like him. He wasn't too keen on the authorities."

"Apparently, he said he needed money in a hurry. But anyway, it meant we knew where he was and I decided to go down to the address he had given. To Ilvercombe. When I got there, I got hold of a waitress and she told me he wasn't there – so I'd wasted the journey and the price of the ticket. I walked along the shore, just trying to think things out, and – well, you know the rest."

And Xan knew that instead of the book she was dusting, she was seeing darkly foaming water and a grotesque, disfigured face.

He was also suddenly aware of a slight lessening of his own burden. Rabbit had got in touch with his pension administrators. He had put a red flag on his own file. To cover it, he said quickly: "What was in David Paradine's file? You said you'd read it."

"Nothing very interesting. And nothing about his death. Just the basics – his training record, exercises he was on, that sort of thing. And that's what worries me. You see, someone at the Department must have re-classified those two files. The same person could have removed anything they wanted to hide. So you see what it means."

Xan saw what it meant. He also saw that to keep his own knowledge back would be deeply unfair. “I think I’d better tell you what I know about all this.”

He went through the main facts of the business, starting with Giles Maybury’s death and including everything except the diary and his theft of Adam Paradine’s letters.

“So it started with Mr Maybury’s death?”

“I think he was the alarm bell. Whatever happened, it happened a long time ago and was hidden very well. Something happened to make them start worrying again – I think Giles Maybury was that something.”

“He may have got in touch with our Branch to ask about David Paradine. Maybe that’s why they reclassified the file. I can check that.”

“I don’t want –,” he began and paused.

She regarded him coolly. “I hope you’re not suggesting that I don’t do anything.”

“You work there.”

“And that’s why I’m in a position to do something.”

He said nothing further. Impossible to give words to his reluctance to involve anyone else in this business and equally impossible to insist on carrying the point. But he was not easy in his mind.

The dog sneezed again and the girl glanced over anxiously. “I hope he’s going to be all right here. Of course, it’s not usually dusty, it’s just the books.”

He reluctantly accepted the change of subject. “I’m just thankful to get him out of my hotel. I don’t think I could have kept him there much longer without the staff starting to suspect something."

Jemima shook her head impatiently. "I expect you'll find they already knew – especially the women."

As he walked back along the road to the station, the stone angels in the graveyard across the street looked at him pityingly. But was it really pity, or was it a warning, he found himself wondering?

CHAPTER 29

It was six o'clock in the morning and Elinor Maybury was sorting through the wardrobe in the spare room. Old age took a lot of things away from you and one of those was the capacity to sleep in, as she was wont to say. So she had occupied herself in clearing out Giles's things, a task she had been putting off for a while.

Methodically, she sorted through the coats. Tweed, winter wool and a hideous full-length fisherman's oilskin Giles had acquired from an agricultural show on the grounds that it would be handy for going to cricket matches in the rain but which had proved so heavy that it felt like wearing a suit of armour. An ordinary Burberry mackintosh was far more practical and Giles had carried his even on the hottest of sunny days, just in case.

Come to think of it, Giles's Burberry wasn't in the wardrobe. Well, of course not. Elinor took herself to task for being slow. If Giles had been wearing it the day he went to Wimbledon... Perhaps the police had thought it more tactful not to return it.

But the descriptions of Giles furnished by the witnesses at the inquest had not mentioned a raincoat. Instead, they had all described his suit and hat. Memory promptly furnished a snapshot of Giles in his drab linen suit with the dark blue shirt and that ridiculous pale blue Panama hat. Yet he had certainly left the house with the Burberry. What had he done with it?

It was probably not important, but it was odd. And odd things were important. She looked at the clock to check it was not too early – other people could not be expected to share her own difficulties in sleeping – then went downstairs to the telephone in the hall.

"His what?" It was a bad line but Xan always preferred to use his room phone when possible. It was much safer to give out a hotel number than a mobile, for one thing. And while potentially damning if the wrong person called your room, hotel extension numbers could not follow you around the streets and track what you were doing.

"His Burberry," Elinor repeated. "His raincoat. He took it with him to Wimbledon but the police didn't say anything about a raincoat."

"He wasn't wearing one when I saw him. He could have left it on his seat – but he didn't."

"So, what happened to it?"

The mystery of the missing Burberry raincoat was an intriguing puzzle which occupied Xan over breakfast.

The coat had disappeared somewhere between Giles Maybury's front door in Egham and Wimbledon's Centre Court. Of course, Maybury might have simply left it on the train by mistake. Elinor had promised to check with the train company. But it was a dull solution and required an element of coincidence.

It would be so much more satisfying if the raincoat had

disappeared for some important reason. And there weren't very many ways a large, durable garment such as a coat could disappear.

You could bury it at the bottom of a rubbish bin, drop it into deep water (but only if suitably weighted), burn it (with some difficulty), or cut it to ribbons. But why would Maybury have done any of those things? Equally, he might have given away the garment, lent it to someone, hidden it in some fashion – but again, why?

And when could he have done any of those things? He had only had the journey between his home and the All England Club in which to do it. A train, a Tube and then the taxi. Not many possibilities there, especially now that most stations had got rid of their left luggage facilities, so tempting to the terrorist.

And what could be significant about a coat? Perhaps a great deal, Xan thought suddenly, if you were a man with a secret who thought you were being followed and feared that your wallet might be stolen. What if Maybury had concealed something in the pocket of his coat and hidden it somewhere on the way to Wimbledon?

He imagined himself in the part of Giles Maybury. Leaving the house in the morning, a little nervy, a little agitated. Not quite sure whether the secret he had stumbled across was real or imagined. Then on the train, thinking he was being watched. Telling himself he was imagining things, but then seeing something that made him certain. A glance of collusion, perhaps, between two of the other passengers. The train drawing into Waterloo. Wondering what to do, how to safeguard the secret. And deciding – what?

Xan's mind roamed vaguely over the usual furniture of stations – fast food cafes, shops and so forth. A post-box? No, too elaborate. Maybury would have had no time to make up a parcel and anything as bulky as a coat would have needed to be weighed at a post office. Had he left it with one of the station shops or cafes? But terrorism had made staff at stations unsympathetic towards customers with parcels they wished to abandon. So what had he done with it?

The thing was a magician's trick. But a magician's trick was only a puzzle you hadn't seen the answer to yet. And as he frowned into space, his eye fell on a notice detailing the Hotel Coronado's laundry arrangements.

Of course. A dry-cleaning kiosk. Most big stations had one. Hand in the coat for cleaning and retrieve it later. And finally, he realised the significance of the clue he had held all along. The little yellow ticket in the diary, marking the page. He was a fool. It had been the ticket – not the diary – that Maybury was trying to pass to him all along.

*

Mr Robinson enjoyed his work managing the Sparkle-Clean Dry-Cleaners at Waterloo Station. His busiest times were in the weekday morning and evening rush-hours, when office-workers dropped off and collected garments on their way to and from the office. They were often in a hurry and short-tempered. They were invariably wearing identikit black, grey, charcoal and navy suits and he often wondered whether it mattered who got which parcel back again.

In the middle of the day and at weekends, you got a more interesting variety of customer and sometimes they were in the mood to stop for a chat. There were girls who had been out to a formal do the night before and would sorrowfully exhibit a smart dress with a red wine spill. There was nothing like red wine for ruining stuff like silk, only of course, few ladies bought real silk these days.

Then there were the old-school ladies and gentlemen who still had most of their clothes made to measure, from the most expensive materials. They were some of his best customers and never in a hurry, like the young ones – but of course, that sort didn't ever have to be in a hurry, Mr Robinson reflected without resentment.

And then sometimes you got someone you just couldn't place. The young man with the odd brown-green eyes appeared just after Mr Robinson reopened after lunch, rather suggesting that he had been hanging around on the station concourse, waiting. But Mr Robinson hadn't seen him doing so. That was the first oddity.

He was a tall young man with a scar running down the left side of his face and a rather lean, hungry look about him. He pushed his ticket across the counter with a quizzical look, as though he didn't know what he expected to receive. That was the second oddity.

The parcel took some time to locate. It had evidently

been left some time ago. And when queried, his customer was vague about the contents. That was the third oddity and rang a definite alarm bell, but after another look at the young man's slightly dangerous appearance and the scar (really, it looked almost like a *knife* wound), Mr Robinson put aside the idea of pressing him.

Instead, he retreated to the back of his shop and hunted around in the section reserved for items not collected. It did happen, with it being a train station. People dropped things there because it was convenient on a journey and then perhaps it might happen that their circumstances changed and it became less convenient, in which case it might be a month or more before they returned.

It was a relief when he laid his hands on the parcel. It was a tempting thought to open it up to see what was so remarkable about it. But a glance through the open door to his impatiently waiting customer made Mr Robinson decide not to risk it. He carried the parcel out hurriedly, before temptation could get the better of him. "Here you are, sir. It was right at the back."

And the young man smiled and thanked him and paid the bill without a murmur, but Mr Robinson had been watching closely as he handed over the parcel and he was quite sure that the expression in his customer's eyes had been curiosity, not recognition.

Definitely something wrong about *you*, he said to himself as the young man disappeared into the crowd. But nothing anyone could get hold of or report. Best to forget about it.

Xan walked over to the river, a disregarded stretch without tourists and therefore also empty of ice-cream sellers and performing street artists. He had given himself away over the parcel, he thought – it had been touch and go whether the manager would refuse to hand it over without a description of what was in it. Some people would have done. It all depended how much trouble they wanted and the little man with the jumpy eyes had not looked as though he wanted any trouble.

He opened up the brown paper carefully. The cream material with the tartan lining revealed itself. He turned the coat over gently, looking first for stains. There was nothing obvious. No reason for Maybury to put it in for dry-cleaning unless he had suddenly tired of carrying it – or if he had some other ulterior motive.

There was nothing in the coat pockets. Of course there wouldn't be, if it had been cleaned. But as he had half-expected, there was an envelope underneath the coat, in the packaging, as though the cleaner who had attended to the coat had found something in one of the pockets and put it by for safe-keeping. The envelope had Maybury's name and address on it. The flap was open. Inside was a photograph.

It must have been taken using an old-fashioned film camera. The setting was somewhere sunny. Three young men stared at the camera, two in Army uniform, the other in ordinary clothes. They were leaning against the side of a large vehicle, perhaps a coach or a bus. Behind them was the edge of a street sign written in Arabic.

Xan studied the faces. They all looked young, in their twenties. They seemed to be having a good time. The youngest, in civilian clothes, smiled rather warily at the camera, as though he was already learning to be cautious of being pinned down by the organisation he had signed up to. Private Robert Hare, before his face was damaged. The taller one in uniform was carrying a kit bag slung over his shoulder. He was immediately recognisable as Corporal David Paradine. The third man was turned a little from the camera, but he too looked familiar. Stocky, square, dark-haired. Older now, of course. But someone Xan had met recently. Talked to.

Xan looked up from the photograph and across the river towards the Palace of Westminster – a golden citadel in the sunlight. It was absurd to think that something could be seriously wrong in Westminster. But Giles Maybury had thought so.

CHAPTER 30

The Records Office for the Department of Security and Defence was on the fifth floor of Westminster House and was a confused octagonal shape, thanks to having being hacked unceremoniously out of bits of other rooms. It had large windows looking out onto the river and was freezing in winter, with a grand ceremonial fireplace that did not work, and unbearably stuffy now, in summer.

Information came into the Records Branch sometimes through the door, in boxes carried by officials surprised by the weight, but more often these days over the internet connection. Once inside, it was locked down in cardboard boxes and concealed in filing cabinets and databases, to be grudgingly dispensed when called for.

As with all Her Majesty's government departments, defence was supposedly becoming digital by default, but this process was occurring in a slow inching fashion and in the meantime, there were always more boxes of papers coming through the door. An earlier generation of records officers had, termite-like, constructed an unwieldy nest structure in the basement of Westminster House to house it all.

Jemima Drury arrived early on Monday morning. Only one of her colleagues was at his desk. Paul always came in to the office early to avoid the crowds on the Tube. As always, he ignored Jemima's arrival, staring intently at the report he was reading.

"You see, I don't really like people, very much," he had once explained to Jemima, his brown eyes nervous and intense. "I like *things*. And records are things. That's why they moved me here from HR."

This morning, his silence was a blessing. Jemima was able to get straight on with checking the log of external enquiries about records. There it was in black and white. Maybury, G. The day before David Paradine's file had been re-classified. Confirmation, if it were needed.

She thought about David Paradine. He had died so very young – younger than she was now. The archives held stories of so many short lives and wasteful deaths that one got used to trying not to think about them, but she was going to have to think about this one now.

There had been no post-mortem report, but that wasn't necessarily as sinister as it appeared. Post-mortems fell into the category of defence data which was not released to the public and they were not filed by subject but by practitioner. So David Paradine's post-mortem might very well be there, down in the archive, invisible to anyone who didn't know where to look. And she knew where to look.

It took her a couple of hours to search the database for serving doctors who had been in Egypt at the time in question. Eventually, she found three. Now all she had to do was to check their files in the archive.

"Jemima, could you attend the directorate team meeting for me this morning?" Geraldine's plaintive voice rose across the room. "I've been called into an audit of well-being practices and training targets. Apparently, we're 3% below where we should be for this quarter."

Geraldine was the Records Manager. She had a rangy appearance like an eager hare and she favoured flowery blouses, voluminous skirts and sensible shoes. Today, she had also adorned herself with a necklace of coral beads which wrapped round her throat three times and still managed to cascade to her waist. Her fingers played with the necklace nervously, perhaps in uneasy anticipation of the looming audit.

"Of course," Jemima said gloomily. Directorate meetings were almost as much of a waste of time as well-being audits in her opinion and usually ran to at least two hours.

This one excelled itself by running to three. It was not until after one o'clock that Jemima managed to dash out for a sandwich. As soon as she had swallowed it, she cast a guilty eye over the unread emails waiting in her inbox and went down to the archive.

The main lift only went down to the ground floor but the goods elevator, while unadorned with posters about forthcoming performance management catch-ups, took you all the way down past the basement canteen and the sub-basement squash courts to the sub-sub-basement. This area was off-limits to the casual inquirer and accessible only by swipecard.

Once inside the archive, Jemima closed the door softly

behind her. Before her stretched the open-plan archive vault, crammed with row after row of free-standing metal filing cabinets that looked as though they would topple over given the slightest encouragement.

There were plenty of secrets here according to the dull official government definition of the word and in the years she had worked here, she had come to take that for granted. But whatever was going on, it had started right here in the archive – and it had led to a man being pulled dead from the sea and another stabbed at a tennis-match.

There were three doctors on her list – Armitage, Miller and Pargiter. The first two were still alive, while Dr Pargiter had passed away nine years ago. This seemed significant, but she decided to check the records in strict alphabetical order. It felt like a vindication when she reached Dr Pargiter's files and found the sheaf of stapled pages labelled PARADINE.

The light in the stacks was poor. Jemima spread out the report, using the open drawer of the filing cabinet as a makeshift desk. It was very slight, just four pages. Many of the documents she would have expected to see, such as the report of an incident review panel, were not there.

She half-expected the post-mortem report itself to be missing too, but there it was at the back. She read with a sense of slight disappointment. There was nothing odd about it to a cursory glance. David Paradine had been shot at the base of the collarbone and he had died in hospital. The analysis suggested that he had been rising to his feet at the time he was shot but gave no indication of what he had been doing before the shooting started.

At first, she had thought the report ran to four pages but then she saw that the last page was another post-mortem – that of the Egyptian who had died, Haresh Khalim. She read it quickly and with an increasing sense of surprise.

It would be a good idea to take a copy but there was no photocopier or scanner down here in the stacks. It would mean going all the way up to the Records Branch. Then she remembered her phone. She pulled it out and took careful pictures of the relevant pages of both Paradine's and Khalim's reports.

"What are you doing?" A childish voice interrupted her.

Jemima almost dropped her phone. "Jade? You made me jump."

Jade was the most junior records officer, a school-leaver with wide blue eyes. She was standing at Jemima's elbow. "Geraldine sent me down to fetch some urgent files."

Jemima closed the file with a slap. "I was just –." She could not think of a remotely plausible explanation of what she was doing. "Looking at some papers," she concluded lamely. "And then my phone buzzed."

Thankfully, Jade seemed to accept this feeble answer. She looked around the archive and shivered theatrically. "It's creepy here, isn't it? I never like coming down here alone, somehow."

It would clearly be impossible to do any more detecting now, even if she had the appetite. Reluctantly, Jemima made the mental transition back from detective to records officer, wondering inwardly if it became more difficult to do so each time.

Back at her desk, she began dutifully to look through her neglected emails, but the significance of what she had read nagged at her mind. She had made no promises about what she would do with any new information she found, but it seemed suddenly impossible to keep this to herself. Impulsively, she rose and pulled on her jacket.

The girl at the next desk glanced up curiously. "Going to lunch? I thought you had already been out."

Jemima seized on the first idea that came into her head. "I'm getting my hair cut."

Alicia stared at her hair. "But didn't you have a trim just a couple of weeks ago?"

Jemima panicked. "Yes, but I've decided I don't like it. I'm going to do something quite different with it."

Alicia tossed her own hair, a neat, shining dark bob that never fell out of place. "Good idea. Ask them for something choppy that will do something about all that length."

"I'll consider it," Jemima said and hurried out to the lifts, taking the main one this time.

Once outside the building, she crossed the road to the park by the river and dialled the number Xan had given her. "It's me. Do you think you could possibly meet me after work? There's something I need to tell you about."

It was only after she rang off that she realised she had put herself in an awkward position – one a male detective would surely never find himself in. And there was really no choice.

CHAPTER 31

Trafalgar Square was not the best place to meet anyone. Whether you chose a lion or a fountain, there were too many of everything, and when the square was crowded with tourists and street entertainers, as it always was on a warm summer evening, you could spend fruitless minutes searching.

Xan thoughtfully positioned himself on the steps that led up towards the National Gallery, from which vantage point it was easy to spot Jemima making her way through the crowd and brushing aside the importuning of human statues, buskers and fire-jugglers.

There was something different about her today – it took him a moment to realise that under a disguising summer hat, she had done something rather radical with her hair.

She said quickly: "Thank you for coming. I've got something to tell you about. But I can't rattle it off in a crowd among people trying to do flame-throwing tricks. We'd better walk down to St James's Park, that's usually quiet at this time of day."

She saw him eyeing her shorn hair and added ruefully: "I can explain that, too. But it's rather a long story and you'll miss most of it unless you're a lip-reader."

The streets behind the Abbey were empty and the park

itself was quiet. Parents had taken their children home and tourists were starting to wander towards eateries and coffee-houses. The sun was caught in the drift-nets of the tallest trees.

By common consent, they began a circuit of the lake. The shallow water was like a mirror. "I found something in the archive," Jemima said. "Unfortunately, I panicked and told my office I was getting my hair cut when I came out to ring you and then I realised I'd have to do it for real. But it was worth it – I think."

Xan smiled. "I found something too. It didn't involve any grooming procedures but I nearly gave myself away to a man who runs a dry-cleaning establishment. So what did you find?"

"I found the post-mortem reports. Paradine and Khalim. But there's nothing odd about David Paradine's death, as far as I could tell. A bullet in the chest, near the collar-bone, when he was getting to his feet. Just as you would expect – at least, I presume you would expect it. I don't know much about these things. But then I read Khalim's file. And that was different. The notes said he was shot in the head 'execution-style'."

"What?"

Jemima said: "That's what I thought. It doesn't make sense, does it?"

Xan shook his head. "If David Paradine was shot first in the chest, he couldn't have taken a shot like that. But if Khalim was shot in an execution-style killing, he couldn't then have shot Paradine either."

"Well, maybe there was someone else shooting."

"Maybe there was," Xan said slowly.

She glanced at him, as though troubled by his reticence. "Hassan Khalim could have been travelling with a friend, I suppose. But that would mean David Paradine got up and shot Khalim in cold blood for some reason and then his friend shot him. It doesn't seem terribly likely."

"No, it doesn't."

"Then," she said, reluctantly, "we know that Private Hare was also on the coach."

"It wasn't him."

She looked at him carefully. "How can you be so sure?"

"Rabbit couldn't stand the sight of blood. That's one of the reasons they kicked him out of the Army. And his shooting was terrible. It wasn't him."

"But there wasn't anyone else."

"There might have been. In fact, there must have been. I was a fool not to spot it before. One of the witnesses talked about two soldiers travelling together. But Rabbit wasn't in uniform."

"Then who was the other one?"

"You'd better take a look at this. I found it today."

He produced the photograph that Giles Maybury had taken so much trouble to protect. Jemima stared at it. Three men smiling at the camera. She knew two of them from their records in the archives. The third –. She looked up from the photograph at Xan's face.

"Recognise him?" he said expressionlessly.

She nodded. "Oh, yes. It's the Junior Defence Minister,

Mark Romilly. I recognised him straightaway. Anyone would who knew him."

*

"It would be useful to know what Romilly's official record says about his Army career. His public biography doesn't mention Cairo, but it's only a paragraph."

Jemima said: "I can tell you that. He was never in Egypt at all. Or at least that's what it says."

They had stopped at a coffee-house, a ramshackle affair close to the lake. A piano in the corner was being half-heartedly played by a shabby man who might have been either an off-duty waiter or a customer.

"At any rate, we know now what they're trying to cover up. It's one thing the defence minister having been there when a fellow-soldier died rather messily. But if he shot Khalim in cold blood – if that got out, it would destroy his career. He's an ambitious man."

"Are you saying that he – but he's a *minister*."

Xan shrugged. "Ministers are people too. But no, I'm not saying he's necessarily involved himself. Politicians have powerful interests around them. Perhaps someone's invested a lot of money in Mark Romilly. It would be useful to know a little more about who's backing him. Whoever they are, they have quite a motive to silence anyone who knew something that would sink his career."

"They?"

"It's got to be more than one person. Giles Maybury at

Wimbledon, Reverend Paradine at his home, Rabbit in Devon. That's quite a reach. And the man who handled Maybury's death was part of a team – the police had a lead on him and he turned up dead in a London street, the same day that Rabbit disappeared."

"You're talking about a conspiracy."

Her voice was dubious, as though it was implausible – but why, he wondered? Once one conceded the act of murder, was it such a big step to a murderous conspiracy?

He considered the complex entity that was Lombard & Black, which had ties both to Giles Maybury's government pension fund and to the charity that had been the net beneficiary of Reverend Adam Paradine's estate. And he thought of a sullen face glaring at him from the window of a car outside Major Phelps' nursing-home.

"There would have to be something big at stake to make it worthwhile taking the risk," Jemima said slowly. "And I've got an idea about that. It's the Party leadership contest next month. He said he wouldn't stand, but of course they always say that. You know – 'if nominated, I will not run, if elected, I will not serve'. It sounds better to have to be persuaded to do it."

"And if they have a leadership contest, anyone who wins would become the Prime Minister."

"Yes."

"I see."

"So, what are we going to do?"

"We need proof. The photograph is only damaging when you know when and where it was taken. I need to find someone else who was on that coach – but the only other passenger who was named was a Jane Griffin who I can't track down."

"She sounds rather a mythical creature. And in any case, I suppose she might have been sitting at the front of the coach and not seen anything?"

"She was one of the few people sitting near the back, in fact. So was Rabbit, but he was asleep, of course." But as he spoke, Xan wondered anew. Had that been a lie? His failure to question Rabbit more closely the one time he had spoken to him seemed ever more disastrous, a widening circle of rippling effect.

Jemima said helpfully: "I could find out more about Mark Romilly quite easily. Everyone in the Department talks about the ministers, they're like minor gods. No one would think it odd that I'd be interested. For instance, he has regular meetings with a Harley Street doctor – Sir Julius Stoke, his name is. One of the girls in the Private Office told me he simply won't see a strange doctor."

Xan turned that over in his mind. Private meetings with a doctor sounded vaguely sinister. But at that moment, his train of thought was interrupted as the piano-player paused in his playing, distracted by the sight of a large man in a too-small suit struggling to open the door to the cafe.

Xan groaned.

Jemima looked at him in surprise. "What is it?"

The chairs shrieked protestingly as they were shoved left and right to make way for the fat man to make his way over to their table. "Well, well, this is nice," he wheezed amiably. "You'd better introduce me."

Resignedly, Xan kicked a spare chair into roughly the required position and turned to Jemima. "This is Billy Dangerfield. A friend of mine. Of sorts."

Billy nodded affably. He turned to the waiter, who was hovering anxiously behind the big man making all the noise. "Black coffee, two sugars," he instructed.

As though taking his own instruction from the words, the piano-player began his tune again. Having lowered his bulk cautiously into his chair, Billy surveyed the scene through red-rimmed eyes. He glanced at Jemima again. "I didn't catch your name. But then, I rather think I wasn't meant to."

"Jemima Drury."

Billy leaned over and shook her hand with the careful attention of someone who may fall off his chair if he does not maintain a cautious eye to balance. "Delighted to meet you." He turned back to Xan again. "Well, how does it feel to be a dead man walking?"

It was then that Xan realised, with a familiar sense of weariness, that Billy was very drunk indeed. "What are you talking about?"

For answer, Billy plucked a pencil out of his pocket and scribbled something on a napkin. A lopsided square like something a child would have drawn, suggesting a building of some sort – a small and ill-favoured one with too many windows and an awkwardly slanted roof.

Xan stared at it. "What's this?"

Billy ran an irritable hand through his hair. "If you

don't know, *I* can't tell you." He stared blearily at the cup that had been deposited at his elbow. "Did I order coffee? I don't want this. Take it away."

The piano-player, as though sensing tension, began to play more loudly. Billy struggled to his feet. "I'm due somewhere. Where?"

He shambled towards the door, gave a wobbling half-wave at the proprietor behind the bar, then fell out of the door, leaving the piano-player and the waiter staring after him.

Xan swore under his breath. Jemima looked at him. "What did he mean about a dead man walking?"

"I don't know." And, not for the first time since he had come to England, Xan wished Billy Dangerfield to the blazes.

*

The city was in darkness now, or its own version of it, punctuated by the amber glare of street-lamps.

He had accompanied Jemima to the Underground despite her apparent amusement at this old-fashioned behaviour and his own irritated awareness of its futility – the dark, lonely route between her local station and her flat was a dozen times more hazardous for a woman walking alone at night than this tourist-ridden central district. He had then taken his own route home to the Coronado Hotel, conscious of a residual exasperation with himself that he would have liked to pin entirely on Billy but could not.

Now, standing at his bedroom window and once more tracing the patterns of lights in the tower-block opposite, he took another swallow of his whisky on ice and dragged his mind away from Billy's crashing foolishness and back to the case.

Now he knew what they were trying to hide and why. The shooting of the Egyptian had been cold-blooded murder. Why? Something to do with the card game? The words snagged in his mind. There was something not quite right about that card game. He groped for the answer and couldn't find it.

Alternatively, perhaps Khalim had pulled his gun first and Romilly had shot him in revenge for Paradine's killing. Again, why? It wasn't clear. But either way, it would be enough to sink a promising politician's career – and also the interests that surrounded it. All the things money supposedly couldn't buy. Votes in Parliament. Changes to regulations. Valuable procurement contracts. All those things riding on Romilly.

No wonder there had been consternation when Adam Paradine decided to clear his attic and stumbled across an old photograph that put Mark Romilly on a tourist coach where two people had died. No one was supposed to know that Romilly had been on that coach. His Army record must have been neatly edited to eliminate the episode.

So, someone had taken the decision that it would be far more convenient if Reverend Paradine was eliminated instead. They had acted quickly but not quickly enough, because Paradine had showed the photograph to his old friend Giles Maybury and asked his advice.

Maybury had poked around, made a few inquiries. He was well-connected, he knew who to talk to and where to look. And then what? He had talked to the wrong person about it. Perhaps it had even been Mark Romilly himself. Romilly would have passed the fact on to his backers. And Maybury would have been doomed.

How much had Romilly known? At the fete, he had professed himself curious about Maybury's murder. He had surely known more about the matter than a casual acquaintance should. But he had been quick to volunteer the fact that Maybury had shown some anxiety to talk to him when they met at the Ritz – no doubt in case someone had overheard that exchange. All in all, it had been an adroit performance, aided by his wife.

There were still questions to be answered, of course. What, for instance, had been the meaning of the Greek tag that Maybury had quoted when he was dying?

And what about Rabbit? After they got rid of Maybury, they must have checked up on anyone else who had been connected with the Egypt incident and who could therefore be dangerous – like Rabbit, living quietly on his boat minding his own business and no trouble to anyone.

What had Romilly known about that particular murder? Had they told him in advance – or more likely, after it was over? Had Romilly had the guts to protest? Xan took another sharp swallow of his drink and carried on looking out of the window.

CHAPTER 32

The phone number that Sir Miles Temperley had given him connected to an automated messaging service. Xan left as short and non-committal a message as he could and within an hour, the answer came. Temperley would see him at an address in Vine Court, SW1.

It was hard to know what to expect. A private flat? An office? But as Xan had found before, London postcodes could be misleading. When he reached the cobbled mews that was Vine Court, he had to walk round the corner to find the entrance and suddenly found himself in the buzzing thoroughfare of the Strand, confronting the front door of the club where he had watched Billy eat breakfast the day after the Wimbledon murder.

There need be nothing wrong in the fact that Sir Miles Temperley was a member of the same club as Billy, but it was disconcerting, all the same. Xan made himself known to the reception desk and was directed upstairs to a room with large leather armchairs, books lining the walls and a cold, dead fire in the grate.

Sir Miles rose out of one of the biggest of the chairs to greet him, the clown face discreetly cheerful. "Delighted to see you, my dear chap. You needn't worry about this room, I've instructed the clerk we're not to be disturbed.

I'm on the Committee, so they generally do as I say. Now, what do you have to tell me?"

Xan had known that there would be currency to be paid for coming here. He produced some small change. "Giles Maybury had offered to look into something for a friend. A man whose son had died on active service. I think he found out more than he was meant to."

"Can you tell me names?"

"Not at this stage. I want some information. I need to locate someone. A witness. I have a name for her, but I don't think it's her real one." This had been suggested by Jemima's remark about mythical beasts. And once he had thought about it properly, the name of Griffin did rather suggest itself as a cover name. "She was in Cairo on a certain date ten years ago. I imagine you can find a list of British subjects who flew home around that time."

"I'll see what I can do, if you think it important."

"I do."

Sir Miles looked at him thoughtfully. If he felt a trifle uneasy, he didn't say so. "I'll have the information for you by tomorrow, my dear fellow. Now, it's nearly lunchtime. Why don't you have something with me?"

Xan declined and took his leave. As he passed down the stairs, a visitor scribbling a note at the reception desk looked up and Xan paused momentarily. He knew that heavy, sullen face.

The toffee-brown eyes were incurious. They passed over Xan without interest. The man exchanged a few words with the reception-clerk and passed through a set of double doors which said Committee Only.

Xan went over to the desk. The clerk was staring down at something. A pencil was lying next to it, snapped in two. "He broke his pencil," the clerk said with awe. "I've never seen Mr Angel look upset about anything before."

"Perhaps he had indigestion," Xan suggested lightly. "Who did you say he was?"

"That's Marcus Angel, sir. Chairman of Lombards. But perhaps you don't know Lombards." The clerk's voice made allowances for Xan's accent.

"Yes, I know Lombards."

"He's on the Committee here. Mind you, once you're as important as him, you get on the committees for everything, it seems. He sits on the Wimbledon Board as well. The tennis club, you know."

Xan said that he knew.

CHAPTER 33

Goring and Streatley, despite its double name, was a single small village straddling the River Thames. Coming out of the small station, Xan guessed which side of the river he wanted and guessed wrong. The swans on the river watched superciliously as he re-crossed the bridge.

He had come here to see a Mrs Jane Kilgetty. After two days of silence, Temperley had produced her name and address without comment.

The house was a sprawling, Victorian mansion and when he rang the doorbell, it was answered by a plump, grey-haired woman in sensible cords and an elderberry-coloured top. She did not look at all like the kind of woman who would know any secrets.

"Mrs Kilgetty? My name's West. I wanted to ask you some questions about a coach tour you took in Egypt."

"Good heavens," she said lightly. "That was a very long time ago."

"I know. But I'm afraid something has happened which makes it important now." He offered her Temperley's card, which Temperley certainly had not authorised him to use in this scenario.

There was some hesitation. Xan thought that Jane Kilgetty was weighing up the risks of talking to him with the risks of closing the door and letting him go elsewhere. At last, she seemed to make up her mind. "I suppose you had better come in. We can talk in the sitting-room. The dogs are in the kitchen."

She showed him into a room and then left him alone, murmuring something about tea. He took the opportunity to look around.

The room had tall French windows looking down over a sloping lawn to the river. It was furnished with antique pieces and what looked to his untutored eye like very good paintings. A large bell-shaped container at the far end of the room with a rug over it struck an incongruous note. In the distance, he could hear the irritable yapping of small dogs.

It was tempting to take a look under the rug but before he could do so, he was warned by a temporary crescendo of barking that the kitchen door was opening. He moved away from the mysterious container as Mrs Kilgetty came in with a tray of the sort of array of teacups and jugs that Xan had learned to be wary of.

"I'll be with you in a moment." She paused by the bell-shaped container. "You don't mind, do you? They could do with some air and light."

Slightly mystified, Xan disclaimed minding anything. She twitched the rug off to reveal a large bird-cage with three small yellow birds perched inside.

"My canaries. I love to hear them, if you won't find them distracting. Now do sit down, Mr – West?" She seated herself on an elegant chaise longue and began to busy herself with pouring tea.

Xan dropped into an armchair. He had heard the faint scepticism in her tone when she used his name. "You're used to dealing with people under different names, aren't you, Mrs Kilgetty? You'd have to be, given your previous employers."

She hesitated. The light glittered off her glasses. But, Xan thought, if she was really averse to answering questions, there would have been no invitation into her house, no offer of tea. For some reason, Jane Kilgetty wanted to talk.

"I know who you worked for – or at least, I can narrow it down to two or three organisations."

She said quickly: "It's best, we find, not to mention any *specific organisations*. We have a formula we use, under which I might advise you that I worked on the *south* side of the river."

He waited. Xan's mind turned to London and its river, and the buildings on either side of it. "I understand."

"Of course, I can't tell you anything about their work. I'm retired now. We retire early in my profession."

"This isn't about their work."

"Then what is it about? That coach trip – so long ago."

"Two men died."

"And the authorities looked into it at the time. Why would you want to ask questions about it now?"

"It's become important."

She still looked puzzled. "And you say it has nothing to do with my former employers?"

"I'm just interested in what happened on that coach. I've looked into the available records, but you weren't called at the inquest."

Jane Kilgetty nodded rather sadly. "That's right. I was hustled away. Protecting an important source. A soldier dead and they just kept saying it was nothing to do with me and not to blow my cover."

"They might have done better to leave you there. Your disappearance looked odd, once I knew what to look for."

"And why were you looking in the first place?"

"I need to know what happened on that coach. And you have a trained, observant mind."

Mrs Kilgetty sighed. "I'm not sure I do any more. Oh, it was a very exciting job and I enjoyed every minute of it, but I've forgotten most of what I knew. You make a clean break, you know – they insist on that. No friends, no keep-sakes. So, you forget everything very quickly."

Xan thought the lady perhaps insisted too much. "If you could just tell me about it from the beginning," he said patiently. "You were travelling to Luxor from Cairo."

"That's right. I had a most urgent appointment and good reasons for not using my own car. As a matter of fact, Western travellers were discouraged from travelling alone through the desert at that time."

"Where were you sitting on the coach?"

"About three-quarters of the way back on the left." She twinkled at him. "I daresay you're thinking there's nothing much wrong with my memory. But that trip was fourteen hours. Plenty of time for things to get stuck in your mind – mostly the discomfort and the heat. And the toilet facilities." She shuddered. "But you won't want to hear about that."

"Did you notice the people sitting behind you?"

"Not at first. I noticed the soldier in uniform playing cards with a friend."

"Just one friend?"

"Yes. There was another man with them, but he was asleep."

"And when did you first realise something was wrong?"

She screwed up her face. "Someone started shouting," she said thoughtfully. "Most people were half-asleep so it came as a shock. I saw that there was an altercation going on behind me. Then two shots in rapid succession. Then the coach swerved and went off the road and we fell into the ditch. Everyone was shouting and screaming. The woman in front of me was muttering in Spanish, I think it must have been prayers."

Xan considered this. The evidence that the two shots had been close together was important. If the second had occurred after the crash, it was additional evidence in support of cold-blooded murder.

"Did you see who fired the shots?"

"The first was Khalim, the Egyptian. And the second was one of the soldiers. Not the one who got shot, one of the other two."

At any rate, that disposed of the idea that Mark Romilly had for some reason deliberately shot David Paradine and Khalim had been an unfortunate witness.

"What did he look like – the soldier who did the shooting?" Xan said quickly.

She shook her head. "I never saw his face. He was sitting behind me, while the other two were across the aisle."

"Then how do you know he had a gun?"

"Because he shot Khalim."

"And the two you could see?"

"The one who was shot went down on the floor and I could see he wasn't going to make it, poor fellow. The fair-haired one by the window had been asleep the whole time. The shots woke him up and he just looked dazed. Then the one behind me took the second shot, just before the coach swerved off the road and we all went flying."

Xan absorbed all this. It held together, mostly. But he was interested in Mrs Kilgetty's precise recollection of the shooting and the briskness with which she described it. And there was one other thing that puzzled him. "How did you know the Egyptian's name?"

There was a slight pause. "Because I read all the newspaper reports, of course. I was naturally interested – and concerned for my cover."

"It's odd, though, that you've remembered that name all these years. And not, apparently, the name of the soldier who was shot."

Another silence.

"There's something about Khalim, isn't there?" Xan said. "I've found it remarkably difficult to find out anything about him. What do you know?"

"He was never convicted of anything," she said quickly. "Anything that would interest us, anyway. He was being watched due to his connections only."

"That's why you were on that bus, wasn't it? To watch him."

"We thought he was small fry. I hoped he'd lead us to someone else."

"But instead, he got into an argument and got shot in the head and your lead was gone. What was the argument about?"

"I can't tell you that, I'm afraid."

"It wasn't about a card game. You were quoted in the newspaper saying that only two of them were playing cards. The two soldiers. The Egyptian man wasn't playing, was he? So, what was the argument about? Was there even an argument?"

The canaries were singing, he realised suddenly. Mrs Kilgetty leaned forward earnestly and spoke in a low voice. "I can't tell you anything officially. It was hushed up. The Egyptian authorities didn't want it reported and neither did we."

"What was hushed up?"

"Khalim nearly blew that bus up. He was small fry all right but the sort that has his own dreams of glory. He'd got tired of being a middle man, passing messages. He'd got it all with him – homemade stuff, of course, but an olive jar filled with diesel and a cigarette lighter will have plenty of impact in a bus full of Western tourists." She shook her head wearily. "If we had had any idea what he was planning, we would naturally have stopped the bus from travelling. As it was, those soldiers saved us all. Khalim managed to shoot one of them but the other one got him right between the eyes."

Xan's carefully-constructed theory lay in tatters. "Khalim was a terrorist?"

Jane Kilgetty nodded.

"Why didn't any of this come out at the inquest?"

"There wasn't any evidence," she said drily. "The olive jar got smashed in the crash and there was enough leaking fuel around to cover it up. A cigarette lighter wouldn't tell you anything. The Egyptian authorities weren't keen to report that someone had nearly set fire to a bus full of tourists. The tourist trade was only just starting to recover then. And as I say, there was no evidence."

"Except for your knowledge about Khalim."

"Yes," Jane Kilgetty said. "But I was under cover and I was hustled right out of Egypt the same day. I made a report to my chief but he said to stay out of it. As far as the authorities were concerned, it was a minor terrorist incident, apart from the death of an unfortunate off-duty soldier."

Xan sat back in his chair, frustrated. The canaries twittered triumphantly in their cage, apparently enjoying his discomfiture. And Jane Kilgetty smiled kindly at him and poured more tea.

CHAPTER 34

The train back to town was slow and jolting. Xan stared out of the window at the changing countryside. Autumn was coming. The fields were full of yellow wheat. Lines of swallows perched on telegraph poles, restless with the consciousness of their impending journey.

His theory made no sense now. Mark Romilly had shot an Egyptian civilian in cold blood, but it was to save a coachload of passengers from a terrorist attack. He was a hero.

So why, then, did the incident not appear in his official Army record? Granted, it had been kept quiet at the time as part of counter-terrorism operational practice, but once Romilly had risen to power, you would have expected something to be made of it. From what Jemima had said, a heroic story like that would be priceless to a politician. Instead, the whole thing remained hidden – not only that, but anyone who found out about it was being swiftly eliminated. It didn't make sense.

His mind too restless to settle, he picked up a paper that a fellow-passenger had cast down on the seat. His eye rested on an unedifying tale of a senior politician undone by scandal in his private life, and the hash that this would make of the upcoming Party leadership contest.

He remembered Jemima talking about the leadership contest. And Fenella Romilly remarking ruefully that a career for a politician was a tightrope these days, always dreading the moment when some past action or inaction would come back to undo you. Given all of that, it would almost be worth –.

The passengers in Coach F, who had grown tired of the view of endless cornfields, overgrown hedges and woods, were enlivened by the spectacle of a young man jumping to his feet and saying something regrettable. The fact that he promptly sat down again did not rob the spectacle of any of its interest.

Some passengers speculated that he had missed his stop, while the ticket collector, who had been collecting fares at the other end of the carriage, eyed the offender severely, under the impression that this was a case of a ticketless traveller alarmed by imminent exposure.

It couldn't be true, Xan thought. It would never work. And yet … A number of pieces of evidence were falling into place. Mark Romilly's sensitivity about seeing strange doctors. Fenella Romilly's revealing remark that her husband had nightmares and woke up afraid that he had talked in his sleep. And Giles Maybury's quoting of an Ancient Greek tag before he died.

It all added up to a single, monstrously absurd idea that would explain why Reverend Paradine had had to die.

And Rabbit. Rabbit must have known. It was no good ducking that point. So why hadn't he said anything? Xan thought he knew the answer to that, but it only made the fact of Rabbit's death harder to stomach.

Once the train reached London, he returned to his hotel, inconveniencing the chambermaid who was trying to do his room, and worked through the information he had amassed on Mark Romilly. Open source had yielded vast quantities of names, dates, photographs and reports. Birth certificates, health records, school records, university and the Army were all watertight, but naturally, they would have dealt with that very carefully. But there might be something they had forgotten.

He paused as he read over Romilly's Army record again. There was something odd about that, after all, wasn't there? The period when he must have been in Egypt was not well covered-up by a plausible story of being elsewhere. It just didn't feature, as though they hadn't thought it mattered particularly.

And what about the date? There must be a date when this had happened – when the phantom Mark Romilly had become real, as it were. Once again, he went over Romilly's official biography. But there was no trace of the 'join'.

He needed proof. And proof was going to be hard to come by in this case. The records that mattered weren't these fabricated ones. Somehow, he was going to need to get on the track of the other man whose identity had been hidden behind all this smoke and mirrors. An ordinary man, probably with an ordinary name, like Tom, Dick or Harry …

Xan pushed aside his notes to reach for the book he had

found in Rabbit's hotel room at Ilvercombe. The collected works of TS Eliot. He picked it up and turned it over, looking at the faded blue cloth and gold lettering. Then he opened it again to read the name scrawled in the flyleaf. *Tom Riley*. Not Rabbit's name and not Rabbit's book. It had come home with him from Egypt by mistake and he had kept it but it had belonged to someone else.

But even if he now had a idea about the name, he was going to need more. This called for a specialist – and one who was alive to the dangers of the industry. There could be no more innocent parties put at risk by this business.

*

"You again." Flannery blew out his cheeks in one of his most dramatic sighs. Since their last meeting, his office seemed to have got dustier and the man himself even fatter, if that was possible.

"I'm afraid so."

"You seem to have been in the wars, if you don't mind my saying so. Ironically, considering that this appears to be where your interests lie."

"It's funny you should say that."

"So, what former soldier do you want to know about now?"

Xan leaned across the desk and spoke. The expression on the face of the specialist in marriages and divorces passed through amusement to incredulity to something akin to seriousness.

At last, Flannery passed his tongue over his lips and said: “You’re pulling my leg.”

“I haven’t got time for that. And anyway, it doesn’t matter to you, so long as I pay you, right?”

“Upfront?”

“No.”

Flannery nodded. “Naturally not. But what I’d like is to know who’s paying you.”

Silence.

“That’s what I thought.” Flannery shook his head sorrowfully. “You don’t look the type, but it comes to us all. Apparently. Hasn’t come to me yet.”

“What does?”

“Sentimentalism. Trying to do, God forbid, the right thing.”

“Are you going to help or not?”

“Sure. Sure, why not? Every instinct’s telling me to steer clear of anything you suggest, but there it is, you apparently don’t have a monopoly on being a damned fool. I’ll see what I can do and get back to you.”

“Thank you.” Xan rose.

It was disconcerting to reflect, as he came out of the door next to the launderette, that he appeared to have made a minor error of logic.

He had decided to make use of Flannery’s skills on the grounds that he would be little loss to the world if anything unfortunate was to happen to him. It was therefore inconvenient to find that he liked him.

CHAPTER 35

Paddington Station had a sleepy air in the middle of the day. Looking up at the vaulted arches soaring to the skies, laced with ornate ironwork, Xan found himself grateful for the fussiness of those engineers and architects who had insisted that even the most utilitarian of structures should be conceived like a cathedral.

The high arches let you look out along the track to the trains heading west. A shiver of rain hung in the air and the dark green trains pulling in were damp, panting and steaming, like dogs racing in from a romp in the woods.

On Platform 1, a bronze Paddington Bear sat eternally on a pile of luggage, his solitude enlivened by a steady stream of tourists taking pictures. What extraordinarily people the English were, Xan reflected, shedding their worldly influence at high speed, yet continuing to weave fairy-tales and nursery-rhymes that held the rest of the world enchanted.

Xan was here to catch a train because a sudden sense of unreality had come over him. The theory he had evolved didn't seem possible. Surely such a conspiracy couldn't hold water for a day, let alone for years. If only there was an academic expert one could refer the question to. And then he had realised that once again, Giles Maybury had been ahead of him.

Oxford at first glance was unimpressive. The area around the station was an ugly mix of cheap buildings catering to the tourist industry and expensively hideous business schools. But gradually, history began to make ground until, by degrees, he found himself in a medieval landscape.

Narrow streets hemmed by stone. Huge doors studded with iron opening into forbidden courtyards. The sense of secrecy, of those locked out and locked in, reminded him of the souks of Marrakesh and Fez. The comparison seemed even more apt when he found a covered market where butchers' shops hung up whole pigs and deer alongside feathered pheasant and duck, and greengrocer establishments fought for elbow room with souvenir shops selling trinkets and leather.

The market's southern boundary abutted onto Coventry Street, a dusty alley which ran along the northern edge of Coventry College. Approaching the edifice, he observed a castellated facade and the inevitable oak door in the wall, with a smaller door cut in it for convenience. From the far side of the street (which was not very far at all), he could follow the roofline as it dropped down to a lower level over which he could make out the lazily stirring upper branches of some type of tree – willows, at a guess. These must be in some inner garden of the college.

All of which would be very useful if he were planning a covert incursion by night over that lower part of the wall. But he was going to have to do this the daylight way.

Disregarding a notice announcing that the college was closed to visitors, he stepped through the doorway into a stone archway. Beyond it was the main quadrangle of the college.

In the porter's lodge in the archway, the man behind the glass considered him alertly. "How can I help you, sir?"

Xan knew he didn't fit the usual range of possibilities – tourist ignoring or not comprehending the Closed sign, student, member of the teaching staff. At the same time, the alert look was benevolent and the 'sir' was positively encouraging.

He asked confidently for the Chancellor, knowing from the website's events page that he was well out of the way delivering a lecture at one of the other colleges.

The porter looked apologetic. "I'm afraid Sir John is unavailable until much later in the afternoon."

"Yes, he said he'd be able to spare half an hour after four. That's all right, I'll wait."

The porter was evidently unfamiliar with current threat assessment levels and offered no argument to this. "If you would just sign the visitor's book, sir."

He pulled out a vast ledger from under a desk and opened it. It looked expensive and handmade, each page whole millimetres thick.

Xan had planned a conversational gambit to distract the porter while he studied the book, but at that moment, the phone fortuitously rang, obliging the porter to turn away. Xan quickly turned the pages back. There it was, Giles Maybury's familiar signature. He had arrived to see a Dr

Murray at ten and left an hour later. An early appointment, suggesting that the matter was been urgent. And it had taken an hour to discuss. Xan glanced up at the wall, where the lecturers' rooms were listed on a carved oak board. Dr Ewan Murray, staircase 7, Room J.

The porter was finishing his call. Xan hastily turned back to the current page and filled in his details in a careless scribble.

"Thank you, Mr West." The porter evidently had form on deciphering scrawled handwriting.

The seventh staircase was, like the others, a winding stone affair with treads that had been worn down over the centuries. What must it be like to live and work inside these walls, cocooned by so much beauty and serenity? Would it lead to a tendency to forget the difficulties outside the walls?

When he knocked on the door of Room J, a young face, all sharp angles, topped by a wavy array of bright red hair peered out at him with a look of surprise.

This was mutual. Xan hurriedly discarded the eccentric and aged lecturer of his imagination as he added up his impressions. Very young, possibly younger than Xan himself. A worn green pullover with holes at the collar, over corduroy trousers of a bright mustard hue. And a pair of sharp blue eyes frowning at the unexpected visitor.

"Let's see. You can't be one of my students, of course – too old. And not one of my esteemed colleagues – at least a couple of decades too young. Not a tourist, surely? The porters can't have slipped that much."

Xan had had a cover story prepared, but on impulse, he discarded it. "I'm afraid I don't have an appointment. I wanted to ask you about a friend of mine who came to see you a couple of months ago. Giles Maybury."

"Oh, yes. I remember. He had some rather interesting questions to put to me."

"I wonder if you could tell me more about that."

"And I'm sure you have excellent reasons for asking me."

"I don't know if you'd call them excellent. But he died about a month ago. I need to know what you told him. I could say that he would want you to tell me – but of course you'd have to take my word for that."

Dr Murray grinned. "I'm a reasonably good judge of character. You'd better come in." He held the door open, then pulled up a couple of armchairs beside a cold, dead and anachronistic gas fire that looked as though it should have a Do Not Use sticker on it, before disappearing into an outer pantry of some kind.

Xan took the opportunity to glance around the room. It was high-ceilinged and oak-panelled, probably part of the oldest fabric of the college. The walls and floor would be stone, making the room cheerlessly cold in winter. It was crammed with books and papers, no computer in sight.

The lecturer reappeared carrying an old-fashioned tray supporting a teapot and two cups. His bony wrists stuck out from the cuffs of his pullover. He poured the tea and then folded himself into the other armchair. "Now, what exactly did you want to know?"

"I need to know what Maybury asked you about and what you told him. If it helps, I can make a guess."

"Go on, then," the lecturer invited.

"I think he asked you about fake memories. And I think he had a particular scenario in mind. A mass narrative imposed on an entire population. He would have wanted to know if it was possible."

Dr Murray nodded. "And I told him that in my opinion, it was. It's a pet theory of mine, of course. I wrote a paper on it. I don't suppose anyone read it."

Xan wondered whether perhaps someone had read it.

"The central thesis is that memories are malleable – astonishingly so. If I was going to set about it myself, there are three main areas to consider." Dr Murray settled back in his chair. "First, the official data. Birth certificate, parents' marriage certificates, school and health records. One individual, however determined and well-resourced, could never falsify all of that. One would need useful connections in each of those areas."

Xan nodded and the lecturer glanced at him with sharp eyes.

"Well, well. Assuming all that is in place, the second element is cultural records. In the old days, that meant newspaper clippings and the like. But that's outmoded now. Everything's online."

"Surely that would make it more difficult."

"That's what most people would think. But in fact, the availability of large amounts of data online makes it more easy to fake."

Dr Murray took another sip of tea and warmed to his task. "The other useful thing you can do online is provide digital verisimilitude to an otherwise unconvincing narrative. Supporting testimony, in other words. Create a profile on all the main social media channels going back years. School. University. Jobs. Get the whole thing on record in black and white with some doctored images."

"But what about the people who actually went to those schools and universities?"

"People's memories are wonderfully elastic things. How well do *you* remember your schooldays? Suppose you bumped into an old schoolfriend and he mentioned another classmate, someone you didn't remember at all. You look up the individual in question online and find his picture in the school photograph and a whole life profile available on social media. Would you conclude that this had all been elaborately faked or that your own memory was faulty?"

Xan began to see. "People rely on the records they can see rather than their own recollection."

Dr Murray nodded. "And if you had the right resources – discreet resources – you might indulge in a bit of memory seeding. In a memory seeding exercise, you identify targets, people who can act as advocates for your false narrative. You might identify men who had attended a specific public school, for instance. Then you send out your people primed with false memories to make contact – it would have to be done obliquely, of course. You go to your club and talk to someone whose brother was at that school and pass the false memory onto them. Do you remember when Burlington tried to keep a live frog in his shirt drawer, for instance. That's the sort of story that gets passed on. No one does remember it happening, because you made it up, but plenty of them repeat the anecdote. No one realises that they don't remember a Burlington and if anyone is puzzled, they can look him up online."

"What about the other way around? What if someone recognises your Burlington as someone else?"

"What of it? People see likenesses all the time. But if the names are different, they assume it's just a chance resemblance. And of course, ageing helps – after a few years, a certain identification becomes far less certain." Dr Murray leaned back in his chair again. "That's how it should work anyway, according to my theories."

"I think it did work."

The room was silent for a long while, except for the ticking of an old-fashioned clock on the wall. Outside the open stonework window, you might have expected to hear ordinary life going on – people's voices, traffic – but there was nothing, as though the college building was wrapped so thickly in cotton-wool that time stopped here altogether.

At length, Dr Murray said: "Of course you can't tell me who your Burlington is. But I'm presuming there is some advantage to their deceit."

"Yes."

"There are obvious advantages in certain areas of public life to having no skeletons in the closet. Politics, for instance. A perfect candidate created out of whole cloth. An ingenious notion. It makes you wonder if it's the first time they've tried it."

Xan stared. "You think –."

"I don't know what to think," Dr Murray said cheerfully. "But one has to wonder about Obama."

"That's absurd."

"Is it? Such an perfect candidate, ticking every box?"

"The records on him are surely incontrovertible."

"Let's say Macron, then. He appeared pretty much out of nowhere. Didn't even have a Party of his own."

"My candidate does," Xan said. "And I don't know how much they know. But it's pretty clear from what you've told me that you couldn't do this sort of thing on your own. The question is, what can I do about it?

"Is it doing any harm?"

"If I'm right, they've killed four people to protect this secret."

Dr Murray's bony face did not change. The red hair flamed brightly. "Well, that does rather make a difference."

"Yes. And what I need to know is – how do I prove what they've done?"

*

It was late afternoon and the shadows were stretching across the cobblestones when Xan emerged from the gateway of Coventry College. He had brought a copy of

Dr Murray's paper with him to read at his leisure.

As he walked down the narrow street, he had a sudden sense that he was being watched. Peripheral vision did not suggest any particular suspect – the student bending over his bicycle struggling with the padlock, the two girls loitering and conferring over their phones, the elderly tourists peering at a map, all looked thoroughly innocuous – yet he could not shake the feeling.

He did not try. Fieldcraft advised you always to follow the advice of your inner alarm systems, even when you couldn't see the workings. He cut through the market and then paused as the narrow street gave onto the wide, sunlit expanse of a main road and a group of cyclists flashed past him six abreast. Now he was certain he was being followed. No, not followed – surrounded.

The first two, a young couple, were loitering thirty yards back in Coventry Street, where he had come from, pretending to check their mobile phones in the shelter of a massive college gateway. The usual watcher's ploy, but less effective when two did it at once.

There was another watcher propped against a doorway in a wall on the opposite side of the road, reading a newspaper. A woman with short auburn hair unlocking her bicycle from the crowded public racks. Then two more to make sure, one outside a bookshop to the right, the other looking into a shop window fifty yards to the left. All the exits covered. But they had been careless to use some of the same people they had used at Wimbledon.

Instinctively, Xan looked at his watch. Quarter to six.

There were still plenty of ordinary people around – walkers, cyclists, joggers, shoppers. And he did not think they would try anything in front of witnesses.

He called up the map of the city he had briefly scanned in the station. This was Broad Street and the busiest shopping streets lay between this point and the station, but eventually the cheap restaurants and souvenir shops gave way to a hideous council building and an ancient castle mound. And between the castle mound and the main station was a dangerous no man's land of half-hearted businesses and far too convenient canal bridges.

If this was his operation, Xan thought, he would have someone posted at the castle mound and someone else at the station itself, in case of any slip-ups.

A large group of Italian or Spanish tourists was swirling along Broad Street towards him, following the shouted commentary of their guide, a man with a red umbrella held over his head despite the sunshine.

"On thees very spot," he announced, pointing at the middle of the road, "the martyrs of the Reformation were burrnd alive."

Xan quietly joined them. He knew he was too tall and too fair to blend in completely, but all the same, this was too good a chance to miss. By staying close to the leader with his umbrella, he could stay out of view of most of the following wolf-pack.

The tour group flowed along Broad Street as one and he let himself be swept along with them. They were heading away from the station, but it was safer than moving alone and he could double back once he lost the wolf-pack.

Exeter College, the Bodleian Library, the Bridge of Sighs – the last a ridiculously quaint, Venetian-influenced archway crossing a narrow street. The tourists milled around taking photos of the bridge, momentarily blocking the view of anyone coming along the main road. Xan took his chance and moved quietly away down the narrow street.

The sun did not reach here. The street was shadowy and silent and he was made uneasy by the sound of his own footsteps. He followed a couple of sharp turns, then unexpectedly emerged into a vast square dominated by an absurdly huge dome.

The place seemed deserted. Only a lone student straightened up from his bicycle as Xan passed – but he had seen that move before and he recognised the face now too, when it was too late. He saw the glimmer of the knife and dived to the left, a desperate feint, kicking over the bicycle and hearing it clatter to the paving-stones as the man closed on him.

For a moment, they were rolling in the gutter, each one struggling for a position of greater gravitational force – but the other man had the advantage because he was armed. The only way to neutralise the flashing knife was to reach for it and hold it fast, while using the pivotal force of your other arm to smash your opponent's head against the cobbles. Then reach with your free hand for his throat and apply pressure on the main artery until he lost consciousness.

Xan got to his feet slowly. Homeland would advise a second blow to the head to make sure. But Homeland had no experience of operating in this land with its Alice in Wonderland logic. He remembered suddenly that the very notion of Alice in Wonderland had been born here in this city and then wondered why he felt so light-headed and was focusing on irrelevancies.

He pulled up his shirt and sweater a little and saw the blood beginning to well from a long, deep cut over his ribs. Hurriedly, he fished in his pockets and found a handkerchief to press against the wound. He needed to get off the street and win a moment to recover and plan his next move.

He went round the vast dome to put it between him and his pursuers, then turned at random down another side-street. It was shuttered by tall stone buildings with closed windows.

No help to be found here. But then, unexpectedly, a break in the roofline. A smaller building in Art Deco style painted white, with an open door from which light and music spilled out. A poster declaimed: 'The Mikado – performed by the University Gilbert & Sullivan Society'.

A piece of musical theatre. It might not be to his taste but it was sanctuary, of a kind.

Xan took a second to gather his composure. The assembling audience appeared to be a mix of middle-class, middle-aged affluence (a flowery dress here, a Fair Isle sweater there) combined with students revelling in their own scruffiness. A heterogenous-enough crowd therefore for him to blend into.

His lack of a ticket seemed more likely to be a problem but it appeared that the Society did not trouble itself with such capitalist concerns. Along with the rest of the crowd, he was swept into a small, whitewashed hall with at one end an unpromising-looking bare stage and a piano and the rest of the space filled with rows of equally discouraging hard chairs.

Xan chose a chair at the edge of a row. A moment later, someone stopped beside him and he braced himself for a challenge. Instead, a kindly woman thrust a glass of wine into his hand.

"It's complimentary with the ticket. I hope you enjoy it. They've been practising for ages, although some of the high notes are still a bit of a challenge."

The wine was a literal life-saver. The alcohol and sugar flooded vigour into his veins to replace the lost blood. He sat still as the hall filled up around him. Then a tall, thin young man slid archly onto the piano stool and struck up a chord.

Musical theatre had never been to Xan's taste, but he was only too willing to let the dramatically declaimed dialogue and the thumping piano accompaniment wash over him while his mind ranged feverishly over what to do next.

There was a sound at the back of the hall and he turned his head sharply to see two men peering into the room. One was short and balding, with black eyes like currants, the other thin and gaunt, with the dead eyes of the fairground hawker. The girl from the front desk was urging them to take a seat.

Someone was singing a ballad that seemed to have at least a dozen verses. At this moment, Xan would have exchanged all his trade-craft for an accurate knowledge of the libretto of The Mikado. When did the damn thing get to the interval?

Another chorus, another solo number and finally a series of bows onstage. Xan kept to his seat until the rest of the audience had begun to get to its feet and mill around. Once again, it was the cover he needed. He pulled himself awkwardly to his feet, discreetly holding the handkerchief in place over his wound with his left hand.

There was no hope of manoeuvring his way through the crowd surging instinctively towards the entrance-hall in the hope of refreshments. And besides, danger lay that way. Instead, he went up the steps onto the stage, picked up the nearest stage prop that could be managed with one hand (a pot-plant) and made his way back-stage with it. The people pursuing him would have little chance of making any headway through a purposeful music theatre crowd bent on purchasing interval refreshments.

He ducked past a couple of dressing-rooms and then set down the pot-plant in a corner as he spotted the hoped-for rear exit. As he tried the door, he heard a commotion somewhere behind him in the auditorium. Perhaps his pursuers had lost patience and decided to try and force their way through the throng.

The door opened and he slipped through and let it fall

softly shut behind him. Outside, there was blessed darkness and silence. Quietly, he began to make his way towards livelier streets where there would be crowds, witnesses, buses to the station.

He found himself in another narrow lane, this time with gargoyles ranged along the roof-tops. Monstrous faces glared down at him in medieval horror, interspersed with scorpions, crabs and less celestially significant squirrels and rats. Then he came out onto the wide, curving High Street, its stone facades ghostly in the moonlight. The shops were closed and there were few people around and there would be no cover in this well-lit street. He became aware that he was getting tired.

A car was coming slowly up the street. There was no reason to suppose it belonged to his hunters, but just in case, he retreated into the darkness of a stone porch. The car slid gently into view – an expensive-looking model. It stopped only a few yards away. The passenger window on his side was open and he saw a hand impatiently drumming on the side of the car. One finger wore a signet ring.

Xan dared not move a muscle. The slightest sound or movement might be enough to betray his presence. But then suddenly, he realised that the big oak door behind him was open and a crack of light showed. He pushed the door a little further open and slipped cautiously inside.

From the outside, the building's purpose had not been apparent. It was only once he was inside that he realised it was a church. High ceilings soared above him. Carved stone faces gazed disapprovingly from walls. Muted lamps were glowing for the convenience of night-time worshippers.

Xan had never been religious. If he had ever felt the pull of it, it had died in him at the time of his mother's funeral. Since then, he had got along very well without higher powers. But now he found himself approaching the altar as though some sort of revelation awaited.

There was nothing there, of course. Candles, statues, paintings, emptiness. But then a woman came quietly out of a doorway. She wore no robes of office, but even in her off-duty clothes and a pair of shabby trainers, her authority was unquestionable. "Can I help you?"

Xan held her eye contact, willing her not to look down and see his fingers pressing the handkerchief against his side. "No, thank you."

"If you want guidance, you have only to ask for it, but I don't think you do, do you? What do you want?"

"Sanctuary." Afterwards, he was not sure whether he had said it or only thought it. But just then, he heard the sound of the motor-car purring away up the street. The way behind him was clear.

The vicar smiled gravely and went back through the door she had come from. No doubt she was accustomed to troubled individuals who wandered into churches and couldn't explain what they wanted.

As he walked back down the aisle, silence surged back into the church and the stone statues seemed to settle back to their centuries of rest. But it was then that he heard the handle of the door turning. The car's departure had been a ruse.

On the left of the main door was a set of stone steps leading upwards. He went up them and found himself in an open gallery that looked down on the whole church. He slipped into the front pew and leaned forward with his arms resting on the balcony wall. He dropped his head onto his folded arms as though to pray and listened, straining his ears.

Footsteps hesitatingly advancing into the church. Two sets, possibly three. If they headed straight towards the altar as most people would, he could make a silent retreat without being spotted. He risked a quick glance downwards, resting his chin on his arms.

The two figures advanced down the centre aisle and then fanned out, the expected move, into the little chapels to each side.

Now was the time to move, but Xan's tired muscles would not do as they were told. And suddenly, there was a further sound from below – the third man he had not been sure about was ascending the stairs. And he had nowhere to go.

Xan cast silently around for a weapon and his left hand closed on a hymn-book. Not very appropriate in a place of holy ground, perhaps, but a book made a heavy and sharp-edged weapon and if it struck right, it could inflict substantial injury. He drew back into the shadows of an alcove and waited.

A moment later, the man emerged at the top of the

stairs. He was one of those Xan had seen at the concert-hall – chunky and balding, with eyes like black currants. His face was dispassionate – this was just a job. The eyes flicked around alertly, looking for his quarry.

Xan moved from the shadows like lightning. The chunky man was quick to see the danger and dodged, but not quickly enough. The heavy book found its mark, smashing into his face. He staggered backwards, but as Xan moved to follow up his advantage, the chunky man somehow regained his balance and came forward again, head down, like a bull. And now it was Xan's turn to dodge the barrelling charge which almost knocked him backwards into the pews.

He dropped the book, which wasn't helping now, and twisted out of the way. His knife-wound from earlier was bleeding freely again – he needed to finish this fast. He pulled himself back to his feet to see that the chunky man had paused to wipe the blood out of his eyes.

It was now or never. Xan bunched his fist carefully – do it wrong and you could break your thumb – and hit the chunky man precisely at the point on the side of the head, above the ear and level with the eyes, where the skull is weakest. The other man reeled back dizzily, struggling to regain his balance, and came up hard against the stone gallery balustrade.

He clawed at the air frantically for purchase, his centre of gravity too high to right himself. Xan instinctively reached out a hand, but it was too late. The other man crumpled suddenly backwards. For one second, he was a floundering, flapping bat in mid-air. The next, he became a huddled heap of clothing on the stone flags below.

When Xan looked over, a pool of darkness had begun to form around the broken body on the floor and the vicar was bending over him, her face horrified. "God bless my soul."

Forgive me, Father, for I have sinned, Xan thought. There would be no sanctuary today.

CHAPTER 36

Jemima was curled up in the sitting-room reading by the light of the shabby standard-lamp she had rescued from a charity-shop. But her book did not seem to hold her attention. Perhaps the rain was to blame – it had been battering the window-panes ever since she got home. The room felt big and dark and full of shadows.

At eleven, she gave up on the book. A decent night's sleep was required if she was going to be any use at all at the office tomorrow. But as she switched out the lamp, a jarring ringing sound reverberated suddenly through the empty flat, making her start nervously. It took a few jumpy seconds to realise it was her own doorbell.

Caution dictated that a single girl living alone did not answer the door at such an hour. At the same time, she reasoned, anyone coming to her door at such a time must have an urgent reason for doing so.

She went downstairs and opened the door cautiously on the chain and found Xan leaning against the door jamb as though it were the only thing keeping him upright.

"I'm sorry," he said wearily. "I shouldn't have come here."

A number of questions sprang to mind but she pushed them all hurriedly aside. He looked terrible – distracted, exhausted, worried, perhaps a combination of all three. Her fingers struggled to undo the unfamiliar catch on the door chain and then she clutched his arm as though he might otherwise fade insubstantially back into the darkness and dragged him into the hall.

Upstairs, the ugly kitchen strip lighting turned the whole room to dazzling white and she could see that it hurt his eyes. She turned off the main light and switched on the oven hood lamp and the stupid ambient display lighting over the worktops instead.

Mags was in his box in the corner. His tail twitched a little, but he did not stir.

She said: "What *happened*?"

"I got caught in a storm."

"Well, I can see that. You'd better have a hot drink – or at least…" She remembered his aversion to tea. What on earth did one do with someone who didn't drink tea? Then she remembered her impulsive decision to make a Christmas cake the year before last.

She hunted in the back of the food cupboard until she unearthed a small, flat bottle that was still half-full. She poured some into a tea mug and thrust it at him. "Drink this."

"What is it?"

"Cooking brandy."

He grimaced a little but swallowed a few mouthfuls, finding that it made things begin to swing back into alignment. For the first time since he had stumbled onto the London train at Oxford station, he could think clearly again.

What the hell had he been thinking, coming here? He didn't remember consciously deciding to do so – in fact, he didn't remember making any kind of logical decision at all after the train reached Paddington. He must have been half-delirious.

He looked across the kitchen and saw that she was watching him steadily. He groped in the back of his mind for some explanation or apology that would make sense but found nothing. Instead, he said again: "I'm sorry about turning up like this."

"Don't be silly. I'm glad you did. You frightened the life out of me," she said without much logic. She added as briskly as she could manage: "Your coat's soaked. You'd better take it off."

He began wearily to pull the dripping raincoat off. But even in the dim light, it was clear that the rain had drenched him well beyond his coat. His sweater was also dark with water. She looked at him in dismay. "You're soaked through!"

"I'm afraid so." He smiled faintly. "I can't remove anything else, though, in the interests of respectability."

"Don't be ridiculous." She took the coat from him and hung it over the banister on the landing. When she went back into the kitchen, he had removed his sweater but he was still standing, leaning against the kitchen counter, as though he lacked the energy to do anything else. And she drew in her breath sharply as she saw the crimson stain spreading over his damp shirt.

"You're hurt. And don't tell me it's just a scratch. What happened to you?"

"I went to Oxford, to talk to a university lecturer. He gave me tea."

"Okay."

He grinned ruefully. "It doesn't sound very hazardous so far, I'll admit. But someone must have followed me there. They jumped me when I came out."

Jemima was proud to achieve a tone of voice that was almost matter of fact. "How bad is it?"

"Not too bad."

She dismissed that as the half-lie it was. "Shouldn't you be at the hospital?"

"I'd rather not. Lots of questions."

"Well, I've got some first aid stuff in the bathroom. Not very much, but it will have to do."

The bathroom was next to the kitchen and was small even for one person. Jemima looked round it helplessly. "You'd better sit on the edge of the bath."

He concentrated on getting his shirt off while Jemima assembled everything from the bathroom cabinet, which was awkwardly-placed at head height. A clean flannel, nail scissors, antiseptic solution, bandage, surgical tape. Her hands were shaking so much, she almost dropped the bottle of antiseptic.

She placed everything as carefully as she could on the wash-basin and ran some hot water into the sink. For a moment, she stared at herself in the mirror, trying to steady her nerves. A strange girl looked back at her, face drained of colour, eyes wide.

Xan glanced at her. “What is it?”

“Nothing. I think you’d be better off with a proper A&E nurse.”

“I don’t want a proper A&E nurse.”

“I’m afraid I’ll hurt you.”

“I wouldn’t worry about that.”

The girl in the mirror looked back at her, disgusted by her lack of courage. She turned away from the mirror and forced herself to look at him properly. She could now see the long cut under his ribs, its edges disguised by blood.

“It’s not as bad as it looks,” he said reassuringly.

And in the event, the clean-up was not as difficult as she had feared. The wound was not a deep one. She tried to think of it as nothing more dramatic than a grazed knee. It was simply a matter of cleaning off the dried blood and bathing the cut with disinfectant solution.

Once the wound was clean and dry, she bandaged it with the gauze and the tape. “There.”

He pulled himself cautiously to his feet. “Thank you.”

“It’s rather amateurish, I’m afraid. But I’m no expert on this sort of thing.”

“It looks good to me. But I’m sorry I put you through it.”

“Don’t be silly. It’s not your fault I’m so squeamish. And do you really think I’d rather you’d gone off to some hospital in the middle of the night where no one knows you?”

He smiled. “I don’t know, would you?”

"I don't know," Jemima said lamely.

There was something in his eyes she couldn't interpret. Then suddenly he was beside her, seeming very tall in the cramped bathroom. He was pulling her into his arms and kissing her in a reckless, impatient way that left her breathless. For a moment, time didn't seem to exist at all. Then he banged his elbow against the cabinet, cursed softly and let her go. "This room is too small."

She laughed shakily. "It wasn't designed for this."

"I shouldn't have done it anyway. I'm sorry, Jem."

"Why shouldn't you?" She was very carefully putting the things back in the bathroom cabinet, as though the world depended on her arranging everything precisely in its place.

"For one thing, because it's late at night and I turned up here uninvited. For another, because you don't know very much about me except what I've told you. And that reminds me – there's something I need to tell you about, if I could keep my mind on my job for five minutes."

"You'd better come back into the kitchen," she said. "I'll make some coffee. And if you want me to listen to whatever it is you want to tell me, you'd better put your shirt back on."

In the kitchen, correctly attired – or as correct as was possible for a man whose torn and bloodstained shirt was past salvaging – he told her about Mark Romilly's secret.

"Are you really serious about this?" She stared at him incredulously. She was leaning against the kitchen counter, holding a mug of coffee she was forgetting to drink. Her newly-shorn hair, too short now to plait or tie back, fell forward against her cheek.

Xan had prudently propped himself against the window on the other side of the kitchen and was stroking the dog's ears industriously. "Completely serious."

"But it's insane."

"Perhaps. But Giles Maybury suspected it before I did. And how else do you explain the photograph?"

"All the same, I simply can't believe it. He's a *Minister*. And besides, I've met him and he's a nice person."

"Well, that's the point, isn't it? He's playing a part. And in any case, I don't believe he was behind the murders himself. In fact, he can't have been. Their whole plan is designed to make him a credible leadership candidate – they would be crazy to risk that by letting him get mixed up in a murder case. I'd be prepared to bet he has an alibi for every single one of these murders – not a suspiciously cast-iron one, just something nicely natural-looking."

"All the same, I don't believe you'll get anyone else to believe this."

"Not without proof. But I have a feeling I know where to get it." He grinned suddenly. "Detectives shouldn't rely on feelings, as you're about to point out. But I'm waiting on a phone-call from a disreputable source."

"Well, there must be something I can do too."

"There isn't." He glanced across the kitchen at her. "I mean it, Jem. You work in Romilly's department."

"It's recess, remember – he isn't here."

"Yes, but someone else in that place must be involved.

Someone who changed the classification for Paradine's file. You can't afford to be noticed." He looked out of the kitchen window that gave onto a rather the ugly back-yard, frowning. "If it comes to that, I don't really like you being here on your own either."

"I have a guard dog," Jemima said encouragingly.

"And I've never seen that dog do anything other than wag his tail at strangers." He took a swallow of coffee and glanced at his watch ruefully. "I'd better go."

"Do you have to? It's the middle of the night?" Too late, she heard her own words and blushed furiously. "I didn't mean that the way it sounded. But you're hurt and it's raining and it's after midnight. And I have a sofa," she offered lamely.

He laughed. "I know, I've seen it."

"It's not nearly as bad as it looks. But I know, you're expecting a phone-call from a disreputable source. Is it your friend Mr Dangerfield?"

"Not this time. And I'm not sure Billy is a friend of mine."

"You ought to trust people more."

"It doesn't really go with the territory."

She started to say something, then stopped abruptly. But people in his line of work were practised, after all, in hearing what people didn't say.

He put down his coffee and came over to her. "On the other hand, all the best detectives know when to break their own rules."

She smiled faintly. "Do they?"

"Definitely."

As he walked back along Columbine Road towards the station, he found that the storm had lessened. And if the stone angels in the graveyard across the street thought anything in particular, they kept their heavenly counsel to themselves for once.

CHAPTER 37

The station waiting-room was cold and dark and Xan was glad of his sweater. From the window of the train, the huddle of stone walls and slate roofs in the moonlight had looked cosy, almost Christmassy, but in the time that he had been dozing on the hard wooden bench, the chill had begun to set in.

After he had left the flat in Columbine Road, he had called Flannery from a phone-box, then waited at King's Cross for a train going north. By the time one rumbled in, drums were beating and bells ringing in his head again and it had been all he could do to pull himself onto the train and drop into a corner seat. He had dozed a little and only just wakened in time to get out at the right stop.

The connecting train he wanted would not come in until half past nine in the morning. Until then, he was as well off here as anywhere. An owl called repeatedly outside, somewhere in the moonlit darkness.

He pulled his coat closer around him and stretched his feet out and let his thought roam outwards through the silent countryside as though he could traverse it like the owl. This other Eden, demi-paradise.

At five, he got up and left the station. The place showed itself by daylight as a small town with a main square and a clock-tower. It was all built in the honey-coloured stone they seemed to use hereabouts for everything and it looked peaceful and a long way from murder.

He suddenly discovered that he was hungry and turned into a lorry drivers' cafe. Tired, unshaven and travel-stained, he looked little different from the haulage men who had been driving all night.

He ordered a substantial breakfast of eggs, bacon and toast. But when he mentioned coffee, the girl behind the counter looked dubious.

"Coffee-maker's on the blink. And we're out of instant. Better have tea."

About to refuse, he stopped himself. Why not, after all? When the food came, he ate it abstractedly, watching out of the window as the dawn routine got under way in the square. Postman, milkman, delivery vans, joggers and dog-walkers. Shop-owners pulling up their blinds and putting their noticeboards out on the pavement.

One could get used to this, he thought – perhaps even become part of the pattern oneself. Give up the security profession, move to the countryside, perhaps even marry and settle down. There was a pleasant warmth in the thought. He was also suddenly conscious of an unfamiliar but agreeable sensation of physical wellbeing that seemed to emanate through his tired muscles. He looked down and realised that he had drunk the entire cup of tea.

He went back over the conversation with Flannery. He had called him from just outside King's Cross at just after one in the morning. "Have you found anything?"

"Do you know what time it is?"

"I'm in a hurry."

A long expiration, or alternatively it could have been a yawn, Xan decided. "Go away."

"Did you find him?"

"I can't be sure what I'm looking for, can I? But yeah, I came up with someone – the only Tom Riley the right age. But good luck with finding him."

"I don't think I will find him. That's the point," Xan said patiently. "I just need to know where he lived."

This time, it was definitely a yawn, an ear-splitting one. "Grew up in a place called Ashbury somewhere in the West Midlands. Sounds a dead-end sort of town."

"Thank you, that's all I need."

"Well, congratulations." And the call had disconnected with suspicious haste. And Xan had gone into the ticket office at King's Cross Station and looked at the maps and learned that the only way of getting to Ashbury without waiting for the northern express in the morning was to take the late Cardiff train and change at Woolbridge.

So, he had taken the late Cardiff train. Now here he was in Woolbridge and it was nearly nine. He walked back to the station and caught the train to Coalport.

The journey north took him into different territory. The landscape became emptier, with wider prospects of land stretching towards hills beyond. Occasionally, the train stopped at large manufacturing towns, whose factories and distribution depots clamoured at the sky and belched chemicals bad-temperedly into wide and sluggish rivers.

He took out the poetry book again and turned the pages, as though reading it would give him some insight into the man he was chasing. At a casual glance, there was little he could readily relate to.

Coalport was, as the name suggested, an industrial port – not on the coast, but straddling a large river with high mud banks and thick, sludgy water. At the station, he bought a single ticket to Ashbury, not having wished to advertise his exact destination to the clerk at King's Cross.

This time, it was a two-carriage train that bumped its way along a narrow track, hemmed in by overgrown hedges and trees on both sides until it began to look as though the woods would reclaim the track altogether. It did not suggest much for the prosperity of Ashbury.

Somehow, Xan had the feeling that he would find what he wanted at the end of this track. But of course, as he had confidently assured Jemima, investigators didn't rely on feelings.

*

When he alighted at Ashbury Station, he found that the place was bigger than he expected. The wide streets were lined with buildings of unexpected grandeur – eighteenth century by the look of them, and yet all with a look of decay. In the grand town-houses, the front doors hung loosely on their hinges and the sash window-frames were rotten, with paint flaking off.

It felt like a ghost town. Many of the buildings had windows boarded up and dusty For Sale signs. He passed an old mill-works. A splendid town hall, also boarded up. Then an ornate pillared building which advertised itself as a public swimming baths For The Health And Physical Benefit Of The Needy, founded 1850 by Sir Geoffrey Bellingham.

A local benefactor, Xan guessed. There were further tributes to the munificence of Sir Geoffrey in the form of a statue in the town square, a plaque on the wall of what had evidently once been a primary school and another one above the door of the public library.

So this was Romilly's home town. What would Romilly think if he came back here? Probably he never would – he must have been warned to stay away. But it was curious to be treading these pavements in his place.

It didn't matter. He had a job to do. What was he looking for exactly? School records? (Hardly, with no school.) Health records? But local authorities didn't keep records like that any longer. And besides, he was not dealing with amateurs. The people behind Mark Romilly had had ten years to cover their tracks and they would have started here, where Tom Riley grew up.

For want of a better idea, he called in at the library.

"I'm afraid," the stooped man at the information desk said apologetically, "we destroyed a lot of our old records a few years ago. So much is stored online that it seemed unnecessary. And besides, we found that in many cases, we were actually keeping it *illegally*. All these confusing changes in the law. I'm sure you'll understand. It was a question of either trying to track down every individual about whom we held any records or destroying it all and we simply don't have the resources."

Xan asked about local newspapers and his informant shook his head regretfully.

"Closed down, I'm afraid, a matter of ten years ago. It's difficult for local media to make a living these days. And their records went with them. Now we have no local newspaper – a great loss to the community. We do have a blog, of course."

But Xan was not interested in a blog. Instead, seeing that the librarian seemed well-disposed to questions, he put a tactful query about the history of Ashbury and its empty streets.

"Same story as a lot of places in this part of the world, I'm afraid. We lost the manufacturing work. And when the jobs went, the youngsters went."

"Where did they go? It must have been tough finding jobs anywhere."

"Hard to know." The librarian gazed thoughtfully at the nearest stack of books as though he might find the answer there. "Of course, a lot of them went to the Army."

In a back room, Xan found a set of old telephone directories. There were one or two Riley families but over the decades, the frequent appearance of an address at No 32 Victoria Street.

It was not too difficult to find Victoria Street, a narrow road that suggested no obvious reason for naming it after a monarch. The houses were small and crowded close together. Number 32 was no different from its fellows.

When he rang the doorbell, it was answered, after a long wait, by an elderly woman with a headscarf bound round her head. When he put a tentative question about previous residents, she shook her head. "Me, I do not know. I am not from here. I come here seven months. I am Polska."

"And your neighbours?" he suggested.

Another shake of the head. "Romanian. Yes, and Turkish. And none here for longer than a year."

It was clear that he would find no one in this street who remembered long-ago Rileys.

In the churchyard at the end of the street, he found, as expected, many elaborate Bellingham memorials featuring marble Bibles and long inscriptions, but no recent burials. Presumably the family had moved away when the local industries failed and taken the wealth of the town with them.

He explored the further end of the churchyard, where the ground sloped sharply down towards the distant river and gravestones looked in danger of toppling down into the ditch that ran alongside the hedge.

Here, a riot of nettles and brambles presided over mossed-over headstones and grass-choked graves. In many places, the ground had caved in, leaving gaping holes. A malicious bramble snagged at his sleeve and as he turned to disentangle it, he saw the name he was looking for, almost illegible, on a crumbling gravestone.

There were only three Riley graves. An Alice Riley born in 1908 who had died in the fifties. A child with no name who had died at only three days old in 1964. And Gerald and Anne Riley, buried together some time in the early nineteen-eighties.

No Tom Riley. But one would not expect that. What, in fact, would one expect? The sun came out with a sudden weak ray of sunshine and a blackbird flew down and perched on Alice Riley's headstone.

"How did they do it?" he asked it. "You can't just make a man disappear. People here must have known him."

The blackbird put its head on one side, as though to consider the matter, and then flew off to an overgrown apple tree.

He left the churchyard by a side gate that brought him out on another empty street. A flyblown pub, an antique shop (closed), launderette (closed) and a museum. He strolled into the museum, where a woman presiding over a dusty reception area looked startled to see a visitor and tried to urge him politely in the direction of the gift-shop.

The museum comprised a few large rooms filled with displays of Roman coins turned up in fields during the ploughing. A shabby staircase led up to the first floor, where – investigators should receive danger money for persistence in the face of this sort of thing, he felt – there were further displays of stuffed animals with sad glass eyes, indifferent watercolours and an exhibition of turn-of-the-century biscuit tins.

Beyond the biscuit tins, a dusty velvet curtain hung,

screening off what appeared to be a lumber room full of rubbish.

Xan pushed the curtain aside to find a jumbled array of chests and boxes, broken chairs piled on top of them, all dimly lit by a small, high window where a bee buzzed forlornly, caught in a cobweb.

He might have not gone any further if it had not been for the bee's agitated buzzing, which prompted him to scramble awkwardly past the piles of boxes to reach the window. The glass was grimy with dust and cobwebs and he had to apply considerable pressure to the catch to force it open. With the aid of a crumpled piece of paper, he manoeuvred the bee free of its gossamer threads and it bumbled noisily out into the sunlight.

To make a job of it, he brushed the rest of the cobwebs and dust off the glass. A hopeful ray of afternoon sunlight illuminated the tea-chests and racks of dusty clothing. It would have been nice if it had suddenly picked out the location of the hidden treasure he was hunting for, but it did not. However, he took advantage of its light to unfold the crumpled piece of paper. It was a label, written in marker pen in the aggressive capital letters that mark out an educational establishment.

ASHBURY ST JAMES PRIMARY SCHOOL –
DISPLAY MATERIALS.

CHAPTER 38

The All England Lawn Tennis & Croquet Club seemed forlorn and empty out of the tennis season. The walkways were quiet and the cappuccino-vendors, strawberries and cream outlets and programme-sellers Xan would have remembered were gone. But the museum and the shop were open and when Jemima asked about a tour of the show-courts, she learned that it was possible, at a price.

Despite her best intentions, she had been unable to face going into the office. She was too disturbed by what had happened the evening before. Her mind showed it to her in a series of melodramatic stills. Xan leaning against the door-frame in the rain looking drained and exhausted. His bloodstained shirt. The bottle of brandy. Her face staring at her in the bathroom mirror. Now he was heaven knew where, looking for proof that would bring a government minister down – a man she knew and respected.

To distract herself, she had tried to occupy her mind with other aspects of the puzzle – for instance, the murder that had started things off, for Xan anyway. This had led her to the tricky question of the man who had come in from outside and she had come up with an idea. And this had prompted a sudden eagerness to see the fabled Centre Court for herself.

She had therefore taken a day off (it was all very well for Xan and his 'I'm on vacation') and taken the train to Wimbledon.

Now she sat high up in the stands on the Centre Court, looking down at the green lawn that was the heart of things as far as the tennis world was concerned. No one seemed at all interested in her presence until a man with sandy hair who had been standing watching her with a quizzical expression for some time at last climbed the stairs to where she was sitting.

"You seem very interested in this seat."

Jemima glanced up warily, seeing that he was not a steward. He looked in his late thirties and had sandy hair and an intelligent look.

He displayed a badge. "I'm an inspector from Scotland Yard. My name is Nash."

Jemima's interest sharpened at once. "Are you here because you've got a new lead?"

The inspector's sandy eyebrows rose. "Interested in the case, are you?"

"Sort of." It seemed unwise to explain her connection with the Department. Instead, she offered an explanation which seemed safer. "A friend of mine was here when it happened and gave the alarm."

Inspector Nash sighed. "You'd be referring to Mr Ross."

Jemima glanced at him uneasily. "You know him? But of course, you must have questioned him."

"I did. And did he happen to mention that he's one of

the most suspicious people in the case?"

"Of course he did. But it's absurd. He'd never met Mr Maybury before. And besides, he said that the murderer almost certainly came in from outside. Well, I've been trying to figure out how and I've got an idea."

"Have you now?"

"There's no need to laugh," she said severely.

"I assure you, I'd be only too thankful if anyone had an idea that would solve the blast – that is, the wretched case." Inspector Nash dropped into the seat the other side of the aisle and looked all ears.

"Well, it seems pretty clear that the murderer couldn't have had a ticket for the same court as Mr Maybury. Unless they went together, that would have been a ridiculous coincidence. But he could have got into the grounds quite easily. I daresay the police have their own ideas about that."

"Perhaps," Inspector Nash said woodenly.

"And once you're in the grounds, you can walk into the outer section of Centre Court without being challenged. I think they knew where Mr Maybury was sitting and which entrance he would use. Then you would just need to wait outside and get onto the court at a change of ends – it didn't even have to be the closest entrance to Mr Maybury's seat. And that's where my idea comes in."

The inspector waited expectantly.

"I've talked to the stewards. When people first arrive, they look after their ticket very carefully, but once they get onto court, they stop worrying about it. And when they go out for a break, they often carry it casually while they're taking off their sunglasses or holding a drink or most likely of all, looking at their phone. It would be easy enough for a professional to pinch someone's ticket without them even noticing. Then you go straight onto the court. The other person won't notice they're missing their ticket until they come back two games later and by then you've gone."

"And the ticket?"

"You drop it on your way out and someone hands it to the steward, so when the real owner complains of having lost it, it can be handed back to them."

Inspector Nash considered the proposition. It was really rather ingenious. "It might work," he admitted.

"Of course it would work," Jemima said decisively. "But the snag is that there's no way of proving it. I mean, you could interview the stewards yourself, but probably all they could tell you –."

"Is that people do mislay their tickets sometimes," agreed the inspector. "And of course, it doesn't rule out anyone who was on the court. Someone who produced a ticket when asked but wasn't too eager to explain where he got it from. Someone in an, er, adventurous line of work. A professional, if I might put it that way."

Jemima said sharply: "If you're talking about Mr Ross again, that's absurd."

"I expect you're right, Miss," the inspector said in the tactful voice people use when they are humouring you. "You seem to have very strong feelings on the matter."

Jemima blushed.

CHAPTER 39

The village of Hamblefield dozed in its fold in the hills, hemmed by fields of ripened wheat and fallow spaces where horses stood switching their tails under oak-trees. Closer to the village, an agricultural show was under way in the main field by the river, with farm animals being herded into pens and people in quilted jackets and caps carrying megaphones.

In the first field, animal pens were crammed together for inspection. In the second, a giant marquee showcased gardening and culinary accomplishments. Beyond this, a ploughing competition was attracting attention from what looked like both professional and amateur experts.

Xan found himself glancing into a box of caged ferrets and they returned his look philosophically. Being caged was not much of a proposition for anyone, man or beast.

Xan was here for a curious purpose. He wanted another look at the man he suspected of being caught up in a murderous conspiracy. An agricultural show might be an excellent spot at which to appraise a man, alongside all those spectators assessing Shire horses, bulls and rams against a variety of measures.

Xan's own measures were not physical but emotional. Steady nerves. The ability to focus. Fast reflexes. And the most important one of all, the capacity to weigh up risk and make a rapid decision. Would Mark Romilly, in short, look like a man who knew that a series of murders had been committed on his behalf in the last two months?

Of course, he might not know what had been going on. But whatever else the Party sought in its leaders, a level of intelligence must surely be a standard requirement.

Xan had come to Hamblefield on the first train after spending the night in a hotel at Coalport. In his jacket pocket, closely guarded, was the proof he had found. It might not be enough on its own, but it was something.

He turned his attention back to the show. According to the printed programme, Romilly was due to make a speech at around 2pm. It seemed a long time to wait.

*

Joining the trickle of civil servants flowing into Westminster House at just before nine in the morning, Jemima felt like an impostor. She was no longer the person they thought she was – she had become someone new, with dangerous, troubling thoughts.

Her mind flashed back and forth between a dead body sprawled on the shingle under a stormy sky, a man she hardly knew leaning against her door in the rain, his face drawn with exhaustion, and another man she knew and liked, who might be guilty of terrible crimes.

She had never questioned her faith in the Department before – it seemed so big and permanent, with its granite and marble. One felt as though the people in it were also made of granite and marble. But perhaps people, like buildings, were made up inside of frayed carpets and peeling wallpaper, fault-lines where you did not think to look.

Now she sat in the big room, listening to the ticking of the old-fashioned analogue clock on the wall, thinking her troubling thoughts and watching her colleagues at work. Each of them sensing the absence like a presence, the ministers around whom this edifice was built. Only she knew that one was a hollow man, a centre that could not hold – not for long anyway, not if Xan found what he was looking for. And then what? In her mind's eye, she saw the grand edifice of Westminster House crumble into dust like the Royal House of Charn.

With sudden impatience, Jemima sat up and turned her computer screen towards her. There were certain things she wanted to know. For one thing, who had changed the labels on the files? It wouldn't have been Romilly himself – the whole point of all this was to protect him. But how many people had the necessary level of access? She had an idea about how to find out. But first, she intended to study the Minister's diary.

She would not be able to access his private diary of course, but there would be the sanitised version published on the Department intranet during Parliamentary sessions and another one maintained by Romilly's constituency office. It would be interesting to see what activities had been put in place for the junior minister to keep him out of harm's way on the critical dates.

After half an hour, she sat back and looked at the notes she had scribbled. Reverend Paradine had died on the day that Mark Romilly had lunched at the Ritz and bumped into Giles Maybury. Was that an incriminating fact or wasn't it? It suggested that Maybury had somehow given not only himself away but Adam Paradine.

At any rate, Romilly had returned to the office after lunch and got through a whole stack of submissions with his Private Secretary. And then in the evening, when Reverend Paradine was killed, Mark Romilly had been at the House speaking in a late debate – an unimpeachable alibi and hardly one that could be stood up in a few hours.

On the Saturday, Romilly's constituency engagement diary showed that when Giles Maybury was murdered at Wimbledon, he had been chairing a traffic committee in Bray.

Those committees were organised weeks in advance, of course. But the day before, Romilly had gone on a fact-finding tour of an armaments factory which Jemima knew for a fact had not been planned at all. Sally, the senior events officer, had told her that the tour had been stood up at a moment's notice. And Romilly himself, Jemima remembered, had complained bitterly about having to go, according to Sally.

What did that prove? Nothing at all. But it suggested certain things – for instance that, as Xan had thought, they had perhaps planned for Mr Maybury to be murdered on the Friday, not the Saturday. And that Mark Romilly had not known what his alibi was for.

Then there was Rabbit's death. Could it really have been only a week ago? At any rate, the entire weekend was blocked out in Mark Romilly's constituency diary, suggesting a private engagement. Perhaps a house party planned months ago, or perhaps just a hastily arranged weekend away, somewhere far enough from Ilvercombe to make it the only alibi he needed.

"What on earth are you doing?"

Jemima started guiltily. Geraldine had paused by her desk. With dismay, she saw the other woman's eyes drop to the piece of paper by her keyboard, on which she had scribbled down the all-important dates.

"I was just looking up a set of contact dates for Pensions Branch," she said hurriedly. And before Geraldine could enquire any further into this spurious story, she plunged recklessly onwards. "I had a call from the security branch. They wanted to know how many people in the building have got administrator access to the records database. It's for a data protection audit."

This, Jemima thought proudly, was a very plausible line. Departmental reviews of data protection processes had proliferated like weeds over the last few years.

As she had anticipated, Geraldine took the question for granted. "Well, I had to trim the list right down last year after the last one. They said there were too many people on it and some of them had no business case for it. So now it's just our team. Just the five of us."

The words echoed mockingly around Jemima's head as

Geraldine moved away. Just the five of them – herself, Geraldine, Paul, Alicia and Jade. Unless Geraldine was wrong or lying, it must have been one of the other four who had changed the classification of David Paradine's file.

But how could it be any of them? Geraldine fretted if a stationery cupboard was left unlocked overnight. A secret like this would terrify her to death. It couldn't be her.

Paul, then. His candidly-confessed misanthropy must be a factor. But would a man who didn't even like attending team meetings become part of a criminal conspiracy?

Alicia was at any rate more of a team player. She was considered too good for records and would no doubt move on soon. But could one seriously suspect a person of being mixed up in a murderous conspiracy just because they were good at collaborating and partnering?

And then there was Jade, who confessed herself 'completely bewildered' by the complex filing system. With her round blue eyes and eccentrically layered hair, Jade couldn't possibly be the one.

Just before lunch, Jemima's mobile phone buzzed in her bag. She glanced at it. It was an unrecognisable regional number, presumably a phone-box. And no one called from phone-boxes any more. She took the precaution of going out into the empty stairwell to answer it.

"Jem? It's me." His voice sounded faint and different, or maybe she had just forgotten what people sounded like calling from telephone-boxes.

"Yes?"

"Is everything all right at your end?"

"Of course, why wouldn't it be?"

"Where are you?"

"At the office, of course. But it's all right, I've left the room. How are you getting on?"

"I've got everything I needed. I'm coming back this evening."

"That's good. That you've found whatever it is, I mean," she added hastily. Really, a schoolgirl could do better.

"What about you?" His voice sounded amused and she hurried into speech.

"Everything's fine. I went to Wimbledon actually. I met a friend of yours."

"That sounds unlikely."

"He's a police inspector. I told him about an idea I've had about how someone could have got onto the court. He said he thought it might be possible. He's very nice."

"Not when he's cross-examining you in an interviewing room." Abruptly, he said: "Your voice sounds rather odd. Where did you say you were?"

"I told you, at the office."

"Yes, but *where* are you?"

"On the stairs." Jemima suddenly realised that her voice must be floating beautifully all the way down the hollow, open spiral of the stairwell.

He said quickly: "Don't say any more. I'll be back in a few hours. Are you sure everything's all right?"

"Yes, of course it is."

There was the clunking sound of a hand-set being placed

on its cradle in a small glass box hundreds of miles away – she had almost forgotten that sound. And at once, she sensed the well of silence surging back around her. And was that the sound of a door softly swinging shut, one or perhaps two levels below?

It was then that she knew how stupid it had been to take the call out here. The middle of the noisy office would have been safer. What had she said? She had mentioned Wimbledon and the police. How much did it matter? Xan must be exaggerating the risks, surely.

She went to the washroom to steady her nerves and while she was in there, thought up an excellent story about a phone-call from her landlord about someone coming to view the spare room.

When she returned to the Records Branch, Geraldine was standing up at her desk, rummaging through the big floral handbag she carried. She was chittering away in an agitated fashion.

"Now, I know I had some ready money for the canteen. I don't like going out for lunch unless I go very *early*, the queues in the sandwich shops are so terrible. But someone came round with a leaving collection and I find I've left myself a little short, which is most annoying."

"I'll lend you some," Jemima said quickly. She picked up her bag from her chair, extracted her purse and found a five-pound note for Geraldine, who twittered gratefully as she stowed it away.

"So much nicer not to have to go out. I'm sure I had to queue for *twenty-five minutes* the other day, it's really quite absurd."

"Someone should do something about it," Jemima said vaguely. She was still thinking about her story about someone coming to see the spare room. But something else was bothering her. Surely she had left her bag on the floor, not on her chair. And she always put her purse in the other side of her bag, not in the inside pocket where it always snagged on the zip.

As she closed the bag, a railway ticket fluttered to the floor and she picked it up, then paused and looked at it again. ILVERCOMBE, DEVON. RETURN.

She sat down at her desk, feeling suddenly unsteady. Either there was a thief at Westminster House or while she had been out of the room, someone had searched her bag.

She had spent the morning suspecting people, but what if someone in this building suspected her? Why? Had it been the phone-call – or something else entirely? She looked around the room and saw them all attentively studying their screens. Paul, Alicia, Jade. None of them paying any attention to her.

Geraldine brought Jemima a cheese sandwich from the canteen and she ate it at her desk, even though she didn't feel very hungry. The thought of spending the afternoon in the oppressive atmosphere of the Records Branch was unbearable. Then she thought of the archive. Since she was stuck here until five o'clock, she might as well do something useful.

When she let herself in using her swipecard, the vaulted

space of the sub-sub-basement was slumbering and silent, as always. She took an armful of the 'fat files' which were waiting to be put away – the bulky records of those with an extensive military career, which did not fit easily in the main filing system. They were stored in a side-room, in a set of large bookcases which had been brought down here for the purpose. It was mind-numbing work and after a while, it began to calm her nerves.

She was not even sure how much time had passed when she was jerked back to awareness by the sound of the main door opening at the end of the corridor. Of course, there was no reason why it should not. But there were only the five of them who had access to the archive.

Perhaps the person who had just come in would call out to ask where she was. If it was Jade, she certainly would. Jade found the archive 'creepy'. But there was silence.

Perhaps she should call out herself, but for some reason, she did not. Instead she stood quite still, her fingers tensed on the file she was holding as she strained to listen.

Then she heard the sound she had been waiting for – the soft footfall of someone walking between the rows of filing cabinets in the main room. Whoever was down here, they were not doing anything with the records. They were looking for someone – for her.

There might be nothing wrong in that, of course. But there was something about those soft footsteps that made her uneasy. They suggested that the person, whoever they were, preferred not to be heard.

Of course, she was probably worrying about nothing.

All the same, she made up her mind. At the moment when the footsteps were furthest from her, she left the side-room where she had been working and began to move quietly towards the main door. As she did so, she pulled her swipecard out of her pocket and clutched it in her hand so that it would not accidentally swing against one of the metal filing-cabinets.

It felt like a frightening echo of a childhood game. She had nearly reached her objective when her elbow brushed one of the cabinets and it teetered, creaking protestingly. At once she heard the footsteps turning towards her.

Panic lent her inspiration. She threw her whole weight against the cabinet and shoved violently. It rocked again and then began to topple, catching the one behind it in a domino effect. She did not stop to see what happened next but ran to the main door and pressed her swipecard against the reader. The door slid open. And as she bolted into the lift and held the button down to close the doors, she heard behind her a crashing cacophony of toppling filing-cabinets.

The lift stopped on the ground floor to let in an influx of reassuringly ordinary-looking people on their way back from long Friday lunch-hours. They were busy discussing their plans for the evening and paid no attention to her. By the time the lift reached the fifth floor, she felt calmer. Perhaps she had been imagining things after all.

When she came into the Records Branch, only Jade and Alicia were at their desks. But as she hesitated in the doorway, Paul came hurrying in behind her. Was there a bruise on his forehead or was she imagining it?

Before she could decide, Geraldine hastened over from the storeroom where she had apparently been sequestered. “Could you just run this down to Private Office? It’s a submission to go in the Duty Minister’s box to be signed over the weekend.”

Jemima glanced automatically at the clock. It was half past two. The box would almost certainly have gone.

“I meant to send it with the internal post but they’ve been round already. And it’s rather important.”

It was another excuse to get away from her desk at any rate. Jemima took the submission and made her way down to the third floor.

The suite of Ministerial rooms, with their oak panelling, thick carpeting and corniced ceilings, were a world away from the shabbiness of the Records Branch. The big room in the middle of the suite was the Private Office, where the support staff to the various Ministers gossiped, filed papers and made decisions on behalf of their betters. It was usually buzzing, but now, on a Friday afternoon in recess, the room was deserted.

Jemima loitered uncertainly in the doorway. Surely one of the Private Secretaries must be in the building, even in the dead days of August?

The door to one of the Ministerial rooms was standing open. Ordinarily the rooms were kept locked while their occupants were absent during recess. Perhaps the PS was in there – the long oak table inside each Ministerial office was just the thing for collating Committee papers, one of them had once told her.

She knocked before she went in, but this room too was empty. The long bare table with all the papers tidied away and the big captain's chair shoved under the leather-topped desk in the corner where the Minister preferred to do his work told their own story.

This was Mark Romilly's room and she had no business being in here. She looked around it curiously – the big windows, the book-case and the ornate fireplace, with its ugly yellow Do Not Use sticker that even Romilly had not been able to get them to remove.

She wandered over to the bookcase. Few government officials had bookcases these days, or the need for them. This one was crammed with serious reference tomes as you would expect in a ministerial office, but they looked dust-free and read – presumably by Romilly himself.

She had not come here to try and find evidence. That was Xan's job. But now she had been presented with an opportunity. These books, if they were his, would have his fingerprints on. So would many of the things in his office, of course, but a book was removable.

Before she could examine any of the books, she heard footsteps in the Outer Office and moved away from the bookcase just as Hugh, Romilly's Private Secretary, poised in the doorway, a surprised look on his handsome features.

Ministerial Private Secretaries were almost invariably well-groomed, ambitious and charming of manner, all three attributes being considered vital for this surprisingly influential role. Hugh was also young for the job, having just graduated from Cambridge, and his expensive suit only partially disguised the build of someone who spends their weekends on a rugby pitch. Sport of all kinds seemed to be the major preoccupation of his life – just now, he was idly tossing a ball of rubber bands from hand to hand.

"There you are," she said with what she hoped sounded like asperity. "Geraldine sent up a late submission for the Duty Minister's box."

The ball flipped from left hand to right and back. "That's Callaghan this week, not Romilly. And the box has gone."

"I thought it had. I was just waiting to check with someone."

Hugh might reasonably have asked why she was waiting inside the Minister's office, but he seemed to have lost interest in the matter. Three high ball tosses in a row. "Geraldine should have sent it up earlier."

Jemima retraced her steps to the Records Branch and relayed this news, rather more tactfully worded, to Geraldine. The older woman's fingers plucked nervously at her choker. "Oh, dear. It was rather important as well."

"I'll check on the roster when the next Duty Minister is in," Jemima offered. But when she tried to log onto her computer, the machine wouldn't accept her password. After the third try, it fell sullenly into protected mode and she swore at it under her breath, then turned to Geraldine. "I can't get back into my computer. I'll have to ring the helpdesk."

She did so, but to no avail. "I'm sorry," the technician said. "There seems to be a problem with your profile. It won't let me restore your privileges." A few keystrokes. "That's interesting. It's not the machine, it's you. Has your role changed?"

"No, of course not."

"Has anything else changed?"

"No, of –," Jemima began again, but then stopped.

"Do you want me to check it with my manager?"

"No. It doesn't matter."

"Sure? I can take it up with the Head of Security."

"No, don't do that."

"I tell you what," the technician added, "you'd better check your swipecard as well. If the whole profile's gone down, next time the system updates it could affect your access rights as well. Doors and everything. You don't want to get stuck in the building on a Friday afternoon."

"No, I don't," Jemima agreed hollowly and hung up.

Geraldine glanced at her. "What is it?"

About to answer, Jemima checked herself. Her thoughts raced ahead of her. She heard herself say lightly: "I tell you what, I'll just run downstairs and see if the box is still here. One of the third-floor secretaries told me it might get held downstairs for a while."

"Are you sure?"

"Absolutely." She stuffed the submission into her bag to add verisimilitude, hoping it wasn't anything terribly important, and hurried out to the lift lobby.

She would have to use her swipecard to call the lift. She did so. Nothing happened. Then she tried the door to the emergency stairs. It wouldn't open. It was as the IT technician had warned her. Someone had switched off all her access rights, disabling not only her PC log-in but her access rights throughout the building.

When had they done it? Her swipecard had worked when she went down to the archive and again on the third floor. It came to her that it had been done while she was wasting time in Private Office and that perhaps that was why she had been sent there, after they had failed to get hold of her in the archive.

Now what? She could feel panic creeping taking control of her mind. Should she trigger a fire alarm? Would that disable the electronic access system entirely? Someone had once told her that it would, but what if it didn't? Or should she go back to the Records Branch and make up some excuse to persuade Geraldine to accompany her to the ground floor? But what reason could she possibly give?

Suddenly, the lift indicator tinged and she looked up in hope. The door opened and Sir Julius Stoke, the medical specialist with whom Mark Romilly had private appointments, emerged. He greeted her cheerfully.

"Leaving early? It's a beautiful afternoon, I must say. I walked over through the park and you could hardly move for sunbathers."

Jemima jammed her finger on the lift button to hold it. The doctor glanced at her. "Is something wrong?"

"Urgent submission for the Duty Minister," she said breathlessly.

"On a Friday afternoon? How unusual. What is it?"

"Fox-hunting on military land," Jemima said at random, as the lift doors closed on him. She kept her finger on the G button until the lift reached the ground floor. When the doors slid open, she expected to see security guards waiting for her, but the reception area looked just as usual.

She did not dare risk the automatic barriers. Instead, she looked around and saw a stack of boxes on the floor – brochures left over from an event. Inspiration struck. She picked up a couple of boxes and awkwardly approached the manual barrier. The guard looked at the boxes instead of at her and waved her through. Then a moment later, the glass entrance doors slid open before her and she walked out into the sunshine.

She set down the boxes on the steps. On the other side of the road, a man was leaning against the railings. Her heart thumped, but it was only a courier critically examining his bicycle. As she passed him, he apparently decided that his machine was all right after all, gave it a final kick, and began to ride after her.

CHAPTER 40

Jemima was walking hurriedly along Millbank. It was only a few minutes to Westminster Station, but she was conscious of the courier cyclist following a regulation twenty paces behind her. He made no attempt to catch up with her.

Would he follow her onto the Underground? These people seemed to specialise in accidents. And if that was what was supposed to happen to her, of course it would be so much better if it wasn't on Civil Service estate.

Perhaps that was why the guard at Westminster House had opened the barrier for her. The Underground would be a much better place for murder. On the crowded Tube platforms at rush-hour, it would be so easy for someone to slip onto the tracks. She had been part of the horrified crowd of onlookers herself at such an incident more than once and seen the red-stained sawdust that was brought up from the tracks in the clean-up work.

Would she even make it safely to the Tube station? The crossing at Westminster Bridge was a huge, four-lane junction which was always a melee of red-light-jumping cyclists, heavy goods lorries and confused tourists. No one would think it odd if there was an accident here.

When she reached to Parliament Square, she looked

anxiously around. On her left was Westminster Cathedral. You could retreat into its dark, calm heart – but then what? Anyone could follow her in there. What she needed was a sanctuary where no one else could follow her. And at that moment, she looked to her right and saw, as if for the first time, the familiar black wrought iron railings and behind them the golden citadel that was the Palace of Westminster. As if in a dream, she came up to the guards and presented the badge that said she was an employee of Her Majesty's Government.

"We're shutting in half an hour, Miss," the security guard said apologetically, as though the Palace were a shop.

"That's all right, I won't be long."

The guard opened the security gate and Jemima walked into the sanctuary of the Palace yard. The gate clanged behind her and the cool black shadows fell over her like an extra layer of protection.

She descended to an underground screening room where she submitted patiently to having her handbag searched, and then re-emerged into the courtyard. Here, pool cars were parked nose to tail in the afternoon sun, many with a driver sitting reading a newspaper with the driver door open and one foot on the ground.

At the eastern end of the estate, the Elizabeth Tower stood forlornly in scaffolding, the world's most famous clock buried somewhere beneath its wrappings. To the west was the tower's larger sister, the Victoria Tower, looking down on the entrance by which the Sovereign came to Parliament. Beyond that was the odd strip of garden known as Black Rod's Entrance. And immediately before Jemima, roughly between the two towers, a double set of oak doors led into the medieval vastness of Westminster Hall.

Inside, the stone flags, bare monastic walls and high vaulted ceilings created the feeling of a church. This was where tours of the Palace started. There were signs to washrooms and the café and gift-shop and people studying statues and sculptures, their hands clasped behind their backs as though they were in a museum.

Jemima took out her phone to call Xan but his phone went to voicemail. As she was about to leave a message, a cacophony of bells rang out, apparently from directly overhead and she gave it up. It didn't matter. If she could just waste some time here until it was safe to leave…

She had her hands clasped, studying the portrait of some obscure former statesman on the wall, when an amused voice broke in on her ear.

"Despite the medium, he's no oil painting, is he?"

She turned and saw a man in his early forties, sunburned with dark hair and very blue eyes. Many casual visitors might have supposed that this was just another tourist. But despite the fact that he was casually dressed in jeans and a shirt, this was very much one of Her Majesty's government ministers.

He was looking at her quizzically. "You're from my Department, aren't you? I'm pretty good at faces, although now that I think of it, your hair looks different."

She had forgotten how young he was for a minister. If one was to meet him in other circumstances, he would seem attractive. He must do sailing or some other VIP outdoor hobby to get so brown in England. And he was smiling at her in a friendly manner that made nonsense of the gap in status.

Nonetheless, one was indoctrinated over the years on how to address a Minister, even one in jeans and an open-necked shirt who addressed you so casually.

"I didn't realise you were in London today, Minister," she said politely.

"Oh, I only came in for my committee papers. A bit under-dressed, I daresay you're thinking. But it's recess and when they said they needed me to come in, I said I was d – er, that I would prefer not to get up in a suit and a tie in the middle of August, just to fetch a few papers." He looked at her curiously. "What are you doing in here anyway? Seeing the sights?"

Jemima hurriedly marshalled her thoughts. Then an idea came to her – an idea with more than one possible application. "There's an urgent submission for the write-round."

"One for the Ministerial box, eh?"

"Yes, but I don't know whether the Duty Minister is here."

"Callaghan left an hour ago. But we can't have a vital submission hanging about. I'll sign it."

"That would be wonderful," Jemima said sincerely. She scrabbled in her bag and for a heart-stopping moment, thought she had nothing to write with. But he had already produced his own expensive-looking fountain-pen.

"It's the signature on the back page that's the really important one," she said quickly. "And if you could note the media and handling lines. Or say you've noted them anyway, that's the important thing."

Romilly laughed. He rested the papers on a flat-topped glass display cabinet and bent over them to casually scribble his name. Then he looked at her with more attention. "You're not from Private Office."

Jemima folded the papers away carefully in her bag. "No – I'm from the records office, someone just asked me to bring the submission over."

"Then you must have a tour of the place while you're here."

At that moment, a tannoy announcement rang out above their heads. "The Palace of Westminster will be closing to visitors shortly."

"Oh, what a pity, it's shutting."

"Nonsense. That doesn't mean our people. In any case, I've got the pass to end all passes. Come along, I'll give you the grand tour."

Romilly conducted her up the steps at the back of the hall, waving away an official who approached with a 'we're closing, sir' expression. He used his swipecard to open the door and led the way along a series of galleries lined with paintings and statues.

"This takes us round the way the Sovereign enters," he said absently, as though part of his mind was on other matters. "The grandest rooms are there, of course."

As they passed along the corridor, Jemima felt a blast of cold outside air and looked through a doorway to see the great wrought-iron gate of the Sovereign's Entrance. Beyond it was the street. A handful of tourists stared curiously at her.

"We won't go through there," Romilly said cheerfully. "It sets off an alarm if you so much as look at the ironwork and there'll be armed guards breathing down our necks inside a minute."

He conducted her instead through the Robing Room and the Royal Gallery and then the House of Lords Chamber, with its famous red leather seats. He looked around it with a critical air. "It's smaller than you expect. Everyone says that. The Commons Chamber is even smaller. My constituents always seem to feel it's a bit of a damp squib."

Jemima wondered why he was taking so much trouble over her. Of course, everyone knew there were plenty of senior civil servants and ministers a girl had to be careful with, but Mark Romilly had never been considered that sort. Perhaps it was nothing more than the opportunity to display his celebrated charm. He could often be seen in this chamber on the Parliamentary television channel, being courteous to the Speaker and deferring graciously to his fellow-Members.

He conducted her into the House of Commons library, which she thought was far more appealing than the stuffy debating chambers and endless galleries they had passed through. It had a quiet, clubbable atmosphere, with cosy leather Chesterfield chairs in warm hues of olive green and bronze and books lining the walls.

Her companion seemed to read her mind. "I'm afraid there's nothing readable here, it's all tomes about tax law and rules of succession." He brandished a block of House of Commons writing paper. "But everyone wants to steal some of this."

Jemima found her voice. "What happens if they do?"

Romilly laughed. "Oh, locked up in the Tower, I should think. Now come out and see the view from the terrace. I'm afraid we've left it too late to get a drink – they shut early in recess, blast them."

They passed through a second door out onto the river-side terrace which she had often looked at from across the river. It had a sad, end of season look to it, with chairs upside down on tables and a closed and locked bar area.

Across the river, the lights of London hung in the dusk – the wrought-iron lamps on nearby Westminster Bridge, street-lamps across the river casting a pool of pale light along the wall of the Archbishop's Palace and further along, the Blackpool-like illuminations of the Millennium Wheel.

Mark Romilly propped himself against the terrace wall, disregarding the Impressionist splendour apparently for the pleasure of studying his companion's face. But of course, Jemima thought to herself, he must come here all the time and the view probably didn't interest him any more.

He fished in his coat pocket. “Cigarette? Of course, one isn’t supposed to smoke but after all, there’s no one here to enforce it.”

“No, thank you.”

“Well, I will, if it’s all the same to you.” He fished a pack of cigarettes out of his jacket pocket and struck a match. The sudden flame lit up his handsome, regular features. His eyes were blank, as though whatever thinking he was doing was not being allowed to reach the surface.

He smoked the cigarette silently and she looked out across the water, wondering about the desperate stakes he must be playing for. What would they do to him if it all came out?

At last he spoke, so suddenly that she jumped. “What are you thinking about? You look very serious.”

She might have come up with some light, meaningless answer. Instead, she heard herself say: “I was thinking about Giles Maybury. Do you remember him?”

Not a muscle of his face contracted. “Yes, of course I do.”

The instinct to warn him had come so suddenly that she had not thought ahead to the next move. She looked away from him, into the water and spoke deliberately. “He was worried about something before he died. He thought something odd was going on at the Department.”

“I see.”

“And then he died. But he told someone about it before he died – a stranger he bumped into casually. And he found out some things."

"I see. And he's the type who'd talk about what he knew, eh?"

"Yes."

Romilly nodded and drew on his cigarette slowly and deliberately.

Jemima stood silent in an agony of indecision. What had she done? Just then, another man came quietly out onto the terrace. She recognised him with a start as Sir Julius Stoke. He looked, she thought, worried. "Minister, we're expected at the opera at eight."

Romilly grimaced. "Hell, I'd forgotten. Look, I'm not dressed for it. I'll have to cut it."

Sir Julius smiled faintly. "Your PS asked me to mention that your suit's back at the office."

"Blast."

The two men looked at each other warily. Jemima watched them, feeling as if she had come into a theatre in the middle of a play. There was something going on here that she did not understand. Romilly spoke first. "Very well, then. But I'd better show my staff-member out first."

"Ah, yes, Miss Drury." Sir Julius turned to Jemima with a remote smile. "The fox-hunting matter – it must have been rather important."

"Fox-hunting?" Romilly repeated blankly.

Sir Julius turned back to him. "I'm afraid I had a second message for you which I've only just recalled. You need to call your constituency office. We'd better go up to the

Members' room."

"Seriously?"

The doctor shrugged. "I understand it's important."

Again, their eyes met and again some silent exchange took place which Jemima could only guess at. Whatever it was, it was Romilly who gave in. "All right, blast you." He turned to Jemima. "I'm afraid I'll have to leave you to make your own way out. I'm sorry."

"It's quite all right. Minister," she remembered to add.

He smiled briefly. "Don't hang about – the place is closed and you don't want to get locked in overnight. And don't go back the way we came – those doors are all swipe-controlled. Turn right once you're out of the library and that will take you straight to the main courtyard."

She nodded silently.

Romilly swung back to Sir Julius. "All right, then. I wish I knew what was so important, though. If it was that urgent, I don't see why they didn't call my mobile."

And as though in answer, a phone shrilled and with a grimace, he turned away, tugging it out of his jacket pocket.

*

Through the library and turn right for the main courtyard. It sounded straightforward but when she emerged into the stone passageway, she paused. To the right there was a sign saying NO ACCESS. SECURITY ONLY. Mark Romilly must have forgotten about that, or perhaps it didn't apply to him. But it would certainly apply to a junior-grade civil servant.

As Jemima hesitated, someone came hurrying from the opposite direction. She was bundled up in a number of large scarves to add to the chokers round her neck and her handbag was looped over her shoulder and slipping off.

"Geraldine?" Jemima stared at her incredulously.

"Thank goodness I've found you. The people at the gate are so stupid. They didn't seem to know if you were still here."

"But why did you come? If it's about the submission, I've got it signed at any rate."

Geraldine did not seem interested in the submission any more. "Then why didn't you come back to the office?"

"Because I bumped into the Minister."

Geraldine stared. "But they told me when I asked at the gate that Callaghan left at four."

"Not Callaghan – Romilly."

All trace of colour left the other woman's face. "Mark Romilly is *here*?"

"Well, he was half an hour ago. But he was late for the opera, so he's probably gone by now."

Geraldine did not appear to be listening. She caught Jemima by the arm. "Then we must leave at once."

"Why?"

"The building's closing. We could get locked in"

Geraldine's fingers were urging Jemima to the left. She resisted. "Mark Romilly said to go the other way."

"But that won't do at all," Geraldine said agitatedly. "It

brings you out through a gate that's only for Members of Parliament. He wouldn't think about that, of course." Her voice held the dryness of the civil servant bred to a hierarchical system.

"But he said that this way, the doors are all access-controlled."

"Never mind. I know a way through."

Reluctantly, Jemima fell into step beside her.

Geraldine led the way along the passage. She seemed in a hurry, skittering along, clutching at her necklaces and scarves. The Red Queen, Jemima thought irreverently. Then she stopped suddenly at a door. "Come along, there's no time to lose."

Jemima saw a dimly-let set of stairs leading downwards. "We're going down?"

"Of course we are. The doors aren't access-controlled at that level – the catering staff use it."

The passageway at the bottom of the stairs was dark and gloomy. There were pieces of broken furniture and other lumber seemingly abandoned in the corridor. "This is the part of the Palace that's closest to the river, you know," Geraldine said absently.

It was true that there was a dank, damp smell and once or twice, Jemima thought she heard the sound of dripping water. "But surely this can't be the quickest way out."

"It's the safest, can't you understand that?"

"What do you mean?"

"Not now – I'll explain later, there isn't time."

But a moment later, Geraldine paused at a doorway.

"Now this is one of the lowest points in the entire estate, I believe. And quite an unusual feature."

Unwillingly, Jemima followed her into a big room with chairs piled on tables and cobwebby dust sheets thrown over bigger pieces of furniture. There was no light except what filtered dimly through a dirty window. Her arm brushed a hanging wire and the movement dislodged a shower of plaster from above.

"Come along," Geraldine said impatiently.

Jemima moved towards the window. A reeking dampness hung in the air and she paused involuntarily. Before her there was a gaping hole surrounded by stone flags, dropping down into the darkness of what must be deeper cellars. Then she saw a dull gleam and instinctively she moved back.

"There's *water* down there?"

"It used to be a well, you know. So very insanitary. Of course, it's never used now. It connects with the main outfall to the river. Anything that goes in gets washed out in the next high tide, I understand."

And that was when she understood that they were not going to let her go – they had never intended to let her go. The only thing that mattered to them was that her death should not come at Mark Romilly's hands.

She ought to have realised the absurdity of an eminent doctor bringing messages about opera performances and dress suits. He had even shown her that he knew the matter of the fox-hunting submission to be a lie. Romilly must have been puzzled, but he had played along. And of course, Sir Julius's and Geraldine's hints of danger had been part of the game. Now was the time when something was supposed to happen to her – now that Romilly had safely left the House and gone somewhere public where he could burnish his alibi.

She looked across the gaping hole at Geraldine. "What have you done?"

"Well, really," Geraldine said crossly. "You say that as though it's not all your fault. You were the one who made a fuss about those files. If you had just minded your own business, we wouldn't be here."

Keep her talking, Jemima thought. "Why did you do it in the first place?"

"*I* didn't do anything. I'm really very unimportant in the scheme of things. But something had to be done. The fallibility of modern politicians had become such a problem. There's always a scandal from the past. They realised that what they needed was someone with no background at all."

"But it's crazy – it could never have worked."

"It *is* working. No one even thought about questioning Mark Romilly – no one, until that bumbling old fool Giles Maybury found out something somehow. And we couldn't take any chances, not with the Party leadership election so close."

"Then what about me?"

"I'm afraid you don't play any part in things at all. They don't record your name on the door when you come onto the Parliamentary estate, or when you leave again –

only you won't be leaving, of course. And you went through all those controlled doors on Mark Romilly's swipecard, so there's no record of you at all. You'll just disappear."

"You're crazy," Jemima said. She took a step back. A cobweb brushed her hair lightly and she remembered something.

"You just say that because you're too stupid to see how clever it all is."

"Is it? It wouldn't ever have worked for long," Jemima said, to distract the other woman from her movements. She took another step back. "It's already going wrong – you know that."

It was a step too far. Geraldine looked at her sharply. "What are you doing? You can't imagine that you'll be allowed to get out of here and go and spread a lot of lies about us?"

Jemima took a third step and then caught hold of the fraying cable hanging from the ceiling and dragged at it. She covered her face to protect her eyes as a shower of white plaster poured from above, enveloping them both.

The collapse was greater than she could have hoped for. Evidently, the ceiling was in a serious state of disrepair. Somewhere in the cloud of pale dust that now filled the room, Geraldine was coughing and floundering. And then suddenly there was an ominous creaking sound from above them.

Jemima jumped for the doorway just as a number of heavier pieces of plaster and bricks came crashing down, burying the room in rubble.

Silence. From the doorway, Jemima stared vainly into the clouds of choking dust. It was impossible to see anything, but she thought she could hear vague twitterings and stirrings from within it.

It didn't matter. There was no time to lose. At the back of her mind was the uneasy suspicion that during their exchange just now, Geraldine had been stalling as much as she herself had been. After all, she might be dangerously unbalanced but she wouldn't have had the strength to deal with anyone alone. Someone else was probably coming.

Outside in the passage, the empty corridor yawned at her sarcastically. Which way? There was no obvious clue, so she turned right at random. But in this direction, the aura of decay intensified. Light-bulbs hung drunkenly from the ceiling. Fallen beams and heaps of bricks began to intrude into the passageway. This was the House of Charn once the cursed word had been spoken.

There must be another way back up to the floor above. At last, she came to a set of stairs. At the top, there was a door into a small ante-lobby. She opened it, then paused, amazed to see where she was.

She was standing in the octagonal Central Lobby – the heart of the Palace, with its four doors leading to the two debating chambers, the library and the great space of Westminster Hall. She had been here before tonight, with Mark Romilly – it seemed a million years ago.

The route through Westminster Hall would be the

quickest way out now, but the door was closed and someone was standing with his back to it. Young, broad-shouldered, suited, his feet widely spaced, tossing a ball of rubber bands to and fro.

"Hugh?" she said incredulously.

He turned and saw her and his eyes widened. She realised how she must look – plaster, dust and cobwebs still clung to her hair and clothes.

"What are you doing here?" she demanded.

He shrugged. "Geraldine asked me to come over. She was worried about you."

Jemima stared. "*Geraldine* said that?"

He stopped tossing the ball of rubber bands. "Sure."

The faint hope inside her flickered and died. He was still standing with his back to the doors. The pose of a sentry blocking an exit. This wasn't the cavalry or even just an innocent witness whose presence would make her safe. This was one of them.

He was studying her watchfully, perhaps wondering what she might do next. She felt the tension stretching between them. He did not know what she suspected – she did not know what he knew. She found herself wondering when and how they had persuaded him to be part of this. Perhaps they had recruited him right out of university, like the spymasters used to do.

Then suddenly, absurdly, the tension was broken by the maddening electronic tune of a mobile phone. His. He turned away from her and fished it out of his pocket to answer it.

Jemima backed quietly away, one step at a time, until she came up against the ornate carved door that led to the House of Lords debating chamber. Her hands behind her back, she reached for the handle. The door opened a crack. She slipped inside and the heavy door swung to behind her.

Velvety darkness enveloped her. In the dimness, she could only just make out the lines of benches, the carved oak galleries lining the walls and the throne. She had been here before tonight, too.

She moved forward hesitantly in the darkness. Beyond this chamber was the Royal Gallery and the way down to the Sovereign's Entrance. Mark Romilly had told her that if you entered that space, it automatically set off alarms. What would happen when it did?

At that moment, she heard the clatter of a phone hitting the marble floor of the lobby and someone yelling her name. She backed away as Hugh threw his weight against the door. There was a crack of light as it opened, then it swung shut and the darkness flowed in again and she could hear him scrabbling for a light switch.

In almost pitch blackness, she blundered through the chamber, trying to remember what the television pictures showed. A table, she thought, and banged her hip against it.

Her fingers strayed across the invisible surface and almost knocked over something smooth and icy cold with sharp edges – something metal. Whatever it was, it would do as a weapon. She snatched it up just as Hugh reached her and smashed it into his face.

There was a sickening crunch, followed by a horrible snarling noise. And then, perhaps on some time-delay, the lights came on and flooded the debating chamber with a brilliant glare.

She dropped her weapon – an ornate silver penwell that appeared to weigh several hundred tons – and stood staring at Hugh. His blonde fringe was flopping over one eye and he was breathing hard. His mouth was bleeding. The veneer of the ambitious fast-streamer had shattered and the young man who looked at her drew back his lip and snarled again.

There was no time now to think or plan. She turned to run, almost tripping over the penwell she had dropped. Through the double doors at the far end of the debating chamber and into the Royal Gallery, then the Robing Room. At the far end, there was a staircase leading down.

The door at the bottom of the stairs was controlled by a button release – presumably, the other side held a keypad, but it seemed oddly casual for access to such an important space as the Sovereign's Entrance. She pressed the button anyway and as soon as she stepped out through the door, realized that she was in entirely the wrong place.

Instead of a grand stone arched entrance and a shrieking orchestra of bells, here was silence and darkness and the smell of rain on earth. Above her, a pale sky. And in front of her, a tall fence with barbed wire at the top and trees behind it. This was Black Rod's garden.

She peered into the darkness for a way out. There could

be no climbing the fence directly in front of her. It was far too high. And to her left, the garden ended against an out-thrust angle of the Palace wall. But to the right, the way to the rest of the estate was only barred by railings. They were lower than the fence before her, presumably because they were inside the Palace estate.

She looked at the railings. They might be lower than the fence but they still looked about eight feet high. They were made of black wrought iron and decorated with elaborate curlicues which might provide footholds.

Afterwards, she knew it was only the adrenaline flooding through her veins that made her try it. She got her left foot up onto the narrow support of the lock mechanism and pulled herself up, using both hands to grip the railings. The metal was slick from rain under her fingers. The railings were topped by spikes, their tips rusty but still sharp. The spikes were disconcertingly at the level of her chin.

She swung her right foot up and jammed it into the gap afforded by two spikes and a horizontal curlicued bar a few inches from the top. From that position, it was possible to swing her left foot over the spikes and brace it in the same position. Then she swung her second leg over. Her arms were starting to ache from the effort by now, but very carefully, she held her body away from the spikes as she jumped down. Then she turned to look for the way out.

There wasn't one. In this neglected corner of the Palace estate, there was nothing but bramble bushes and a tall brick wall – too tall to climb, this time – with a door that didn't move an inch even when she threw all her weight against it.

She was trapped. And as she turned back, she saw Hugh step out into the courtyard through the door she had come by, breathing heavily. Blood was dripping from his face and spattering his white shirt. He looked up and saw her, then he closed the door carefully behind him, as though to block the path of any witnesses.

He came slowly over to the railings. He tested his footing on the lock box and began to climb the railings as she had done.

He pulled himself up to look over the railings, bracing himself for the effort involved in swinging himself over. But something was wrong. Jemima saw that the foothold he had wasn't big enough for his boot and his foot was slipping.

She saw his fingers tense on the railings as he glanced down to see what his options were. Then suddenly, a burst of bells ringing out from a nearby church jerked him into involuntary movement. His foothold gave way and his fingers scrabbled ineffectually on the rain-soaked metal as he slid downwards.

It was only a few inches before he was suddenly and dreadfully halted. There was not even time for a scream, only a scarlet splatter of blood. He hung in mid-air, like a puppet. One of the iron spikes had entered the base of his chin, pinning him as securely as a butterfly and killing him instantly.

Jemima pressed back against the brick wall as far from the fence as she could get and covered her face with her hands.

CHAPTER 41

Two hours earlier, Xan had descended from the early evening express at London Paddington, reflecting with some irritation on a wasted journey to Hambleden.

At just after two o'clock, a party of local dignitaries had squeezed their way self-importantly onto the makeshift stage at the agricultural show. Mark Romilly had not been among them. And when Xan trudged over to inquire at the information tent, a hearty woman in a quilted jacket and a scarf with clocks on it had looked put out.

"Called back to London, it seems. Urgent Parliamentary business, they *said*. When Parliament isn't even sitting."

There had been nothing for it but to return to London himself. He went to the station and was fortunate enough to catch an express. His ribs were aching again and he took two pain-killers washed down with a bottle of water. The train was busy and he missed his phone ringing.

When he reached Paddington, the evening rush-hour had already begun. Suddenly impatient, he took a taxi to Romilly's London place. The Georgian town-house with its view of the park looked expensive. The front door was answered by a housekeeper who turned a blank face to his inquiry. "I'm afraid Mr Romilly's not here."

"I've just been down at his country place – they said he

had come here."

"Oh, he did, a few hours ago. But he didn't stay. Changed his clothes and went out again almost at once."

"Did he say where he was going?"

"He didn't say, sir. But he'd got his briefcase, so it looked as though he was going to the House."

And Xan had gone hurriedly back down the steps to catch his taxi. But the evening traffic meant the journey was a slow one and in the end, he lost patience, paid the driver and walked through the park. Now here he was at the front desk of Westminster House, where the evening shift receptionist looked warily at the tall young man with the impatient look.

"It's recess, sir, all the ministers are away."

"I know that. But Romilly came back to London today. Is he here?"

Perhaps this well-informed visitor was a Ministerial driver or even, the receptionist thought, part of the police protection unit. He looked the type. Perhaps this was something to do with a security alert. Over the last few years, the constant barrage of security levels moving up and down and instructions revised almost weekly had created uncertainty in his mind. He suddenly felt unequal to stalling any further. "No, sir. They unlocked his office for him, but he didn't come in after all."

"Then where is he? His housekeeper said the House."

The receptionist felt a sudden weight lift from his brow. "Oh, then he'll be at the Palace of Westminster, of course." Catching his unwelcome visitor's questioning look, he amplified: "The Houses of Parliament, sir. Just across the road."

One could hardly drag a minister out of Parliament to answer questions. Xan asked about Jemima instead and was told that she had left over an hour ago. It was then that he remembered his phone. He fished it out and saw that there was a message. He played it back, but there was no voice, only the insistent chimes of what sounded like a church clock.

Eager to be helpful, the receptionist said: "Is that the Victoria clock, sir? I'd recognise it anywhere."

"What?"

The receptionist pointed across the road. "The clock in the Victoria Tower. It's very distinctive. But it only sounds like that from inside."

"Inside?"

"Like I said, sir, inside the Palace."

*

"I'm afraid the Palace is closed to visitors, sir." The uniformed guard in the little lighted security cabin was apologetic.

Xan spared a moment to wish he had cajoled or forced someone at Westminster House into lending him their authority, whether it came in the form of a security pass or their presence. Instead, he would have to try a bluff. "I've come over from Westminster House. The Minister asked me to come and collect some papers. I didn't bring my pass, I'm afraid, but it's very urgent."

The guard shook his head regretfully. "More than my job's worth, sir. I'm afraid you'll have to go back and get your pass."

"Look, do you realise how urgent this matter is? The Minister won't be at all happy."

The guard looked wary. "Which Minister?"

"Romilly. He's over here now. He called me himself, not five minutes ago."

The guard's expression inexplicably lightened. "Here he comes now, sir, you can speak to him yourself."

Xan turned sharply. Mark Romilly was making his way down the steps into the courtyard. His driver was with him. Romilly looked worried. Then as though aware of being watched, he looked over and met Xan's eyes. There was a flash of recognition.

Unaware of the sudden tension, the guard contributed his piece. "Mr Romilly, this gentleman says he's one of your staff and that you asked him to go in and get some papers."

Romilly considered Xan thoughtfully. Again, their eyes met. Xan did not move – the situation had progressed faster than he was expecting. In his mind, he rapidly reviewed options – only to find that what happened next wasn't covered by any of them.

Romilly was nodding briskly. "That's right," he said impatiently. "Let him through, what are you waiting for? I can't stop, I'm afraid – late for a reception."

He turned away towards the line of pool cars. Trying to

disguise his astonishment, Xan submitted to a brief search and went through into the Palace grounds.

He entered the building through the set of doors from which Romilly had emerged. Before him, chamber after empty echoing chamber presented itself. The building seemed entirely deserted apart from the guards at the gate – almost as though the place had been deliberately emptied of witnesses.

Of course, Romilly had left the building too. But that thought wasn't particularly reassuring. If something bad was happening here, Romilly would be kept well away from it.

He had reached an octagonal chamber with four sets of grand doors opening off it. A ball of rubber bands rolled inexplicably under his foot. He glanced at it, wondering how it came here. More disquietingly, a mobile phone lay on the floor. He took a careful glance at it to ascertain it was not Jemima's, but did not pick it up.

One of the four sets of doors was slightly ajar and he went through. The room was in darkness and he switched on the light. It illuminated an ornate debating chamber which he recognised from television news. But he was not interested in that. Here was a second sign of another presence and this time more disturbing – a bloodstain, not on the floor, but on the white painted wall, at hand height.

And at the precise moment that he stared at it, a scream rang out suddenly from somewhere near at hand, then stopped with an unpleasant gurgling sound.

Xan went fast in the direction of the scream. There was a

long gallery full of paintings, then another room and a set of stairs. He went down the stairs too fast to think and kicked open the door at the bottom to find open air and darkness.

It was only when he emerged that he saw the railings and what hung on them. The grotesque parody of a man, a scarecrow hanging in mid-air, spattered with blood.

Hurriedly, he approached the railings. "Jem?" he said urgently. Then he saw her, standing against the wall. She pulled her hands away from her eyes when she heard his voice.

"Are you all right?"

"Yes. But I can't climb the fence again."

"What about the door behind you?"

"It won't budge. I tried it."

"All right. Hold on a moment." He was testing the railings experimentally.

"What are you doing?" Her voice was suddenly sharp with alarm.

"Well, you can't get out, but I can get in."

"Please don't."

He smiled at her reassuringly. "If you can do it, I can."

He swung himself over quickly and expertly, avoiding any contact with the dead man. Then he jumped down the other side. And a clock somewhere, that must have been a few minutes out of step with the bells, earth-shatteringly began to strike half past nine.

CHAPTER 42

The Palace security guards were first on the scene. There were sharp exclamations and a general tendency for the guards to unship their weapons and watch Xan suspiciously. It had been refreshing to be in this green and pleasant land for so long and not see any guns but now there were nearly half a dozen of them, all pointed at him and Jemima.

And then within minutes, the police arrived. Whoever had been on patrol closest to the scene, he guessed, and again there were exclamations and now questions. In the bright lights of the guards' torches, the body on the railing looked more gruesome than ever, the blood still trickling down and dripping onto the ground.

And then, while they were all arguing among themselves about what should be done and in what order, more police arrived who seemed to have different instructions and then the door in the wall was unlocked and they were ushered through it. And then a man with a sad, clown-like face came down the steps and said: "I'll take it from here, Bob," and opened the door of a black limousine.

*

The neat Regency house in Kensington seemed the kind of place where no crisis was so serious that it could not be solved by sitting down for tea. But the man with the craggy face pacing up and down over a carpet of delicate blue fleur-de-lys wore a worried expression and a crooked tie. "This is all rather unfortunate, Mr Ross."

Xan was leaning against the mantelpiece wondering how long this would take. He felt bone-tired and the last thing he wanted was to be in this well-appointed room, looking at flower-patterned wallpaper over a century old. He looked over at Jemima – she was leaning back in a wing-backed armchair of a ramrod straight disposition and he could not see her face properly.

"Yes, it's all very unfortunate," Sir Miles said again. "The press may get hold of it and that will make matters worse, of course."

Xan wondered if he was expected to apologise. "More unfortunate for some than for others," he said rather drily.

"A Ministerial Private Secretary dead in Black Rod's Garden. It's the kind of thing the papers would make a great deal of, if they got the chance. Thankfully, someone had the sense to call me. And that's why you're here and not giving statements at a police station. And to cap it all, Romilly crashes his car and puts himself in hospital."

"What?"

"Leaving Westminster this evening. He wasn't hurt, thankfully. Odd thing – his car seemed to plough straight into a lamp-post. Avoiding a bus filled with people, as I understand. Romilly was driving. He's not badly hurt, just shaken up, I gather, but he says he's stepping down from public life, effective immediately. Well, a brush with death – it takes some people that way."

"I would have thought," Xan said, "that a man who had spent time in the Army would be used to brushes with death."

"Quite so." Suddenly Temperley wasn't meeting Xan's eyes. "At any rate, that's what the press have been told. Perhaps some hint of over-work and ill-health, too."

So Romilly was retiring at forty-two. An abrupt end to his ambitions of leadership. It could only mean he had realised his position was untenable. Either that, or others had realised it for him.

"And you're quite sure about this story you've just told me. You must realise it sounds rather incredible."

"Yes, I realise that," Xan said wearily. "But as I told you, I have evidence."

"What kind of evidence?"

"The kind the police like. Fingerprints. On a child's school art project, labelled with Romilly's real name. He would have been about seven, I guess."

"You've tested the fingerprints, I suppose?" Temperley said sharply.

"Not yet. I'm not a chemist."

"And of course, you don't have Romilly's own fingerprints to compare them with."

"No, but –."

Jemima came back to herself from a long way away at the sound of their arguing. It was midsummer and the warm night air came in through the French doors but she still felt cold. The chair had a high straight back and raised arms and it felt as though those were the only things that were keeping her upright. She said: "I've got his fingerprints."

"What?" They both stared at her.

"I asked Mark Romilly to sign a submission today. His fingerprints are on the paper, along with his signature."

Xan glanced across at Sir Miles. "Well?"

"We'll see when both samples have been tested," Temperley said cautiously. He held out his hand, but Xan shook his head. "I don't think so."

The clown face split in a smile. "You don't trust me."

"I don't trust anyone right now."

"Very well. I can arrange for those samples to be tested in front of independent witnesses. In the meantime, I'm sure you'll both understand the importance of absolute discretion." Temperley was glancing at his watch. "I need to talk to Scotland Yard again. They're upset. The Home Office will smooth them over, but in the meantime, we don't want too much fuss."

Jemima said: "Will everything be investigated properly now? Will they find out what happened to Mr Maybury and Reverend Paradine and Mr Hare?"

"Well, one has to consider public interest, Miss Drury. There's no evidence to speak of, you know. Nothing to link – er – a certain person with anything."

"So, nothing's changed."

"Oh, yes," Temperley said. "Everything has changed."

CHAPTER 43

The week following what the authorities referred to obliquely as the Palace of Westminster incident, the weather changed abruptly, as though someone somewhere had pulled a lever. Sunshine gave way to bleak, drizzling rain and a sharp wind that blew nobody any good.

The political fall-out from the Palace of Westminster incident was extensive, but as the public was concerned, the matter was kept under wraps as far as possible. No briefings to the press were given other than a statement communicating Mark Romilly's sudden decision to retire from politics. It would of course have a dramatic impact on the forthcoming leadership contest. The press pack raced away enthusiastically in pursuit of this new hare.

Xan Ross found himself, for the first time since his ill-advised foray to Wimbledon, at a loose end. There was nothing for him to investigate. Sir Miles Temperley had urged him not to feel the need to stir up any more trouble. Jemima appeared to be unavailable due to pressures of work. Now what, a voice in his head asked?

Feeling restless, he went to Waterloo and caught a slow train to Egham. The train was quiet and he had a window-seat. The countryside slid past – dripping wet woodlands of slender silver birch trunks under a steel-grey sky.

When she opened her front door, Elinor Maybury had expected one of the various drearily familiar sights she was becoming used to as a widow. Her sister-in-law. The vicar, who still seemed convinced she needed spiritual salvation. When she saw Xan, she was relieved. "You've taken your time."

"I'm afraid it's a long story."

"Well, you'd better come in and tell it. I've given Giles's whisky away to the golf club raffle but I've got sherry."

The well-appointed sitting-room seemed a curious place for the story he had to tell. It sounded outlandish, absurd. Xan found himself glancing again at the adventure novels that Giles Maybury had favoured. Had it pleased Maybury in a small way that at last something exciting had happened to him?

"What I've got to tell you is classified," he said apologetically. "I shouldn't be telling you at all, in fact."

Elinor smiled at him. "You're not fond of playing by the rules, are you?"

When he concluded his story, she nodded with some satisfaction. "So, poor Giles wasn't just in the wrong place in the wrong time. And what about that girl? She must have been brave – and intelligent, which is far more useful, of course. I'd like to meet her."

"I'll tell her that."

"Do better than that. Bring her to see me."

The young man in front of her went slightly red under his tan. "I'll ask her."

*

On his return to London Waterloo, Xan walked through the urban jungle of Lambeth until he reached a deserted park where tall trees towered over empty grass and an immobile fairground had ceased its mechanical clamour. There was something disconcerting about the monstrous machines – roundabouts, Dodgems, a helter-skelter – all paused in motionless silence.

He stopped beside a carousel of golden horses frozen in mid-gallop. A figure emerged from the shadows – a stout man stuffed into a suit that was being strained beyond bearing by the poor fit.

"Hmmm, melodies unheard are sweeter, eh? Hardly worth a ten-minute walk from the taxi drop-off point."

It was true that Billy's voice was a little breathless and his face a little rosy. "There's a bench under that tree," Xan suggested diplomatically.

Billy waddled to the bench and lowered himself onto it with painful deliberation. Xan sat on the extreme other end as a counter-balance. "Well?"

"I see you're attracting the attention of the Government's greatest and good."

"Who exactly is Sir Miles Temperley?"

"He's a fixer. Works for a deniable department, which is handy for him. Never has to explain himself and none of the paperwork can be circulated."

"Well, what does he want?"

"What they all want is to make sure this business

doesn't embarrass the Government. It's caught them by surprise and they don't like that."

Xan stretched his legs out and stared at the galloping horses. "How much did you know, Billy?"

"I didn't know anything for certain, dear boy. The merest suspicion, picked up from my contacts, that Mark Romilly had got a long way in a remarkably short time and some interests must be pushing him. Those same interests took a hit when Giles Maybury died at the All England Club."

"What interests?"

"I told you. The Crooked House." Billy grinned at Xan's expression.

"Who are they? His party?"

"Well, I daresay some of them are in it, but they're much more than a political party. They're best described as a set of combined interests. And they backed Mark Romilly."

"They did more than that, they created him. You wouldn't have thought anyone would have had the nerve."

Billy shook his head. "You should have left the thing alone. I did try to warn you."

"It was your damned ticket. Where did it come from? You never answered that question, but you can answer it now."

An extraordinary expression was crossing Billy's face. It took Xan a moment to realise it was embarrassment. "I told you people gave me things," he said defensively.

"This was from an old job of mine. Twenty years in one office – people remember things like that. There was a retirement dinner. Charity raffle. You know the kind of thing."

Xan did not.

There was that faint and further creasing of Billy's rumpled features which represented a grin. "Well, I won that ticket. Didn't even bid for it, must have been some kind of sweepstake I entered without knowing. I'd had a few drinks."

Naturally. "Are you saying it came from the *police*?"

Billy shifted his bulk awkwardly. "That's the point. I wasn't always a policeman."

"Well?"

Billy looked away through the trees. "Twenty years in the Mount Pleasant sorting office. I was a postman."

Xan looked at him incredulously. "You've never mentioned that before."

Billy shrugged. "Didn't fit the image at Homeland. I said twenty years in the police but it was a lie. Five was enough. I wasn't cut out to be a policeman."

"I don't suppose you were the ideal build for delivering letters either," Xan said rather unkindly.

"Truth is, I didn't want the Grand Order of the Charitable Trust to know I'd given away the ticket. Turned out it was the top prize and there was hot competition for it." He grinned again suddenly. "Of course, they wouldn't have made such a fuss if they'd known what came with it, but there it is."

"I ought to wring your neck." Xan thought about what had come with the ticket.

There had been a point during in the investigation when he had even wondered about Billy himself. It had not just been the ticket. There had been Billy's vagueness about whether or not he had known Giles Maybury personally. The fact that an attack by hired thugs had come a couple of hours after Xan had called Billy from a public call-box. His strange mood when they had met under the shadow of Traitor's Gate. It would have been like Billy to choose somewhere so apposite to betray a friend. Now he discovered that Billy's dark secret was a hidden past as a postman.

"Well," Billy was saying, "you were never really the vacation type. Talking of which, what are your plans now? Have you thought about when you're going back overseas?"

"Should I?"

"I'd have thought it was advisable, yes. I told you, the House always wins."

Xan said nothing.

Billy shook his head impatiently. "It's not as though you belong here. You don't belong anywhere. And people who know about the House don't tend to live very healthy lives. They'll have taken a sizeable hit over this. And you're on their radar, They can make things very difficult for you here if they want to."

"And what if Jemima is on their radar too?"

"If that's what this is about, you're a bigger fool than I

took you for. Temperley will look after her. It wouldn't look good if anything happened to a respectable civil servant. But it's not his job to babysit you. And then there's Romilly himself. How must he be feeling?"

"Romilly's out of the picture now."

"Is he?"

"Of course he is."

But despite his assurance, Xan wondered.

*

There was another call to make – to a coffee-shop, where that hard-working police officer Inspector Nash was indulging in a quiet mid-morning cappuccino. He looked up when Xan strolled over and pushed out a chair for him. "Join me, Mr Ross. I gather you're no longer a subject of interest to the Metropolitan Police."

Xan sat down and found the inspector looking at him quizzically. "You seem to have turned into something of an untouchable. File removed from the Met database, no questions about you to be brooked, inquiry lines closed all over the place and anyone who was anything to do with the case moved double-quick onto something else. I've never been so busy. And there's always the chance that if I ask too many awkward questions, they'll promote me to keep me quiet."

Xan smiled. "I hope so."

"They think they've rounded up most of the small fry. And that reminds me, if I were to show you a couple of pictures, do you suppose you could pick someone out?"

"More small fry?"

The inspector did not reply. Instead, he extracted a brown envelope from his jacket pocket and removed a set of five photographs, all of them blurry shots of affluent-looking men in suits. "Well?"

Xan looked over them carefully. At last, he indicated the second from the left. "I think he was seated two rows behind me on Centre Court."

"I'm much obliged to you." The inspector gazed thoughtfully at the visage of the man second from the left.

"Does he have a guilty secret?" Xan asked curiously.

The inspector nodded. "Of a sort. He's the secretary of a tennis-club – one of those fancy places where you can't play if you've not got the right sort of accent. Huge membership fees. It turns out he never mentioned to his members that the club had been allocated Wimbledon tickets in the ballot. He used them himself and took a young lady friend. Thought no one would find out. The perfect crime. It was his bad luck that it was the day there was a murder on Centre Court."

And Xan looked down at the plump, pleased-looking face – the face of a man who has stolen a march.

CHAPTER 44

The morning sunlight was rising over the angels in the churchyard when Xan came down the road. Their stone faces looked pinched and disapproving, as though they knew he was coming here uninvited. As he reached No 37, he saw a new estate agent sign outside the front door, indicating that a flat was To Let.

Jemima answered the door. Her face and hands and quite a lot of her dress were dusty. Her short hair was still resisting settling into a decided style. She smiled ruefully. "You always come when I'm in the middle of doing something messy."

He couldn't find an answering smile. And, as if somebody somewhere considered he required a little moral bracing, a sudden cacophony of bells from the nearby church issued a stern reminder of his purpose here.

Jemima glanced at him thoughtfully, looked as though she was about to say something, then checked herself. "You'd better come in."

As he followed her up the stairs, he said: "I'm glad you're here. You've been very hard to find over the last week."

"Yes, I'm sorry about that. Lots of conversations with the police and then debriefing sessions with Sir Miles.

And then Human Resources got on to me about redoing the confidentiality module in the Civil Service learning and development suite."

He smiled. "I've had much the same, although not the last one."

There was a cardboard box and a pile of books on the landing. In the kitchen, the dog jumped up and wagged his tail at the sight of Xan, then flopped down again in his basket.

Jemima said: "I'm packing my books up. Since I've now suddenly got time on my hands."

He leaned down to stroke the dog's ears. "Why have you got time on your hands?"

"Oh – gardening leave." Seeing his baffled expression, she said: "It's what the civil service call it when you've blotted your copybook in some way and it's less embarrassing for everyone if you just stay away from the office."

"*You've* blotted your copybook?"

"You needn't sound so outraged on my behalf. Sir Miles said no blame was to be attached to me."

"Well, that was good of him."

"The Department's in an absolute flap about losing one of its Ministers so suddenly but everyone's been told not to talk. Sir Miles has cooked something up about a mishandled propriety issue which means a lot of people have had to resign on immediate effect. Including Geraldine." She shivered. "And Mark Romilly's gone to his country estate. Another sort of gardening leave, I suppose. No press statements. Everyone in Whitehall pretending frightfully hard that he never existed in the first place, which is rather ironic, in the circumstances."

"I saw him at the Palace of Westminster, you know. He was coming out when I was arguing with the guards at the gate. He told them to let me in."

She looked startled. "He did? Why on earth?"

"I think he wanted me to find you,"

"It's true that he argued with Sir Julius about me," Jemima said slowly. "But it doesn't make sense. He'd already let so many people die. He couldn't afford to let me go."

"But you're a member of his own Department. And perhaps he could already see it unravelling and decided to cut his losses." As he spoke, he wondered again what cutting his losses might mean to the man who called himself Mark Romilly.

She said briskly: "Sir Miles wants me to move out of here. That's the other reason I'm packing my books. He seems quite worried about me."

"He should be."

"He says his team will find me a well-appointed flat somewhere suitable. I think his ideas of what qualifies as well-appointed and suitable are likely to be rather generous, don't you, judging by what he calls his London pied a terre? So, with luck that means room for all my books." She smiled faintly. "To say nothing of a dog."

He looked up quickly. "Are you sure?"

"Well, I've got used to him now."

So, at any rate, he had taken care of Rabbit's dog. The

harder fact remained – that that other England which had briefly taken shape before him had vanished, gone in a welter of instructions from the authorities and papers and lies and Temperley looking disapproving and saying he didn't think that that would do at all.

She was watching him. "What is it?"

"Temperley wants me to leave the country."

"Yes, he told me that too."

This was disconcerting. She didn't sound as though it was of any particular consequence to her. Perhaps it wasn't. "He says he thinks my presence in this country compromises the government."

"I know. It's absurd."

"I could just disappear," he suggested lightly. "Then Temperley won't be able to find me to deport me."

"And when they take away your visa?"

"They can't do that. I'm a British citizen. I'm here on my own passport. Even Billy doesn't know that."

She smiled at him. "So it really is your real name?"

"It really is my real name."

She looked down at the dog, her smile fading a little. "But you're still going to go."

Impossible to explain that this wasn't about his name. He thought fleetingly of Adam Paradine's stolen letters, but it wasn't really about that either. This was about his Homeland work.

Billy had hinted as much. If they were to drag all that into the open, everything in his past would be laid bare to anyone who cared to inspect it. And Billy had warned him about that too. *She doesn't know anything about what you really are.*

Jemima didn't say anything more. He stopped stroking the dog's ears and crossed the kitchen to where she was standing. "Do you mind, Jem?"

And in theory, she knew the answer to that one. All the books on her shelves said the same, from Jane Austen onwards. A woman never admitted how much she minded. On the other hand, it seemed to her that she was dealing with someone who hadn't had much experience of people minding.

"Yes, of course I do. If it comes to that, lots of people will be sorry, far more than you like to pretend. Inspector Nash and Mrs Maybury. Even your friend Billy." She thought about that. "I don't mean in the same way I will, of course."

He grinned. "I should hope not."

"When do you fly out?"

"The day after tomorrow. I have to go to a place called Blythwich first."

"Why?" She looked up, catching the change in his tone.

"It's where my mother is buried."

And she did not know then why a chill came over her. People talked about a goose walking over your grave. It wasn't her grave, or his – but something she couldn't put a name to made her feel cold.

CHAPTER 45

When Xan returned to the City Coronado Hotel, it was the first day of September and it was pouring with rain.

As he stood apologetically just inside the door, letting the water drip off his coat onto the mat, Leah looked up and saw him. As she described to her colleagues later, she felt a terrible premonition right away. "You've come to check out, haven't you?"

"Yes – I'm going back overseas."

Leah thought he didn't sound particularly cheerful about it. "Well, you've picked the right day. You've had the best of the weather here."

Xan glanced at the steady rain outside the window.

"You know what I mean. It's been a lovely summer."

"I suppose it has." He was thinking about death at Wimbledon and in a vicar's swimming-pool and at an old-fashioned English seaside resort.

"Going anywhere nice?"

"I'm not sure yet."

"I see you found someone to take that dog, anyway." And she smiled demurely at his startled expression. "You seem to think no one but you has any eyes in their head, Mr Ross. All us girls knew about him but the management wouldn't have stood for it for a second, not if they'd ever found out about it."

"I suppose not," he said, chastened.

"Oh, I almost forgot. Someone called for you. Wanted to know if you were still staying here."

And Mr Ross suddenly looked quite different – not dangerous, exactly, but formidable. "Did they give a name" he said, quietly enough.

"No. He said it didn't matter. He said he was going into the country himself." She looked at him anxiously. "Is something wrong?"

"No, of course not."

He took the Volvo from the same garage as before. It was a cool autumnal day, with wisps of mist in the fields either side of the motorway. He made good time, branching off the North Road towards the bulge of East Anglia well before midday.

The next stage took longer – by his calculation, there was no major road, not even an A-road, going directly towards his destination and he was forced to pick his way along a series of B-roads and tiny, unmarked lanes that radiated out like seams across the cornfields.

The corn slowly gave way to flatter, wider fields rimmed by deep ditches, the contours so low that only clumps of trees and the occasional church spire broke the flat line of the horizon. And when the fields began to merge and blur together into a wetland of bulrushes with water shimmering below the surface, he knew he was nearly at the sea.

There was still a climb to be done, though and a narrow

road took him grudgingly to the top of the ridge, where a bleak little township huddled on the high ground, buffeted by the wind off the sea. This was Blythwich. In the valley below, the River Blythe wound lazily east through the marshes towards the river-mouth.

Of course, they had moved around a lot. This place was just like the others. The only reason it was significant at all was because it had been the last place.

He left the car in a side street. The small houses looked grim and desolate and Windrush Road seemed the greyest and dreariest street of all. He had not thought that he would remember the house itself but there it was, No.17, with its mean windows staring out.

He had had the room at the front at the top and his mother a small room at the back. The landlady had been silent and hostile, sensing his mother's illness and determined that they should leave before she was left saddled with an eight-year-old boy.

He turned away from the house and walked along to look at the river meandering east towards the invisible sea. On the opposite bank, on a rise of higher ground, a big, grey church stood incongruously with its sentry-guard of tall trees, too big for its parish.

There had been a boat that took passengers across from this shore to the church if you rang a bell. There still was, although the rowing-boat had been replaced by a small engined contraption that belched out blue smoke. The ancient ferryman who piloted it might have been the same man as before or he might not. He did not seem inclined for conversation, which suited Xan.

He was the only passenger and he sat in the stern and followed the river-course with his eyes. Upstream, he knew, it narrowed into a fast hill brook. Downstream, it widened into an indolent estuary, its power draining into salt-marshes and mud-flats. A sudden shadow touched his mind and was gone again before he could get hold of it.

The boat was nosing at the small jetty that served the church. He paid the ferry-man and walked up the road to the church.

The churchyard was green and sodden and dripping. There were few new graves and the old ones seemed neglected, the headstones crumbling and their inscriptions illegible. Brambles were invading from all sides – a stone saint carrying a large, open book gazed despairingly as they clawed at him and threatened to swallow him up.

The place was on the furthest side from the church, close to the river-wall. Her headstone was weathered like all the others, with green moss growing on it. He bent down and traced with his fingers the letters he knew were there.

Margaret Ross
Aged 32

He had not brought anything – you were meant to bring flowers to graves. He had never subscribed to the idea. What comfort was it to someone dead to have flowers on their grave? It was meant as comfort for the living and it was a long time since he had been in the market for that commodity. All the same, he found himself breaking off a shoot from a white-flowering sapling to put on the grave.

As he came back to the churchyard gate, he glanced across the river. A figure was standing on the jetty – a man, his arms folded, presumably waiting for the boat to take him across. Of course, any inhabitant of Blythwich might have a perfectly respectable reason for wanting to visit the church. But Xan felt a sudden tremor of something – what? A premonition?

He stood and watched as the old ferryman hastened from his cottage. The newcomer stepped into the boat, which began to tack slowly towards the northern shore. As the boat drew closer, the face of the passenger became clear. Romilly.

So what were his intentions? Obviously, some sort of reckoning – he had reason to think he was due it. But this was exactly the kind of thing Temperley had wanted to avoid. It would be better for Xan not to allow himself to be found and give Romilly the space to recover from the blow to his ego.

Which was all very well, but there was no road away from the church on this side of the river – only small paths seaming the fields and marshes stretching away to the north and the river running east to the sea. However, it should be easy enough to make his way on foot across the fields.

It was fortunate that a belt of stunted oaks and wind-blown ash-trees surrounded the church and that a thick hawthorn hedge led to a more substantial stretch of woodland to the west. He could circle round using this cover and cross the river back to Blythwich for the car once the baulked Romilly had given up.

He made his way along the bridleway and then up the side of a recently ploughed field. A sense of the absurd assailed him. This was all ridiculously melodramatic. It was surely possible to appeal to reason. Perhaps he should stop and wait for Romilly and try to settle this in a sensible fashion.

He was still turning this possibility over in his mind when he came to the gap he was looking for in the hedge. It came in the form of a stile with a gap beneath it for the convenience of dogs. He was just reflecting on the old-fashioned eccentricity of this arrangement as he climbed it. As he jumped down, there was a loud echoing crack and a bullet struck the fence-post a few inches away from his cheekbone.

Instinctively, Xan dropped out of sight the other side of the stile. By the time he had worked his way down the hedge to the tree-lined ditch at the bottom of the field, he had come to certain conclusions. 1 – the shooter was Romilly. 2 – Romilly was an excellent shot. 3 – he was using an ordinary hunting rifle so that an eventual kill would look like a hunting accident. 4 – a hunting rifle was quite good enough to kill a man, even at this range, if you got your aim right.

The game had changed. No longer did Xan contemplate stopping to reason with Romilly. Instead, he worked his way silently and quickly through the wood, aiming for another hedge the other side that would give him cover. The hedge bore off at a north-west angle that would take him in the right direction – but as he made his way up beside it, he caught a movement on the brow of the hill above him.

He tried a different tack, going up the other side of the wood with the intention of making a bigger circuit, but a moment later, he was checked again. Whatever Romilly's soldiering experience had been, he was good at hunting.

There was no choice but to work his way back down to the river he had left. As he scrambled down through the belt of trees, he realised that he was tired. And he could not afford to be tired. There was no safety here. On the right, the river glinted. It looked sluggish and shallow, but he knew it was deeper and more dangerous than it looked.

As he paused to catch his breath, another shot whistled close past his head. There was no time for strategy now. Romilly and Romilly's gun were keeping him pinned to the river. Every time he tried to move away from it, he was driven back again. What was the other man's plan? To drive him down to the river-mouth, by the look of it. And then? Well, it was a quiet spot for a murder.

Half a mile further on, the river widened suddenly into an estuary and before him was the sea. Flocks of water-birds flapped irritably into the air as he approached. The tide was out and the estuary was a desert of smooth, flat sand, the river spilled across it like water across a table-top. On his left, the cliffs soared steeply upwards.

As Xan looked across the sandflats, shading his eyes, he felt a chill. He had been here before. This was the place of his dreams. He had forgotten it, but it had not forgotten him – it had been here all the time, waiting for him.

The flat, smooth reaches of sand looked innocent, but Xan knew they were deceptive. The sand-flats were their own world, shaped, collapsed and reshaped by the river and the tides. Within that mile of sand, there were hidden gullies and lagoons, fast-flowing channels and pockets of mud.

The warning signs along the edge of the bay made it clear: Keep Off. Danger. He remembered a trick from his childhood – a safe passage through the sand that could not be seen but had to be remembered via a sequence of markers. The fencepost, the coastguard station on the cliff, the far point of the headland. The trick was not to veer too close to the river-mouth, but to head towards the sea, where the river's power was dissipated. Because of this, the path could only be negotiated safely when the tide was out.

He turned to look back along the path by which he had come. There was no sign of Romilly – but he was not foolish enough to imagine that he was not somewhere close at hand. He hesitated only momentarily and then set out across the sand, disregarding the warning signs.

The fencepost, the coastguard station, the headland. What came next? On the opposite shore, a stunted ash-tree, a five-bar gate, and in the dim distance, a lighthouse on the point. And then as he paused to orient himself, something flew past him with a zip like an angry wasp, making the water-birds fly up with a beating of wings. Back on the shoreline, a man's figure was faintly visible.

It was difficult to turn his back on the gun-sights, but he forced himself to do so. He was almost certainly out of range at this point – Romilly evidently knew that too and was now saving his ammunition. Xan was safe enough, therefore, so long as he kept going. If he could reach the southern shore and disappear into the landscape, Romilly would never find him.

A moment later, he dropped down into a gully and splashed across a stream. But when he emerged the other side, Romilly was making his way across the sand.

Now it was hard to control the urge to move faster – but he must not forget the markers. He went carefully, skirting the shallow depressions which indicated quicksand and the quivering stretches like the surface of a sponge cake before it was baked which meant mud. Whenever he looked back, Romilly was there – following in his footsteps, but not gaining.

He himself was two-thirds of the way across the bay, he calculated. Why was that important? His tired mind groped for the answer and then had it. The tide was turning. And once it came, it would come fast, blotting out the wide estuary.

He stopped and turned. Romilly was some fifty yards back. He had lost the rifle, somewhere out there on the flat sands. Xan cupped his hands to his mouth and shouted. "Go back."

Romilly paid no attention to him.

"You won't make it all the way across. You'd better turn back. The tide's coming in."

The other man turned his head to glance at the glimmering line of the water in the distance. "Well, that's handy," His voice floated over the mudflats. "Shroud, coffin and grave in one handy package. By the time they find your body, no one will recognise it. But then, there's no one much to recognise it anyway, is there?"

"Go back, Romilly."

"You don't get it, do you? The level of organisation. At first, you came as something of a surprise, I'll admit. But we soon got you figured out and I've had people watching this place ever since. It was a reasonable guess you'd come to visit your mother's grave. A sentimental gesture – but then, you are sentimental. It's a flaw of yours. I've looked up your record. You walked away from Homeland because you didn't like the level of casualties."

Xan said nothing.

"Of course, the ferry-man will remember you. But he didn't recognise me. I was lucky there. I'm always lucky."

"Your luck's running out, Romilly."

Romilly didn't answer. He was looking down, testing his feet. "What the hell is this?"

In talking, the man had forgotten to watch where he was going and had blundered into a patch of softer sand. Xan felt a sudden thrill of disquiet that he could not entirely account for. "It's quicksand," he said. "It's like a house of cards until you step on it. Then it collapses, pulling you in."

Romilly sneered. "You know a lot."

"I've been here before."

"Then tell me, how does one get out of this stuff?"

"You can't. Not without help."

"Well, how deep does one sink?"

"Not very far – no further than your waist."

Romilly grimaced. "Well – checkmate, I suppose. Once you get across the bay, you might call out the coastguard to come and get me."

"Yes, I could do that."

Romilly watched him peevishly. "I'm pretty thirsty," he grumbled. "You don't have a bottle of water you could leave?"

"Yes, I do." But Xan didn't move.

"Well, come on, then – I can hardly come and get it."

"I don't trust you."

Romilly's lips drew back suddenly in a snarl. "You're damned right. I lost the rifle but I've still got my revolver. If you had come any closer, I would have blown your head off."

Xan said: "There's something you've forgotten."

"What's that?"

"The tide. It only takes a few minutes in this part of the world and it covers the whole of this bay."

All colour ebbed from the man's face. He looked east at the glimmering line of the advancing tide. "You're sure about that?"

"Yes."

With an effort, Romilly regained his nonchalance. Xan felt an unwilling respect for him. "How deep does it get here, would you say?"

"About seven feet. Deep enough to drown you."

"Not a very pleasant way to meet one's maker."

Xan looked from the northern shoreline to the southern one and then out to the advancing sea. Romilly didn't stand much chance – any chance at all. And as he said, it would be an unpleasant way to die. The decision to leave him began to seem more difficult. Wearily, he said: "Chuck your gun away and I'll come and help you."

Romilly grinned wolfishly. "Not a chance."

"Then there's nothing I can do. I'm sorry, Romilly."

He was looking out to the east. The sea was coming fast. Due to the square shape of the wide, flat bay, there were no white-topped waves rolling in. Instead, the water came in flat surges across the sand, sometimes from one direction, sometimes from another. Where it met the river flow, it spread in all directions at once as though someone had left a tap running. As he watched, a wide finger of water stretched and flexed like something alive and ate up a space of sand to come pooling in around the man trapped in the sand.

Mark Romilly looked down. His skin was a greyish hue. He looked up again at the other man. "It's the thinking time that gets to me. I remember standing on a mine once. Waited forever before they got anyone out to me. All kind of thoughts go through your head. You might keep me company."

Xan made sure the high sand-bar he was positioned on was far enough away to be out of reach of a bullet. "Tell me about Giles Maybury."

"He tried to catch me out. He thought he was so clever, trotting out that line of gibberish at the Ritz. It turned out it was some Ancient Greek tag from the school I was meant to have gone to. Of course I'd never heard it before and I showed it."

"So that was it."

"That was it. But he'd let me know he knew. He saw he was in danger then but he was careful. We had to do it at Wimbledon, it was the only place. It might not have come off, but it did."

"What about the Crooked House?"

The water was flowing in swiftly now, swirling around Romilly's knees. He glanced down at it, then away again. "They've been around forever. They adapt, when they need to, but they don't evolve. They're interested in wealth, political power, land, whatever moves the levers."

"What made them pick you?"

"They wanted a clean-skin. It had to be someone with no close ties." He glanced over at Xan. "It could have been you, had you thought about that? We're not so different. No family. No past. No opportunities. You make what you can of life using the only thing you're good at. Violence."

"Was it worth giving up your own identity?"

Romilly laughed. "Sentimentality again. You never met Tom Riley. You wouldn't have wanted to. He amounted to nothing. I saw the possibilities, all right."

"And the risks?"

"I didn't believe it would work, but they'd figured it out damned well. I didn't want the defence brief, of course, but they could see the advantages of a defence minister with Army service, so I couldn't avoid it. And they would have made me leader at the next election. Then Prime Minister. And that's when the fun begins."

"And Rabbit?"

Romilly winced a little. "I never wanted that. They didn't tell me until after that was done." He glanced down again at the water that was now up to his waist and shrugged. "Well, there it is. Maybe this is retribution of a kind. I don't think it will take very long now."

Xan did not think so either. "Are you a religious man, Romilly?" Not many soldiers were, in Xan's experience, but it was curious how many, when they were dying, wanted something. Words, thoughts, visions of an after-life, whatever comfort you could give them.

Romilly grimaced. "Do I look it? And no last messages, either, thanks. I'm not the sentimental one here."

A silence stretched between them, with nothing but the steady lapping of the water and the crying of the birds. It was Romilly who broke it again. "Funny thing is, I keep thinking of a line of poetry. It used to stick in my mind whenever I read it, I don't know why." He glanced over at Xan. "Now what the hell are you doing?"

Xan had remembered something. The poetry-book was still in his rucksack – he had forgotten to take it out after the visit to Ashbury. "This is yours. It was with Rabbit's things. He'd kept it for you."

Romilly twisted his head again awkwardly to look. "I'll be damned. I thought I'd lost it after the crash. I'd ask you to bring it over here, but – well." He considered the matter. "Since you can't, there was a poem that used to go through my head when I was on guard duty. Something about a veiled sister who prays for those who walk in darkness. It's in Ash Wednesday, near the end. You might read that bit."

And it was an odd way to mark the death of a man one didn't like, but Xan found himself leafing through to the right page and reading the words aloud.

Romilly listened attentively. "I never understood that bit," he said again. "Funny thing, poetry."

Xan closed the book. There didn't seem to be anything else to say. Suddenly, Romilly turned his head sharply, not to look, but to listen. "What's that?"

A faint thrumming seemed to fill the sky. Xan looked up and Romilly followed his glance as best he could. "What the hell is it?"

"A helicopter. Someone must have spotted us."

A moment later, the thudding reverberations seemed to fill the bay as it came into sight – a red, mean-looking machine. The birds scattered.

Romilly twisted round and peered up at it. "Army."

"The Army do sea rescue around here?"

Romilly shrugged. "I'm not too fussy at this point."

The helicopter began to manoeuvre closer. A man in

uniform opened a window and leaned out. "Mr Romilly, sir. It's lucky we found you."

Romilly said through chattering teeth: "Unfortunately, I don't believe we have time for the social niceties."

"No, sir. How deep are you?"

"It's up to my knees."

"Mud?"

"Quicksand, I'm reliably informed."

The co-pilot glanced at the tide. "We haven't got very long. I'll come down to take a look."

It took a few minutes for the man to winch himself down close to Romilly's level. Xan watched from his safe position on the shingle bar. The winchman was talking to Romilly in soothing tones. "This will be no problem, sir. We've got specialist equipment for this."

"What are you going to do?" Xan said. "He's stuck pretty fast."

The soldier glanced at Xan. "You'd better get well back to the shoreline, sir. We don't need a second casualty."

"Oh, I don't know," Romilly grinned.

He's got guts, Xan thought. He knows he's up against it. "Good luck, Romilly," he said, and turned to make his way towards the shore. The tide had come in strongly while he had been watching Romilly – the water around him was now above his waist and came in strong, regular swells that threatened to knock him off his feet.

Halfway to the shore, he turned back to watch. The winchman was being raised to the hovering helicopter. With sudden disquiet, Xan saw a wire cable that ran down from the chopper to the sea. What kind of rescue technique was this, exactly?

Driven by a sudden impulse, he began to wade back, but in the short space of time, the water had risen higher, up to his chest. He struggled to make any headway.

"Hey!" he yelled up at the helicopter, as though the machine itself had ears. Both machine and pilots were deaf to him. Suddenly frantic, he cupped his hands and shouted to Romilly. "Get that rope off you!"

The man could not hear him, or did not understand. The water was nearly up to his neck and his face was pale and set. The helicopter was thrumming in a purposeful manner. The engine note became higher. The men in the machine were conferring together. Xan opened his mouth to shout again but a huge swell of water rocked into him, knocking him off his feet, dragging him under.

He clawed his way upwards and surfaced, spitting saltwater and blinking water out of his eyes. The helicopter was a giant blurred insect. He couldn't see Romilly, but the rope was quiveringly taut and someone was screaming. Then the helicopter engine noise changed to a high-pitch whine. As though synchronised, the scream rose higher and was suddenly cut off.

Another swell came, this time from the west, and dragged Xan under again. This time, he stayed down and began to swim steadily out to sea.

THE END

About Annabel Frazer

I live in Berkshire, close to the River Thames. I live with my family and two cats, one of which likes to walk across the keyboard as I am writing. Any typos can therefore be ascribed to him.

For everything else, I am grateful to my family for their patience and support. I'm sorry to my husband for setting a particularly violent fight in the church where we got married and to the All England Lawn And Tennis Club for my temerity in borrowing the hallowed setting of their Centre Court for this book's first murder.

I am also the author of:
The Day The Earth Caught Cold
The Sea Raven

You can find out more about me or tell me what you think of my books by visiting my author profile at www.goodreads.com/annabelfrazer.

23573059R00246

Printed in Great Britain
by Amazon